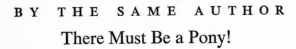

Good Times / Bad Times

A NOVEL BY

JAMES KIRKWOOD

SIMON AND SCHUSTER / NEW YORK

FIRST PRINTING

LIBRARY OF CONGRESS CATALOG CARD NUMBER: 68–25750
DESIGNED BY EDITH FOWLER
MANUFACTURED IN THE UNITED STATES OF AMERICA
BY H. WOLFF, NEW YORK

To Lila Lee and Mary Murphy With Love

1

IT WAS such a short time ago that Jordan and I read in the papers you were going to defend the Wilk girl. That's why I took your phone call; I knew of your reputation, of course, not only from the Wilk case but from several other cases I've followed that you've been associated with. I have a morbid curiosity, and if there's an unusually ripe murder trial I'm bound to get hooked on it.

Right now I'm a little put out with Caroline Wilk, because if it weren't for her you'd be here now. You said her case should be over within a month or so and I certainly hope so.

The only thing I have to say about the timing of your call is a simple—miraculous. I don't know what would have happened if you hadn't made it. Things were getting pretty sticky here. Although, funnily enough, I don't mind being in jail. What with all the gory publicity I'd much rather be here, being stared at by the police and this tight little jail community than by thousands of civilians every place I went.

You certainly come across on the telephone, which is unusual. I liked your sense of humor. That more than anything else put me at ease and gave me a certain sense of security I've been needing badly. When you said in the meantime to jot down all my thoughts on what happened and I said it was torture for me to write in longhand, also torture for anyone trying to decipher it, and you said, "Well, I just had the prescription for my glasses changed last week, perhaps we'd better arrange for your typewriter." Also when you bawled me out for knocking you and Caroline Wilk off the front pages the opening day of your trial. And when you asked me what my most immediate problem was and I gave you that stupid answer "I'm depressed!" and you came back with "Must be one of those days."

Anyhow, in case you don't know it, you have real pull. Not two hours after we talked, I was moved into another cell around the corner from everyone else, my typewriter was brought in, and also the prescription of Dexamyl I asked for. They are also treating me with one hundred percent more respect. Speaking of the Dexamyl, it's working now and I have that sort of fluttery feeling inside my stomach. I think this comes not only from the pill but from knowing I've found someone I can tell the truth to.

When you said I should open up and put down anything I felt, my most secret, innermost feelings—"What you might believe to be your blackest thoughts," you said—and it would go no farther than you, I believed you. So I hope you believe me when I say I have no impulse to draw back and the way I'm feeling now, at least, I'm just going to spill it out. As best I can.

Having said that, I don't know where to start. I somehow want to spill it out all in one great blob. I really don't want to delve back into my childhood in detail, so I won't. This really concerns Jordan and Mr. Hoyt and me. So I think I will just begin with how I happened to go to Gilford and arriving there.

(Unbelievable to think it's not even five months ago. Unbelievable to think the best thing in my life happened since then and the worst.)

As you may know, my father is an actor. As you also probably know, from the little digs in the papers, he has a drinking problem. I love him more than I hate him, which I suppose is not too bad, the way everyone is walloping their parents these days. I'll put it like this: in many ways I understand him. That isn't to say I haven't wished from the very beginning that I had been sired by almost anyone else. My mother is dead; that happened when I was six. Of cancer. She was very beautiful, that's mostly what I remember about her. But there's no real need to talk too much about her because that's long ago. Except to say that my father was very much in love with her, and although he was always, from what I hear, a heavy drinker, he was in control of it before she died. The combination of her death and his career—acting—is what turned him into an alcoholic. Acting alone could do the trick. Especially when you've been successful at it, a star, and then you lose it.

If someone waved a ten-year unbreakable contract for movies in my face at a guarantee of fifty thousand a week, I would turn it down. No, I wouldn't. I'd take it and then, at twenty-eight, which I would be in ten years, I would take all the money I'd saved and go into business or whatever. But I wouldn't count on a penny more or one day more employment in that business. It's treacherous, the saddest profession in the entire world. Someone said whoring is the oldest and also the saddest profession in the world. It may be the oldest, but it loses out on being the saddest. Acting is.

I'm afraid Dexamyl makes me go off on a tangent. I will try to control my tangents.

My father still works, when he's taking care of himself and when he's offered something, although he's usually insolvent and I'm afraid always will be. He has long periods when he doesn't touch a drop and then he might get the road company of a Broadway show or a summer stock package or even a supporting part in an independent movie now and then. But it's hit-and-miss.

It's hard to raise a son that way, although he's had me with him whenever he possibly could. I put in two years at a Catholic military academy run by The Little Sisters and Brothers of Eternal Punishment (my name for them). And one period of a year I spent with my father's father, who is ninety-one, in Tucson, Arizona.

My father's been married once since my mother, but that only lasted two years. I liked my stepmother at first and she liked me. Liked me—it was as if she was courting me, instead of my father.

9

"You're my fella!" she'd say, hauling me to movies, amusement parks, the beach, flooding me with presents, forever interested in whatever *I* was interested in.

I was hoodwinked (I was also younger then) and I was the happiest kid on the block when they got married. Everything was still dandy for a while, one long honeymoon, until she became pregnant with my half sister, Linda.

It happened very quickly: she was in her seventh month and I was practicing the piano (her idea originally, the piano lessons), and I saw her out of the corner of my eye walk into the living room from her bedroom. I didn't look up from the piano because I had finally mastered the little Italian art song I'd been practicing and I wanted her to be proud of me. She stood at the end of the piano for a minute or so and I was playing away, concentrating for all I was worth. She suddenly slammed the wooden part of the piano that comes down and covers the keys—slammed it down on my fingers, and ran sobbing to her bedroom.

She broke two of my fingers. Later that day, when I got back from the hospital, she apologized and wept and my father and I put it down to pregnancy. And I, I might add, gave up piano lessons. But it was never the same.

After Linda was born she turned on me full force. It was like I'd been a stand-in for a child in the house and now that her daughter was there, the *real* child—what was I doing there, too? When she started resenting my *father's* presence, they got divorced.

But enough of that; what I want to tell about is this immediate problem. Problem! That must come under the heading of Department of Understatement.

So, this last summer, my father had been up for the part of a judge on a television series; he missed out by an inch and it hit him hard and he lost control. We were living in a tacky apartment on Argyle Avenue in Hollywood. Two pulldown beds, a kitchen, bath and so close to the Freeway my father and I used to kid about being run over in our sleep.

Every day he would go to The Masquers and play cards and

drink. His cronies love him there. If he has anything—it's charm. There's a great camaraderie between the men who belong to that club; they really love one another. Mostly people in movies or television. One retired actor, Milton Bigelow, is especially fond of, and good to, my father. He's been out of the business and in used cars in San Fernando Valley for years. Anyhow, his son went to Gilford a long time ago, and he offered to send me there for my senior year. Being that my father was unsettled and thinking of coming back to New York to see what he could find on the stage, he accepted Milton Bigelow's offer and that's how it happened I was sent off to Gilford Academy.

Henry, the guard, just brought me the Boston papers and I'm still on the front page.

Random thought: Many times I've seen pictures in newspapers of young guys who have killed people. So often they're Boy Scouts, all-A students, or they sang in the choir, or they taught Sunday school—then suddenly they stabbed their mother to death thirty-eight times with a bread knife because there wasn't any peanut butter in the kitchen. It always seemed so unreal, so out-of-left-field.

Now I glance sideways from this little table they've set up for me and I see myself staring up at me from the paper and, even though it's me and I remember every second of what happened, it seems even more unreal.

God, suddenly I had a cold splashing moment of not believing it at all. Not at all!

Still, I look back down and on the front page is a huge blowup of a snapshot Jordan took of me on the tennis court. I'm reaching across the net, smiling and shaking hands with Ed Anders and looking very All-American Tennis-Anyone. Directly next to it there's one of me being hauled up the steps of this jail. In this one I look all kind of mean and hunted. The caption over the tennis picture says: ANOTHER NORMAL TEENAGER TURNS SLAYER. The caption over the other picture is a very sly: OR IS HE?

The story is sickening and snide and the implications are incredibly dirty. I hate it. The other papers aren't exactly handing out bouquets either. HEADMASTER BRUTALLY SLAIN BY STUDENT. In another: NEW HAMPSHIRE'S SAVAGE CRIME OF THE DECADE, with a gruesome picture of the body right after they found him, that I could only glance at a second and that seems to give truth to their adjectives and adverbs. It's those words that make me shiver. The papers also feature articles and pictures of Jordan and Mr. Hoyt when they were alive.

"Both gone . . . ," as my father mutters when he's watching a scene on "The Late Show" with two actors who have died.

Another paper is still quoting the policeman who said I laughed right after they showed me the body at the morgue, that he didn't think I was sorry I'd killed him. I refer to this particular policeman as My Buddy.

Of course I'm sorry.

I'm also sorry I got off on the wrong foot in jail. I might as well tell you—there have been these little catastrophes ever since I got here.

It was dark by the time they brought me in. I was cold and numb and bruised, with a sprained ankle to boot. I don't think it's stretching a point to say I was in shock. More reporters, policemen, fingerprinting, questioning, and it was a few hours before I was finally put in a cell with another prisoner, a tall, thin, emaciated man in his late thirties. He had posture like a curve, his head jutting out as if he'd sprained his neck, and thin dirty-looking hair that hung down and got in the way of his eyes, which bulged.

I remember him asking me why I was there and the guard saying "Murder." The prisoner let out a long, admiring whistle. "Murder!" he said. "Murder!" he repeated and then made a series of clucking sounds. "Murder—boy, you—" He just broke off, whistled again and shook his head.

Even in the state I was in, I remember thinking of that old joke, the punch line being: "You don't *look* Jewish." Not that it made me laugh or anything, but I remembered it.

They were busy taking my clothes away and giving me dungarees and a T-shirt and slippers; while they were doing this he was very quiet, sitting on a stool and watching me. As soon as we were alone he told me he was in jail for robbery. I didn't want to talk, I wanted to be alone. There was a double-decker bunk. When he saw me looking at it, he quickly told me he slept in the upper one. I lay down on the bottom part. When I'm depressed the first thing I want to do is sleep.

I lay there and he started to whisper—"Hey!" I ignored him at first. But he kept whispering "Hey! . . . Hey! . . . Hey! . . ." with urgency, as if he had a big secret to tell me. Finally, after about twenty "Hey's," I turned my head and looked over at him, his neck all craned out, hair falling down in front of his eyes. When he saw me looking, he leaned way forward and whispered, "You got any pot?" I shook my head and he said "Awwwwww." Very long and disappointed.

Then he started in with the "Hey's" again. He kept on at me and I kept staring up at the mattress above, hoping he would stop. Then I was aware of him getting up and coming over to stand right next to me. "Hey!" he kept whispering, until I finally had to look at him. "You don't got any pot?" he asked.

Oh, dear God, I thought, on top of everything they've put me in here with some poor, sad cuckoo of a guy. I looked at him, straight in those bulging, empty eyes, and said, "No, I told you!"

He stepped back away from me. "Okay, you don't have to get mad. Okay . . . okay . . . okay," he muttered, going back to his stool. After he sat down he thought for a moment. "Huh," he snorted. "I heard you the first time. Huh—you could do murder, you could tell a lie."

I told myself to turn him off, to make myself unconscious and go to sleep. There was nobody in the cell across from us, but I could hear snoring from someplace. I closed my eyes and synchronized my breathing with the snoring, pretending it was my own. I actually made it; I was vaguely aware of pressure on the bunk, of him climbing up to the top, but I was in that half-state just before you drop off.

Then I *was* asleep until something started to nag me awake. For a long while I was blocking it out, but then I could hear him whispering again. At first I couldn't make it out, didn't want to, hoping he would stop. But then he started in with the "Hey's" again. Pretty soon I was wide awake, but I didn't open my eyes. I kept thinking he'd get tired and give up. Not him. The longer I didn't respond the shorter and sharper he'd hiss out "Hey! . . . Hey! . . . Hey!"

Finally I snapped my eyes open. "What? What do you want?"

His head was hanging down off the bunk; he brushed his hair out of his eyes and then he said, "Are you scared?"

I moaned and moved over toward the wall, turning sideways to face it. "Leave me alone! Jesus, leave me alone!"

He didn't answer, but I could tell he hadn't moved his position, that he was still staring down at me, because there was no movement at all from above. Somehow, the fact that he was staring at me made me furious, even more so than when he'd been whispering. I could feel my heart beating faster and faster.

After a while he whispered, "Are you?" I clenched my teeth and my fists, begging that he would stop. Then he went on. "Are you?" he kept asking, allowing for a space before each one, then gradually decreasing the space until he was chanting, still in a whisper, "Are you? . . . Are you? . . . Are you?"

I leaped out of the bunk and shouted at him: "Stop it! Stop it! Stop it!"

He started screaming for help and I began screaming for him to shut up and all hell broke loose. Two guards came, the lights were switched on, the prisoners all down the corridor woke up and began yelling, too. It was a madhouse. The guards opened the door and came in, pistols drawn, asking what was going on. Lanky, up on top, was all hunched up in a ball, cringing back against the wall. "He did murder! He did murder!" he cried out, pointing to me. One of the guards, the older of the two, looked at me and said, "Okay, what's going—" But I didn't let him get any farther. I quickly told him what had happened, while the younger one went out to quiet down the other prisoners. There wasn't any expression on his face and I was wondering if he was believing me but when I finished he looked up at the other guy and said, "What are you—some kind of nut?"

"*He* did murder!" he said, sort of childish and accusingly.

"All right, let's keep it nothing but calm. I don't want to hear a sound," the guard said, turning and walking toward the door.

The same moment I felt panic that they were going to leave me with him, I caught sight of the empty cell across the corridor. "Put me in there," I asked him, pointing over to it. "Please put me over there!"

The guard didn't even have time to answer when my friend in the top bunk mimicked me: "Please put me over there!" he whined, and that was the crowning touch. He was beginning to repeat it, when I couldn't help it. I cried out "Jesus! Oh, Jesus!" Absolutely screamed it out.

"Steady, lad," the guard said, coming to me and putting a hand on my arm. "Steady," he said, looking across at the empty cell. "The can in there's on the fritz," he said. (They have a toilet just sitting there in the corner of each cell.)

"That's all right. I won't go, honest I won't. Please, let me sleep in there!" I just held on to him, begging, until he said all right and took me in there. He was very decent about it, even promising to get the john fixed first thing in the morning.

Something funny: You think that was the last we heard of the other guy? Oh, no. By this time I was worn out; after I got settled into the bunk I was just about dropping off when I heard this loud whisper: "You're scared, aren't you?" I couldn't believe my ears. I opened my eyes and looked over and there he was, clutching the bars and staring over at me. When he saw me looking he got all excited and started nodding his head. "You're scared, aren't you?" He only got it out about twice more when the younger guard stepped up and gave him a hard crack on the knuckles with a club. Then all I heard was whimpering until I finally went to sleep.

The next morning I could tell he was sulking; a couple of times I glanced over and he'd quickly look away. They took him away that morning and I haven't seen him since.

But you see, what I don't understand, around noon the sheriff

15

passed my cell and glanced over at me. He walked on by a few steps, but then he came right back. "Kilburn," he said, his face very stern, "I hear you caused a ruckus last night. None of that around here!" he snapped and walked away. I know it seems a minor point, but I got upset wondering why the guard hadn't told him it wasn't all my fault. Also, he didn't let me explain, just walked away.

The sheriff had been considerate when he first brought me in: Was I cold? Was I hungry? My father was on his way. Etc. But that morning was a change, and that was only the beginning.

2

WHICH BRINGS ME to my father's visit; he arrived late that afternoon. It would have been much better if he hadn't; it broke my heart to see him.

He'd been drinking, I could tell that. I don't mean that day, I don't think he had, but recently and heavily, too. For the trip east he'd gotten himself all pulled together and dressed up. I notice that when men who are heavy drinkers suddenly pull out of it and get all scrubbed up, they have almost a boyish look about them. Like boys on Sunday on their way to church. Although my father's sixty-eight, he doesn't look more than in his early or mid-fifties. Good lean build, erect carriage, long, straight nose, something noble about him. And, this time, when he was brought into my cell, he actually had this boyish look to him. His complexion is ruddy anyhow, and he'd had a close shave. His brown hair, which is still with him, was all combed and slicked back. But he does have a wild little cowlick way back at the end of his part and right there, in the middle of all the slickness, were these ten or twelve hairs sticking up. His eyes were the giveaway; they weren't bloodshot so much as the rims were edged in red. And his hands were unsteady, his whole body, actually, was trembling when he hugged me.

He simply hugged me and kept saying "My boy, my boy!" He

has a very theatrical voice, anyhow, but now it was full of quavers and I could sense he was about to cry. So there I was, in jail for killing someone, patting him on the back and telling him, "It's all right, Dad. It's all right, it's all right." I took his hand and squeezed it.

Up until he arrived I'd been very nervous, anticipating his visit; now that he was here, I felt suddenly calm and in control.

I led him over and he sat on my cot, taking a handkerchief out of his breast pocket and wiping off his face. After he composed himself he looked up at me and said, "You didn't do that, did you? You didn't do that?"

There had been no doubt that I'd done it from the very beginning, and if anyone else had put this question to me, I wouldn't have understood why. Being it was my father, I sort of understood. He's not always too much in touch with the reality of certain things, especially in times of crisis.

When I said yes, he groaned, a very low, stricken groan. Then he mumbled "My boy" several more times and put his head in his hands. I went over to kneel by him; I put a hand on his leg and we stayed that way for quite a while, until he finally cleared his throat and raised his face. "I suppose you'd better tell me about it," he said. But the way he said it, like the moan, his voice low and sad, with a tone of hopelessness about it, indicated he was not really looking forward to taking on such a heavy burden. Thinking about this, I didn't answer him right away; I just stared down at his black shoes and the high polish on them. "You'll tell me about it?" he said, more resigned than asking me.

"Yes," I replied, but the tone of his original sentence stuck with me and took away any desire to do so. I stood up and walked away from him, trying to work up some momentum for even beginning to tell him, but I couldn't. So I just paced back and forth for a while.

Suddenly he stood up. "Would you like a priest? Perhaps if we had a priest!" I almost grinned; I knew he was reaching back into some old movie, or play, for the theatrical thing to say, for some way to avoid the reality of facing his only son and, in so many words, finding out how and why he killed a man.

Also, I had a weird sensation, looking at him, standing there, his face all lit up, waiting for my answer about a priest. It was this: even though he was right there physically, standing before me, I got an intense pang of homesickness for him. Homesick for perhaps some good time we had, diving off the pier at Santa Monica and swimming in to the beach, or going to the circus, or him baking bread, which he loves to do, and wreaking such havoc in our apartment, messing it up so much just baking *one* loaf of bread that you practically had to move out. The good, small times are the real times with him. The big moments he usually plays all half-melodramatic and distracted, trying to act out what he imagines would be the average, right, real-father emotions.

He spoke again. "Peter, would you like a priest?"

"No," I said, "not actually. Not right now."

His face fell; he was disappointed; not because he's so religious (although he's becoming more and more so with age), but because he had lost a good, honorable dodge to avoid facing the facts of what had happened. He said, "Well, then . . . ," and just stood there wagging his handsome, matinee-idol head back and forth. "You know, whatever happens, I'm behind you, Peter. You know that."

"Yes, I know."

His face lit up again. "And the men, all the men at the club, too!" He said this with great excitement, like this was really meant to cheer me up. "They sent me back first class on the plane. They told me I wasn't to worry about a thing. Not a thing." He reached into his pocket and took out his money clip, which was full of bills.

I swung away from him. "God—don't!" I said.

"What?" he asked.

The idea that something I'd done had caused him to accept even more charity than he already had, killed me. When a man his age can't even come to see his son in jail without it being charity! I didn't answer his question and he didn't press me. I think he knew what I was feeling. And when I turned around he'd put the money away.

"But a lawyer, you'll need a lawyer," he said. "They're arranging for a lawyer, from New York, a good lawyer. You knew that?" I told him I heard a lawyer was being engaged. "Oh, yes, the Masquers is behind you one hundred percent!" He rubbed his hands together. "They're a great bunch of boys. Lovely men . . . lovely." (I always get a kick out of him calling a man "lovely." He's extremely masculine; it's incongruous and a little dated, I suppose, but good to hear.)

He suddenly let out his laugh, which is more like a lion's roar. It was too much for him and he went into a coughing spell. I walked over and slapped him on the back. When he stopped, he nodded and thanked me. "The damndest thing happened at the club last week. We had a Pipe Night and Percy Doolittle—" He chuckled. "Oh, Lord, that Percy— He's a—he's a lovely fellow." But he never finished. I think the combination of a reverie over Percy Doolittle and the realization that this was perhaps not the time to tell a funny story stopped him. He just sort of wound down.

He took out a cigarette; his hand was trembling so he could hardly get the lighter together with it. Almost in answer to this he said, "I didn't take a drink on the plane. Not a drink."

I knew he was dying for one, and I knew this meeting was more painful for him than it was disappointing, no matter how much expected, for me.

"They showed a movie on the plane." He exhaled a long stream of smoke. "Imagine that, seeing a movie all those—oh, I don't know how many—thousands of feet up in the sky!" He shook his head about that and I agreed with him that it was pretty wild. He looked around the cell, spotted the toilet in the corner, walked over and dropped his cigarette into it and flushed it. He stood there looking down at the cigarette disappear, as if this, too, were a miracle. When the flushing had stopped, he turned around to me. "Well, Peter," he said. "Now, tell me, boy. Isn't there something I could do for you? Something . . ."

"Yes," I answered, getting an idea.

"Yes!" he repeated with enthusiasm. "You just tell me. What?"

"I'd like a tuna fish sandwich—and a couple of boxes of Good and Plentys."

"You would, would you?" He laughed, his lion laugh again. "Well, that shouldn't be too difficult. You really want one of your tuna fish sandwiches, do you?"

"Yes," I said. I'm crazy for tuna fish and I'm addicted to Good and Plentys, my favorite candy.

He was delighted; I think he was getting a kick out of me, at a time like this, being composed enough to ask for things like that. He was also thinking he had an excuse to leave.

A sudden feeling of anger at myself—that all this sounds like I'm patronizing him. I don't mean to. I understand him. It's just that I've seen him go through so many disappointments with his career, seen him suffer so many knocks and degradations that would make you cringe. And he takes them quietly, like a man, no self-pity. So that no matter what, I have to help him.

He got over his enjoyment about the sandwich and candy and down to facts. "Yes, well . . . would you like them now?"

"Sure, why not?"

"Well, then, we mustn't keep this young man waiting," he said, as if talking to some third party. He walked toward the cell door. The guard, who had been standing a few discreet feet away, moved to open it. "Shouldn't be too hard to come up with," he added, with just that tinge of doubt edging his voice that they might not be found in the first place he went to.

"You might have to try around," I said.

"Mmn, but I'll be coming back soon."

The guard let him out and he turned back to me. Before he could say anything, I said, "I'm all right here, Dad." I was telling him goodbye for now and not to worry, go on his binge.

He didn't acknowledge that, but busied himself buttoning up his overcoat. Then he said to the guard, "I'll be coming back in a while," and walked on briskly down the corridor.

Oddly enough, listening to his footsteps fade away, I felt great affection for him. I suppose the affection was for a scene we'd played out before. I was on old familiar ground with him and at least it was comfortable in some damn screwy way. You see, I really feel like *his* father sometimes. In the clinches. And although right now I could use one of those fathers you see in insurance ads—what can you do?

Of course, I haven't seen him since. It's only been three days; I don't know what he could be doing in Concord, New Hampshire, for three whole days. Yes, I do. When he gets like that he doesn't really know where he is anyhow. Maybe he's gone down to Boston. I give him another few days and then he'll show up. I get dizzy thinking about the remorse we'll have to go through.

So, to get on with these little difficulties I've had here. Early that evening I was brought to a room, like a smoking lounge, next to the sheriff's office. The sheriff wasn't around, but one man in civilian clothes introduced himself as the state's attorney. His name is David Gerstein. I liked him—tall, easygoing, prematurely gray, nice homey, lived-in face. One of the policemen that accompanied the sheriff when he first brought me here was there and another man, Mr. Gerstein's assistant. Mr. Gerstein did all the talking, very nice, low pressure. He said he had a statement he wanted me to sign, a formal statement.

When he said that, I asked him, "You mean a confession?"

He smiled, a warm smile, also a bit amused. "Well . . . let's call it a statement of fact."

I'd been told my lawyer would be arriving the next day and I remembered so many movies and TV shows where the defendant is always being bawled out by his lawyer for having signed a statement or talking too much, so I told Mr. Gerstein I thought I'd better wait until my lawyer got there.

"Peter, this isn't anything you'd object to, I'm sure. It's simply a statement fixing the exact time, place, and circumstances of the"— he hesitated for a second—"of the man's death," he added. I thought how considerate that was, not using "murder" or even "crime." "You're not changing your original admission to the sheriff, are you?" I told him I wasn't. He seemed a little relieved and

22

slid these stapled papers over in front of me. "In that case, why don't you read this, Peter? I don't think you'll find anything to object to."

Now I'll tell you something. In spite of what I said about my father's visit, I was not all that cheered up when he actually *didn't* come back. Added to that, knowing I wouldn't sign anything until I talked to my lawyer, I thought I would rather not read about the whole thing in black and white. So I told Mr. Gerstein: "If you don't mind, I'd rather not read it."

"Why not?" he asked.

I leveled with him. "I don't want to get any more depressed."

He looked at me for a moment and then he smiled. He took out a cigarette and asked me if I wanted one; I told him I didn't smoke. He said he understood my father had arrived, and complimented his acting, saying he remembered him from pictures. He asked me if I was being treated well and I told him I was. He asked me once more if I wouldn't reconsider and at least read the statement. He was so nice about everything I actually thought maybe I'd better, but just as I was hesitating and looking over at the papers, he said, "All right, Peter, that's all for now." He shook my hand, said "Take care" and the interview was over.

When I was back in my cell I was actually sorry we didn't talk more.

No trouble there, but the next afternoon my lawyer, Lawrence Hartl, showed up from New York. For this meeting they took me to another private room, on the second floor, with just a long table and a few chairs and that awful, unfinished picture of George Washington, in which his expression is kind of mean and prissy, like those wooden false teeth of his must really be killing him.

I'd only been in there a minute or so when a policeman opened the door and in Mr. Hartl breezed. Some people, when they come in from the outside, bring in cold air with them that's refreshing and welcome, like that old phrase—a breath of fresh air. Others throw off just plain damp cold air and make you shiver. He belongs to the latter group.

He's a short, stocky man, lots of wiry, sandy hair and energy, a rasping voice, and an annoying habit of never really looking at you. He'd hardly got in the door and introduced himself when he was at the table, opening up a large briefcase and pawing through a lot of papers, putting some on the table and some back in the briefcase and talking steadily all the while, telling me about his one friend at the Masquers who had phoned him in New York. He also said he didn't much like to take cases out of New York, but he was doing this as a favor to his friend, making it all seem—I don't know—*remote,* from me.

I know what put me off: he didn't take the time or trouble to look at me, to size me up, see what kind of a person he was dealing with.

But he raced on, using some legal terms I didn't understand, explaining what the procedure would probably be, complaining about a bad cold he had and the trip up from New York. At first I kept wishing he'd sit down and *settle* down and focus on me and maybe we could talk. Then I'm afraid I really stopped listening to him; all I remember was a pulling-away feeling and thinking I wasn't really going to be able to communicate with him.

Finally he did take a seat. He blew his nose and I thought maybe this fidgeting amounted to his usual preliminaries and they were over with, but then he said "Just a minute" and delved into some more papers, skimming over them, like he was gleaning facts here and there.

After a while he put them down, wiped off his glasses, and actually looked at me. "I suppose this man Gerstein's been to see you," he said. I told about our meeting and he was pleased that I hadn't signed anything and called me a "smart kid." Just as he was going back to his papers he mumbled, "I hear he's one of those smooth Ivy League kikes."

I'm afraid that brought the curtain down. I said, "I liked him." He didn't answer or even react to that; he was involved in his papers again. I couldn't help thinking how much better I liked Mr. Gerstein and wishing it were the other way around, that he was my

24

lawyer and this Mr. Hartl was on the other side—or not there at all.

During my thinking, he asked me a question, which I missed. When I excused myself and asked him what he said, he got testy, looking at his watch, saying it was three-thirty and he had to get a five o'clock plane and we didn't have a lot of time to waste. I wanted to suggest he could make an earlier plane, if that's the way it was going to be, but I didn't have the nerve.

He asked me a few questions, which I answered, mainly about any chances of premeditation. Then he said he'd like to get down to the heart of the matter with me. But *he* was the one that did the talking; he began telling *me* what had happened. He had talked to various teachers and a few students at school, and he had a copy of the very first police report, and just from those he was making up a whole version of what happened. He started making assumptions, like the worst of the newspapers, right from the start.

Suddenly I knew it was impossible; we could never work together. You see, no matter what I did, there is a specialness about it, about Jordan's and my friendship, and about Mr. Hoyt, that is *so* special I don't think I could tell it to many people. He finally asked me a question and then answered it *for* me and his language was so crude I found myself standing up and saying "No."

"No—what?" he asked.

All I could do was shrug and say, "No, I can't—" But because of his personality, and even though I didn't like him, I was still cowardly about telling him I didn't want him for a lawyer. I made him drag it out of me, which I hated myself for.

"No, you can't—what?" he asked.

"—tell you."

"Tell me?" he repeated. Then he shrugged. "I'm afraid you'll have to."

"No, talk to you," I said, looking down at the floor and loathing myself.

"What?" he asked again. Then: "Oh," he said knowingly, "you mean about . . ."

25

I knew what he was leaping at; I looked up at him then and saw an expression which allowed me to keep looking at him and say, "About anything." There was a silence and I looked away and said, "I'm sorry."

Oddly enough his tone changed a bit for the better. He told me if I wanted help I'd have to tell someone. I wanted to ask him why, if this was so, *he* was telling *me,* going off on his own version, but I only nodded in agreement. He finally said something about how I'd better start cooperating, that I was "in a big enough heap of trouble already."

"Don't!" I said. He looked confused. "Don't scare me," I told him. "I'm scared enough already."

That ended it. He sighed, said "All right, all right," and began putting his papers back in his briefcase while I stood there, embarrassed, hoping he'd leave quickly, which he did, wishing me luck and saying, "I'll tell Leon"—his friend at the Masquers—"this was entirely your decision."

When the guards took me back to my cell I lay on my cot, feeling relieved and frightened at the same time, wondering what the next step was. A half hour later the sheriff came to my cell, wanting to know what happened. I told him I just didn't think Mr. Hartl was the right lawyer for me and he asked why. I wanted to say because he had no sensitivity but I shied away from that word due to its implications, simply saying I felt I couldn't really talk to him.

I was hoping he might be able to help me out, and when he said, "Mmn, well let's see now . . . ," I stood up from my cot and started over to the bars. Then he came out with "Who *would* you like? Clarence Darrow?"

I stopped, looked him straight in the eye and said, "Yes, if you can dig him up!"

He made a little sound, indicating I was pretty sharp, and walked away. The way I looked at it, I was being honest about something fairly important: who is going to defend me. That's not anything you want someone to be flip about. Also, frankly, I was worried. This made me nervous, so I got flip back at him.

That evening it got worse. After dinner they took me to the

showers, along with seven other prisoners, men in their late thirties, forties or early fifties. One of them, a husky man with a lot of black curly hair, whom they call El Greco, stood at the spigot next to me. He's a house painter and one of the jail's "regulars." Every few months he's brought in for wife and/or child beating.

At first he sang in Greek; actually he's got a pretty good voice. Then he started looking over at me to get my reaction to his singing. I smiled at him and nodded and he smiled back, but pretty soon he was soaping himself up and leering at me, singing *to* me, making sly little gestures, and getting a big kick out of it. I naturally avoided looking at him after a while. When I did this, he got an even larger jolt out of it and stopped singing and spoke to me in Greek. His tone was very insinuating. I turned my back to him and he gave a loud wolf whistle and slapped me on the ass. The two guards, who were standing in the doorway to the long, tiled shower room, laughed at this. The other prisoners, too. I told myself to keep cool. But then he started singing "I've Got a Crush on You" to me, in broken English, but he knew all the lyrics.

Well, I've got a sense of humor and because of the implications in the newspapers and me being eighteen I can go along with a joke. But then when the six other prisoners joined in and one of the guards as well—the other one was too busy laughing to sing— then it got a little heavy-handed.

What are you supposed to do—just stand there in the shower all wet and naked and sing along *with* them? I finally decided to turn around and face him, like a man, and maybe he'd get embarrassed and stop. When I did that, he applauded and leered even more and I kept wishing I could turn off my blushing and just stand there with a whole lot of poise, as if I were taking a shower alone.

I couldn't turn off my blushing, though, but I figured out something else to turn off. What I did, when El Greco turned his back on me to lead them conductorlike in a big crescendo ending to the song—I quickly reached over and switched off the cold water. I knew he wouldn't really get burned, because he'd jump out of the way as soon as he felt the hot. He took off in one big leap, yowling and cursing; when he landed a few steps away he slipped, his feet went out from under him, and he took a pretty hard and comical-looking pratfall. Immediately the other prisoners and the guards began laughing at him. The man nearest him leaned down and said something—I didn't get it—and the next thing El Greco had scrambled to his feet and butted him in the stomach with his head. For a moment I thought there was going to be a wild free-for-all right there in the shower, but the guards rushed in and broke it up and we were all hustled out and back to our cells double time.

It wasn't long before one of the guards came for me and marched me to the sheriff's office. When I walked in, he shook his head and asked me for an explanation. I told him about El Greco, about the gestures, the slap, the cracks he was making in Greek, and about the big community sing. When I was all finished he still looked at me and said, "Yes, I realize that. But why did you turn the hot water on him?" I couldn't believe it. I'd just *told* him why; I thought that was obvious. "Well, speak up!" he said.

By this time I was beginning not to like the sheriff. "He sang off-key," I said.

For a split second I thought he was going to slap me, but then a strange and very slow smile crawled over his face. "Oh, you want to be funny, do you? All right, we'll see if we can't provide you with a few laughs while you're here."

It's odd that I would talk back to him. You may not believe it but it's true: I'm usually very shy around people I don't know, unless it's someone I take to immediately. Then I can become quite forward, as far as trying to get to know them. But I don't usually sass people. I don't know what came over me.

Perhaps when people treat you as if you're a shifty character, you don't want to spoil the picture, so you kind of carry on the myth. Anyhow, at this point, I thought: Oh-oh, watch out, don't get in trouble with the guy that runs the place.

That evening was when I decided to go on a silent binge. Not absolute silence. I mean I would answer a question now and then. Or even ask for something, if I wanted it badly enough. But I decided I wouldn't discuss the case, wouldn't answer back the other prisoners, wouldn't talk if I could help it.

I was, by this time, confused and miserable, and I told myself I'd better keep to myself until I figured out a pattern of behavior that would keep me out of any further trouble. I lay awake thinking of the best person to contact for help in getting a good lawyer. I didn't think of you right off; I suppose because I knew you were busy on a major case.

It wasn't until about two A.M. that I thought of my father's doctor, and mine, in California. A great man, intelligent and always very concerned. The next morning I asked Henry, the most decent of the guards, to ask the sheriff if I could send a wire in regards to getting a lawyer. He came back with word that I could not, that they were trying to locate my father, and nothing would be done until then.

Shortly after lunch I heard a lot of whistling from down the corridor, a few come-on Greek phrases from El Greco, and Henry appeared with Marjorie Koff, a writer for one of the Boston papers. I understood why the commotion; she's what you would call a very attractive package. Though she's probably close to fifty, at a distance you would swear not over thirty-five. The essence of femininity, tiny, very pretty legs, smart dresser, pretty chestnut hair, little white gloves, little flowered hat, big wide smile, dimples, soft voice —but watch out for the eyes: steel-blue bullets. Such a piercing look, right off, that you would swear her eyeballs were pointed.

She actually carried a little jeweled tape recorder and a box of chocolates. Henry introduced her, saying she was here to do an interview with me, and started unlocking the door. Right away I stepped up to the bars. "No, please," I said, "no interview."

Henry hesitated, but Miss Koff laughed very girly-girly as if it were a joke and said, "Come on, Henry, open up."

"No!" I said firmly.

She just waved a gloved hand in the air and said, "Oh, *Henry!*" as if: don't pay any attention to *that*.

He told me she was a good writer. I just shook my head and right away he turned to her and said, "The boy doesn't have to give an interview if he doesn't want to, Miss Koff."

"He will, he will," she chirped. "You just go on down the hall and leave us chat a minute." He hesitated and she gave him a play-ful shove. "Go on, Henry!" He walked away and she turned to face me through the bars. "Well, Peter," she said, "you're even better looking than your pictures, you know that?" I glanced away from her, thinking surely she'd put it as a rhetorical question because what could I possibly answer. But she spelled it out, as you would to a child: *"Do you know that, Peter?"* When I looked back at her she said, "Oh, I know many a girl would give her eyeteeth for big blue eyes like that." When I didn't answer she gave me a very pro-fessional look of appraisal and said, "You know what I've got fig-ured out about you? With all your blond hair and fair skin, I've got it figured out you have the strong personality of a brunet." She went on, all smiles and charm, telling me how we were going to be good friends and how the feature article she was going to write would do me a lot of good, ending up with, "Now why don't you tell Henry to let me in, and we'll just have a heart-to-heart."

I was very polite but firm. "I've decided not to talk to anyone about it until I've spoken with my lawyer."

The smile didn't leave for a minute; the eyes just got a little sharper. "Fair enough," she said. "We won't talk about anything you don't want to. We'll just have a chat, get to know each other, strictly off-the-cuff." She had changed her tactics, no longer patroni-zing, but speaking to me as an adult. Still, I thought that anyone who could work their eyes so independently from their face was not to be trusted. I had a strong hunch and stuck to it, wanting to end this meeting before I got into hot water.

"I'm sorry, I'd really rather not." I walked over toward my cot.

"Peter!" she called out, and when I turned around she held the box through the bars. "At least you can accept the candy I brought you." She smiled at me. "I imagine the food's not too exciting," she added.

She was right. Besides, I have a sweet tooth and I wanted the chocolates, but I figured if you're not going to talk, don't take the candy. "No, thank you," I said.

That did it. For one moment her smile snapped shut and the rest of her face matched her eyes and I knew I'd been right. I'm sure the moment was involuntary, like a power failure for one second during a storm, because the smile came right back on. Although she was annoyed, she was smarter than to show it. "I'm sorry we can't get to know each other, Peter." When I didn't answer, she added, "You may not know it, but a good journalist can do you as much good as a lawyer." She took a card out of her purse and slid it under the ribbon on the box of chocolates. "I'm leaving my card and number, Peter. If you should change your mind, if you should need any help or want anyone—just to talk to—tell the sheriff. He's an old friend of mine, and he'll get in touch with me."

The way she said it was so nice I almost had second thoughts as she bent down and set the box of candy between the bars and gave it a little shove with the tip of her toe. But I kept thinking of her eyes. No more nudging, she just said goodbye, turned and walked away. I suddenly thought at least she hadn't threatened me with a bad review or tried to scare me. I stepped quickly up to the bars—just in time to hear her hiss to Henry: "Little bastard!"

I wanted her to know I'd heard it. I gave the box of chocolates, with her calling card, a savage kick and sent it slamming up against the bars of the cell opposite. I couldn't see her or Henry but their footsteps stopped for a minute before continuing on until they were drowned out by El Greco's whistles and catcalls.

I quickly straightened up my cot and combed my hair, waiting for a visit from my friend, the sheriff. He didn't disappoint me. My refusing to give her an interview griped him more than anything I'd done or said before. He really read me the riot act, ending with, "You'll get no help, no help from anyone, if you continue to act this way." He started to walk away.

A real moment of panic struck me and I called to him. He turned around and I leveled with him. "Mr. Clay," I said, "I'm not actually feeling so well—all messed up—I'm sorry."

He seemed concerned and took a step back to my cell. "You feel sick?" he asked.

I didn't want to plead physical illness, didn't want to lie to him.

"No," I said, "just me, inside, I feel all mixed up and—" I was going to finish and say that's why I might act funny now and then, but he cut me off: "I should think so!" He shrugged and walked away.

Damn it, you see, if he'd stayed and let me finish and talked to me, I feel . . . well, that we could have *talked*. Bad timing, all along with him. That afternoon was the low point. I sat there getting into a deeper and deeper funk, thinking: No lawyer, no father, no friends. The self-pity was nauseating enough, but the feeling of fear was even more sickening. I had one window in that cell, high up, so I could only look up into the bare branches of a tree and by the time it began to get dark I was actually feeling physically ill, numb and shaking at the same time. I was actually thinking about calling for the sheriff and telling him, all right, I'll do anything you want, talk to anyone, reporters, the state's attorney — anything.

Which brings us to your phone call out of the blue. I never would have thought to get in touch with you, knowing you were just starting on the Wilk case. The fact that you got interested from all the newspaper publicity and sensed certain things between the lines and then called *me* is still a miracle in my eyes. God is *not* hiding out in Mexico City. That was three days ago. I haven't seen my friend, the sheriff, since, but Henry is very impressed that I've got you and, as I said, everyone is treating me with kid gloves. I even got a private shower last night, if you call being stared at by two guards private. At least nobody sang to me.

So now, as Mr. Hartl said, "to get down to the heart of the matter."

3

BOARDING STUDENTS were supposed to arrive on Saturday or Sunday at the latest at Gilford. I didn't leave California until Monday, so I was a full day late. My father was sick from a heavy bout of drinking, and the superintendent of our apartment building, a Mrs. Mosley, who's more like a den mother and very nosy about what goes on with all the tenants but very fond of my father, was away visiting her sister and wouldn't be back until Monday. I didn't want to leave him alone. She's very good about stopping in and seeing he's all right, even bringing him food.

Riding out in the airport bus, 1 had mixed feelings. I couldn't wait to get out of California. Everything tacky and sad and disappointing, that's what California represents to me. Because of my father and the way his career has gone, the way we've had to live, some things I've seen there. Also, my best friend, Boots, had moved north to Oakland that spring so there wasn't much there for me. On the other hand I was concerned about leaving my father, especially in the condition he was in, but even my regrets were mixed. It's not much fun being around him during these periods and the last month or so, since the series fell through, had been rough going.

To be honest, I was much more glad than sad to be leaving. By the time I was up in the plane, I was almost manic. I was just giving myself up to the adventure of what was happening. I'd never been to a prep school, so there was that to look forward to. I'd been to Boston and Martha's Vineyard with my father but never farther up into New England, and there was that. The main thing I was looking forward to was making a best friend. In case that sounds mawkish or Tom Swift Goes to Prep School, I'll have to let it stand. If I'm a fanatic about one thing, it's having one particular best friend that I can really connect with. Although I can make friends easily, if the signals are right, I've never really wanted, nor had, a large circle of just plain friends. I've never run with a pack or been part of a gang. Give me one good close friend any day. I suppose I'm what you'd call monogamous when it comes to friends. So, that was what I was really looking forward to.

The trip was great, lunch, a rotten Doris Day movie, changed planes in New York, on to Boston where I had dinner and then got the train for Brewster, New Hampshire, the nearest train town to Saypool. After two jet planes, stepping onto the train was like stepping back in time. It was incredibly old-fashioned, paneled wood, worn green seats, funny lighting fixtures, and the musty, closed-in smell of train steam. Even the conductor and the few passengers had an antique look about them, like figures out of a wax museum. It was night but the moon was out and I could make out the dark, wooded hills as we crossed over into New Hampshire. I let the combination of the train and the countryside turn my imagination loose. I wasn't going to prep school in New Hampshire. I was traveling backward into the last century, just crossing over into Transylvania, where, as they say, little did I know what awaited me at the Castle Frankenstein.

If I'm giving the impression I had some premonition of what *was* awaiting me, I'm not. It's just that in hindsight, something strikes me. The irony of it, perhaps.

The train stopped often and for long periods of time. A few people would dribble off now and then and many times it looked like there wasn't even a station. I was in the middle of a gory paper-

34

back, and when the conductor finally called out Brewster, I looked at my watch and it was a few minutes after eleven; we were an hour and forty-five minutes late. Nobody got off but me and if I'd thought the other passengers had been getting off at dinky places, I stepped off into Nowhere, U.S.A. Nothing but a long shed, a small, locked-up waiting room with about a five-watt bulb and a barred-up ticket window at the end. In the distance I could barely see lights in two or three old houses up on the side of a hill. After the train pulled away and I'd become accustomed to the dark, I could make out a crossroads about fifty yards away and on the other side a darkened store and gas station.

The sheet of instructions from the school said, among other things: "Taxis available at all times from Brewster to Saypool, a distance of twelve miles." That gave me a laugh—not really, I was feeling a bit lost. While I was debating what to do, a truck zoomed by the crossroads, shaking the platform I was standing on, and right after it went by a light went on over the store. I took that as a sign to go over. I left my typewriter and one bag and decided to carry the other suitcase so whoever answered wouldn't think I was a burglar or a bum. Just as I was a few steps from crossing the road, a car came tearing by going about seventy. The headlights shone on me and I jumped back. There was a wild screeching of brakes and for a moment I thought the car would skid off the road. The taillights did swerve from side to side but the car finally stopped, slammed into reverse and backed up so fast I stepped back off the road again.

I was certain it was some kind of New England hot-rodder, but not only did I hear the driver call out "Taxi, Mistah?" in that strong New England accent but when I stepped up to the car I saw that he was at least as old as the miles per hour he'd been going.

I put my things in the back seat and started to get in front with the driver. "This is a taxi, Mistah—in the back." I thought, Oh-oh, here's a testy character. But not at all, as it turned out. He does have that one rule and he is one of your most definite characters, but he's a gem. The only description for Cutler Barnum is: he

35

looks like an old billy goat, skinny and wrinkled, little wisp of a chalky-gray goatee and old-fashioned round metal-framed glasses. From his looks, you'd think he'd just about be able to manage a Model T at fifteen miles an hour, but he's a speed demon. First thing he said to me after he'd reached a speed between sixty and seventy was "Lucky for you I just happened to be driving around."

I smiled. If he just happened to be driving around at that speed, I wondered what it was like when he was on his way someplace specific in a hurry. "Day late for Gilford," he said. I answered yes and asked him how he knew. He laughed and said, "Where'd you think I was takin' yah?" It suddenly struck me I hadn't even told him where I was going. We became friends right off. And have been friends ever since. Not so incidentally, he would be a good one to call for a character witness from up there. Jordan and I took his taxi almost every weekend. When the time comes, please get in touch with: Cutler Barnum, Saypool, taxi phone: 7649.

The road from Brewster comes into Saypool at the edge of the village, the main part being off to the right and down the hill. The school is about the equivalent of three blocks to the left, so I didn't see the village that first night. Not much of the school either, as it was mostly dark. Cutler Barnum pulled up by a two-story colonial house set back a ways from the sidewalk, with only a night light on the porch. "Headmaster's conked out early, but there's lights on over there," he said. To the left and set way back, the ground-floor lights were on in a large, three-story wooden building. "Lincoln House," he added.

"That's me," I answered. I paid, thanked him, and walked down a wide, neatly mowed piece of lawn that led past the headmaster's house straight to what I could tell was the large, granite school building up on a rise. To the left and halfway to it was Lincoln House. As I stepped up on the porch, a man got up from an easy chair and came to the door, opening it for me.

"You must be the boy from California!" he said, shaking my hand. I didn't much like that tag, but the way he said it made it seem almost exotic, like: Oh, the boy from Mars! We went through

36

small talk about the trip and a few questions about California, then he realized he hadn't introduced himself. "Oh, I don't know where my mind is, beginning of school and all. I'm Carl Kauffman, two f's, history and Glee Club." He chuckled and added, as if he were letting me in on a little joke and a secret at the same time, *"And* your housemaster. I know we're going to have a dandy year."

Right away I got the feeling of primness about him. He's actually not a bad-looking man, in a sort of thin-faced, lean-framed way, with his horn-rimmed glasses. He has a pleasant face, regular features, and extremely tidy, little waves to his brown hair that hugged his head and never got out of place. He asked if I'd like a glass of milk before turning in. Not being a milk fan, I asked for a Coke. "Oh," he said, giving me a playfully reproachful look, "Cokes are bad for our teeth."

Carl Kauffman should have been a male nurse. He has that kind of antiseptic personality. He's one of those people who invariably use the plural "we" when he's really talking about "you." "Now, why did we do *that?*" "We must *think* before we answer the question." There's nothing basically mean about him, more a feeling of tightness. You wouldn't want to spend a lot of time with him.

He said he supposed he should call the headmaster and tell him I was there but then he looked out the window. "Lights all out," he said. "Well, you must be tired, Peter—all the way from *California!*" He said it as if I hadn't had the benefit of plane or train.

We'd been standing in the large parlor, comfortably furnished with two sofas and lots of easy chairs and three awful paintings of seascapes with gallons of purple and lavender in them. Behind it was the dining room with six large tables, all neatly set for the morning. After pointing it out, he started upstairs. When we hit the second floor he nodded to a door to the left. "My room," he whispered. "Eight boys on this floor, twelve on the top." We went on up to the third floor. There was a long wooden hallway, uncarpeted, with three light bulbs along the way. The doors to all the rooms were closed, except the large bathroom. He indicated for me to peek in there: four washbasins, three showers, two booths and two

37

urinals. Then he tiptoed to the end of the hall and opened the far door on the left and I followed him inside.

It was a single, corner room with two windows and a fire escape leading down from one. A maple bed, dresser, desk, desk chair, and an old brown leather easy chair. He switched on the desk lamp and turned off the overhead light. "That's better," he whispered. He asked me if I liked my room, walking to the corner and showing me the large closet. I told him it was fine. He looked at his watch, clucked, said good night and that it was good having me at Gilford and tiptoed out. While I was thinking he wasn't going to be an all-time favorite of mine, he opened the door and stuck his head in. "Do you sing?" "Sing?" I asked. "Yes—for Glee Club!" I quickly told him no. He snapped his fingers, said "Darn it!" and left.

I wasn't too sleepy; I was feeling the excitement of being in a new place. I unpacked, set my typewriter up on the desk and told myself I'd start a journal, now that I was away at school. I never did. God, how I wish I had.

When I was getting undressed the door opened a crack and a fellow in bathrobe and pajamas stuck his head in. "Hi," he said, looking down the hall as if he were being followed, "my name's Dennis Vacarro. I'm down on the second floor; I just came up to say hello." I introduced myself and walked over and shook his hand, which was extremely damp; his face was sweaty, too. I said to come in but he looked back down the hall and said, "No, better not, it's pretty late." He glanced down at the floor, then up at me and added, "I could sneak up later, though, and we could talk."

"Later?" I asked, confused by his saying it was late but that he could come up even later.

"You know, when everyone's asleep?" Again he looked down the hall.

I knew there was something strange. In this short time I'd noticed his eyes never stayed in one place. They'd go to me, then down to the floor, back down the hall, back to me, etc. "Well . . ." I said, not really knowing what to say.

"Only talk, I don't mean anything else but just talk," he said, making it a dead giveaway. Before I could answer he looked down the hall again, said "Oh-oh!" and took off. I heard footsteps and Mr. Kauffman's voice whispering to him in a stern way but I couldn't make out the words as they both went downstairs.

While I was brushing my teeth in the bathroom, a very good-looking boy with a dark complexion and tons of black hair came in and stood at the washbasin next to me. He said "Hi" and immediately took a brush, comb, and a small bottle of hair cream out of his bathrobe pocket and went to work. We exchanged names and made a little small talk but he never gave me his undivided attention, concentrating completely upon the ritual of combing his hair in the mirror, applying the lotion very gingerly and sparingly, patting it lightly upon his hair and then snatching his hand away as if he'd been stung, so he wouldn't get too much on, then combing his hair straight back, then snatching at bits of it with a very fine metal comb and twisting a swirl of it here, picking out a single curl with the fingers of his other hand and arranging it over the swirl. He did it quickly and adroitly, like a professional barber. By the time I finished washing up, he was still hard at it and I'm afraid I became engrossed. I was putting things back into my toilet bag slow motion. He glanced at me, not directly, but in the mirror, and said, "I'm an actor." I said "Oh!" and he added "Yes!" In another moment he finished and backed away from the mirror, took a long, admiring look at himself, sighed and said, "Well—gotta get to bed." He gathered up his things, said good night and left.

I had to smile, all that preparation for going to bed. Then I thought, Well, listen, maybe he has some pretty wild dreams and wants to be ready for them.

Lying in bed, I reviewed Carl Kauffman, the damp fellow with the nervous eyes and the actor and, as far as friends were concerned, couldn't help but think—well, that's three down.

The ungodly noise of shouting woke me up the next morning. It seems like all the guys on my floor wake up yelling. At first I was frightened; I even thought there might be a fire, but it was only everybody getting up and washed and making up their rooms.

I noticed there were a few double rooms and was glad I had a single. There were a few quick hellos in the bathroom but that was about all. When I followed everyone down for breakfast, Mr. Kauffman was waiting in the parlor for me. He took me in to my table and introduced me to the six other fellows, all seniors, already sitting there.

The "actor" was there, but I was relieved to see that the fellow with jittery eyes, Dennis Vacarro, wasn't. The following thumbnail sketches pretty well describe the group at my table:

ED ANDERS: Football, basketball, hockey, skiing and baseball star. Room like a sporting-goods store. Had fallen on the ski slope two years ago and stuck his metal ski pole into his intestines. Great bowel trouble because of this. Drank tons of mineral oil, very flatulent, goes to the john about twenty times a day.

WILEY BEVAN: Had actually had a sexual experience with a waitress the previous summer and couldn't get over it. Riveted to that one experience and, because of it, a certified sex maniac.

PHILIP SIMMONS: From a lower-middle Boston family. A new student, so excited to be away for his senior year at a prep school you'd have thought he was an exchange student at the University of Peking.

LEE GALONKA: The actor, going to be a movie star (he says). Brought his own three-way mirror to school to put on his dresser, five hairbrushes and about fifty combs. Mostly combs his hair—a hair-combing major.

JIMMY GREER: Sad, stutters something fierce, always looking like he wants to please so badly, hoping not so much to be included as hoping not to be *ex*cluded (if that makes any sense); still wets the bed occasionally. (Why do most stutterers wet the bed? Is it a package deal?)

40

LOGAN TINNEY: Fifteen, but a senior. Photographic memory, brilliant at book learning, loves to argue about anything he's read. Or hasn't read, for that matter. A born debater.

That was the cast. Ed Anders and Wiley Bevan had been at Gilford their entire high-school terms. The rest of us were new. With that many new students at one table, everyone was making his own point and the conversation was incredible.

Ed Anders got right to sports and was disappointed that I only played tennis, a game that fits in with my preference for an activity you can engage in with one friend, as opposed to a pack. Wiley Bevan let it be known right away that he wasn't a virgin. Philip Simmons told me immediately this was his first year away at prep school and asked if it was mine. He was delighted it was but a little of the edge was taken off when I told him about military academy. When he asked where I'd gone to school the year before, I simply said in California, not wanting to drop Hollywood right off.

Lee Galonka picked California up like a bloodhound. "Not Hollywood?" he asked. When I said yes, his reaction was so violent he knocked a glass of milk into poor Jimmy Greer's lap, who apologized to *him* for getting wet. Lee Galonka immediately wanted to know if I knew any actors personally. I thought if I told him my father was an actor, he'd knock over the whole table, so I didn't let him in on that until much later. Even when he found out, he didn't know the name; my father's brief heyday was way before Lee's movie-going time. When he asked me which movie stars I knew or had seen in person, actually wanting me to rattle off a string of names right there in front of everyone, I crossed him off my list. I told him I'd fill him in later. "Yeah—yeah!" he said, practically panting.

As for Logan Tinney, his beady little IBM eyes were tracking me from his baby-fat face; he was studying me, not diving right in. But he was ready to dispute almost everything anyone else said. The group at my table didn't seem to be too exciting or original and I was mildly disappointed.

41

After breakfast, Mr. Kauffman, who sat at another table, walked me around and went over the points of interest on the campus. Besides the headmaster's house, up front by the street, and Lincoln House, where I lived, there was the large, brown granite three-story school building sitting up on a small hill, only slightly larger in area than the building itself; below and behind on a flat surface, two tennis courts; to the left of the school building and also on a rise, a small gymnasium; then the grounds sloped gently downhill for about five hundred yards until they leveled off at the athletic field. To the right of the field is the shore of Big Pine Lake, which the entire campus slopes down to. There's a small strip of sand making a beach but then beyond the football field the shoreline turns into a heavily wooded area running for a curved mile or more around this side of the lake. On the other side of the school building from Lincoln House and halfway down to the lake are two large, brick dormitory buildings, Madison and Logan Halls, where the rest of the boarding students and several teachers live. A few other teachers live in the village. The school was much smaller than I'd imagined.

That September day was beautiful, warm and cloudless, and the view looking across the lake from the school was exceptionally peaceful, flat, wooded lands bordering the lake with a few scattered summer lodges and cottages and then beyond, wooded foothills leading up to rugged mountains, thick with trees themselves. My impression of the campus and surrounding country that morning could be summed up in two words—clean and, somehow, innocent. Innocent sounds odd, maybe unspoiled would be more like it.

Mr. Kauffman took me to the headmaster's office where his secretary, Mrs. Mason, an extremely well-organized woman, gave me my schedule of classes and my books. She explained that the headmaster, Mr. Hoyt, was with two of the teachers and would see me later.

After that Mr. Kauffman took me to the combination assembly hall–theater. Every morning before the first class, there is a brief chapel period with a prayer and hymn, nondenominational, but certainly Protestant in feeling, followed by announcements of various school activities. We talked for a few minutes while the auditorium was filling up and then he suggested I take a seat down front where the seniors sat. Somebody hissed at me; Lee Galonka, the actor, had saved me a place. I sat down and he immediately asked me if I knew Sandra Dee. I told him no, and was sorry I'd sat next to him.

Just then Franklyn Hoyt strode out onto the stage from the wings and I had my first look at the headmaster. A tall, lean man, he had a walk that struck me right off as being unique. He tilted forward, springing ahead with each step off the balls of his feet. Although I later learned he was fifty-one, the walk was extremely youthful, belonging more to a lanky adolescent, except for the urgency in it. He radiated energy, hardly ever walking as if he were just walking, always as if he were going from one specific spot to another and without a lot of time to waste. Because of the tilt and the springing motion, you always thought he was going to overshoot his mark. Like that morning, I thought he was going to end up way beyond the lectern in the middle of the stage, but he had a way of stopping suddenly, and then pivoting around to face you.

That morning, as he was walking, I also particularly noticed his hands. They were huge and seemed to swing independently of his body, even of his arms, like they'd been sewed on at the wrists. When he'd taken his place behind the lectern he cleared his throat and began right away with a prayer. His voice was low and almost theatrical in tone; there was a sternness about it, a determination that made it compelling to listen to. After a few lines, he glanced up and paused for a second, checking to see if we were all paying attention. There had been some small sounds of settling down but his look stopped all that and the auditorium became deadly quiet. He returned to the prayer and read about a dozen more lines before he looked up again. His gaze struck the center of the auditorium and then he looked over to the left, where I was sitting on the aisle. When his eyes came to me, he stopped. I thought I detected a small frown, probably because I was new, but then I thought this was only the second day of school and quite a few of the students must

43

be new. I might have made the frown up, because of his unusually thick eyebrows and deep-set brown eyes, but I know I didn't make up what he did next. He looked to see who I was sitting next to, Lee Galonka, and then back at me, before he went on with the prayer. Even Lee Galonka, who is not overly perceptive, noticed it, because I felt him looking over at me and then back up at Mr. Hoyt.

After the prayer, Mr. Kauffman stepped up onto the stage and sat down at the piano. Mr. Hoyt looked down at me once more when he announced the hymn which we all stood to sing. He didn't look at me during the hymn, however, and that gave me a chance to study him. He actually had a handsome face, rugged and strong, with good coloring. His eyebrows, although they were thick and dark, were not shaggy but neat and well defined. One focused on them first and his eyes. His nose was straight and long, good chin, prominent cheekbones, but it was his mouth that marred his looks. It was too small for his face and his lips were thin. As he was singing he moved his head and the right side of his face caught the auditorium lights. It was then I noticed a raised portion, like a carbuncle, about the size of a quarter, up over to the side of his forehead, close to the hairline. It had a slightly heightened reddish color, more than the rest of his face, although it wasn't exactly what you'd call angry-looking. His hair was medium length, parted on the left, and brown, although any bright light showed up some copper-reds in it.

After the hymn, he introduced Mr. Ingersoll, geometry, algebra and also football coach, who made some announcements about signing up for the football team. Mr. Hoyt walked to the side of the stage and took a chair next to the piano. Next Mr. Kauffman spoke about tryouts for the Glee Club and while he was talking I felt that Mr. Hoyt was staring at me. I glanced over and he was, but looked away, diverting his attention to Mr. Kauffman when our eyes met. I didn't look at him again during the assembly, because I could feel that he was, from time to time, looking at me.

My first class was French with a great old teacher, Mr. Lomax

44

Piper. It was my first year of French because I'd taken Spanish and Latin in California, so there were mainly younger students in the class. I hadn't been in there ten minutes when the headmaster's secretary opened the door and said, "Would you excuse Peter Kilburn for a few minutes?"

I couldn't explain it, but I had a shaky feeling in my stomach as I followed Mrs. Mason down the empty hall to the headmaster's office for my first meeting with Mr. Hoyt.

4

MRS. MASON ushered me in, simply saying my name and then ducking back out and shutting the door.

(Now, setting this first introduction down, a certain warped part of my mind thinks, What if she'd said in a very matter-of-fact voice: "Mr. Hoyt, this is Peter—he's here to kill you.")

He rose from his desk and leaned forward to shake my hand. My hand got lost and his grip was firm. The strong scent of bay rum pushed forward from him. When I think of him now, I can almost smell it. He indicated an old leather armchair which looked to be comfortable, but gave so much when I sat on it that I ended up practically sitting on the floor.

He took his chair and I immediately felt slightly uncomfortable, having to peer up over the desk at him. He picked up a pencil, twirled it over in his fingers and said, "Peter, you're a day late. Why is that?" I was just about to reply when he continued. "Actually two days. We asked that the boarding students be here on the ninth, the tenth at the latest."

"My father was sick and I didn't feel I should leave him."

"Oh, I'm sorry," he said, and there was concern in his voice. "Nothing serious?"

I wasn't going to tell him the reason, so I said, "No, just a sick spell."

Right away his voice took on the same sternness as when he was reciting the prayer in chapel. "You're not making up an excuse?"

"No, he was in bed for over a week. He still is, as far as I know." I felt a twinge of resentment that he would presume so early in our meeting that I was lying. I was hoping he'd welcome me to the school, say it was good having me there, etc.

He kept his eye on me, trying to decide whether I was telling the truth; I felt again the disadvantage of sitting so low. "If your father's ill, surely there must be someone to take care of him."

"Not really," I told him. "He's divorced from his wife and—"

"Divorced?" he asked, picking up a folder which I guessed was mine and opening it up. "I knew your mother was—" He glanced inside, then down at me. "Catholics, aren't you?" There was something about the way he used the plural that indicated he was not all that fond of *Catholics*. I told him yes and he repeated "Divorced?" again.

I didn't know what to say so I explained about the superintendent, Mrs. Mosley, being away and that I'd waited until she had returned, that she would look after him until he was on his feet again.

"This superintendent, this Mrs. Mosley, she's married and has a family?"

"No, she's a widow."

"But she lives with her children?"

"No, she doesn't have any." I was in the middle of wondering why he was interested in something so remote from me when I suddenly understood.

"I see," he said with distinct distaste, his lips pursed up as if he'd tasted a lemon.

I was so shocked that he had whipped up some nasty little story in his mind so quickly that anything I thought of to say that would clarify the situation wouldn't come out.

"Even so," he said, twirling the pencil again, "you could have sent a wire and advised us."

I had thought of it actually, but being we were not too flush and

47

my father's always being dunned by the phone company, I refrained. "I'm sorry," I told him.

"Sorry," he repeated, not actually sarcastic or mocking it, but as if the word were fairly ineffectual.

A feeling of uneasiness came over me, sitting in that strange office, in a strange school, with this strange man. I'd only been in there a few minutes, yet I had a feeling I wanted to go out, come back in and be introduced again, and start over. I also felt I didn't want to get off on the wrong foot with him, not at all. I decided to be honest. "Actually, my father is not too well off financially right at this particular time," I said. He kept looking at me until I felt compelled to add, "That's why I didn't send a telegram." Still he didn't reply and I thought maybe I'd try to lighten the conversation. I smiled at him and said, "I figured every little bit helps."

He didn't smile back but he accepted my reasons and nodded. "Yes, I'm aware that your tuition is being paid for by the father of an alumnus." He didn't say it with any feeling of put-down to it, simply stated it and went back to scanning my folder.

I happened to look at the raised spot on his forehead, trying to figure out if it was the result of an accident or if he'd been born with it. He started to turn a page, then glanced up quickly and caught me by surprise. I naturally took my eyes away, but I knew he was aware of what I'd been looking at and I silently cursed myself for being so stupidly juvenile as to *have* to look right then.

"Still," he said, "you could have had Mr. Bigelow send a wire."

Again he surprised me. Couldn't he realize that accepting tuition and spending money for a whole year was enough, without calling up someone and asking them to send a *telegram* for you? I had money and I was saving it, but I wished I'd sent the wire. I also wished he'd let me off the hook about it. "I suppose I didn't want to bother him," I said. Then I decided to throw myself on the mercy of the court. "I realize I should have sent a wire. I'm sorry I didn't."

That placated him. That was what he wanted—capitulation and a full apology. He closed the folder. "Well, you're here," he said,

48

nodding. "I would like to speak to you about your curriculum." (I'd picked out my schedule through the mails.) "I see you've had three years of Latin. However, you failed Latin last year and now you've elected to take first-year French instead of making up your Latin." I remembered from the brochure that he was the Latin teacher and I knew I was on tricky ground. I told him I'd done well in Spanish and right away he said, "And the reason you did, of course, was your two-year background in Latin."

It wasn't true, but I agreed with him, going on to say that although I respected Latin, I'd gotten all muddled up in it and felt I could achieve much more with a new language, starting in fresh at the very beginning. I actually felt Latin was—is—a dead language and consequently I couldn't work up interest in it; also my third-year Latin teacher was not interested either and was in no way inspiring.

Then he said that from the transcript of my school records he knew I had an exceptionally high IQ but that I was a year older than most seniors. He asked me why that was, but not before telling me it was a sign of laziness and that Gilford was anything but a lazy school. I explained to him that for one year I was traveling with my father, the last time he toured in a play. This didn't set well with Mr. Hoyt; again his mouth pursed up and his face became very tight. He said that was against the law. I didn't explain all the reasons to him, and there's no use going into them now. But that's how I lost a year. He went right back to the IQ, looking at the transcript and saying that my grades weren't what they should be except for Spanish and English.

I felt on a tightrope with him. Again I wanted to level with him. "Last year was not a good year for me. I had a part-time job in the evenings and on weekends."

"You had a job?" he said, showing surprise. He leaned forward in his chair and repeated the phrase.

"Yes," I went on, feeling a little annoyed that he presumed I wasn't the type to work. "That took up a lot of studying time, but I don't think that was the entire reason for my grades."

"Oh?" he said with interest.

"No, I'm afraid I didn't like Hollywood High School." Again he looked surprised, but pleasantly so. "It's too big, too flashy, I felt lost there. I didn't really take to my teachers, except for English."

"And Spanish, you did well in that?"

"I wanted to learn it badly enough, so I applied myself."

"Let's hope you apply yourself here."

"I will," I told him.

"Good!" he said and for the first time he smiled. His smile was frightening; it always was to me. It came too quickly, seemed to strain his entire face, and left just as quickly. Oddly enough, when he smiled at me that first time, I felt more uncomfortable than at any other moment during our interview. But then it snapped shut and he asked, "And you didn't like Hollywood High School?"

"No, I wasn't really happy there."

"In that case, I hope you will be happy here at Gilford."

I told him I was sure I would be. He asked me what activities I was interested in, but just then Mrs. Mason came into the room with some more folders. Mr. Hoyt stood up, said I'd better get back to my class, that as I had missed coming to his house the afternoon before with the rest of the seniors, I should come by at four that afternoon.

When I left I felt not so much at ease with him, as I did on probation. I didn't like the way he put me immediately on my guard. Although I'd felt quite peppy that morning, my short interview with him tired me out.

As I said, I am preoccupied about having one best friend. So during my classes that morning I paid more attention scouting for candidates than I did to the subjects or the teachers. I naturally hadn't met all the boarding students and I had no way of telling them from the day students. I had a hunch about which were which and it proved mainly to be right. Actually, the day students, who far outnumber the boarding students, have a more open, honest and healthier look about them.

Still, that day, I didn't spot anyone, either boarding or day, that I had an immediate, strong hunch about. I didn't let it bother me too much, though. I know it takes time.

Lunch was a duplication of breakfast, as far as the talk went. Lee Galonka asked me if I knew Ann-Margret; Ed Anders asked me if I was going out for the tennis team and criticized the school for not having a swimming pool, which reminded Wiley Bevan of a choice bit about him and his waitress friend "making it" in the swimming pool at the resort last summer. Philip Simmons wanted to know how I liked being at prep school and Logan Tinney told Lee Galonka he'd better start thinking of changing his last name if he was going to be a movie star. Jimmy Greer stuttered along, looking intensely interested at every word anyone said.

I began scanning the other tables, trying to spot someone worth cultivating. While we were eating dessert, the room was extremely noisy with talk and suddenly a hush came over it, like someone had turned off the sound. I looked up and Mr. Hoyt was standing in the doorway. His smile flashed on, he said "Hello, boys!" and turned and walked out of the house. Nobody commented on it or him and gradually the conversation got back to normal, but I thought how strange he had the power to quiet everyone down when actually nobody was doing anything wrong.

After lunch was when my troubles really began. I had gone up to my room, and when I came back down to walk over to school, Jimmy Greer was standing on the porch. I said "Hi" to him and he smiled and fell into step alongside me. Just then Mr. Hoyt was striding along with that strange tilting-ahead, bouncing-off-the-balls-of-his-feet walk of his. He was on the gravel path at the far side of the lawn and ahead of us by maybe fifteen yards. Jimmy Greer tried to say something but his stutter made the words stick in his mouth. To clear the air I said something, I forget what, probably about the weather or lunch.

By this time Mr. Hoyt had gone up the steps and was tipping along the last few yards before going in the front door of the school.

"He's got a fa-fa-funny walk, huh?" Jimmy said. He wasn't laughing when he said it, just commenting on it.

I answered yes and said, "Kind of like this." Then I swung my arms out from my sides and took several steps, springing off the balls of my feet. I swear to God I wasn't making fun of him; I was just trying to figure out how he did it. And I did; I got into the swing of it and then Jimmy Greer giggled and said, "Ya-yes, that's it."

He went on giggling, but the giggle turned into a gasp and he stopped dead in his tracks, so suddenly that I glanced over at him and the expression on his face made me look immediately toward the school. Mr. Hoyt was standing in the doorway, one hand holding the door open, on his way back out again. I suppose he had forgotten something. He, too, froze for a moment, as I did, one leg ahead of me, my arms cocked out from my sides, in the middle of a step. It was a brutal moment. I could see the expression of anger and distaste on his face, even though we were a good distance away from him.

Finally he let the door close and started forward to the steps; for a second I thought he was going to come down them and over to us, but there's a gravel path on either side of the lawn and as Jimmy Greer and I started walking soberly forward, heads down, I could tell he was going to take the path to our right which led to his house instead of the one we were on. I was relieved in a way; yet in a way I wasn't.

I had an immediate urge to explain that I hadn't meant to make fun of him, so as not to let the awkwardness of that moment drag on, but I had no idea of how exactly to do it. When I felt he was about even with us, on the far path, I glanced over. He was walking straight ahead at a fast clip, eyes forward. I could see that his face was red and I also noticed that the raised spot on his forehead stood out white, drained of its color.

When Jimmy Greer felt that Mr. Hoyt was past us, he said, "I think he sa-saw." I replied yes and neither of us spoke again as we climbed up the steps. Walking into the dark hallway, I was numbed by what had happened; I don't even remember Jimmy leaving me, but after a while I found myself just standing there by my locker while school was coming to life for the afternoon classes.

I remembered I was to be at his house at four and right then I

52

knew I couldn't stand the suspense. I decided to try somehow to explain it hadn't been my intention to make fun of him. I walked down the hall to wait for him to return but as soon as I got even with the front door I caught a glimpse of the top of his head bobbing up the steps.

The surprise of seeing him coming back so soon and the coward in me sent me into an abrupt about-face, tearing down the hall and around the corner.

The afternoon session was a total loss. I might as well have been sitting in a closet. I wasn't able to pay attention to the subjects or to the teachers. I wasn't even scouting around for a potential best friend. I wasn't doing anything but sweating out my predicament. I started planning all sorts of explanations to him. But my concentration was shot, and I'd no sooner think of something like "Very unusual walk . . . admiring it" and lies like "Walk like my father . . . couldn't help but notice" when I'd cancel them out, realizing that just from our first interview he was not the kind of man to take any comment about a personal trait from a lowly student. Then I'd sit in a daze, my thoughts all muddled, hating myself for having done such a stupid thing, hating fate or whatever for letting a tiny thing like that happen on my first day and also hating myself for being so nervous about it.

Looking back, I should have followed my first impulse and attempted an explanation right then before classes started, though it would have been a difficult scene at best. Still, it would have been much better than the scene I was headed for. You probably think I was wildly overreacting but, you see, I might have been unsure about many things, what to do, what to say, but I was sure of one thing: I was in trouble.

Before I get into that, my father showed up back here at jail this afternoon with a woolly story about not feeling well the day he was here and thinking he'd just better get down to New York and consult a good doctor. The reason I didn't hear from him was, if he turned out to be terribly sick, he figured I had enough troubles and he didn't want to worry me about that. But now he's fine and not only that, he's got a great part in a picture.

Of course in his conversation today he kept mentioning this actor and that "lovely" fellow at the Players Club in New York. So what really happened, he probably got to "not feeling well" as soon as he left here and somehow found his way to the airport and a plane to New York to be with his buddies at the Players, the East Coast contingent of his Masquers pals in Hollywood.

The movie job is a charming example of the workings of Hollywood. In it he plays a kindly ex-schoolteacher turned derelict Bowery bum who has gasoline poured over him and is set on fire, just for kicks, by a gang of juvenile delinquents on the Lower East Side. The leader of the gang, parentless and a tough customer, gets pangs of conscience and finally goes to the hospital to look in on their victim, who was sleeping in a doorway when the gang set him on fire and wouldn't recognize him. The bad egg pretends he's visiting someone else in the hospital and they become buddies. At the end of the picture when the old bum gets out of the hospital, the kid lets him stay in his cold-water flat and, of course, finally tells him he was one of the ones who turned him into a crepe suzette. In turn, the old man tells the boy he knew all along. "But how?" asks the kid. "You were in a drunken stupor." "I recognized your voice, when you were shouting to the other fellows to get out of there before the cops came."

After my father had told me the plot, I said, "And the two of them open up a lemonade stand, become millionaires, and found Boys Town!" You know what my father said? "Peter, you mustn't let this stay in jail make you bitter!"

I love him.

I bet the producers of the picture are getting ulcers staying up nights thinking of ways to spring me so I could play the boy. The opening day of my trial, they could premiere the picture simultaneously in 2,871 theaters across the country in a saturation booking.

I kill a man and my father ends up making $1,750 a week with a six-week guarantee. If we didn't have the war in Viet Nam, we'd have a depression. You keep knocking 'em off and the money rolls in.

As Jordan would say—enchanting!

Anyhow, my father never connected his job with the publicity, never acknowledged it, that is, and we actually had a great visit. He's happy and relieved that I have you and impressed with all this typing I've done. The sheriff and I are more or less friends again and he, along with all the guards, is getting a big kick out of me whacking away at this machine for hours at a time.

My father just left for the coast an hour ago. P.S. He never once asked me about what had happened. But he did bring me three tuna fish sandwiches and tons of Good and Plentys.

5

BY THE TIME school was out that first afternoon I'd got myself so worked up about having imitated Mr. Hoyt's walk—I told myself nothing could be that bad. There was a half hour between the end of the last class and the time I was to present myself at his house and I used it to spruce up. I took a quick shower and put on, for the first time, one of the sport jackets I'd picked out with my father. It was a fairly loud black, brown and off-white plaid jacket with some burnt-orange threads woven into the pattern. I hadn't been all that sold on it; my father was the one who was crazy about the coat, so I ended up with it.

The time I arrived at Mr. Hoyt's house wasn't left to chance. I made certain I got there at four sharp, not a minute early and not a second late. I walked up the wooden steps and rang the bell while the town clock was striking.

That was when I met his wife, Mrs. Hoyt, first name, Miriam. Old-fashioned, long lace curtains covered the windows next to the front door. I saw her pull a panel to one side and peek out before she opened the door, which she did quickly and then immediately glanced behind her.

It was done so furtively I thought she was going to whisper some secret message in my ear and quickly shut the door in my face.

Instead she cleared her throat and said, "I'm Mrs. Hoyt, please come in." I introduced myself and shook her hand, which was extremely damp. She made no pretense at smiling and said to take a seat. I thought she might sit down, too, but she only stood there, nervously clasping her hands together and pressing one upon the other in little short squeezes.

She was extremely ill at ease, looking behind her several times toward the heavy maroon drapes hanging in the doorway leading off to a hall and the stairs up to the second floor. After a moment she took a quick little step over to a chair, looked down at it, touched the arm and then stepped away again. Then she glanced back toward the hall and stairs once more. There was something spylike about it all, as if we were in dangerous territory where we might be apprehended and executed without a trial.

At first I attributed her conduct to what I'd done, figuring Mr. Hoyt had told her I'd mimicked him. Later, I realized that was her way. She was always nervous. Looking at her then, I thought she had a hump on her back, but she didn't. She did have extremely bad posture. She walked hunched over, bent forward, head ducked out slightly; and when she was outside, walking around the campus, she'd cast quick little glances from side to side, as if she were expecting someone to jump out from behind a bush or a tree and shout "Boo!"

The house was deadly quiet. As I was wracking my brain trying to think of something to say to break the silence and get us talking, she glanced at the drapes again, looked back at me, attempted a smile, which really came off as a nervous twitch, mumbled something I couldn't make out, wheeled around and scooted through the curtains and away.

I was left sitting there in the parlor, which was dark and furnished heavily, with lace doilies on the arms of everything and Oriental rugs, not the thick plushy kind, the thin almost shiny variety. The pictures on the walls were of Victorian couples, all of whom looked like matching parent sets. It wasn't a room that made you want to spend time in it.

57

I remember thinking, No, that couldn't be the headmaster's *wife;* she must be the housekeeper. She did look like a housekeeper, plain face, almost dowdy, blondish stringy hair, flat on the top of her head, watery pale-blue eyes. But then I remembered distinctly her saying she was Mrs. Hoyt.

Without the sound of footsteps or any movement, I heard a voice: "Is my father here?" I almost jumped up from the chair. I turned and standing in the doorway to what was a study I saw a short, dark-haired boy with glasses whom I recognized vaguely from one of my classes. I said he wasn't and he walked into the room toward me, extending his hand. "I'm Headley Hoyt," he said, formal yet polite. I introduced myself and he said, "Do take a seat." I noticed that in spite of his manners, his dark suit and his glasses, he didn't seem to be more than fifteen. I knew he was in one of my classes and I wondered if he could possibly be a senior. "Are you waiting for my father?" he asked me. When I said I was he immediately started for the doorway. "I'll tell him you're here."

I spoke without thinking. "No, that's all right," I said, not being anxious at all for the confrontation.

He stopped and turned around with almost a surprised look on his face. "Oh, but he'll want to know you're here," he said and left the room.

I could hear him going up the stairs and then hear footsteps above me. Headley Hoyt! I thought what an unfortunate name to stick on anybody. It just sounds like the owner would be the kind of person who'd be kidded; and although he turned out to be the kind of a boy who was eminently kiddable, nobody kidded Headley P. Hoyt. Not with his father.

After a minute or so I heard vigorous motion above me. Then I actually felt the approaching presence of him, beyond the actual footsteps which I could tell were coming in a straight line from wherever he'd been to me. By that I mean I could sense the energy rushing toward me. I felt a quick moment of panic. But I told my-self—steady, that of course I'd put myself in the position of the underdog and it really was probably much worse in my mind than it was in his. I took a deep breath as I heard him step off the last step.

I was wrong. He practically charged into the room, stopping dead at the sight of me and swaying back, rocking back on his heels from his frontward tilt. He made a sound, a little snorting sound. His face was red and the raised spot on his forehead was white, drained of all color. I learned to watch for this sign of his anger.

Suddenly I remembered I hadn't stood when he entered and I got to my feet. He kept on staring at me. His mouth was pursed up with what I thought was distaste, then suddenly he smiled and not only smiled but let out a short burst of laughter. For an instant I thought he was going to come over and take my hand, tell me it had all been a great big joke, that he knew his walk was odd and that everyone was always trying it on for size.

Wrong again. He did laugh, but he cut it off sharply. Then he flung an arm out toward me. "Look at you, just look at you!" I looked down at myself and he laughed again. "Yes, look at yourself." I was confused and glanced up at him, I suppose questioningly. "Yes—you!" he said, taking a quick step toward me, a hostile step. I felt he actually wanted to grab me or hit me. I stumbled back against the chair, lost my balance and sat down clumsily. He laughed again. "Is that your best jacket, that horse blanket? Did you think you could make an impression with your best jacket?" I was surprised and, at the same time, angry with myself for wearing it. He walked a few steps away from me and when I didn't answer he wheeled on me, demanding, "Well, did you?"

"No," I said, barely audible. I was stunned because, you see, I realized it was worse than I had imagined.

"No—what?" he asked.

"No, sir."

"You'll learn a thing or two here, you can be sure of it. We'll teach you some manners!" He sort of snorted and looked toward the hallway beyond the drapes. Then he made a gesture with his hand and spoke sharply. "Up, get up!" I stood and he nodded his head, indicating the study. "In there," he said. He let me walk ahead of him and I felt uncomfortable with him behind me. I almost felt he might shove me.

The study-library was completely different from the rest of the house in that it was comfortable: wall-to-wall thick beige carpeting, huge desk, an overstuffed sofa and two leather armchairs, and the walls, except for the one with the large windows, lined with packed bookcases.

He closed the door behind him, which made me feel even more uneasy, and gestured for me to sit down in a chair by the corner of his desk. He paced for a while and just as I was pulling myself together, trying to find the words for some kind of an apology, he sat down abruptly at his desk. "Trash!" he muttered. I looked at him and he said, "Yes—trash!" and suddenly stood up again.

Then he started pacing back and forth from the far side of the desk past the windows to the door and back again. I couldn't help but wonder, with him in the mood he was in, how the house could have been so quiet until he made his appearance. I would have thought he would have been upstairs smashing inanimate objects.

"We make it a rule not to take theatrical people. Did you know that?" I shook my head. "Oh, we've had an experience or two—all disastrous. We wouldn't have accepted you for a minute, not with your background, not with a father like yours."

There wasn't time to object, even if I'd had the courage, which I didn't, because he kept right on. I can't be sure of every word but one thing I'm certain of—I'm not making it worse than it was.

"We wouldn't have considered a little Hollywood snip like you if it hadn't been at the request of the father of an alumnus. Added to that, of course, more or less a charity case. Gilford has always held itself open to a few charity cases. We have three boys here now on half-tuition, but at least they're decent boys, good students, not"— he flung an arm out toward me—"a little smart-snot like you! Even so," he went on, "we wouldn't have given you a second thought, not so much as a nod, if our boarding quota hadn't been low this year. You can be sure of that." He had a way to emphasize by chopping the air sideways with his flattened-out hand and he did it then, adding, "However, having made a commitment, albeit a risky one, the school will not be marred by the character of a single"—he broke off, searching for an adjective; not finding one to fit me, he simply said—"student. Rather the student will rise to the standards of the school and make no doubt of that!"

He went on pacing back and forth, continuing to repeat how the school felt about "theatrical trash," always connecting me with Hollywood, warning me what was going to happen to me if I didn't shape up to Gilford's standards, rubbing it in that I was a charity case (I wondered whether he was referring to my tuition being paid by Milton Bigelow, or whether I was on half-tuition besides), and, most of all, forever dropping innuendoes all over my father.

It was obvious he knew more about him than he'd let on in his office—for instance, the drinking thing.

The more he went on the more stunned I became. He wasn't giving me a chance to defend myself, not even a word. Just as he was repeating about how unwholesome I was, I heard footsteps and some rattling sounds and the door opened. Mrs. Hoyt stood there carrying a large silver tray with cups and silver tea things and a plate stacked high with cookies. "Franklyn, I brought—"

He waved her away with a hand. "No, Miriam," he said.

She winced and ducked back a step, looking at me and then at him and said, "But I thought—"

"Not now," he said, turning away from her and waiting for her to leave.

"Yes, Franklyn," she said and backed out of the room.

He turned around and looked at me closely. I remember thinking: No tea and God only knows—no sympathy.

"What?" he asked. But his voice was no longer sharp or sneering. His wife had interrupted his anger and he spoke almost with humor. "Something on that nasty little mind of yours?"

"No," I said, wondering if I could possibly have been smiling, even faintly, but doubting it.

"Now," he said, going on in a perfectly matter-of-fact tone, as if he were going over my curriculum, "I suggest, if you have a dirty little bag of tricks up your sleeve, you just forget about them. The boys here may not be sons of great men, they may not come from the wealthiest families, but they're clean, decent boys. Most of them come from good solid New England families and I don't want them contaminated." He looked at me. "You understand what I'm talking about?" I shook my head to the negative. "Oh," he said, picking up a pencil and fingering it, "I imagine you do. Any nasty little adolescent practices you might have picked up along the way in Hollywood."

I was so dumfounded by this last statement that I stopped listening to him. He wasn't ranting any more, just talking on in a perfectly normal voice about the school and standards and studies (I believe) while I was wondering how anybody could condemn a person's entire character without knowing them. I remember suddenly wanting to get to a mirror, to look at myself and see if there was something in my face, something I wasn't aware of, an expression or just my looks even, that helped him form such an opinion of me.

I just sat there numbly thinking how I'd really expected *Goodbye Mr. Chips* and Greer Garson to be his wife and tons of students like great friendly puppies swarming all over me, and I don't know how long he went on speaking, except I remember one time he finally sat down at his desk just as I was beginning to sift through what alternatives were open to me.

There weren't many. I could just leave. I had one hundred and forty dollars I'd saved and that would get me home, at least on a Greyhound bus. But then I would be immobilizing my father as far as him being free to come to New York to look for work, and that might mean going to live with my father's father in Tucson and, although he's fairly spry for ninety-one, we really don't have much in common. His whole life now is built around his canary, Tippy, and the only thing Tippy does is spill his seed out of his cage. He doesn't even sing. My grandfather's forever warning him *not* to kick his seed out and then clucking over him fondly—and getting a big bang out of it when he *does*. My grandfather also gets mixed up occasionally and talks to me as if I were my father and we were decades back in time and that can be sad-making.

If I did leave, I couldn't just say I didn't like the school, which my father would never accept because he knows me and knows I would have specific reasons. But I could never tell him what Mr. Hoyt said about him. It would do one of two things: simply hurt his feelings badly or else my father would get into one of his elegant rages and call up either the head of the Screen Actors' Guild, the Governor of California, Cardinal McIntyre or try to get ahold of the President of the United States and demand such a headmaster's resignation.

Then I could just run away in general, but that seemed melodramatic and, of course, my father had enough problems without that.

Or I could stay. That alternative was far from pleasant. The bottom had really fallen out of Prep School as far as I was concerned.

I heard Mr. Hoyt say, "—will you?"

I had no idea what the question had been, but I took a chance and nodded yes and to my surprise he seemed to be smiling and stood up and reached out his hand. I couldn't get over it. I shook hands with him and he said, "You may go now, Peter."

The interview was over. He even walked me to the front door, saying something about what time dinner was. If he thought I had a a bag of tricks up my sleeve, he was full of surprises.

I didn't go to dinner that night. No appetite. Mainly, I wanted to reach a decision. I was too confused by what had happened to go along not knowing what I was going to do. Shortly after everyone had gone down to the dining room, Mr. Kauffman appeared at my door. "Dinner, Peter." I told him I wasn't hungry. "We still come to the table," he said.

I truly wanted to be left alone. I took a deep breath and said, "I really don't feel like it."

"Oh," he said, "I see." He paused a moment. "You're not happy here?" he said, half-statement, half-question.

My resistance was so low that I said, "No, I guess not."

63

"Well," he sighed, "any place takes getting used to, a new school especially. After all, this is your first day here. Then, too, we might just be a little homesick, mightn't we?"

I didn't answer and he left, taking my silence, I suppose, for an admission. Homesick? For Hollywood and that one dumpy room with the pulldown beds hanging over the Freeway! And then, of course, I realized I was. Gilford, at that point, would have made me homesick for a damp cellar.

For a long time I sat there trying to sort out my thoughts but not really getting too far, even with the quiet that came with study hours. It must have been shortly after nine when I heard footsteps hit the top landing and come on down the hall and I knew who they belonged to. There was the same direct lope about them, a ka-plick-kaplock, ka-plick-kaplock. I was so certain I even stood up as the door was flung open. Mr. Hoyt's face was red again and the raised spot on his forehead stood out white. "So!" he exhaled. He looked at me for a long time before continuing. "You didn't come down for dinner?"

"I wasn't feeling hungry."

"You weren't feeling hungry!" he said, and now *he* was mimicking *me*. "You weren't feeling hungry and you don't like it here." (Thank you, Mr. Kauffman.) "Too bad about you," he went on, "but those aren't the questions. The fact is, you are not in your own home. This is a school, an institution of learning, and you will obey the rules. The school will not operate on your schedule, rather you will operate on Gilford's schedule. Do you understand?" I was feeling heavy and hopeless and when I hesitated answering for a moment, he demanded, "Do you understand?"

The joke or whatever, this second assault, had gone too far. He hadn't even allowed me time to catch my second wind. I was suddenly feeling close to tears and I confessed: "I'm afraid, Mr. Hoyt, I don't understand anything." And I meant it.

This infuriated him even more. "You don't, eh! Well, you will, you have my word for it. See yourself as some sort of a—maverick, a rebel, do you? All good and well! I'll take that streak out of you. I'll break you of that—believe me!"

64

Right away, I decided to pack up and pull out.

He swung around, took one step away, and then turned back to me. "Unless, of course, you decide to leave, to go back to your Hollywood. Wouldn't put it past you, the sort you are, I expect. As long as you don't get your way. I imagine that must be intolerable! Spoiled—" He snorted and was gone, loping on down the hall.

And just as quickly my decision was unmade. I'd be damned if I'd let him call the shots on what I'd do. It's strange how suddenly things happen, a click and your mind's made up and a whole plan of action comes to you. Now, whatever I was feeling, the confusion and disappointment—to be frank, downright unhappy and miserable—was turning to anger, which at least I could understand. And even use.

I swore to myself that I would break *him* down, show *him,* convince him he'd been wrong about me and even make him, in some way or other, apologize.

Now there wasn't even a thought of running away. After all, it's pretty silly to think of running away when there really isn't any place you want to run to. The more I thought about Mr. Hoyt, the more angry I got. I practically tore around the room, straightening away my things, rehearsing my behavior, planning my strategy. Although I didn't have many clothes, one of the first things I did was to wrap up that loud plaid sport jacket in a plastic bag and put it away in one of my suitcases. I told myself he'd never see me in that again.

Toward the end of study period, Lee Galonka sneaked into my room, wanting to know if I knew Tony Curtis. When I told him no, that was three down, what with Sandra Dee and Ann-Margret, and I believe he seriously began to doubt that I actually came from Hollywood. Right after study period, Dennis Vacarro, of the damp palms and nervous eyes, showed up in my doorway. "Hi, Peter— do you ever have nightmares?" I told him yes. "So do I," he said, looking around the hall. "Maybe some time we can—"

With that the door across from me opened and Ed Anders stepped out. "Hey, Dennis, leave him alone!" Dennis turned and hurried on down the hall. Ed kind of spread his legs and standing there, looking right at me, let go with a thunderclap of flatulence that would have knocked pictures off the wall, if there'd been any up. "Pete," he said and smiled at me and turned and went back into his room.

Just before lights-out, Mr. Kauffman appeared again. I somehow wanted him to know I knew he'd told Mr. Hoyt what I'd said, so when he asked how I was feeling, I looked him right in the eye and flashed a great big smile. "Fine!" I said. He was surprised and hesitated. "Good," he finally replied, "we're all subject to our moods, our little depressions now and then."

He started to walk away. "Oh, Mr. Kauffman, I really think Gilford's a swell school," I called out overenthusiastically.

"You do?" he asked, thrown, I could tell.

"Yes, I really do."

He gave me a little confused smile and left. When I was undressing, a kid I'd never seen before stuck his head in. "Hey, you're the new guy, huh?"

"Yes."

"You want to sneak out and come over to Betty Thorn's with us?"

"What for?" I asked him.

"You know . . . ," he said, making a fist with his right hand and giving a few short little jerking-off strokes.

"No, thanks," I told him.

"Okay," he said, "I'll tell her some other time." Then he left.

I thought Gilford may not be my idea of prep school, but there are certainly some odd types around. They even picked up my spirits a bit. With my decision made and my battle plans drawn up, I was even beginning to feel pretty good—I told myself. So after the lights went out, I got into bed, had a good cry for myself, and went to sleep.

The next morning I started right in on my program. I buckled down to studies as I never had before. I was determined to get excellent grades. Although I didn't volunteer for special activities, I did everything that was expected of me and, while I didn't make

66

any great friendships, I avoided making enemies and stayed out of trouble.

Recently I'd been reading a novel in which the leading character kept telling his buddy, "Keep your cool." I took that for my slogan. Keep my cool, no matter what. If someone or something got on my nerves I'd count to five or ten or five hundred, if I had to. I'd force myself to deconcentrate from anything that might rattle me and make me lose my cool.

As far as grades were concerned, the school was built for them, the schedule, too. Every evening from seven-thirty to ten-thirty you were locked (not literally but for all intents and purposes) in your room with complete solitude. There was nothing to do *but* study. And I ground away at it, except it turned out to be not that much of a grind.

I found out when you want to learn something, if you absorb every little bit of information given to you each day from the very beginning on a certain subject, it becomes easy. There are no gaps, no holes in your knowledge of that subject to trip you up and confuse you as you continue, so that your concentration is clear and pinpointed as you go ahead gobbling up more information and filing away additional facts and data. I suppose it's that old thing about the foundations being solid, then the house won't fall down. It's much easier, actually, than just getting by in a subject. With the result that schooling came along well from the very beginning. In all fairness, this was due not only to my application but also to the almost complete lack of any fascinating distractions at Gilford.

This includes a best friend or what you'd even call good close friends. You see, I did keep an eagle eye out, but although there were a couple of fellows I liked, Skedge Miller and Barry Sargent, both seniors, there was a natural gap between boarding students and day students, which they were. After two weeks it became clear that, barring a miracle, there was going to be no one special friend.

So I fell into a routine; one day was almost precisely like the other. The only extra activity I went out for was tennis. There were elimination matches and I ended up on the team. Actually I think I was the best player they had; I could beat the captain, Burt Springer, and the coach, Mr. Hines. We were due to play our first match on a Saturday afternoon in September.

In the meanwhile, Mr. Hoyt and I had not exchanged one word. I didn't have him for any subjects, so that lessened the chance of contact between us a great deal. But that didn't mean we weren't keeping close watch on each other. I could sense him eying me in morning chapel when I was looking down at the hymnbook and I, on the other hand, checked him out when he was reading a prayer or looking down at his notes of upcoming school activities.

Several afternoons before our first tennis match I was playing doubles with Burt Springer against Mr. Hines and Len Hyers when Mr. Hoyt came tilting down the hill from the main school building on his way to the gym. I was serving and although he didn't stop he did slow down and I could tell he was watching. I do have a good serve, hard and fast, from years of just practicing by myself. It just so happened I aced Mr. Hines while Mr. Hoyt was watching and then, serving right away to Len in the other court, I slammed one past him, too.

Mr. Hines, whose face was a little flushed from being aced, turned to Mr. Hoyt and said, "I think we might have a winner."

"Good," Mr. Hoyt said. Then he nodded and said a pleasant "Boys . . ." to no one in particular and continued on.

In fifteen minutes or so, Mr. Hoyt came by on his way back to the school building; again he slowed down and it was obvious he was watching the play closely. It was about a half hour later—I was serving again in the court facing the school—when I threw the ball up for my service that I noticed a form standing behind the slightly opened Venetian blinds in a schoolroom on the third floor. Then the ball was served and in motion and I couldn't take time to look. When the point was over and I served again, I glanced up and the person hadn't moved. I was fairly sure—I could tell by the posture and size of the dark form—it was Mr. Hoyt. He remained there all during that game and one more, until we traded sides, and by the time we returned to the shady side, he was gone.

68

But I remember thinking how strange of him to watch from behind the blinds in a schoolroom way up on the third floor.

By that time, however, I had learned some things about Gilford's past and Mr. Hoyt which were beginning to clue me in on the strangeness of the school and also the character and quirks of its headmaster.

6

IN SPITE OF falling into the routine, I was far from what could be called happy there. In the beginning I would have used my old stand-by "tacky" for the school, but after a week or so I realized— rather, began to *feel*—there was something else about it. When you looked around the campus, especially in the fall, it was really a pretty, almost graceful-looking school. Still, there was something petrified about it. I felt some of its insides were missing. I sensed, from little things I heard, there was the ghost of a much better, healthier school hanging over Gilford.

Then, and this must have been a day or so after Mr. Hoyt had passed the tennis courts, Wiley Bevan took time off one night from the tales of his sexual exploits and, aided by his roommate, Chuck Rhodes, told a couple of us newer students a story that helped explain the shaky personality of Gilford I'd felt.

Seven years ago, and this I believe was Mr. Hoyt's fourth year there as a teacher, not headmaster, the school was top-rate. I don't mean like Exeter or Andover; it was never a large school, or say in the top five, but it was a sound, well-thought-of prep school with a good standing. They still took day students but they were in the minority. The boarding quota was full, with a waiting list.

The then Senator Craig had a son attending Gilford. He was,

from all reports, one of the most popular fellows at the school, attractive, great sense of humor, a good student, along with being a bit wild and manic-depressive at times. Right around graduation time, he wasn't seen for a few days. The headmaster at that time didn't report the boy to his father because he did have a record of taking off every now and then and classes were officially over anyhow. The day before the Senator and his wife were due to arrive at the school—he was giving the graduation speech—a janitor found the boy's body in a corner of the boiler room at Logan Hall.

He'd hanged himself with a belt. No note was left, but his mother found a diary among his things. He'd been having a relationship with his roommate (also captain of the football and ski teams) all year. His roommate had recently told him he was getting engaged that summer and planned to be married and they'd better not see one another after the end of school.

The Senator started out from Washington to attend graduation and ended up at his son's funeral. Although the suicide itself couldn't be hushed up, they tried to hide the specific reason for it. As far as the newspapers were concerned, they were successful, but a local scandal around the school and village was impossible to suppress. The fact that nobody ever suspected what was going on made it a great item for gossip.

The current headmaster received a certain amount of blame for allowing such things to go on under his nose (what was he supposed to do—take turns hiding under students' beds?) and was on his way out. The next fall Mr. Hoyt was headmaster. Changing headmasters didn't help all that much, however, and the school went into a decline. The next year the boarding quota wasn't filled. The stigma couldn't be erased and Gilford had been limping along ever since, struggling to regain its former status.

It was obvious Mr. Hoyt had dedicated all of his efforts and energies, which were considerable, to pulling the school up by its bootstraps. He was its St. George, ready to slay any dragon that might foul the air with its breath, its watchdog, which explains why he was so on the alert for anyone who might taint the school.

On the alert but not, as he told me, so unsusceptible to taking in less than exceptional students. I believe he would have enrolled a certified leper if one had applied. And, of course, having to compromise like this must have galled him all the more. What happened to the school was reflected in the quality of the students. The boarding students rarely came now from outside New England, a few did, but most were from New England families who either couldn't afford or whose sons didn't qualify for one of the top schools. The rates had been lowered, along with academic standards, and the town people had been wooed to send their sons to Gilford as day students instead of to public high school in the neighboring larger town of Everett, where the town girls, the ones who didn't go away to school, went. The tuition for town students was very low.

I heard that one of the larger private endowments for Gilford was dependent upon the number of students attending and that if attendance fell below a certain figure—no more money from that source. There was also a rumor that the town of Saypool, though its growth through the years was small, was finally planning to build its own public high school. If this happened that would knock out most of the day students and unless Gilford could regain its former position as a grade-A prep school, it would be finished.

It was a sick school, crippled and limping along with the shadow of death hanging over it. And Mr. Hoyt was the doctor.

Now, I'm sure, it's had the coup de grace. And perhaps mercifully so. When I think about it—in killing a man, I also killed an entire school. For all poor Gilford's worth now, they might as well dig a huge hole and shovel it in for once and for all.

God, suddenly I'm flattened by homesickness for the good times I had there, for Jordan especially, whom I miss so much I could cry for a year steady. And, oddly enough, even a little for Mr. Hoyt.

Strange, how every so often the reality of what happened leaps up and smacks me in the face (as if I were sitting here behind bars for some dumb thing like jaywalking or spitting in the subway). Still, that's almost the way it is. Then—wham! Like now, I leap ahead to how it all ended and in a second I'm trembling all over and my fingers are so icy-cold I have to stop typing for a while.

One hour later and it's too unhealthy sitting here in this cell without an activity. My nerves start machine-gunning me and I begin imagining all the worst that could possibly happen. So I took a Dexamyl and told myself to get on with it. While it makes me shaky, it's a different sort of shakes than I was feeling a while ago. These are the kind of energetic, outgoing shakes instead of the lonely ones that make you feel you're going to crumble into pieces and cave in on yourself.

I might as well leap right into our strange relationship, Mr. Hoyt's and mine. To do this I'll tell you about the Point System. This was the second year of a seven-school league in the area for sports and other activities, such as debating and Glee Club. Each time two schools played a match, the winner scored ten points. In Glee Club and debating it worked a little different in that, for each one, there were three meetings during the year in which all the schools competed over a period of a couple of days, scoring a certain amount of points for first, second and third place. At the end of the year all the points were toted up and the number of points each school had determined its standing in the league. In the first year Gilford had not done too well; it came in sixth place—in other words, next to last.

Mr. Hoyt was determined that the school would better its position this year. If he could work Gilford up to fifth or fourth or especially third place, the Board of Trustees would be impressed. This would be a sign that the school was gaining ground, not sinking farther into oblivion. To this end, Mr. Hoyt was a master organizer, verging on the fanatic. Hardly a morning assembly went by that he didn't speak of the competition, didn't urge every student to go out for any sport or activity in which he could help the school better its record.

As the first matches grew near, he spent a lot of time getting together a cheerleading squad. He got two guys we later named

The Terrible Twins, Ronald and Rodney Lantz, to head the squad. Although on the surface the boys didn't have the ideal personalities for cheerleaders—they were proper and prim and not what you'd call gregarious—the idea turned out to be not bad at all. They were truly identical, dark, good-looking, on the short side but with good builds and intense faces and clefts in their chins. God only knows, they were professional twins; you never saw them apart, they always dressed the same, walked together, ate together, took the same subjects, went to the movies together, and are the kind of twins who will naturally *marry* twins, even if they don't like them, just to compound the nauseousness of it all. For contrast, Mr. Hoyt picked a tall thin blond day student, Leonard Bean (obviously known as Leonard String-Bean, poor guy) to work between them. They made a striking trio.

In spite of his early hostility toward my father and his aversion to my "Hollywood" background, there was actually a theatrical streak in Mr. Hoyt as wide as it was surprising. He was quite a showman when he wanted to be. He even had two special assemblies to unveil the cheerleading squad and for the student body to rehearse the various cheers. The first assembly was sort of funny. The Terrible Twins weren't used to this kind of showing off—they were accustomed to showing off by just walking down the street or going into a store—and they were nervous. They led cheers about as joyfully as a pair of Red Chinese generals. Talk about grim! They also weren't used to having anyone between them. All during the routines they'd automatically start converging, working in toward each other and squeezing poor Leonard Bean right out of the line-up. By the second assembly, however, they were well rehearsed in regards to spacing, courtesy of Mr. Hoyt, and the twins were catching on to the hang of it spiritwise. The response of the student body was wholehearted. Actually, The Terrible Twins got hooked on cheerleading after a few football games and would jump up and start going through their paces if anyone even happened to look their way. I'm surprised they didn't take an ad in the local paper: "Cheerleading for births, weddings and wakes!"

74

Our first athletic contest was a football game with Stockton at our field on a Friday afternoon, the day before our first tennis match. I could tell from Mr. Hoyt's manner at morning chapel that he was excited. He whipped through the morning prayer and the hymn he picked wasn't much longer than a limerick. Right away he launched into a pep talk. He was really quite jaunty and for the first time it seemed he was looking out over us with a certain amount of affection and without suspicion.

Stockton was a much bigger and more prosperous school and had finished second in the league the first year, but Mr. Hoyt's attitude was "C'mon, boys, we can do it! Miracles are possible!" He reminded me of Gregory Peck in one of those war movies you see on "The Late Show" where the commander of a lone American submarine is trapped in some gulf and about to do battle with half the Japanese fleet.

He made a strong plea for a heavy turnout at the game, so practically the entire school flocked down to the athletic field at three-thirty. It was a beautiful fall day and the setting was equally beautiful, with the lake, all calm and silver, right next to the fields and the thick woods, the leaves a flaming batch of fall colors, stretching away in the background. You'd have sworn planes had flown over and dumped great buckets of yellow, orange, red, copper and maroon paint down on the trees. It was awesome to think leaves could turn that way all by themselves.

The minute the Stockton team came jogging down the hill from the gym I had an uneasy feeling. They were, outside of Ed Anders, our captain, and maybe two other players, much bigger, taller and more powerful. When you saw the two teams lined up opposite each other it looked like a college team had shown up to play a junior-high group. Still, the Gilford side was all optimism at the beginning. The Terrible Twins and Leonard String-Bean were knocking themselves out, leading us through our repertory, and if our team looked scrubby in comparison to Stockton, they at least expended a lot of energy the way they tore around having their private warm-up.

Then the game started and within five minutes Stockton had intercepted a pass, scored a touchdown, kicked the goal, and then scored a touchback. From then on it was pure slaughter.

Mr. Hoyt was sitting with his wife and son, Headley, who, in spite of being at a football game, was wearing his dark suit, white shirt and dark tie and his ever-present glasses. I was keeping an eye on Mr. Hoyt because that very noon the grades had been posted on the bulletin board for the first few weeks of school. The top three students in each class had their names lettered in gold, the rest of the passing students were listed in order of their grades in black print, and if any student was failing, his name was inscribed in red. I had my name in gold three times, second in French, second in English and third, to my surprise, in history-current events. All this time, Mr. Hoyt and I hadn't exchanged a word. Now, with the grades out, I wanted to see if he would at least acknowledge me in a look.

I could see him wilting as the game wore on. If prize fights can be called because of a technical knockout, this football game should have been stopped in the name of humanitarianism. They were mopping up the field with our players. Ed Anders and a day student, "Big Andy" Hepple, a halfback, tried everything in the book, outside of digging a tunnel and going underground, to score a touchdown, but the rest of our guys were so demoralized and beat up that all the teamwork went down the drain and they were left alone. Whereas I'd started out as a more or less disinterested spectator, I began to take the game to heart. I began praying for Ed to somehow crash through and score, just so the defeat wouldn't be all that total. I have to say one thing for Ed: he may not be the best player or the most fascinating guy in the world, but he's a slugger. I found myself feeling proud of him even though the score ended up a dismal forty-something to nothing.

There wasn't even a large victory celebration on the part of Stockton. Even they, I think, felt embarrassed, the way a professional fighter would feel after beating hell out of a bus boy. Most of all, I'll never forget Mr. Hoyt. After he'd spoken a few words to the

76

coach and consoled our team as they limped off the field, I saw him turn and look across to the Stockton side. He took a deep breath, straightened up his shoulders, and away he went, tilting across the torn-up sod and then shaking hands and speaking with Stockton's headmaster. Mr. Hoyt was the epitome of good losing, smiling and bobbing his head. Then they shook hands again, said a few more words, and the other headmaster turned and walked over to his car. As Mr. Hoyt looked after him, his body gradually slumped and he stood there deflated, as if he'd been stuck with a pin and all the air had been let out of him.

In the meantime, his wife and son were crossing the field to join him. He was unaware of their approach. When she took his arm he turned around abruptly in surprise and she let go of him. Mrs. Hoyt looked unhappy, but his son, Headley, started to walk briskly up the hill, swinging his arms as if he were happy as a clam. Mr. Hoyt stood looking after his son, who found something on the ground, bent down to inspect it, and then went on his way. I think I noticed Mr. Hoyt shake his head ever so slightly. In that moment I made up my mind that Mr. Hoyt didn't really like his son.

Then he and his wife started walking slowly up the hill. I passed them eventually and glanced over at him, but if he was aware of me, he didn't acknowledge me. The next day was to change all of that.

Saturday afternoon was our first tennis match—with Stonehenge at their school. Mr. Hoyt had arranged to have three school buses available to transport the team and its supporters the twenty-some miles over there. Most all of the boarding students filled up one and a half buses; they were stuck on campus, so they had to go. Sitting in the bus waiting to leave, I saw Mr. Hoyt standing up on the hill next to the school building looking off in the distance for a whole pack of day students to come racing up at the last minute. They didn't. A few straggled along and Mr. Hoyt held up the departure for almost a half hour before finally dismissing the third bus. The catastrophe of the day before had a dispiriting impact and that's why hardly anyone showed up.

Stonehenge is a beautiful school stuck in a gorge in the foothills of the White Mountains and they had two good clay courts. I was surprised to see the heavy turnout; they had a small grandstand, which was filled, and there were a lot of students sitting on a grassy bluff on the other side of the courts. Two of their players had the flu so we were only playing three singles and two doubles; the school that won three out of the five matches won the event.

One of the courts was still being rolled. I was scheduled to play number two singles, so I sat on a bench while our number three player, Myer Clausen, began his singles. Unfortunately, Myer got an extreme attack of nerves and could hardly hit the ball; he really froze up, playing it very careful so it was not good tennis to watch. I could tell from the expression on Mr. Hoyt's face that he was bracing himself for another complete rout. Also, the students who were watching were getting restless from the sloppy playing. I remember my one big concern was that they all might begin drifting away. Actually the more people that are watching, the better I play. If there's no one around, I just get to feeling happy about being out in the fresh air, playing a game I like and am good at, and getting the exercise. On the other hand, if there are people watching, especially strangers, I'm self-conscious about looking at them and my attention is forced right smack on the court and the game I'm playing, and I try my damndest to make a good impression. In a way, a certain shyness causes me to be a show-off, if that makes any sense.

So I was sitting there more concerned about whether the natives were getting restless than whether Myer was going down in total defeat. The two men with the large roller hadn't even got off the court when I was up like a shot and out there, being introduced to my opponent, a good-looking blond guy, big wide-open face, not too husky but lean and hard. I thought right away: If he plays like he looks—trouble. We started to volley and he had a good strong forehand and moved well.

Just as we stopped to spin for first serve, Myer lost his first set and I noticed a whole group of Stonehenge kids looked like they were about to get off the hillside and leave. Damn it, I thought. I won the flip and chose to serve. I slammed the first one as hard as I could and it went by him—an ace. Someone in the stands gave a loud approving whistle and this caught the attention of about a dozen kids who had by this time started drifting away. I served hard again and my opponent, by luck, had started to move up to the net too soon. The ball had a top spin on it, just touched the service line, then spun up and hit him in the chest. It made me look very flashy and there was applause—the first of the day. None of the kids were leaving now. Right away I had a psychological advantage and I didn't look to the left or right, just kept on serving like the ball couldn't do anything *but* go in, and won a love game without giving him a point.

As he started to serve I could sense the whole crowd was watching us, not the other match, and I could feel Mr. Hoyt's eyes on me. The guy I was playing had a good first serve, but if it didn't go in, his second was weak. We had some good volleys, which pleased the spectators, but I won the second game. I took my service again and that made three. Just about that time Myer lost his match on the next court and that made me fight even harder to win. I played like a demon, and although my opponent won two games, I finally took the first set.

There was healthy applause when we changed sides. I sneaked a glance at Mr. Hoyt. He was leaning forward on the bench with his elbows braced against his knees. His grim expression had been replaced by a sort of interested, quizzical one, like: hmn, what's happening here? I also looked over to see how Burt Springer, our number one singles, was matched and noticed that although his opponent was a good strong player, he seemed to have flat feet and I hoped Burt would keep him running and wear him down.

Our second set was even better than the first. The fellow I was playing, although I think he sensed he was going to lose, never let down in spirits, even when I moved into the lead six games to five. Our last game was exciting and went on forever: my add, deuce, his add, deuce, match point again and so forth. Finally, he made an almost impossible return, which he was only able to lob back high, and I rushed up to the net and slammed the ball past him to take the match.

We got a big hand. As we were leaving the court, I saw Mr. Hoyt stand up and start walking toward me, but our coach, Mr. Hines, being in front of and not seeing him, rushed over and put his arm around my shoulder. I was glad of this and quickly turned, pretending I hadn't seen Mr. Hoyt, and led the way to the water fountain.

I was feeling proud and happy but I thought: No, Mr. Hoyt, you massacred me and I turned both cheeks and jumped through the hoop, played good dog for you, but I'm not that anxious to accept a pat on the head and wag my tail and pretend that our first meeting never happened. I felt I was beginning to occupy a new position in his eyes, but if there was going to be anything like a treaty signed, there was something satisfying to me about prolonging it.

Unfortunately, our captain, Burt Springer, lost his number one match by a hair, and with the singles over we weren't in the best position. They'd won two and needed only one more victory, which meant we had to take both doubles matches to win the day. I was pretty sure Burt and I could grab our match but I was worried about Myer and Warren Glover taking their number two doubles.

However, I could only concentrate on one thing at a time and after Burt took a brief rest, during which I managed to stay far away from Mr. Hoyt by keeping preoccupied with my racquet and straightening my socks and retying my shoelaces, we teamed up to play my former singles opponent and the fellow Burt had just lost to. I was right in my hunch. Burt and I played very well together and I found a great weakness in his former opponent—a very shaky backhand. I whispered to Burt to hammer away at it and every chance I got I hit the ball so he couldn't make a forehand shot. It got him rattled, and in trying to run around the ball and make a forehand shot out of a natural backhand, he bumped into his partner and they had words. That's the best thing that can happen in a doubles match—if you can get your opposition scrapping. We did and it worked, enabling us to win the match in two straight sets. We were now even with Stonehenge. The last doubles match would decide the event.

Although it was verging on the obvious, I took my chances and again avoided Mr. Hoyt, who was continually watching me, by pretending to be intensely interested in the outcome of the number two doubles. And I was. Here we were within one match of winning and it looked like we might not pull it off. Warren Glover was slugging away but he had to pull Myer Clausen along after him. They'd lost the first set, and I was beginning to sweat.

And why was I nervous? Because I suddenly wanted us desperately to win so Mr. Hoyt would have his precious ten points and at least be off to an even start in the league competition. A man I told myself I never cared to even speak to. The mind is a crazy place.

Then, in the fourth game of the second set, and luckily for us, Myer Clausen took a really nasty spill running for a ball and twisted his ankle. It was obvious, after he tried to put his weight on his foot, that he was through for the day. Everyone gathered around him, including Mr. Hoyt, and they helped him off the court. I was already taking off my sweater and getting my racquet out of its press, as if anyone had asked me. When Mr. Hines saw this, he trotted over and asked me if I wasn't too tired. I told him no and to please let me get into the match; he whacked me on the back and out I ran.

I was a better player than either of the other two, but they were ahead a whole set and it was tough going. I kept whispering fighting words to Warren and we began inching ahead gradually until we finally won the second set. If I ever played for blood, I did it then. It was the deciding set of the day and everyone knew it. The spectators were extremely quiet and I could feel Mr. Hoyt watching us like a hawk and *willing* us to win. I was hoarding points like a miser would money, one at a time, until suddenly it was our match point. I pretended it wasn't, though, so I wouldn't draw in and play it careful. The result was I slammed the ball right between the two of them and each thought the other was going to get it and neither one even swung his racquet. It was an upbeat ending and sort of comical and, most important, we'd won.

The play had taken it out of me and I was both elated and tired. When both teams gathered to shake hands and say their goodbyes along with the coaches, there was no longer any possibility of avoiding Mr. Hoyt. He came up to us and he was smiling and I could tell he was happy and excited. He thanked us as a group and then looked over at me and said, "Very good, Peter."

"Thank you," I said, trying not to appear too grateful and at the same time trying not to seem offhand or rude, just keeping my voice even.

After all, these were our only direct words since that first day.

Then a bunch of our boys came up to me and patted me on the back and said how much they enjoyed the matches and one or two commented upon my serve. When I got on the bus, Ed Anders said, "Hey, Pete—here!" Hardly anyone ever calls me Pete, but I was glad that he wanted me to sit next to him. He was very complimentary and said that if I could play football the way I played tennis they sure could use me on the team. I assured him I couldn't. In a way Ed and I were the two heroes of that weekend's events. For the first time I felt I was out of limbo. I had a feeling of fitting in, even though I wasn't absolutely sold on the place into which I was beginning to fit. It was a good ride back; I felt that the New England chill was beginning to thaw a little.

That evening there was a special movie on South America being shown in the recreation room at Logan Hall, along with refreshments. Although I wouldn't have minded basking a little more in my first rays of glory at Gilford, I somehow didn't want to come to Mr. Hoyt, that is, present myself at a function all bright-eyed and bushy-tailed where I could be sure there would be some kind of confrontation but couldn't be sure of *what* kind, because there would be too many people there to insure that it would take place on my terms. True, we had exchanged words at Stonehenge, but we hadn't really talked. So I decided to stay home and read.

Shortly after nine I heard these familiar footsteps coming up the stairs and ka-plick-kaplock down the hall. I quickly shoved *The Boston Strangler* in my desk drawer and picked up the paperback of Dante's *Divine Comedy* which I'd been toying my way through. I heard him stop outside my door and knock. "Yes?" I said.

The door opened. "Oh, Peter—I thought perhaps you'd gone to the movie in the village."

"No, sir," I said, standing up.

"Sit, sit," he said, motioning with his hand, and I did. "You played very well. I'm afraid Gilford owes its first league points to you."

"I'm glad I could help," I said.

"That you did," he added. He stood there for a moment, then repeated: "I thought perhaps you'd gone to the movie in town."

"I've seen it, so I thought I'd stay home and read."

"I see," he said. He just stood there for a while and I could sense he was slightly ill at ease. Finally he said, "Well, we're having that South American film in about twenty minutes. I hear it's excellent. Why don't you drop by Logan Hall and take it in? After all, it's Saturday night and you played very hard today. And well," he added, *"very* well. I suppose you learned how to play tennis in California."

"Yes," I said, "that's one thing California's good for—playing tennis." Immediately after I'd said it I thought: Oh-oh, does that sound sarcastic, I mean considering all the aspersions he'd cast on my background. I hadn't meant it that way; I was merely being honest. I don't think he took it wrong, although he didn't speak for a moment. I realized his hesitancy was caused by not knowing what to say. You see, down deep inside him I believe he really wanted to form some words of—perhaps apology is too strong—but some words that would not require too much decoding to let me know that he'd called a cease-fire and was making a reappraisal. But this was difficult for him.

He stood there so uneasily that for a second I had an impulse to leap in and take the initiative, say something that would open up a direct line of communication. But I quickly reminded myself not to jump in on impulse, not to act like a puppy. If I did I'd probably end up making a mess like a puppy.

He looked around my room. "You keep a tidy room," he said.

"It's almost a compulsion," I replied.

I must have mumbled the last part because he asked, "A what?"

"A compulsion," I repeated. "I mean I like to have things straightened away."

"Oh," he said. Another short pause. "I believe this is one of the nicest single rooms in the house."

"It's a good room," I agreed.

"Yes, a corner room, windows on two sides, that's what makes it a . . . particularly nice room."

"Yes," I said, "I like windows."

"Yes, it gives the room an . . . open feeling."

"Yes."

"During the day the light's good for reading," he added.

He was not one of those people who can talk from their heart. It might start out from the heart but then it gets all tangled up in some kind of Rube Goldberg contraption inside and comes out all about a nice room.

The room was exhausted as a subject and after another pause he said, "Peter, if you'd care to take an hour or so off from your reading and drop around to Logan Hall, we'd be pleased to have you."

"Yes, perhaps I will."

"Fine," he said. Then: "Well, fine. We'll look forward to seeing you there." He turned and was off down the hall.

I was relieved that our conversation was over and I harbored a little feeling inside, almost a smile, that I hadn't blown it, that I might even have won. Not in so many words or in any large sense, but I had at least kept my cool and, after all, he had sought me out. There was satisfaction that I had sat there composed, outwardly, at least, and he had stood in the doorway, not exactly *un*composed, but then again not exactly sure of himself.

That was the night that I decided there must be a human being living inside there someplace.

I then felt free to go to Logan Hall. We'd had our meeting, our first really face-to-face since the outbreak of hostilities and I had a specific invitation. There was a good turnout of teachers and stu-

84

dents at the movie, which was great if you like endless shots of natives scraping out logs for canoes. Although we didn't speak together alone, Mr. Hoyt complimented my tennis playing to several people, among them our football coach, who hadn't been to the match.

When I went to bed that night I thought: Well, the ice is broken and now we get into another phase of our relationship. But I certainly had no idea how deep that phase would get or how unexpectedly the course of it was to run—talk about your ups and downs!

7

MR. HOYT and I didn't have occasion to really speak for a week or so, but he would now and again look my way at morning chapel and there was acknowledgment in his glance that he was actually seeing me and I acknowledged him, too.

The next Saturday we played our tennis match on campus against McCauley School. Mr. Hoyt attended with some VIP's on the Board of Trustees; he was very much on his toes when they were around, even nervous. The football team had been massacred again the day before and I could tell he was most anxious to have us win our match. We did, and I could see the relief written all over his face.

One night in the middle of the following week, Mr. Kauffman came to my room during study hours and asked if I would like to join the Glee Club. I thought we'd been through all that. Besides, they'd already had tryouts and were rehearsing. I told him I didn't sing.

"Not at all?" he asked.

"Hardly at all. About all I can do is croak."

"You don't have to be an expert singer, Peter." Then he chuckled. "That is to say—no Meistersinger." That joke so tickled his fancy that he had quite a little laugh for himself. When he recovered he said, "You know *Die Meistersinger,* Peter?"

I wanted to say, "Not personally—that is, I never sang with his combo." Something about Mr. Kauffman made me invariably want to shock him. But I told him I'd heard of it.

"Well, as I said, you don't have to be a Meistersinger," he repeated, chuckling again.

I reiterated to Mr. Kauffman that I couldn't carry a tune. This was a lie. I can carry a tune and I do like to sing, in the shower, in the woods, or walking along the beach—things like that. The main point was I don't like Glee Clubs, I don't like the songs they sing, and I didn't much like Mr. Kauffman, so the last thing I wanted was to be standing up on a bench in his Glee Club belting out "Massa's in de Cole, Cole Ground."

He wasn't about to give up though. "We're badly in need of a few more members," he want on. "Mr. Hoyt especially wants to make a good showing in the competition. He wants Gilford to have a strong Glee Club."

"I'm afraid I'd only weaken it," I told him.

"Oh . . . well, that's a shame," he said, and finally left.

I thought for sure that had ended it. But sometimes I don't use my head. Almost everyone seems to break into song in the john and I'm no exception. Now I'll tell you something that will make me sound weird. I'm not really an opera fan at all, except there's one opera that I'm a fanatic about—*Turandot*. I happened to hear it once on the radio, part of it, that is, on an FM station in Los Angeles. I was instantly hooked. They didn't announce what it was afterward, so I looked up the station in the phone book and called right away to find out. A friend of mine's aunt is a great opera buff, so I asked her if she had it and she did. I used to go over a couple of times a week and listen to her album. The music kills me, it makes my spine ripple, it's spooky and sad and dramatic and, I think, the most beautiful music in the world. Eventually, when I sensed this friend of mine's aunt was beginning to question my sanity over *Turandot,* I bought it myself, even though my father and I don't have a phonograph. (They make him nervous, records do— why I don't know—also we couldn't really afford a phonograph.) So there I was in Hollywood with my *Turandot* album running around to anyone who had a set and playing it. Included in the album is the complete libretto, and I've learned several of the arias in Italian.

The very next night after Mr. Kauffman's visit I was blasting out my favorite, *Nessun Dorma* ("No One Sleeps"), in the shower. Philip Simmons was singing some Beatles song in another shower, Lee Galonka was combing his hair, Ed Anders was in a booth trying, as he always says, to have a "movement," and poor Dennis Vacarro, whom some of the cruder guys called "The Vacuum Cleaner," was just hanging around the shower room, pretending to file his nails or clean his teeth with dental floss or rinse out a pair of socks but actually just hoping to get a peek at somebody. In other words, the scene in the community john on the third floor was normal, if I may use the word.

I heard Phil turn off his shower and step outside and abruptly stop singing. Suddenly there was absolute quiet except for me. For a moment I thought Mr. Hoyt had walked in. When the quiet continued I stopped singing and parted the curtains to see if everyone had dropped through the floor—only to find Mr. Kauffman standing in the doorway, ears up.

"Oh, Peter," he said, like he'd just discovered who really assassinated President Kennedy, "I was wondering who was singing."

"Singing!" I laughed. "That's the first time I ever heard it called that."

Several of the guys agreed with me. "Um-hmn," Mr. Kauffman said, mouth all tight, having swallowed the canary, and left.

I actually didn't think any more about it. I saw him at dinner and he usually made the rounds at least twice during study period and once more before lights-out, but he didn't say anything and neither did I.

The next morning during French class, Mrs. Mason came into the room and asked Mr. Piper if I could be excused for a few minutes. From her attitude you could never tell whether you were being summoned to receive the Croix de Guerre or if you were being led to the guillotine. She ushered me into Mr. Hoyt's office.

He was working over some papers and right away he looked up and gave me a smile. "Good morning, Peter," he said, as Mrs. Mason withdrew, "won't you sit down?" I took a seat and he immediately said, "How would you like to be in the Glee Club?"

I was taken completely by surprise. "Well, I—"

"Mr. Kauffman tells me you have a very strong tenor voice."

I wanted to brand Mr. Kauffman a liar and a spy but I said, "I really can't carry a tune."

"Why, Peter," Mr. Hoyt said pleasantly, "I'm sure you sing quite well."

I decided to play the whole scene through for real. I was doing well in school and I was holding up my end in tennis, helping to win valuable league points. I didn't want to be in the Glee Club and I didn't want anything to do with Mr. Kauffman. "The only way I can sing at all is if I'm imitating someone."

"Peter, I can hardly doubt Mr. Kauffman's word. He said you were singing in Italian, loud and clear."

"Yes, but I was imitating someone. If I can mimic someone singing a song I like, I can at least get through it and make some noise."

"Would you mind telling me who it was you were imitating that so impressed Mr. Kauffman?"

"Jussi Bjoerling," I said immediately.

"Hmn . . . ," he mumbled, then he flashed a smile at me. "Couldn't you just go on imitating Jussi Bjoerling for our Glee Club?"

"No," I smiled back at him, "I don't think I could sustain it."

That was the first moment of real rapport we had.

He chuckled, but then he surprised me again when he stood up from his desk, indicating that he was bringing the interview to an end. "I suggest you see Mr. Kauffman after school and I'm sure he'll find a place for you in the Glee Club."

Although he was being tenacious, he was also being amiable, and as I was unable to detect any undercurrent which might lead me into a trap, I decided to make an attempt to end the Great Glee

Club Conspiracy for once and for all. "Mr. Hoyt," I said, looking him straight in the eye, "may I be completely honest with you?"

This seemed to make its point. "Why, Peter, I would hope you would always be completely honest with me."

"I really can't sing," I told him, realizing full well I wasn't saying anything I hadn't already said, but I wanted to be absolutely serious and attempt to win out by steadfast repetition. I could tell he still wasn't completely sold and as he opened his mouth to say something I just plunged in and raced on. "Mr. Kauffman must have heard me on key by accident. I actually can't carry a tune. I think Glee Clubs are great; I'd like to be in a Glee Club if I weren't next to tone-deaf."

"It seems to me," Mr. Hoyt said, "if anyone were tone-deaf, he might struggle along trying to imitate . . . oh, say, Frank Sinatra, but to go in for someone like Jussi Bjoerling, that's a different matter."

"I'm sure lots of people admire opera stars and have favorite arias who can't anywhere near sing them." I wasn't giving up. "Mr. Hoyt, it would really embarrass me to struggle along and try to keep up with the Glee Club and sing in public. I'd only make a fool out of myself and mess things up."

Oddly enough, that did it. He thought this over and said, "If it would embarrass you, if you feel that strongly about it—"

"I do," I cut in.

"Then I'll speak to Mr. Kauffman." We shook hands, said good-bye, and I walked out of his office dripping with relief.

And who ended up performing with the Glee Club? Me!

A week or so passed and in the meantime life went on as usual. I was studying hard, minding my own business, reading a lot—still no best friend; I'd completely given up on that score—and playing tennis regularly. The football team hadn't won a game and Ed Anders was racking up Purple Hearts every Friday afternoon, but we'd won three out of four tennis matches.

It was a Wednesday afternoon that I was again summoned by Mrs. Mason, one of the few times I ever noticed her showing any kind of emotion. She was excited. On the way down the hall she even turned to me and said, "How are you liking New England, Peter?" I told her just fine and she smiled and said "Good."

Mr. Hoyt wasn't working on any papers or reading; he was waiting for me. He quickly stood up from his desk. "Peter," he said, "sit down." Whereas his eyes were usually solemn and suspiciously grave, like he was about to detect something that would displease him, this afternoon they were sparkling. I could sense he was excited, almost as if he were going to tell me I'd won the Irish Sweepstakes or a prize of some sort. Then he suddenly looked up from the desk top and said, "Peter, your father's an actor!"

He said it with enthusiasm and as if he'd just found out this fascinating piece of information, and almost as if *I* hadn't known it myself. I was confused, but I said "Yes . . ." I couldn't think what else to say.

"I have an idea," he said, "an idea to augment the Glee Club performances."

"The Glee Club?" I asked, not really believing my ears that I was still being badgered about the goddam Glee Club.

He sensed my concern immediately and made that little chopping motion in the air with his flattened-out hand. "No, no—you don't know what I have in mind," he said, indicating it was going to be nothing but good news. I certainly *didn't* know what he had in mind, so I just sat there waiting for him to tell me. He smiled at me and then slapped a hand down flat on top of the desk. "Hamlet!" he exclaimed. He let his smile hang open during the pause that followed and then he added, sitting back down in his chair, "What do you think of that?"

What I thought was that I might be going crazy, or I'd blacked out and missed a whole section of the conversation. "Hamlet?" I asked.

"Yes, Hamlet!" he said, smiling even more, as if he'd just given me the secret word. He leaned forward over the desk and said, "I want you to speak Hamlet's soliloquy."

"Hamlet's soliloquy?" I asked.

"Yes, Peter—yes! Don't you think it's a splendid idea?"

I thought it was probably the worst idea I'd ever heard in my life, but he was so enthusiastic, he was really looking about sixteen and just out of the shower, that I didn't know how to break it to him. "Where?" I heard myself asking, stalling for time.

"Where?" he repeated. "Why, with the Glee Club." He said it incredulously, like it should have been perfectly obvious.

I still was not getting a clear picture. "With the *Glee* Club?" I realized I was beginning to sound like a parrot—Hamlet? Me? Where? With the *Glee* Club?

"Yes, Peter, on the program with the Glee Club, don't you see?" He frowned just slightly that I wasn't right along with him. "You'll either—I haven't decided yet—but you'll either speak the soliloquy at the beginning of the second half of the program or toward the end of the second half before their last number, a medley from *Sound of Music.*"

"Which soliloquy?" I asked, not even thinking about what a screwy double bill Hamlet and *The Sound of Music* would make.

" 'To Be or Not To Be,' " he said, eyes lighting up again. "It will be a splendid addition to the program, don't you think?"

I felt trapped. I'd already nixed the idea but I'd been taken so completely off guard, by his enthusiasm as much as the idea itself, that I hadn't a clue how to get out of it.

He stood up and began pacing back and forth, talking about how it was going to add just the right extra touch to the performance, how he didn't know why he hadn't thought of it earlier, but that he'd just that morning come across an article by the leading drama critic in Boston reading the riot act to a visiting English company because their Hamlet was forty-six years old. This critic said Hamlet should be able to bring a blush to his cheeks "without the aid of rouge pots."

The more he went on, the more stunned I became. He was so *for* the idea that it was like bucking a hurricane. I was only trying to concentrate on ways of getting out of it, but I couldn't pull my thoughts together. They were one big splatter in my head. I was also confused by his switch in attitude toward the acting profession. Whereas that first day to be an actor or come from an acting family was unspeakable, now suddenly it was—whoopee! The fall meeting of the league Glee Clubs was only a month off and he started getting very practical, asking me if I could have the soliloquy ready by then and, without even waiting for an answer, *telling* me that I could, that he'd counted the lines and there were only thirty-five.

The next thing I knew he'd shoved a book, *The Complete Shakespeare,* into my hands. He said he didn't want to keep me from classes but that he knew I would be just great and that I was to meet him in the auditorium after school and we'd start working on it right away. As he ushered me out, Mrs. Mason was bubbling over about what a fine idea she thought it was.

The next thing I knew I was standing in the hall with *The Complete Shakespeare* in my hands.

I don't suppose I have to add I didn't hear one word of what was going on in any class for the rest of the afternoon. Every moment of my time was spent plotting. By the end of classes I was armed with several ideas, none of which I was sure of, but all of which I was willing to try.

When I walked in the rear door of the auditorium, Mr. Hoyt was already up on the stage dragging the lectern off into the wings. "Oh, Peter!" he said, catching sight of me and striding back to the center of the stage. I mounted the steps and he came over and took my arm. "Now, Peter," he said, all wound up and ready to dive in, "I think—"

"Mr. Hoyt, could I talk to you for a minute?"

"Of course, Peter—I imagine you've come up with some ideas of your own, haven't you?"

I had and none of them included me as Hamlet. "Mr. Hoyt, I actually have never wanted to be an actor."

After a pause, he said, "Yes . . . ?" Like: go on.

"What I mean is, I'm not really fond of acting."

"Even though your father's an actor?" he asked.

"Especially. I think it's a very shabby profession."

"I'm surprised to hear you say that," he said.

I was surprised to hear him say he was surprised to hear me say that. So often Mr. Hoyt and I seemed to miss one another in conversation. "What I mean is," I said, taking the plunge, "maybe it would be better to get somebody who really *wanted* to be an actor to give Hamlet's soliloquy."

He frowned. "You mean you don't want to do it?" He looked the closest to hurt I'd ever seen him.

"Well, not exactly that," I said, feeling the warm flush of cowardice creeping over me. "It just seems you might get more, you know, of a performance out of someone who's really interested in acting."

"Whom would you suggest?"

"Say," I said, as if I were just thinking of it, "what about Lee Galonka? He—"

Mr. Hoyt threw back his head and had a good laugh for himself. "Oh, Lee Galonka doesn't want to be an actor; he wants to be a movie star! I doubt if he's ever heard of Hamlet." He laughed again, saying "Lee Galonka!" and waving the whole idea away with his hand.

That suggestion was down the drain. He certainly had Lee Galonka's number and he must have known I had it and I began to feel stupid for having suggested him. I was thinking which one of several approaches to use when Mr. Hoyt suddenly sobered up and asked, "What do you want to be, Peter?"

I didn't want to change the subject, so I said, "Almost anything but an *actor.*"

This didn't set too well with him. "Why do you discredit your father's profession?" he asked.

That's what I mean about *missing*. I was taking my cue from his attitude that first day about acting. But that's where he'd fool you. You could never be entirely sure of what he'd say or what he was thinking. Just when you'd start anticipating what he'd say or do, he'd throw you a curve and not just for the curve's sake alone; it

94

was just the way he was. (This is not to say he couldn't throw curves when he wanted to; he could, and he had a couple of dillies lined up.)

I would really like to have crawled inside his head and just sat there for a day to see what really went on. Jordan, who will be coming along soon, once said maybe he had a brain tumor, a baby one that only pressed on him occasionally. Anyhow, I began to feel on touchy ground again, so I said, "Not because it's my father's profession necessarily, simply because I've been around the business and from what I've seen I'd rather be in almost any other occupation."

"That's surprising," he said. "I would have thought you might gravitate toward it." And now a compliment. "You have the face and build for it."

I was embarrassed. I don't know why, but receiving a personal compliment from him was unsettling. "All I know is, I have no desire at all to be an actor."

Another curve, but not a planned one. "That's rather gratifying to hear," he said, nodding. Then right away, as I began to see the light at the end of the tunnel, he snuffed it out. "But we're not talking about careers. We're only talking about your participation in the school's activities." Now he was anticipating *me*. "Oh, I know . . . the tennis team, but what about the rest of the year? Tennis weather will soon be over. I take it coming from California you won't be going out for the winter sports, at least the teams—skiing or ice hockey?" Before I could answer he quickly said, "Or perhaps you will, perhaps you've spent sufficient time in the East."

"No," I said, "I've never been on skis and I'm not very good on ice skates."

"So I'm sure you won't mind doing your bit by speaking thirty-five lines with our Glee Club. After all, you are a senior and I expect our seniors to set good examples by showing their leadership, by participating in as many school activities as possible."

I knew he was dead set on me and "To Be or Not To Be," but I was dead set against it so I forged right ahead. "Mr. Hoyt, I'm afraid if I took something like this on, it might interfere with studying and my grades would drop."

"Why, Peter," he said, like he'd caught on to a bad plea, "I'd bet money on you memorizing thirty-five lines in one evening."

He was equating the task of performing Hamlet's soliloquy with memorizing thirty-five lines and I thought that was unfair. "It's not the memorizing that would take time away from—"

"What is it then?" he asked rather sharply.

I knew that was a warning that I didn't have much time left to agree to do it; I remember wanting to look at his forehead to see how that raised spot was coming along, but I didn't want to get caught at it. I continued, on my guard and searching for the most diplomatic words to make my point. "It would be all the time rehearsing it, trying to find the right way to act it." That didn't do anything to him; he didn't bat an eye. "Actually, what would distract me from studying would be all the worrying about—"

"Worrying?" he asked. "What worrying?"

"Well, you know, about the actual performance." Now I decided to throw myself on the mercy of the court. "I would be scared— you know, stage fright. I have a one-track mind about things like that and I'd be dwelling on it twenty-four hours a day. You see, Mr. Hoyt, I don't have any real acting talent and I'm sure—"

"Why, Peter," he said almost sarcastically, "you're a splendid performer. At least you're a born mimic. You gave a perfect imitation of the way I walk your very first day here."

Whammo! Curve! Bull's-eye! (The first, last, and only time he ever acknowledged that little episode.) I knew now he wasn't fooling around.

And now he opened up with his biggest gun. "And your imitation of Jussi Bjoerling was excellent—on key, loud and clear. You have a fine voice." He was looking for my expression like a hawk and caught it immediately. "Oh, yes, I heard you. I was standing in the hall on the second floor speaking with Mr. Kauffman. I sent him upstairs to see who was singing so well."

Zonk! Now I felt he'd really been playing cat-and-mouse with me.

"At any rate, if you're confused about how to do the soliloquy just pick out your favorite, say Richard Burton or Laurence Olivier, and imitate the way he would do it. Now suppose I leave you here for a half hour or so while you decide if you won't be willing to help out by reciting thirty-five lines with the Glee Club."

He turned and started to walk toward the stairs. "No, wait," I said. "I'll do it. I mean—I'll try."

He swung around. "I knew you would," he said, smiling, no leftover traces of sarcasm or anything, and I thought—excuse my language—You're goddam right you knew it!

So there I was, standing on the stage, much to my surprise, discussing ways to perform Hamlet's soliloquy.

Now there were no more curves from him. Although I was feeling uncomfortable and trapped and branded as a liar, he was going ahead with enthusiasm, as if we'd never even had the round that led up to it.

After a while he suggested we sit down and I simply read it for making sense. I went through the "thirty-five lines," giving the words lip service only. When I finished, Mr. Hoyt asked me what it all meant to me.

I told him, to me, it was Hamlet's thoughts of suicide, of ending the torture of being on earth, weighed against his doubts of what happens after death. "Which doubts?" he asked me. "Well, whether we simply sleep forever, unaware for eternity, or whether we find out there's a heaven or hell or reincarnation or we end up ghosts or even something worse."

"What could be worse than being in hell for eternity?" Mr. Hoyt asked.

"I don't know," I said. Then I added, "Neither does Hamlet and that's what spooks him!"

"Ah-hah, precisely!" Mr. Hoyt said, taking me by both shoulders. "That's exactly the point. You have it!"

I wanted to mention that just because a person can grasp what a character or a speech is getting at doesn't mean he can hop up on a stage and act it out, but I knew I was up against an immovable object.

"Now the thing to do, Peter, is to go through each word, each sentence for any specific use of the language you mightn't understand." He went on telling me to jot down any word that I wouldn't know how to use myself in a sentence and that tomorrow afternoon when we got together we'd go over them, ending up with a smile and, "I'm glad we got this straightened out. Any questions?"

"Mr. Hoyt, how do you suppose Hamlet will go over with the students?"

His answer surprised me. "It doesn't really matter how it goes over with the students, although I'm sure it will. What matters is how it goes over with the committee of judges."

"But if it doesn't go over with the students, the judges will notice their reaction and that would influence them, wouldn't it?"

"I'm sure it will 'go over,' as you say, with students and judges alike, Peter, if you perform it with expertise," he said, dropping the ball in my lap, right where I didn't want it. "Why, what is it, Peter?"

"Nothing," I said, "except I would hate it if the audience got restless and began coughing and—"

"And what?"

"Laughing, for instance."

"You worry about that?"

"Yes, of course. It's just that Hamlet's been done so much, and by some pretty brilliant actors. I worry about *me* being Hamlet, not Hamlet alone. Also, it might seem old hat."

"We'll see that it doesn't," he said. Then he added, "Unless you can think of another Shakespearean speech you'd prefer. Or perhaps one of his sonnets, or even some other bit of poetry; it doesn't necessarily have to be Shakespeare. If you come up with something else, I'll certainly give it consideration. You let me know," he said, perhaps just a mite testily that I had voiced my doubts, and left.

This last indication that he would give consideration to another choice didn't do too much to cheer me up. For several reasons: I didn't have anything else of Shakespeare's in mind and I don't have any taste or appreciation of poetry, but mostly I knew, as sure as death and taxes, that I was going to be standing up on a stage making an ass of myself come time for the Glee Club competition.

I remember clearly that I didn't have much of an appetite for dinner that night. It was during study hours later on that the idea hit me. I don't know why it hadn't occurred to me immediately but it hadn't. I suppose because I'd been too stunned by Mr. Hoyt's plan to think clearly. I literally jumped up from my desk when it did strike me. I tore off a quick letter to Frankie Spiro at the Masquers in California and went right down to Mr. Kauffman's room to buy stamps for a special-delivery airmail letter. He reprimanded me for not waiting until after study hours, but I told him I was sending away for something for Mr. Hoyt and it was important that it get off immediately. I also said I had something to discuss with Mr. Hoyt and asked if I could have permission to go over and see him.

"During study hours? I don't know if I can take it upon myself to grant you permission, just like that," he said. Poor Mr. Kauffman was all bound up by rules and procedure and frightened and— he's really a nervous mess.

"Could you phone and tell him I'd like to speak to him?"

"Well, yes, if it's all that important," he said, picking up the phone and dialing. "My, my," he clucked. When Mr. Hoyt answered, Mr. Kauffman said, "Young Kilburn's in my room in a highly agitated state and insists on speaking to you." He wasn't letting himself in for any trouble, no sir.

When he handed me the phone and I said hello, Mr. Hoyt asked me, with distinct humor, if I were in a highly agitated state. I had to smile; he not only had Lee Galonka's number, he also had Mr. Kauffman's, and maybe he wasn't such a terror after all. I told him I wasn't, that regarding our talk that afternoon I'd just had an idea and I wanted to tell him about it. I asked if I could come over and speak to him now and he said yes, that would be all right, and to tell Mr. Kauffman.

When I rang the bell to his house, Mrs. Hoyt answered the door as if it were the next thing that happened after a flying saucer had set down in the front yard. "Oh . . . oh, Peter," she said, putting a hand up to her chest. "Come in." Then she whispered, "Is Mr.—ah—" She broke off like she'd forgotten his name. "Is he expecting you?" I told her he was and she seemed relieved.

Approaching his study, I heard Mr. Hoyt say in a loud, stern voice, "And I suggest that you, sir, are blatantly misrepresenting the facts as known in this case!" As Mrs. Hoyt knocked on the door she whispered, "For the debating team."

When she opened the door, there was Mr. Hoyt seated at his desk and his son, Headley, sitting at a card table opposite him. They each had a legal pad, pen, file cards and a glass of water in front of them and there was something immediately funny and sad about the picture of the two of them propped up opposite each other so formally, rehearsing for the debating team.

Mr. Hoyt greeted me warmly. "You know Headley," he said. I said yes, and Headley said hello. Then Mr. Hoyt said, "Upstairs, Headley." The tone reminded me of the way you'd speak to a dog —Down, Rover! Then he added in a completely different voice, "And remember, son, don't allow your emotions to take over. Once you become emotional in debate, you've lost."

"Yes, sir," Headley said, gathering his things together. I couldn't possibly imagine Headley being emotional about anything. He was a tidy little cipher in a blue suit, that's all I could see. I was immediately curious about what he'd been emotional over and I would have given anything to see a display of the same from him.

When we were left alone, Mr. Hoyt turned to me with a smile and said, "Peter, what is it that's got you in such a highly agitated state?" We both chuckled in acknowledgment of Mr. Kauffman. "Now, what's on your mind?"

I jumped right in and told him about Frankie Spiro, who is a combination character actor and comedian. He has a little stutter that makes almost any story he tells funny, but he has some special material that's funny by itself. He's always been a favorite of mine; whenever the Masquers has a night featuring entertainment for the members and I hear Frankie Spiro's going to appear, I tag along with my father just to see him. One of his best numbers is a takeoff

100

on Hamlet. I told Mr. Hoyt I'd sent off a special-delivery letter asking for a copy of it, but I'd heard it so many times I knew most of it by heart.

"He starts off doing 'To Be or Not To Be' deadly serious. He does the first six or seven lines completely straight, except for his stutter, of course. Then he breaks off and says, 'Listen, don't laugh at the poor guy. This Hamlet really had problems. In the first place how would *you* like it if *your* uncle came over for dinner and made a pass at *your* mother?' That always gets a laugh," I told Mr. Hoyt, who wasn't even smiling. "Then he follows it up right away with 'Especially if he's your *mother's* brother!' An even bigger laugh," I told him.

Now Mr. Hoyt winced, but I continued because I was all wound up and I was sure I'd get him with me as I went on. " 'And those old castles, they were drafty. Everyone always had a cold and Kleenex hadn't even been invented. That's why everyone had long, bulky sleeves with lots of extra material. And the plumbing in those old castles—it was criminal. I don't think they bathed from, oh, I'd say Halloween to Shrove Tuesday, which is either in April or Montana.' " (This kind of non sequitur kills me.) " 'That's a long time without soap and water, from whence cometh the saying: There's something rotten in Denmark.' "

Mr. Hoyt was not looking pleased and I had a sinking feeling in the pit of my stomach that I wasn't going to get him, that—as my father so quaintly says—I'd just pooped in the elevator.

But I was in it and some madness made me go on. " 'And at night what was there for Hamlet to do? This was back in sixteen hundred-something, so you know television reception was pretty rotten. What did the poor Prince have to look forward to—just the ghost of his father clanking around? Oh sure, he had his girl friend, Ophelia. But I mean the name alone, Oh-feel-ya, would be enough to put you off. Not only that but'—at this point Frankie Spiro would look from side to side as if someone might be listening, tap his head and whisper—'she was not quite all there, a few loose hinges in the attic.' "

Mr. Hoyt was now looking pretty grim, so I decided to cut it short. "Anyhow, it goes on for about three minutes with a lot of good laughs; then he has a great get-off. Toward the end he says, 'And you wonder why they had so much trouble and ended up with all those murders? They were all *sick!* Everyone in that castle— Hamlet, his mama, Ophelia, the uncle—they all suffered from terrible migraine headaches. You see, they had constant wracking headaches from figuring out how to say everything in iambic pentameter. No wonder they were all nutsy!' Then Frankie Spiro would start walking off, bobbing his head, trying to get the beat of iambic pentameter and mumbling, 'For*sooth,* I *needs* must *go* down *to* the A and *P!'*"

To my surprise the A and P exit line got a laugh from Mr. Hoyt and I thought maybe he'd just been putting me on, testing me out by being grim-faced. "It really goes over very well. I've never seen it fail," I assured him.

"I'm sure some of it's quite amusing," he said.

"What do you think?" I asked him.

"Yes, I can see where at a men's club the reaction might, in a crude sort of way—"

"No," I said. "About me doing it. I could try it out at our own Glee Club assembly before—"

"What?" he asked, leaning forward over his desk. "Peter, you mean you were suggesting you do *that* instead of the real speech?"

Talk about missing!

"Well, yes, I thought we could give it a try and—"

"Oh, no. No, I'm afraid not. Don't you think it's slightly disrespectful to the genius that was Shakespeare's?"

I thought for a good while before answering, but in the end I decided he was being both terribly square and unfair. "Not really. All satire is kidding. If the thing that's being kidded isn't famous, and it would have to have real worth to become so well known, then nobody would bother doing a takeoff on it. In a way I think it's a compliment to—"

"No," he said, standing up from his desk and paying no attention to what I was saying, "it's out of the question. I'll see you tomorrow at five in the auditorium and we can put in a good hour before dinner."

With that I was dismissed. I knew come hell or high water, even if he had to drag me out onto the stage chained and in a cage, he was going to have me doing Hamlet's speech at the Glee Club competition.

That night before I got into bed, I glanced into the mirror and said, " 'Good night, sweet prince'—you poor bastard!"

8

WE BEGAN working at least an hour a day. The prospect of having to do the speech in front of an audience became an obsession with me. I couldn't clear my mind of the idea that I was going to lay an embarrassing egg.

I was so hoping against hope that something would happen to prevent me from actually having to go through with Hamlet that I didn't tell anyone about our rehearsals. Mr. Hoyt was treating it like it was some glorious surprise to be kept under wraps and that was all right with me. Mr. Kauffman knew about it and Mrs. Mason and probably some more of the faculty but, as far as I knew, none of the students.

Not having anyone to talk over this current problem with wasn't good and once more brought into focus my lack of a good friend and renewed my earlier dissatisfaction with the school and the students, too.

A few days after Mr. Hoyt sprang his Hamlet plan, the Glee Club gave an assembly for the students and teachers to try out part of their program. To my surprise they sounded good for a small group, sixteen, with Mr. Kauffman as their Leonard Bernstein, high blush in his cheeks while he was conducting, flourishing his arms, giving them wild dramatic cutoffs and weaving back and forth to the music when he was pleased. He turned out to be quite a performer himself. The selection was fairly square except for a snappy version of "I Won't Dance" and "Lazy Afternoon" from *Golden Apple,* which was great, and their last big medley from *The Sound of Music,* which was so sugar sweet you could have gotten a major toothache from it.

Frankie Spiro sent me a copy of his takeoff and a note wishing me luck. The parts I hadn't gotten to tell Mr. Hoyt were even funnier than I remembered and I learned the whole thing, hoping to spring it again on him if I ever caught him in a distinctly "up" mood or also if he began to sense that we were heading for disaster with the *real* Hamlet.

But he didn't appear to be worried at all, even as rehearsals wore on and nothing was happening. I thought he'd turn out to be a taskmaster and drill me until I dropped, but instead he was almost complacent. Within a few days I'd memorized it completely, but the big problem was to find an emotional line to hang it on. How to act it out. When we'd have rehearsals Mr. Hoyt would sit right up on the stage fairly close to me. Now and then he'd stop me and suggest that I find a gesture for a word or a phrase. At first I'd try perhaps a motion with my hand or some sort of movement but I was convinced that my problem wasn't one of gestures but of finding the right emotional chord and striking it.

It's all good and well to know what something means, but then you have to make a choice as to *how* you're going to deliver it, a choice of attitude. You could say the speech like a crazy man, like someone in a daze, you could spit it out sardonic and bitter, you could do it like you were really trying to figure out a problem. That, as a matter of fact, was Mr. Hoyt's choice. He said it should be quizzical, questioning myself and the world and weighing the decisions. That seemed a little general to me, it was hard for me to *act* being questioning.

After a while I began to feel closed in, constricted by Mr. Hoyt being up on the stage so near me. Then one afternoon, when nothing was happening as far as I was concerned, I started to get severely depressed. I felt trapped, put upon, and a lot of other things—most of all inhibited. I was about in the middle of the speech, third time through, and I suddenly thought I'd have to ask him to sit out in the audience so I could feel free to—I don't know what—start experimenting or just not be so under his microscopic eye.

I stopped and turned to him. He was sitting backward on a hard-backed chair, his hands on top of the curved wood, and he was staring at me, but not at my face, at the middle of my body—by that I don't mean anything dirty, not at that part of me—just sort of at my side. And although he was staring at me I could tell he wasn't really seeing me either. He had a glazed look across his eyes and even when I stopped speaking and looked over at him—he was only about seven or eight feet from me—he didn't move or acknowledge by his expression that I'd stopped reciting the speech.

After what seemed like a long, long silence I said, "Mr. Hoyt . . . ?"

"Mmn . . . ," he mumbled, still without focusing his eyes on me.

"I was wondering—"

He raised his head in a little abrupt movement and spoke as if I hadn't said anything. "You have a pleasant voice," he said, "a very pleasant voice. Go on, Peter, you're doing fine."

I wasn't doing fine and I knew he still wasn't aware that I'd stopped to ask him something. I said his name again, but I realized he'd already gone right back into his, almost like, reverie. I spoke again. "Mr. Hoyt . . . ?"

Then came a big surprise. In a very soft voice, he said, "Call me Frank."

"Frank?" I asked.

He shook his head and snapped out of it. "What? . . . Oh, what is it?" he asked almost sharply.

I knew he thought he was speaking to someone else and that he hadn't really meant for me, Peter Kilburn, to call him Frank.

"I wonder," I said, "if I could try rehearsing with you sitting out in the audience." He looked confused. "I mean, so I would get used

106

to projecting out there, instead of holding it in up on the stage. I think it would help me."

"Oh, yes—certainly," he said, rising and walking toward the front of the stage. But then he slowed down and when he put one foot on the top step he stopped and turned around and I could tell that for a split second he'd forgotten where he was going. Then he gave his head a little shake and cleared his vision, looking right into my face, and I could see the light going on and he remembered. "Yes, yes," he muttered and went on down the steps. Instead of sitting about halfway back, as I'd hoped, he sat in the middle of the second row; still it was better than having him on top of me.

I started in at the beginning again and by the time I'd gotten three quarters of the way through the speech I glanced down at him and his hands were clasped together in front of him, chin resting upon his fingers, and he'd gone off into this strange trance in which he was staring at me but not really seeing me and certainly not hearing me. I knew I could have recited "Hickory, dickory, dock, the mouse ran up the clock," and it wouldn't have mattered.

This added to my depression. For a while I wanted to stop and just tell him it was impossible, I couldn't do it, and if he thought that was terrible, then I'd better leave school. I felt that strongly about it. As I was weighing the consequences, he stood up, brushed a hand across his forehead and said, "I'm a little tired. That will be all for this afternoon, if you don't mind. Unless you want to stay and work by yourself." With that he turned, walked up the aisle and out, mumbling, "Fine, it's coming along fine."

For some unknown reason I started to cry, just standing up there on the stage, almost the minute he'd gone. I began swearing, which I usually do when I get trapped into crying, so I just stood there swearing and crying for a while until I ran down and stopped.

Talk about tired—I was immediately bushed. I had just about enough energy to drag myself back to Lincoln House and up to my room, where I fell into a nap of depression.

I woke up even more depressed. Also, the nature of my awakening was anything but pleasant. Ed Anders was having a severe attack of flatulence. His room was right across the hall from me and he had a charming habit of stepping out in the hall when he felt an attack coming on and letting it go there. He could have done sound effects for a thunderstorm without any trouble at all and sometimes various small-arms fire. This early evening it was thunder followed by a few rat-a-tat bursts of antiaircraft. This awakened me and then everyone who happened to be on the third floor started yelling the way they always did when Ed Anders graced us with a concert.

Wiley Bevan would invariably launch into a newscast: "In Asia, the Viet Cong opened up with a mighty barrage twenty miles north of Saigon. Casualties were running high when . . ." Etc., etc. Lee Galonka, in his only mildly funny bit, would do a dying scene. "Oh—ah, they got me, right in the left gut. Mom! Mom! Oh, God, Mom—tell Bonny I loved her. Oh—ah, the pain. And, Mom—one last thing before I go— Oh, it's starting to get dark— The money's in the—it's behind the— Ohhhhh!" And he'd fall dead. Philip Simmons would start hawking gas masks, Logan Tinney would snort out a few words like "Charming! That's really charming!" Jimmy Greer would giggle. And Ed Anders would rebut with "Jesus Christ, you guys, I can't help it if I got a ski pole rammed through my intestines!"

Everyone would yell out "Neither can *we!*" or "Why don't you contaminate your *own* room?" or "Hang your ass out the window."

There's a saying that people who are sick run a fever and get delirious late at night. Well, the rule's different for guys away at boarding school. They run a high fever in the early evening for a half hour or so right before dinner. All hell breaks loose, everyone's yelling and horsing around and it's pure bedlam.

At the dinner table I got into a deeper funk than ever. I realized the conversation hadn't progressed an inch from the very first day I arrived. Ed Anders was talking about some new dynamic-tension equipment, a tensalator he'd sent away for. He turned to Jimmy and said, "You know, Jimmy, you'd have a good build if you'd exercise. I'm going to start you in on my tensalator."

"Who—ma-me?" Jimmy asked, dropping a boiled potato he was dishing out on the floor.

108

Wiley Bevan was talking about going down to Florida over Christmas vacation to "ball" his summer waitress, who was working there in the winter. Lee Galonka was rapping Paul Newman, Philip Simmons was trying to decide what college to go away to, and Logan Tinney was alternately knocking the virtues of dynamic tension, praising Paul Newman and suggesting that Philip Simmons might as well forget about college altogether.

I got to thinking what a long, dull, dreary winter it was bound to be and how far away June was—not knowing, of course, it was going to be anything but boring and I wasn't even going to make it through January at Gilford.

The next day things got worse instead of better. Breakfast featured chipped beef, which I love. I'd no sooner taken my first mouthful when a fellow at another table, Henry Samish, threw up smack in the aisle next to our table as he was dashing to get out of the dining room. I can't tell you the aversion I have to anyone vomiting, myself included. I know nobody thinks it's charming, but it really demolishes me. I had to excuse myself and go upstairs and lie down, feeling hungry and sick at the same time.

That was only for starters. The night before, I'd been in such a mood I hadn't done my homework. I went to my early class, French, unprepared for the first time. It was also the first time there were two men monitoring the class, newly appointed members of the Board of Trustees from Boston. Mr. Piper called on me right off the bat, giving me English sentences to translate into French using a new verb form. I tried to bluff my way through and got completely bungled up, making an ass out of myself and disappointing Mr. Piper a great deal, I could tell. I was miserable all morning because I'd let him down.

Not having eaten breakfast, my stomach was looking forward to lunch. There's one thing I can't stand and that's tongue and there it was staring up at me. I ate around it, but it really puts me off my feed, and I realized I had to have edible food, so I left the table and cut across the campus to the village and a soda fountain. I'd no sooner sat at the counter and ordered when one of the town characters, called Crazy Andy by the students and the similarly crude townsfolk, sat at the counter two stools from me. He's a skinny fellow about thirty with the disease that kills off the coordination, where each step is about as regular as falling down a flight of stairs and the speech is all twisted and garbled. Because of this, naturally, he's a compulsive talker. Unfortunately his vegetable soup came before my cheeseburger, and soup is about the last thing he should order in a public restaurant. It was a mess, all down the front of him and awash on the counter and at one point, right after my food arrived, he even flipped a whole spoonful right up onto the side of his face, over his left ear, getting it into his hair and everything. He also never stopped talking, not for one second, which made it even more brutal, because you couldn't understand a word of what he was getting at.

I managed to get down my cheeseburger and drink my orange soda but it was just bulk I was putting away, there was no taste involved. The minute I'd paid my check the heavens opened up and you never saw such a downpour. I wasn't dressed for it and ran like a madman back to Lincoln House. When I got back to my room, drenched, I looked into my mirror and said, "This is not your day." I felt like going to bed right that minute and skipping the rest of it. I found a Boston paper and, for the fun of it, looked up my horoscope for the day. Leo: "A good day for financial investments and for straightening out romantic entanglements." That, at least, gave me a good laugh. I really had a lot of financial investments to attend to and slews of romantic entanglements to straighten out.

The afternoon was grim, too. The sky was leaden gray, the rain poured down so hard I couldn't keep my mind on any of my studies, only on my problems and discontentment, which was growing by leaps and bounds, with myself and the school. And if I'd thought I'd hit the bottom of my depression about Hamlet I was mistaken.

When I got to the auditorium Mr. Hoyt was on the stage with a shapeless lump of a man in Army fatigues and a knitted black cap. Mr. Hoyt introduced me to the man, who looked like a mole, all squinty-eyed, as Mr. Rush. Mr. Rush said hello, then chortled, "So

110

this is our young Hamlet!" He had a good chuckle about that and then they got into a big conversation about lighting me.

So it was going to be a real production! This was bad enough, but when Mr. Rush, who owned a hardware store and was interested in amateur theatrics, asked what the setting would be, Mr. Hoyt said the Glee Club would be standing behind me humming.

Humming! What would they be humming?

Then he dropped the last bit of good news by saying I would be wearing a black shirt and black tights.

"Very effective," said Mr. Rush.

That was the last crushing blow. As they went on discussing this pinpointed spotlight they wanted, I thought it better be pretty damn pinpointed so I'm not seen in a pair of black tights, which would really set me up for laughs. While my mind was working overtime trying to whip up some kind of an out, I suddenly thought of trying out Frankie Spiro's monologue on him again. He was in a very "up" mood, speaking with Mr. Rush and gesticulating how he wanted the light to hit me. I could hardly wait for Mr. Rush to leave, that's how anxious I was to engage Mr. Hoyt in conversation, any conversation that might lead to abandoning Hamlet. When Mr. Rush did go, his parting shot to me was a snickering, "So long, Hamlet—see you around."

Not if I can possibly help it, I thought.

"Peter," Mr. Hoyt said, handing me a cardboard box before I could open my mouth, "Mrs. Hoyt picked up some black tights for you in Concord. She couldn't find a decent black shirt, so she's going to make you a black jumper. What's your shirt size?"

"Fourteen and a half, thirty-three. Mr. Hoyt—"

"Try on the tights now and we'll see if they're a good fit." I hesitated for a moment. "Go ahead, Peter," he said energetically, "you can step around back of the drapes if you want."

I did, and changed into them. Unfortunately, after a bit of tugging and straightening around which I knew he would do if I didn't, they seemed to fit. I walked out onto the stage and Mr. Hoyt was standing down in the orchestra, right in front of the stage apron,

111

looking up at me. "Mmn, mmn," he muttered, "they look fine. Turn around and hold your shirt up." I did and he mumbled his approval. When I had turned all the way back around he was focusing on me closely. "Are those jockey shorts you're wearing?"

"Yes."

"Yes, they show through your tights. We'll have to—perhaps Mrs. Hoyt can dye a pair of your shorts black." He kept staring at me. "Step over closer here." He motioned to me and I stepped up nearer to him until he was looking right up at me. "Or perhaps you should wear an athletic—"

"Mr. Hoyt, do I have to wear black tights?"

"Why?"

"Well, I don't know . . ."

"Why, Peter," he said, almost amused. "You're not embarrassed? You have good legs, nothing to be embarrassed about. Hamlet can't very well stand there in a sport jacket and striped tie."

"But if you're just planning to keep a spotlight on my face—"

"There's bound to be some light spreading out and I think the black will be—"

"I have a dark suit," I quickly offered. See how you get trapped? Here I was planning to hit him with Frankie Spiro's monologue and if that didn't work, quit, leave school, and suddenly I'm saying I have a dark suit I'll wear.

"We'll try it this way," he said, looking me over once more. "You'll get used to them, it's the strangeness. I think it would be a good idea if you rehearsed in them from now on." He smacked his hands together and said, "All right, now, Peter, boy! Let's have a good rehearsal. Try to just let yourself go. See if you can't throw yourself right into it this afternoon. See if you can't *be* that confused Danish Prince."

I was confused all right, but without the Danish Prince part. "Mr. Hoyt," I blurted out, "I'm afraid I'm just not up to it."

"Peter," he said, moving forward, "you're not feeling well?"

"No, I'm—Mr. Hoyt, I'm just afraid I won't be able— I can't pull this off!"

112

"Pull this off?" he asked in a cool voice.

"I don't think I can."

Another tone, pleasant, friendly. "Why Peter—I thought it was coming along so well."

"No, I really don't think I can do it."

Now, after a pause: "You don't *think* you can do it? Or you won't do it?" There was an edge of warning in this last sentence.

"No, I don't mean that."

Snap: "Then what do you mean?"

"I mean I don't think it will come off well," I said candidly. "I think it will hurt the Glee Club's performance. It'll do more harm than—"

"You let me be the judge of that. And let me tell you this, young man"—now he was speaking almost in the same tone as that first day—"you're here on half-tuition and you have an added obligation to do your share. And do your share you will. I'll tell you another thing: two of the schools are having extra attractions this year added to their Glee Club programs. Moulton is having a harmonica soloist and Stonehenge has a magician. Gilford is not going to be outdone, not by any means."

So that was it! That's where this crazy Hamlet idea was hatched from. Now I really felt I was being used. Harmonica music does less than nothing for me, but it's certainly a broad type of entertainment and any kind of magic is an audience pleaser. Hamlet, though, is a far different matter. Just as I'd decided to go into this with Mr. Hoyt he spoke up, "Are you going to have a sulk for yourself?"

"No."

"Spit it out, what's on your mind?"

"It's just that Hamlet's not the same kind of entertainment as—"

"I don't want to hear another word about Hamlet!" He turned and walked up the aisle a few steps. "What I want to hear now is Shakespeare's words."

It's heart-warming when someone asks you what's on your mind and the second you open your mouth tells you to shut up. It's great for mood setting and my mood was sinking deeper and deeper.

113

There I was, standing up on the stage in black tights, with a white shirt, a striped tie and a pair of brown loafers. As if Mr. Hoyt sensed my own mental picture of myself, he suddenly said, "Tuck that shirt in."

I did and when I finished I suddenly felt that hot flush behind the eyes that comes before the dam bursts. But the way I was feeling I wouldn't have let him see me cry if I was undergoing brain surgery without anesthesia.

"What are you doing?" he asked impatiently.

Oh-oh, I said to myself, you've got a choice, either cry or get mad and you haven't much time. "Preparing!" I said a trifle sharply.

"Preparing to what?"

"Preparing to get inside the Prince of Denmark!" I said.

"Watch yourself!" he warned, taking a forward step down the aisle.

I launched into the speech, and I was furious. I put my emotions to work and kept thinking of swearwords all the way through it, paraphrasing the swearwords with the real text, like this:

> To be, or not to be: that is the [goddam] question:
> Whether 'tis nobler in the mind to suffer
> The [fucking] slings and arrows of outrageous fortune,
> Or to take arms against a [shitty] sea of troubles, . . .

And so forth. This was a Hamlet pissed off at the world. If my thoughts had been translated into words, I'd have been shot on the spot. When I got through, my ears were practically smoking I was so worked up. And I thought: There, what do you think of that, you sadistic bastard!

Mr. Hoyt broke into a huge smile. "That's more like it," he said. "Perform it that way and we'll pick up some points for sure."

"I don't think I could."

"Why not? Give it emotion. Oh, I see," he said, laughing again. "You don't think you could stay angry with me, is that it, Peter?"

114

His laughing annoyed me and I took a chance. "I'll do my best," I said.

He stopped laughing abruptly and stared at me. I couldn't tell if he was going along with me or if he was going to let me have it. I felt like I was hanging on a cliff. I didn't know where we'd go next and I never did find out because the rear door of the auditorium opened and Erwin Cranshaw, a blob of an unfortunate-looking, overweight kid, whom Jordan later nicknamed "Mata Hari," stuck his head in the door. "Mr. Hoyt?" Erwin came panting down the aisle. "Mrs. Mason says to tell you . . ." but I couldn't hear the rest. Erwin was Mrs. Mason's errand boy and spy and always spoke in a whisper if he possibly could. Everything was extremely urgent and top secret with Mata Hari. After Erwin finished hissing in Mr. Hoyt's ear, Mr. Hoyt turned to me, excusing himself and saying to continue on and keep up the good work. Mata Hari waddled up the aisle after him, shooting little glances back at me, and I knew he didn't know what was going on and it was bugging him something terrible. One thing: He told Mrs. Mason everything he could get his hands on, but Mrs. Mason rarely told him anything.

I stayed there for another twenty minutes or so, just sort of fooling around in my mind, thinking of placing a call to my father in the evening, after the rates changed, and feeling him out on whether he was coming to New York soon and maybe he'd like me with him. Even public school in New York City was looking better than Gilford.

Then Mata Hari came back in and jiggled down the aisle with the earth-shaking news that Mr. Hoyt had said he wouldn't be back, that I was to go on working alone and he'd see me tomorrow afternoon. When he got to the steps, he squinted up at me and whispered, "Hey, Peter—what are you doing?"

"Standing up here on the stage."

"Yeah, but what for?"

"I like it."

"No, really, what for?" No humor, he just had to find out. "How come the black tights?"

"Dracula!"

"What?"

"Dracula!"

"What do you mean?"

"I'm doing readings from *Dracula.*"

"You are? No you're not. Are you—really?"

"I just told you."

"When?"

"Special assembly, next week."

"No kidding, that's wild!" he whispered, turning and lumbering up the aisle, eager to spread the word. "My God—*Dracula!*"

His efficiency as a news outlet was proved the next day when at least a dozen kids asked me about the readings from *Dracula.* How come? Why? When? Etc.

The minute he left the auditorium I got out of my tights and into my clothes and went to Lincoln House where I found a letter from Mrs. Mosley, the superintendent of my father's building, saying my father had asked her to write, that he'd had a "nasty little spill" and broken his wrist, but not to worry, it was in a cast and would heal but he wouldn't be able to write for a while and wanted me to know. She was taking good care of him, he sent his love and hoped I was liking school. I couldn't very well call my father and add to his misery just when he'd broken his wrist. Also, this accident indicated he was on another binge.

I stayed in my room staring out at the pelting rain, which hadn't stopped since noon, wondering if it would ever end and if my streak of freakish luck at Gilford would ever end. I even got to the point where I began telling myself at least I had my health and a roof over my head and three meals a day, that I wasn't blind or deformed, that sometimes you hit a losing streak but you're bound to start winning sooner or later. I tried to blot out the early evening bedlam on the third floor as I continued this tired lecture to myself. I'm afraid it didn't do much good because I was grim by the time dinner came around and I started downstairs, where the conversation was bound to beat me down further.

When things are bad I usually think of a way out of them in terms of a "surprise." It could be in the form of something good happening to me: A limousine pulls up and my real parents, who have finally tracked me down, step out, looking like Yves Montand and Simone Signoret. After a lot of hugging and tears, I mention that I better pack my things, but they say "Forget it!" and whisk me off. Or the surprise could be in the form of something perverse happening to someone that's giving me trouble. For instance, Mr. Hoyt's house catching fire and burning down would have been a titillating surprise at this point. Now, as I went downstairs, I thought: Wouldn't it be great if my whole table was empty and I could eat dinner by myself, just this once, alone with my thoughts.

There was a surprise, too. Not the one I was thinking of. I'd no sooner sat down when I heard Mr. Kauffman clear his throat. I looked up to see him standing opposite me, at an extra place that had been set, and next to him—a completely new face.

9

MR. KAUFFMAN introduced him. "We have an addition to our senior class—this is Jordan Legier." He rattled off our names and we all said hello. Jordan Legier (pronounced Luh-zhay) sat down and Mr. Kauffman went back to his table.

Most new students would be a bit nervous being tossed in with a strange group. But I observed that, if anything, he seemed either completely detached or bored. He'd said hello with a certain coolness, sat down and began eating his meal, not much of it and not heartily, as if he'd already been on a long voyage with everyone there and had decided to abdicate as far as active conversation was concerned.

The first thing I noticed about him were his lips: well formed, not thin, but they had a bluish tint to them. Then his eyes, set wide apart and a dark deep-ocean blue, almost cold. Light-brown hair, chestnut, I suppose you'd call it, parted and combed over to the side so some of it crossed over his forehead. And his nose didn't really go with his face, which had good cheekbones and narrowed to a finely chiseled jaw and was really a sensitive face. Although his nose was prominent, it wasn't too big for his face, but it had a flattened plane for a half inch or so angling from the center of the bridge down one side, and the end, instead of coming to a point, was a little blunted. A fighter's nose, not a punchy one, more a novice fighter's nose with maybe one good fight behind it that made it a little off.

Most of all, it was his poise I noticed. As I said, he never began any conversation; on the other hand he wasn't rude; he did answer when a reply was required, and he listened.

The group came through as expected. You could have dropped an Eskimo or a chimpanzee down at our table and it wouldn't have altered the conversation.

ED ANDERS (*to Jordan, shortly after the introduction*): You go in for sports, fella?

JORDAN: No.

ED ANDERS: You kind of look like the tennis type.

Jordan remained mute; he'd already answered the question

WILEY BEVAN (*picking up the ball*): Louise (*to Jordan*)—this waitress I balled at Camp Comega this summer—(*back to the group*) played tennis all the time. After the lunch shift, she'd always play tennis. (*Snicker.*) That is, when *we* weren't playing. And I don't mean tennis. (*Shakes his head, expels a large breath.*) Christ, she was the end! I mean, she was—(*Whistles.*)

That's the first time Jordan looked up; our eyes met and he didn't sigh but his eyes had the expression that that's what he was feeling. I tried a smile at him. He didn't smile in return, but looked back down and continued eating his meat loaf. I thought maybe I'd made a mistake.

ED ANDERS (*to Jordan again*): You don't go in for *any* sports? Ice skating, skiing?

JORDAN: No, I'm afraid not.

LEE GALONKA: God, did anybody see that winter carnival picture with Troy Donahue? (*Shakes his head.*) And he's supposed to be a movie star! I don't understand some of these guys! I don't understand the whole system! (*Sigh, another head shake.*) Even

119

Cary Grant—and I'm not knocking him—but he's old enough to be my grandfather!

WILEY BEVAN: I wonder if stars like Joan Crawford and Bette Davis still ball a lot? I mean it's not like an Ann-Margret or—

LOGAN TINNEY: Ann-Margret can't act. Ann-Margret's a zombie.

WILEY BEVAN: So—who's talking about acting? (*Giggles, pokes Jimmy in the ribs.*) Huh, Jimmy?

JIMMY GREER: Ya-yeah.

Because of his stutter, poor guy, and not being able to originate long sentences, he's delighted to agree with any statement that's directed to him. If you said, "That Hitler, he must have been a prince, huh, Jimmy?" he'd give you an enormous grin and say, "Ya-yeah." Then he'd think it over, realize Hitler *wasn't* a prince and frown, but he wouldn't say anything.

PHILIP SIMMONS (*to Jordan*): You ever been away to school before?

JORDAN: Yes.

PHILIP SIMMONS (*excited*): You have? I haven't, this is my first year. Where?

JORDAN: Maxton.

PHILIP SIMMONS (*even more excited*): Maxton! That's one of the Big Five.

LOGAN TINNEY (*reaching into his IBM brain*): Scholastically, it ranks number four.

ED ANDERS: Maybe scholastically, but they're nowhere in football any more. Not since they lost their coach, Hank Forman.

WILEY BEVAN: I know a guy went to Maxton. Christ, his sister's a knockout. Flaming-red hair. I never balled her but I danced with her once at a party in Cambridge. Emory Houston. Did you know him?

JORDAN: Yes . . . Emory.

WILEY BEVAN: You did? Ever meet his sister, Esther?

120

JORDAN: Yes, I know Esther.

WILEY BEVAN: You do? (*very lascivious.*) Hey, Jordy—

JORDAN: Jordan.

WILEY BEVAN: Yeah, Jordan, I mean. Hey, did you ever ball her?

JORDAN (*a long look at Wiley, then very quietly*): Not that I recall.

I love answers like that; Wiley Bevan looked so confused it really tickled me. At this point, Jordan glanced over and our eyes met again. I took a chance and smiled once more and he smiled back, not a big smile, just a twist of the mouth over by one corner.

I was becoming excited—a prospective friend on the horizon. I didn't want to louse it up, though. He'd already made such an impression on me that I was vitally concerned that I make a good impression on him. I decided to keep my cool and not push. Actually we didn't speak a word to each other all through the meal except for the initial introduction.

The conversation went on with Philip Simmons saying he was reading a novel about a prep school and there was a part about them putting saltpeter in the food, especially in dishes like meat loaf. He wondered if this was true and began a search for lumps in his meat loaf. Wiley Bevan got excited because that would surely put a crimp in his "balling." He, too, started digging through his plate. Logan Tinney apprised us of the fact that saltpeter was "nitrate of potassium, the symbol being KNO_3."

The conversation was so typical that you'd have sworn it was being piped in from a television comedy series about a prep school. Several times before the end of the meal I would look up and watch for Jordan's response and several times our eyes would meet and I could tell we shared the same reaction.

After dinner we all straggled out into the parlor. I kept an eye on Jordan, who found a chair, sat down and lit a cigarette and was surveying the scene as far as some of the seniors who'd been at other tables were concerned. Mr. Kauffman, who can smell smoke miles away and had probably been up on the third floor, materialized and walked over to him. "We don't smoke in the house, Jordan."

"Oh," said Jordan, looking at his cigarette, but not putting it out.

"I believe you'll find smoking is frowned upon here at Gilford. However, if we—"

"Smoking cuts down on your wind," Ed Anders said, sitting down and at the same time, and purely by accident, punctuating his remark with a short, sharp burst of flatulence.

The timing was perfect. Everyone broke up, including Jordan, except for Mr. Kauffman, who went red in the face and looked pained. Jimmy Greer was in hysterics, clutching at his stomach, and I thought he might fall down to the floor and just roll around for a while. Wiley Bevan said, "Maybe you ought to take up smoking, Ed. You got more than enough wind to go around." At this Jimmy was forced to run upstairs to the john.

When things calmed down, Jordan looked up at Mr. Kauffman. "If we do smoke, where do we do it?"

I had to smile; he didn't lay any comment on the sentence, didn't hit the "we"—just said the words.

"Not in Lincoln House, certainly not in our rooms," Mr. Kauffman replied, careful to avoid using "we" but forgetting and using "our rooms." Then he added, "Any smoking that's done is done outdoors."

"Thank you," Jordan said, rising and walking outside onto the wide front porch.

After a while I wandered outside and stood at a distance from him while he inhaled on his cigarette. He seemed to be taking great pleasure in it, seemed to be concentrating on it one hundred percent, the way real smokers do. Although the rain had stopped and the early evening sky was breaking up in patches of gray and steel-blue, leftover raindrops still blipped down from the trees and the roof. And the air, as it usually is right after a heavy rain, was clean and crisp, like it had been put through a washer.

Standing on the porch as we were, just the two of us, I was

122

positive he was aware I was there. I thought he obviously didn't want to talk or he'd look over and say something, so I figured don't press it.

Several guys came out of the house and walked down off the porch just as I saw Mr. Hoyt coming over from his house. As he drew nearer, I noticed he was looking anything but happy. He had seen Jordan standing on the other side of the porch and he was focusing on him, which left me free to look at Mr. Hoyt. The raised spot on his forehead was white and the rest of his face was highly colored. Walking up the steps, he surprised me by glancing over and smiling. "Good evening, Peter," he said. Then, once up on the porch, he stopped and turned to face Jordan, who was standing in profile to him. Jordan sensed this and turned, not quickly or slowly, just casually, to face him. I was sure they would speak until I noticed the almost bemused, yet detached look in Jordan's cold-blue eyes, as if Mr. Hoyt were in a glass cage and he, Jordan, was observing his behavior pattern. I couldn't see Mr. Hoyt's expression, his back was to me, but I did see the veins in the back of his neck pulsing and tugging, almost causing his ears to wiggle. They each stood like that for what seemed a long time but was probably no more than a few seconds, until a gust of wind swatted the big tree in front of the porch, releasing a shower of raindrops on the roof. This broke it and Mr. Hoyt turned and walked inside.

Immediately I figured they must have had a rocky first meeting, maybe even similar to mine. Having noticed their attitudes with each other, I had to control myself to keep from saying something. It occurred to me I'd been standing there long enough. I didn't want to appear to be bird-dogging him. I started to walk down off the porch when I heard Jordan say, "Balled anyone lately?"

I couldn't help smiling. Then I thought to say: "Not that I recall."

He laughed and said "Walk?"

I said sure and he followed me down off the porch.

I led the way to the path that crossed over the hill the school building sat on. When he was walking next to me, ever since he'd

123

gotten up from the table, in fact, I was amazed at his size. His voice was extremely low and easy on the ears, a slight drawl to it, and his face was set in a mature way, so he gave the impression of being much bigger, taller while he was sitting down. I'm five-eleven and now I saw that he was actually only five-seven or eight. Very early on I realized he had the voice and face and personality of a man in a boy's body. It turned out he was twenty, several years older than the average senior.

When we'd climbed up the path and were standing on the hill, I noticed he was breathing heavily. He stopped and took in the view, looking over to the gym, then down at the tennis courts and beyond at the long grassy slope leading to the football field, the lake and the thick woods. "Pretty campus," he said.

"Yes, it is," I agreed, looking around me, back toward the front part of the campus, the headmaster's house and Lincoln House. It was getting dark but I saw the unmistakable form of Mr. Hoyt standing on the top step of the porch and looking toward us.

"Oh," Jordan said, "cigarette?"

"No, thanks." I felt slightly uncomfortable with Mr. Hoyt on the porch like that. We had almost twenty-five minutes until study period so I led the way across the top of the hill and down the far side. Jordan had lit another cigarette and was enjoying it as much as the first. The longer we walked the more my curiosity was killing me. Finally I said, "Have you met Mr. Hoyt?"

"Mmn," he said. He exhaled a long puff of smoke and spoke in a very flat voice, "Enchanting." (He actually said it like two words: "En*chan*-ting.")

I laughed and he gave me a little quizzical look, like: what was I laughing at? I wanted to ask him what happened but that was a little forward, so I said, "He's a tough one to get to know."

"I could never get to know him," Jordan said. "He's from Mars —or I'm from Mars. No native tongue in common."

I wanted to tell him about my first meeting and all about Hamlet, but that was such an epic to leap into that I held it back.

"Your first year here?" he asked. I told him it was. "Hmn," he said, like he was simply confirming his own thoughts. After a few

124

more steps he stopped and turned to me. "I didn't get your last name."

"Kilburn."

"Not from New England." It was a statement.

"No, California."

"San Francisco?"

"No, the southern part."

"L.A.?"

"Yes, Hollywood."

"There's an actor, Thomas Kilburn."

That was a surprise. "My father."

"Your father?"

"Yes." I was happy and proud that he'd come up with his name. "How do you know him?"

"When I was thirteen, on a trip to Chicago, I saw him at the Studebaker Theatre in *Winner Lose All.* He was excellent. I've seen him in several movies and on television, not much lately though." Then he asked with concern, "Is he all right?"

"Yes." I thought there wasn't any need of going into all that now.

"Your father," he said. "Here, let me see." He took hold of my chin and turned my head sideways. I had to keep from shivering or pulling away—his fingers were ice-cold. "Yes, same nose, almost same profile." He let go of me. "Very interesting." We walked on toward the edge of the lake. When we got to the water, Jordan turned around and stared up at the school. "Tell me, is this place . . . ?" He broke off and didn't continue.

"Is it what?"

"As—sad as it seems?"

How's that for perception! He'd only arrived at two o'clock that afternoon. "Yes, I think it is," I told him. "Sad," I added, "that's a good word for it."

"Hmn," he mumbled and kept staring up the hill. After a while he said, "That group at the table, is that a fair sampling?" Then he quickly added, "Am I stepping on friends?"

"No," I assured him.

"Who writes their dialogue?" he asked.

"I'm afraid they do."

He shook his head. "Where do they keep the charmers?"

"I don't think there are many."

"No—no charmers?"

"I haven't spotted them."

"Shame. What about the faculty? They couldn't all be like Caspar."

"Caspar?"

"Milquetoast—Kauffman."

"No, they're not. They're not too much better though."

"Not possible," he said, frowning.

I gave a rave to Mr. Piper and a fairly good review to Mr. Hines, but there wasn't much to say for the rest of them, except Mr. Hendrix, the biology teacher who was such a character he was fun to have around. I told him the kids were not all as bad as at our table, that some of the day students seemed to be all right but that you didn't see them much outside of classes. I filled him in on a little of the schedule at school and the village, the movie, things like that. When I realized I might be talking too much I pulled in and brought it to an end.

Jordan swung around and looked out over the lake. "What do you do here?" he asked.

"Not much, I'm afraid." I don't know what made me come out with the next but I did. "Actually, I've been thinking of leaving lately," I told him.

"Oh, stick around," he said. "We'll liven things up." I got a kick out of him saying that. Then he turned around and looked back up the hill. "We won't let it bother us," he said.

"What?" I asked.

He nodded his head up toward the school. "Its—tackiness," he replied.

He'd used one of the magic words. We were going to be friends and I knew it. The relief was so great I let out a little laugh.

"What?" he asked.

126

"Nothing," I said.

The bell rang, indicating study hours began in five minutes, and we had to hurry to get to our rooms on time. Again I noticed he was breathing hard by the time we got to Lincoln House. He didn't say anything but "See you" as he went in the door to his room, which was the first one at the top of the stairs, mine being at the opposite end of the hall.

All during study hours I was so manic I couldn't get much homework done. I was gloating over my luck. Talk about *deus ex machina*—the Big Joker in the Sky had dropped a friend right down my chimney. And I thanked him for it.

After study hours, I was thinking about journeying down the hall to Jordan's room when there was a knock on my door. "Yes?"

"Peter?" The door opened and there stood Jordan in a wild green Oriental kimono with a huge gold dragon emblazoned on it.

"Come on in," I said.

"Just for a second." He stepped inside and pulled the door to, but didn't really close it. I noticed his lips were very blue and his face was extremely pale. "Just came by to say I'll see you tomorrow. I'm not feeling too well."

"Anything I can do?" I asked.

He shook his head and tapped his chest. "Tricky pump. I'm bushed—the trip."

I could tell it bothered him to even talk. "I hope you feel better tomorrow."

"I will—nothing unusual." He shrugged.

Just then Ed Anders stepped out into the hall and let loose a major display of fireworks. Jordan winced and looked toward the door. "Ed Anders," I said.

He nodded and turned back to me. We both said "Enchanting!" at the same time and laughed. I told him again I hoped he'd be feeling better and we said good night.

I went to sleep happy.

10

THE NEXT MORNING I was glad to see him looking rested. His skin was always white but there was a glow to it, almost like ivory, when he was in good health. When he was tired his skin looked dry. Also his eyes, which had that dark-blue shine to them, became watery if he was feeling badly.

During breakfast we eyed one another whenever we'd get a kick out of what one of the "Knights of the Square Table," which is what Jordan named them, said. We sat together in chapel that morning and I was aware that Mr. Hoyt took notice of it.

This isn't being put down with hindsight, because right there, in chapel that first morning, I had a sneaky little feeling that somehow the combination of Jordan and me spelled trouble to Mr. Hoyt. The extent of the trouble—no, not at all, but a twinge of awareness about *something.* I was so happy to have a friend I didn't dwell on it, simply sensed it and shoved it aside.

It turned out we had two classes, English and biology, and one study period together. By the end of Jordan's first full day at Gilford, we were locked in total friendship. No declarations had to be made; we just fell into it as easy as you'd fall into stride with someone walking down the street.

He was a special person. I'll try to make it short, this rave on

Jordan, but it must be put down for the record. Also, in view of what happened, I want to be completely honest with you about the extent and also the nature of our relationship. There hasn't been anything that *hasn't* been said about it, I'm aware of that, but you will know the exact truth with all the shadings.

When I say he was special, there were many facets of his specialness; not only his personal qualities, but his circumstances and background. First off, his heart. He'd been born with a bad one. Although he let it be known without any fuss that he had heart trouble, because it was obvious from what he could and couldn't do there was *something* wrong, he never discussed it further—not the specific nature of it, anyway. He'd undergone surgery when he was sixteen and it had helped but I gathered no more surgery was possible, that it was really just a bum heart all the way around and not the kind that can be fixed by new parts, a plastic valve or whatever. I was curious to know if there wasn't something more that could be done, especially now when you read all about the patch jobs and transplants they do on people, but since he didn't like to talk about it, not even to me, I didn't pursue the subject.

That, of course, was the reason for his color, his bluish lips at times, and why he was so thin and his body so boyish-looking. Because he couldn't exercise, couldn't really do anything but take walks. And I've been with him when he gave out just walking.

Probably this inability to engage in any sort of strenuous activity is what gave him his cool, cool poise. Nothing ruffled him; perhaps it would be more accurate to say that he didn't *allow* anything to ruffle him. I rarely saw him lose his temper or become really agitated. But he was no slug either. He had curiosity and enthusiasm and he did have energy, but he would siphon it out steadily, like a delicately balanced steam valve, instead of letting it out in bursts.

His father came from a poor family in New Orleans. He went into the construction business when he was a young man, worked hard at it, and by the time he was thirty he'd formed a small company with a partner and married a girl, Jordan's mother, from a well-to-do family, against their wishes. Through a contact in that business he got included in on a real-estate deal where he made a small killing. He parlayed it into another land deal and is now a millionaire a couple of times over.

I've seen pictures of him and he's a big, good-looking, husky man. Here's the sad part: Jordan's brothers and sisters, four of the former and two of the latter, are all healthy specimens, and most of them were excellent at sports. His father was a nut about health, his mother, too. They were disappointed with Jordan and ashamed of spawning a sickly person.

Jordan was the youngest of their seven children. Here's an example of the great home life he had. On the evening before his father's sixtieth birthday, Jordan was coming downstairs late at night to get something from the refrigerator. He'd been sick in bed for several days and hadn't eaten much; he was better and starting back to school the next day and he was hungry. As he was passing the drawing room, he heard his parents, who were looking over the proofs of some family photographs they'd recently had taken, talking about him.

His father was high and he heard him say, "Look at him, just *look* at him! Maybe we should have stopped after Georgie"—number six—"maybe the juice thins down, gives out." Then Jordan heard his father swear and throw something, something made of glass that broke. He heard his mother cluck over the breakage, then go to him and comfort him about Jordan. Finally he heard his father say, "Christ, it's like he was strained through a sheet!"

Not enough to have a bad heart, you have to hear *that*.

When Jordan was going back upstairs, his mother came out of the parlor, having heard footsteps, and called out the maid's name. His father asked her what she was doing and she said she thought she heard someone. Jordan froze in the upstairs hall, and when she went back into the parlor, he went on to his room.

To show you what spunk he had—about five that morning Jordan went downstairs to the parlor to see what it was his father had broken. He looked all over and finally found the pieces in a wastebasket, an expensive crystal ashtray from a fancy jewelry store in

New Orleans. Jordan was only fourteen, mind you, but that afternoon he went downtown and bought one just like the one that had been broken. He had it gift wrapped and that evening at his father's birthday party he gave it to him. When his father opened it, it didn't strike him right off. Then, as he was holding it in his hands, turning it over and looking at it, Jordan's mother, glancing at the hallway and remembering the footsteps she thought she'd heard, let out a little gasp of comprehension. His father looked at his mother, then to Jordan and Jordan held the look. He said "Happy birthday" and just looked his father in the eye for as long as his father could look and longer, until his father finally glanced away, placed the ashtray down and mumbled "Thank you, son."

The party went on, and when it was time for Jordan to say good night, his father took him in his arms and hugged him, something he hardly ever did with Jordan. When Jordan thought the hug was over he started to pull away but his father kept holding him until his mother broke it up with a remark about it being way past his bedtime.

When his father did release him, his mother walked him out of the parlor and as he started upstairs, she whispered, "I hope you're pleased with yourself, upsetting your father like that!"

Having parents like that is undoubtedly what gave Jordan his cynical slant to life, also his wide streak of wanting to be independent of them. But Jordan didn't hate his family. He wasn't madly in love with them, but he was philosophical about them, often referring to them as the "Little Foxes," which I got a kick out of. I marked his mother down as the villain of the piece.

(I used to get all misty-eyed about not having a mother but now I'm beginning to think I'm not so unlucky after all. I can do all the harmless fantasizing I want about what an angel she was—but at least I'm not stuck with the reality of a nag or an alcoholic or someone with snakes for hair.)

His parents showered money on him, making up in generosity what they withheld in true support and affection. The reason he'd been taken out of Maxton was not a matter of economizing. The

131

school was geared too high for Jordan and also, being so close to Boston, it was near the high life of the city. His doctor suggested a smaller, quieter and less spectacular school. Gilford certainly fit that bill.

Except that, as Jordan suggested, we did manage to liven things up. On to that in a minute.

Jordan had two members of his family he loved. His next-to-oldest brother and his maternal grandmother. She adored him, too. She had money, and when she died two years ago she left him some outright—spending money, she called it, although it was around twenty-three thousand dollars—but she also left him a couple of hundred thousand to be turned over to him when he finished high school. He didn't have to go through college, but she was always insistent upon a formal education, and because he'd been in and out of school for so much time, I suppose she put this in her will as an incentive for him to at least graduate from the twelfth grade. He wanted this money so he wouldn't have to depend upon funds from either his father or his mother.

To get back to Mr. Hoyt. The afternoon of Jordan's first day in school the sun was out and the courts were dry enough to play on, so I was due to meet Mr. Hoyt in the auditorium at five, after tennis practice. After school Jordan asked me what I was doing and I told him about tennis, so he came down to watch. He lay on his side in the thick grass near the top of a small slope that ran past one side of the courts. I wanted to make a good showing and I was knocking myself out against Burt Springer. Burt himself was playing as well as he ever did, which was quite good, and it made for an interesting match.

When I looked up at Jordan I noticed the way he was lying, curled on his side, legs bent at the knees, hand cupped in his chin, and that he looked extremely delicate, almost effeminate. Yet, otherwise, I never got that impression.

At the beginning of the second set I saw Mr. Hoyt coming down the big hill from school on his way over to the gym. He crossed the drive, came up two or three steps and walked along the path at the top of the slope. Jordan was still lying there in the grass only a few feet from the path. Mr. Hoyt was watching us play as he walked and nodded a greeting right before I slammed one, trying to by-pass Burt, who tipped the ball with his racquet and sent it flying off into the far court. Then Mr. Hoyt stopped on the path, right above where Jordan was lying, and as Burt was retrieving the ball he said, "Peter . . ." I said hello and just as he started on his way he suddenly caught sight of Jordan lying there below him. He was surprised and took a little step backward.

Just then Jordan glanced up at him, turning his head slightly and rolling his eyes but not moving his position other than that. He didn't speak and that, together with no other movement and the casualness of his position, gave a definite insolent touch to Jordan's manner. Mr. Hoyt didn't speak either, but I could tell he was furious, not only at Jordan's attitude but because he'd been surprised and because Jordan was there watching me in the first place.

Burt Springer called out my name, and we started to play again. Mr. Hoyt walked on, and though no one had spoken, there had been a moment. Sometimes moments are much more telling, much more memorable than an exchange of words or even an argument. I remember that moment clearly.

I took the second set, which was a relief and pleased me, and when Jordan and I were walking back to Lincoln House he complimented my playing and asked if I wanted to walk down to the village after I showered. That's when I told him about Hamlet and my rehearsal. At first he thought I was kidding, but when he saw I was leveling with him, he settled down and listened seriously. When I got through, he asked me why I'd agreed to do it. I told him about the league and the Point System. Again he asked me why I'd agreed. I told him as briefly as possible about being on half-tuition and I also said that, in a way, I felt sorry for Mr. Hoyt.

"You do?" he asked. Then he added, "Well, you know him better than I do." He sat there thinking for a moment, then he shook his head and almost agreed with me. "Yes, I can understand that." There was a long pause and he said matter-of-factly—the way he would have said "He's a tall man"—he said, "He's a sick man."

"How do you mean?" I asked.

"I'm not sure, but he is. Are you going through with it?"

"I don't know."

"Maybe you'll like it. Maybe you're a good Hamlet."

"No."

"How do you know?"

"I just feel it."

"If you're sure you're not—don't do it. You may be on half-tuition, but you didn't sign a contract saying you'd perform Hamlet with the Glee Club, did you?"

"No, but it's hard to get out of."

"Why?"

"I feel trapped."

"Why trapped?"

"Because, by this time, it's like I promised."

"Did you?"

"Not exactly. But—"

"But what?" Jordan was extremely candid and he liked people to be candid back. Sometimes he would seem abrupt the way he'd snap out Why? When? What? How do you mean?

"He's got his mind made up it will help the Glee Club."

"Do you think it will?"

"No."

"Do you trust your feeling or his?"

"Mine."

"Well . . . ?"

"He's counting so on it."

"Do you like him?"

"I don't think so."

"Don't you know?" he asked, a little surprised.

"I think I don't like him more than I do like him."

"Still, you're willing to go out on a limb?"

"I feel sorry for him."

He looked at me for a long moment, then his mouth curled into that peculiar smile of his and he said, "You're a quaint fellow."

"So are you," I replied.

We both laughed and I had to hurry to shower and meet Mr. Hoyt.

Usually he would be standing up on the stage waiting for me. When I came in the rear door of the auditorium he wasn't there and the place was dark. I walked down the aisle and up the stairs and turned the stage lights on. I wandered out onto the stage and was standing there mulling over my conversation with Jordan and trying to sort out my feelings.

"Whenever you're ready, Peter."

I must have jumped noticeably. I looked out into the auditorium and there he was, sitting way back in the darkness over on the right side.

"What is it?" he asked.

"Nothing—I didn't realize you were there."

"I see."

I just stood there. I'd been frightened and I was pulling myself together, also wondering why he'd been sitting way back there in the dark.

"Are you just standing there or are you preparing?" he asked, using my word and I thought being a little sarcastic.

"Preparing," I lied.

"Where are your tights?" he asked.

"In my room."

"Don't you ever use 'sir'?"

Oh-oh, trouble. "Yes, sir."

"Why in your room?"

"I forgot them, sir."

"I see," he said. "Wear them next time." Then he said, "Any time you're ready."

I began the speech and he did nothing but pick at me. His attitude had made me self-conscious and he stopped me first for being wooden. This rattled me further and, though I knew the thing letter-perfect, I fluffed a line or two. He asked me where my concentration was. Then I concentrated only on saying it correctly and he suggested I might as well be reading off a grocery list. This went on

135

and I realized nothing I could do would please him that day, just as it hit me the true reason for his annoyance was Jordan.

Then, as I was beginning to get depressed, I had a moment of lightheadedness. It came over me in a wave and I thought: What the hell, you have no power to depress me any more. You can't get me down, the school can't—nothing can, not even Hamlet.

I have a friend and friends take all.

Having someone like Jordan made you see and enjoy all the good things around you, but even better than that, it made you thumb your nose at the bad things.

The next thing I knew I was whipping through "To Be or Not To Be" with some sort of bravado I didn't even know I had.

11

FROM THEN ON the only marring note about being at Gilford was the steady approach of Hamlet. But I didn't even let that get me down too much.

Jordan and I spent all our spare time together. Our best times were weekends and after study hours at night. The minute they were over I'd go down the hall to his room. He traveled heavy— portable stereo, record case, electric typewriter, transistor radio, a great wardrobe, subdued clothes, not flashy but expensive: cashmere sweaters, very tailored slacks and really smart jackets, custom-made shirts, etc. His room was a good-sized single, almost like mine, and his bed was larger than the small beds the rest of us had, moved in especially for him.

When I'd get to his room, he'd put records on and we'd sit around and talk. Usually he'd have a drink of bourbon. He said he was allowed this for his heart. That always struck me as peculiar— a bad heart and smoking and drinking. But, you see, I think way deep inside he knew he wasn't going to stick around forever, so he was good to himself. He indulged himself, which was another part of his specialness. He did, by and large, exactly what he wanted when he wanted to do it. This didn't come under the heading of selfishness; his whims hardly ever affected others. And if they did, as in my case, being his best friend, you could either go along with him or not. He'd seldom try to force you to do anything; he'd simply tell you what his plans were and you could take it from there. And outside of not saying something that might hurt someone's feelings, he'd usually say exactly what he thought. And although he never could have come out on top in the event of a fight, he wouldn't let anyone get away with anything.

For instance, there's a senior who lived on the second floor, Frank Dicer, a born rat-bully. Oddly enough, for a guy with his rotten personality, he kept tropical fish in his room. He was nuts about them, no friends, just fish. Jordan said it would have to be something like fish, who are trapped in a glass aquarium; any other kind of a pet would either run or fly away from him. Frank Dicer would use anybody's shortcomings, make fun of anyone. He mimics Jimmy Greer's stutter, calls another kid, who wears bifocals and can barely tell night from day, "The Mole," is forever taunting the poor Vacuum Cleaner: "Hey, Dennis, how many did you knock off last night?" Although he's not a big bruiser like Ed Anders, he's a wiry, scrappy little guy always ready to back up his rottenness with a fight. He met his match with Jordan, though.

Frank Dicer used to love to slide down the banister from the second floor to the parlor. One night we were going down to dinner, toward about the end of the second week Jordan was there, and Jordan was holding on to the banister. We were about five steps from the bottom landing when I heard Frank Dicer call out, "Hey, Blue Lips, clear the railing!"

Jordan stopped dead in his tracks and Frank yelled out again, "Hey, Blue Lips—clear it!"

There were about three other guys who had just reached the parlor floor; they must have sensed something unusual because they all swung around to watch. Jordan turned very slowly and stared back up the stairs at Frank. He allowed for a good pause, and when he spoke, his voice came out low and easy. "What did you say?"

His look and timing were enough for Frank, who, though he avoided using the epithet again, nevertheless attempted to save face by shouting down, "I said clear the way!"

But Jordan wasn't going to let him off the hook. "That's not what you said."

Suddenly it got very quiet. I could tell Frank was confused, being challenged like this. "What do you mean?" he asked. Then he quickly waved his hand at Jordan. "C'mon, move it!"

I put my hand on Jordan's arm, but he pulled away from me and asked once more of Frank: "What did you say?"

Frank was already at a disadvantage, having dodged the issue, so he sort of shrugged and tossed it off casually like he hadn't really meant it, but his face was red. "Blue Lips . . ."

"That's what I thought," Jordan said. I sighed with relief, but Jordan wasn't finished with him. "Come here," he said, his voice still very low and quiet.

"Jordan, come on," I said, knowing he'd get murdered if Frank ever decided to pounce on him.

Jordan didn't acknowledge my presence, let alone answer me. "Come here," he repeated.

Frank shrugged and came down the stairs as cockily as he could, until he stood a step in front of Jordan, who never took his eyes off him for a second. "What do you want?" Frank asked, looking at me and hunching his shoulders, as if to say "What's the matter with your friend here?"

"You ought to do the world a favor," Jordan said.

"How's that?" Frank asked, really confused now.

"Stick with your fish," Jordan said. "Don't have kids—have yourself sterilized."

Talk about bad hearts, mine did a few nip-ups at that point. A couple of the guys at the bottom of the stairs laughed. It was just beginning to dawn on Frank, the implications of Jordan's remark, and I wondered where we'd go from here when Mr. Kauffman walked in the front door and said, "Come on, boys, don't block the dining room," and the fellows at the bottom straggled through the doorway to their tables. Then Jordan turned around, and we came down the stairs, and Frank never said a word. He never called Jordan "Blue Lips" again, either.

After study hours we'd sit around and listen to records and talk.

Having been confined to bed a lot and excluded from other activities, he was extremely well read. Reading was a great pleasure to him. We discussed books, plays, movies—he was a great movie buff—ideas, politics and personalities. And our own private theories about everything from sex to outer space.

One thing we never discussed and that was death. He never allowed the conversation to get anywhere near that. At first, before I caught on, I brought it up by means of asking him if he thought there was anything going on after death—a query that constantly pops up in my thoughts (Hamlet wasn't the only one), especially when I'm lying in bed at night—but he clammed up, didn't seem interested. When I pursued it, telling him what I thought and diving right into the subject, he suddenly turned to me and said, "Peter, did I ever tell you about the time I threw up at the dinner table?"

You see, I'd told him about how depressed I'd been before he'd shown up on the scene, especially the day he arrived, which, in turn, included the episode with Henry Samish and the chipped beef —one of *my* aversions. So he was, in his own inimitable way, letting me know there was one subject he didn't want to kick around. I respected his wishes and steered clear of it after that.

I also got around to telling him about my first meeting with Mr. Hoyt. I thought it would shock him and make him angry. Not at all. He listened very calmly and when I got all finished he merely said, "It figures." That threw me. I told him it certainly surprised me and asked him *why* it figured. "I told you," he said. "He's a sick man. I wouldn't be surprised at anything he did."

At this point I couldn't help asking him about his first meeting with Mr. Hoyt. "About like yours, only different," he said.

"How different?" I asked, warming to a good story.

"We didn't see eye to eye."

"About what?"

"About anything," Jordan said and then he changed the subject. When he didn't want to discuss something, which was rare, that was it.

Some of our best talks came from trading backgrounds. He

140

would pump me about my life in Hollywood with my father and my job as doorman at Grauman's Chinese and my feelings and memories of childhood and California and actors and various schools I'd attended. He, in turn, would tell me about his childhood and stories of his family, his two trips to Europe, one with his grandmother and the other with his parents, about the South (where I'd never been), and an affair he had with the daughter of their laundress in New Orleans when he was only fifteen years old.

It was rare if we ever ran out of conversation. There was less than an hour to talk between the end of study period and lights-out and many times, if we were onto a subject and hadn't finished with it, I'd sneak down to his room after lights-out and we'd sit in the dark, or he'd lie in bed, and we'd talk until one of us got sleepy and then I'd stagger back to my room.

We also had some good times in class. For instance, there was biology with Mr. Hendrix, who is not a bad teacher and certainly dedicated to his subject—a little too much, especially when he starts dissecting things. Then his eyes dilate, his nostrils flare, his breathing becomes intense and you can sense he's beginning to salivate.

The first time he dissected anything—it was a frog—Jordan and I were standing together at the back of a group of students gathered around this combination desk–biology table, where Mr. Hendrix was performing his little operation. He was all hunched over this poor little frog, talking as he was carving it up. It was scary. His sentences began coming in short gasps, as he was describing the anatomy of the frog, and every so often he'd glance up at the class, but only for a split second because he couldn't take his eyes off the thing. You could see—or we liked to imagine we could—the madness in his eyes. Toward the end of the operation, he suddenly brushed his fingers across his nose, like it was itching, but I got the idea that what he was doing was smelling his fingers. I quickly looked to Jordan just as he glanced over at me and we both shrugged, as if we were saying: Could it be? Then we looked back to Mr. Hendrix and sure enough, he did it again. This time you

141

could even hear a little sniff. We looked at one another and wrinkled up our noses and nodded, as if to say: Yeah, that's *just* what he's doing. Then Jordan leaned over and whispered, "I think he's getting close!"—meaning he was about to have an orgasm.

That did it. I started to roar with laughter, so much so that Mr. Hendrix looked up and called me on it. I was so thrown when he snapped at me, "Kilburn, what's so funny?" that I blurted out, "I was just thinking"—laugh-laugh, snort-snort, trying to pull myself together and come up with an excuse—"maybe we'll have frog's legs for dinner tonight."

I don't know where that came from, but it sounded so fantastically stupid that it about killed Jordan. He started to laugh uncontrollably and that set me off again and we were both excused from class to pull ourselves together. We staggered down to the locker room in the basement and all Jordan could do was repeat, "I was just thinking, maybe we'll have frog's legs for dinner tonight!" Then he was a jibbering wreck, laughing and waving me away. Within a few seconds he was panting and gasping for breath and he kept saying, "No, my pump, my pump!"

It worried me and I stopped laughing and after a while he calmed down, too, but not before he popped one of those little pills in his mouth and lay down on a cot for a while. Then we pulled ourselves together and went back to biology class.

Mr. Hendrix was known after that as the "Mad Scientist," along with the Terrible Twins, who broke Jordan up every time he saw them, and Larry (Olivier—Lee Galonka), Caspar (Milquetoast—Mr. Kauffman), Jack the Ripper (Wiley Bevan), Captain Dynamite (Ed Anders), Mata Hari (Erwin Cranshaw), and various others. They were our characters and we had fun with them.

For instance, there was the little diversion we whipped up for Jack the Ripper. It was a ratty thing to do, but we couldn't help it. Wiley Bevan was such a bore, forever spinning out lurid tales about "balling" this waitress, Louise, all summer long, in bed, on the floor in front of the fire, in a car, in a rowboat, on the pine needles in the woods, on the beach by the lake, *in* the lake itself, standing

142

waist deep in the water, every place but up a tree. He probably would have had them doing it inside a grand piano, if we hadn't stopped him.

It happened like this: Wiley kept a diary and his roommate, Chuck Rhodes, found it one day under his mattress and started to read it. He got hooked on it, read the whole thing for the last year, summer and all. This was a rotten thing to do, but he did it. Being Jack the Ripper's roommate, Chuck had to suffer many more of these "balling" stories than we did, so naturally he was interested to get the real scoop.

He did. The diary revealed that Wiley and his waitress, his big Swedish-Movie-Type-Night-and-Day-Summer-Romance, were a fraud. He and Louise had only done it once, and there was an honest description of what happened. Wiley didn't lie to his diary. It had taken place in her cabin and our friend Jack the Ripper had gone at it so fast and furious she had said, "Don't hurry it, baby! Stretch it out, make it last." But he apparently couldn't, he was too excited. It was all over with in about two minutes. After that, she teased him and called him Rabbit-Ass. All summer long he tried to nab her again, but she was going with the tennis pro and he never made it.

I have to tell you that Jordan was annoyed when Chuck Rhodes told us he'd read the diary, bawled him out and made him promise not to tell anyone else. Chuck admitted it was rotten, but we figured what was done, was done. So this is what *we* did.

Wiley knew the waitress had a winter job in Palm Beach at some restaurant. Jordan's family had friends in Palm Beach, so Jordan wrote to their son and asked him to buy a picture postcard of Palm Beach and send it to him. When we got it, we addressed it to Wiley in red ink and the message read like this:

DEAR RABBITT-ASS,
You know in your heart of hearts, we only balled once, on July 11 at 4:00 P.M. Word has reached me that you are spreading it around the Gilford campus that we balled all sum-

mer long. I would appreciate you ceasing and desisting this rumor. Or next summer you won't even get it *once,* Rabbit-Ass!

Sincerely,
LOUISE

Jordan sent the card in an envelope to his friend in Palm Beach and asked him to mail it, *sans* envelope, back to Wiley. We could hardly wait. We always got our mail when we went back to the dorm after school. It so happened that Wiley, the day it arrived, was the first to get to the large bowl containing the letters. He pawed through it, saw the card from Palm Beach, turned it over and must have seen the signature "Louise" before he saw anything else, because he shouted out, "Hey, I got a card from Louise in Palm Beach!"

"Yeah?" I said. "What's she say?"

His eyes flicked to the top of the message and he only got this far: "Dear—" The "Rabbit-Ass" stopped him cold.

"What's she say?" Chuck Rhodes asked.

"Nothing— I mean—" Wiley broke off, his face one giant frown. We watched him read the message. He could hardly believe it. When he was finished he started to read it again, then he quickly looked up to see if we were watching him. We were, of course, and he turned around and walked very quickly up to his room.

It just about killed him. He couldn't fathom it. After he got that card it seemed like his eyes were perpetually narrowed, always trying to figure out an angle that would explain it. I don't believe he suspected one of us wrote the card, but I'm pretty sure he believed one of us knew Louise or a friend of hers and had repeated his tall tales, because he came to everyone in the house in turn, and, in as subtle a way as he knew how, he'd bring up the waitress and the resort where she worked summers and gradually lead around to questions which would tell him if you'd ever been there or had ever met Louise, or perhaps a friend of hers.

He never told another story about her, though. At first it was a

144

relief but, you know, as time went on we began to miss his little fantasies. So did the other guys who weren't in on what happened. They would always ask why he didn't talk about her any more. Especially our movie star, Lee Galonka. Larry Olivier would always say, "What's the matter, Wiley, was that a Dear John card?" He kept after him so much that I'm sure Wiley thought it was Lee who somehow snitched on him.

Jordan was forever dropping fake news items in front of Mata Hari (Erwin Cranshaw), who never trusted me again after the *Dracula* rumor. But Jordan was great; he could really put him on. He wasn't obvious at all, cool and deadly serious; he could invariably get Mata Hari worked up to a nervous sweat of excitement. Rumors like: Headley Hoyt, the most unlikely candidate, was seen sneaking into Betty Thorn's (the town harlot) apartment late at night. Lee Galonka had whipped off a photograph to Columbia Studios and they were sending a talent scout to look him over. The Government was thinking of building a missile base on the site of Gilford, in which case the school would be condemned and torn down. Mr. Hoyt had caught the Terrible Twins whacking each other off in the shower and they were on probation.

So, we were having our good times. If it seems we were having them at the expense of others, maybe; but I must tell you Jordan had a definite sense of right and wrong, a strict morality about who to have fun with and who not to. Two cases in point being Jimmy Greer and Dennis Vacarro, the Vacuum Cleaner.

12

JORDAN WAS as gentle and considerate of Jimmy Greer as if he'd been his older brother. From the first he made a point of always speaking to him, or winking at him to include him in on a joke. Then Jordan found a short story in an anthology about a boy who stuttered, a real loner who gave up socially and applied himself to his studies and became a genius in the field of science. He won a nation-wide prize in college, and soon after, he began to lose his stutter. Jordan gave the story to Jimmy to read. What he was trying to do was to get Jimmy to stop trying so hard to be accepted as one of the gang and find something he could do well and liked and to concentrate on it.

Don't you know when Jimmy Greer got to trust Jordan he asked him if he could show him something and he dragged out a caricature he'd done of Mr. Hoyt. Jordan called me in to see it and it was terrific. For some reason he'd caricatured him as a minister, standing at a pulpit with one hand raised threateningly in the air. He'd exaggerated all the right things—the thick eyebrows which gave him that hooded, intense look, the zealot expression in his eyes, the jutting forward of his head and, of course, the raised spot on his forehead. After Jordan and I had both praised it, Jordan asked Jimmy why he'd made him a preacher.

146

"Ha-ha-hell and ba-brimstone" was Jimmy's reply.

"That's it, that's *him!*" Jordan laughed, slapping me on the shoulder.

"What's him?" I asked.

"Reverend Davidson—from *Rain,*" Jordan said.

And from then on, Mr. Hoyt was Reverend Davidson.

Anyway, we talked to Jimmy, who had done the sketch with only a regular crayon and on plain paper, and asked him how long he'd been drawing. He said for years. Did he have any more? He said no, and when Jordan asked him why, it came out that he used to have hundreds at home but his mother burned them; she'd make his father give him a whipping whenever she caught him drawing. She said he'd do better to spend time on his studies and develop his brains instead of drawing childish pictures.

Jordan told him a native talent like that was worth developing, that in the end it would serve him better than Latin or geometry. That afternoon Jordan went to the village stationery store and bought him a large sketching pad of good rough paper and some charcoal sketching sticks. He gave them to Jimmy after dinner and you never saw such excitement. I don't think Jimmy was used to receiving many presents. He couldn't get over it; when he was excited, his stutter would hardly let him get a word out.

Then Jordan told Jimmy he'd pay him two dollars for a caricature of Mr. Kauffman. Jimmy giggled and nodded his head, but then his face suddenly clouded over. He put the sketch pad and charcoal sticks down on Jordan's bed and I thought he was actually going to cry. Jordan asked him what was the matter and he just said "Na-nothing" and started to walk out of the room. Jordan had to drag him back in and grill him to find out what was wrong. Finally it came out: Jimmy had the idea we wanted a caricature of Mr. Kauffman to somehow *use,* to show it to Mr. Kauffman or post it someplace.

Jordan was furious for a second, but he realized Jimmy had been a fall guy so often he just naturally expected a plot. Jordan ended up putting his arm around Jimmy and reassuring him, finally saying

147

to skip Mr. Kauffman, if that would make him nervous, and do a sketch of me.

Jimmy did one but he couldn't do such good caricatures of people he liked. He was afraid of exaggerating their features and hurting their feelings, afraid they might get upset and be angry with him. But you should see the one he did of Frank Dicer as a Gila monster. He did a great one of Lee Galonka, too. Mainly hair, swirls and swirls of coal-black-hair and a tiny, tiny face underneath.

A sad thing Jimmy confided to Jordan later on: His parents, who didn't have much money at all, had all but gone into hock to send him away to school, actually because his mother couldn't stand him stuttering around the house.

Then there was Dennis Vacarro. Jordan never kidded him, never referred to him as the Vacuum Cleaner. He realized he suffered from a compulsion and needed help and I know he had several long talks with him, although I wasn't present.

Having brought up Dennis Vacarro, I might as well tell you he was wild about Jordan. In a boarding school there are no secrets about who's built how and Jordan might have had a boy's body, slight and frail, but one part of him was definitely well developed and probably seemed even more so because of the rest of him. Dennis Vacarro had checked this out right away and was after him. Frank Dicer was even heard to say (although not to Jordan's face) that that's why he had a bad heart. When he got an erection all the blood rushed to his cock and he blacked out.

(Time out for semantics: I think it's far more preferable to use the word "cock" instead of penis. Cock is clean, forthright and sort of jaunty. Penis sounds like something you'd only touch with a pair of tweezers.)

So, in the course of his campaign to get Jordan, Dennis and he had many conversations and Jordan finally got him to tell how he started out. Of all people, Dennis' father had initiated him into sex, had made him perform certain acts when he was very young, like six or seven; Dennis had grown to like it and, at first, he even

148

believed that's the way it was, that all good little boys obliged their fathers. (Jordan said: "How about *that* Boy Scout Father-and-Son Jamboree!")

When Dennis was fifteen, his father up and walked out on his mother and him and settled down to live with a painter (male) in Key West, Florida. Jordan said Dennis was still looking for a father, still trying to please every male he could.

Put Dennis' parents, Jordan's and Jimmy Greer's together. From the picture—Parents Can Be Enchanting!

Jimmy and Dennis are only two examples of Jordan's—well, compassion is what he had. Compassion for the screwed-up people of the world. And scorn for the rats, especially the smart rats who know they're rats and go on being ratty. He was out to get them in his own quiet way.

The weekends were the best for us; any boarding senior could sign out Friday and Saturday evenings as long as you were back by midnight. Jordan and I took advantage of this every weekend. We'd go to one of three alternate restaurants: Thorgan's Lodge or Little Pine Inn or the Flame Room of the Dorset Hotel right in the village of Saypool. We could walk to the Flame Room but if we went to Thorgan's or Little Pine, Jordan would call Cutler Barnum and away we'd go.

The first Sunday Jordan was at school we checked out in the afternoon and Jordan hired Cutler for two hours to drive us all around the area. Jordan wanted to know exactly where he was and what surrounded him. Cutler started off going between sixty and seventy and Jordan had to impress upon him several times that we were just sight-seeing, not trying to skip the country. The whole region was beautiful and Cutler, who got a kick out of Jordan and his cool Southern style, provided us with a colorful running commentary. If the countryside—the villages and lakes and farms and hills and woods—seemed removed from the pitfalls of civilization it was a false impression. Not at all—it wasn't far from *Peyton Place* country and it was just as raunchy, according to Cutler.

149

Passing the Dorset Hotel: "Patti Knowles runs the place alone. Husband, Ty, used to run it. One Friday, rich society lady from Boston checked in for a weekend of skiing. Monday morning checked out with Ty. Town of Saypool hasn't seen hide nor hair of him since."

Passing a farm: "Sumner Bean's place. Caught his oldest boy molesting one of their heifers out to the barn. Fractured his jaw. Folks say it was 'cause the heifer was *Sumner's* gal."

Passing a ski slope: "Ed Anders went over the ridge, top and to the side there, stuck his ski pole smack in his belly. Fahts every five minutes. Won't take him in the cab no mow-ah."

Passing another farm: "My cousin, Langley Cutler's place. Wife died of can-sah. Married a widow with a seventeen-year-old daughtah. Widow fell down the well over tah the vegetable garden they-ah. Langley up and married his stepdaugh-tah."

That wasn't all by a long shot, but that will give you a good idea. Jordan and I had to laugh, especially at the part about Ed Anders.

The first Friday night Jordan had Cutler drive us six miles out to Thorgan's Lodge, which was built on the side of a mountain, overlooking the largest ski slope in the area. It was on the order of a Swiss chalet with a fine view and excellent food. Even though it wasn't ski weather yet, there were a fair amount of people there. The next night, Saturday, we went to Little Pine Inn, also in a beautiful setting, built out over the water about a mile across the lake from school. The food there was excellent, too, but the waiters and the hostess tended to hover over you a little too much.

You're probably wondering how I could afford all these dinners out. I couldn't. Jordan knew this because I'd told him the story of our apartment over the Freeway, etc., and he insisted on picking up the check. For the first two weeks I kept trying to pay for at least one dinner. I really wanted to, but Jordan wouldn't hear of it. He could always get me to stop doing something by acting completely bored. One night he sighed a long, drawn-out sigh and said in his most flat voice, "Peter, you haven't got money—I have. I enjoy having it. I want *you* to enjoy it. I would appreciate it if you would stop complicating my weekends. Will you do that?"

150

I sat there not replying. I did want to pay once, just as a token.

He sighed again. "Let me put it this way. If the situation were reversed, if you were flush and I weren't, wouldn't you—for my charming company alone—at the very least take me to dinner?"

I looked him straight in the eye and said in *my* flattest voice, "Never in a million years."

That broke him up. But you couldn't win the check game with him, so after a while I stopped. The weekend after we'd been to Thorgan's and Little Pine Inn we tried the Flame Room of the Dorset Hotel and that turned out to be our favorite.

The Flame Room had leather booths and the table tops were too high, almost under your chin when you ate. It was so dark you had to feel your way from your baked potato to your salad, the walls were some kind of brick contact paper, the banquettes of the booths were separated by metal planters featuring fake leaves and artificial flowers, the menu was limited to steaks and chops and the vegetables were straight from cans or the freezer and completely unseasoned. But it had a big fireplace and most of all, it had Patti Knowles. Or Fat Patti as she called herself. Fat Patti was not really fat, more pleasingly plump. She had a gorgeous complexion, peaches and cream with a glow to it, enormous, pretty pink breasts, three quarters of which she displayed to excellent advantage, a mouth she could purse up like Mae West's, and a mass of dyed red hair, for which she had the blueprints for about twenty complicated hairdos. She also had shapely legs, but her biggest asset was her personality.

She'd started out in Greenwich Village as a pianist–singer, got married, retired from bars, got divorced, went back to work and met her last husband, Ty, in New York twelve years ago and came back to Saypool as his wife. The story Cutler Barnum told was true, and having been deserted like that, she at least got the hotel, a small four-story affair which did excellent business in the summer and also during the ski season. She claimed to hate New England, but she really loved it. And the natives had come to love her, mainly because of the way she took the breakup of her marriage and the fact that she stayed on to run the hotel.

151

Fat Patti played and sang at a small piano whenever she got the urge. When we started going there it was after the summer people had gone and before the winter ski crowd arrived, so the place was fairly empty except for the regular locals, and she was at her most uninhibited fun.

She'd sing show tunes and she'd also knock out some special material, a few risqué songs and little dated ditties from her Greenwich Village days. When someone would ask her to sing one, for instance, "Violate Me in Violet Time," she'd throw back her head, shake her red hair, purse up her mouth like Mae West and cry out in a high giggle, "Oh, no—not that old chestnut!" As soon as she stopped giggling, she'd promptly belt it out and when she'd finish she'd throw back her head again and laugh as loudly as anyone in the place.

She'd take almost any popular song and by simply changing "you" to "yours" or "me" to "mine" turn the song into a risqué ditty. She'd whip off about ten songs in a row, singing only a line or two of each, and they'd come out like this: "I'm in love with yours, baby, say you love mine too, baby!" or "I've got yours under my skin!" or "Why can't yours behave?" or "Yours is too beautiful for one man alone and I have an eye for beauty!"

Things we loved about her: She wore costume jewelry by the pound and she must have had a trunk of it because you hardly ever saw the same item twice. When she'd sit down to play the piano she'd ceremoniously lift her hands in front of her and very daintily extract one ring at a time—she'd wear at least three, usually more —and set them down on the piano top in front of her. Jordan began the custom of applauding the ring-removing ceremony and she'd bow low and then roar with laughter. Then, although she'd been madly in love with her husband and everyone knew it, every so often she'd sing a real torch song, like "The Man That Got Away," do it very seriously, and then, after the last note, slump over the top of the piano dramatically. She'd hold it for just a split second, then raise her head and laugh out: "The son of a bitch!"

Whenever we came in and she happened to be at the piano, she'd break off whatever she was playing or singing and launch into a march version of the Jack Armstrong theme, from the good old days of radio, before I was born:

Make the fight for Hudson High, boys,
Show them how we stand!
We're the solid team of champions
Known throughout the land!

Then back would go the head and out would come the laugh.

We loved her, and she loved us, being especially crazy about Jordan. He'd always buy her a drink and she would send one to Jordan, who had somehow managed, when he was at Maxton, to get a Massachusetts driver's license saying he was twenty-one. Jordan would order a double bourbon and ginger ale and I'd order a plain ginger ale, then he'd pour a splash of bourbon in it.

Patti would break us up every so often by suddenly going into a surprise announcement: "Fat Patti, New England's oldest living chanteuse, will now regale you with a few select art songs." Or "Miss Patti Knowles—[aside.] Didn't I used to be Mrs.?—is now accepting drinks from strangers. Dry martini, Beefeater's, straight up, olive on the side." If no one made a move, she'd lift her arms up in front of her face as if she were being stampeded. "Don't rush me, boys," she'd say. Or: "This is Fat Patti coming to you direct and in person from the world-famous Flame Room of the Dorset Hotel in the heart of downtown Saypool." This would get a laugh because Saypool has one large shopping street, the highway that runs through it, actually, with two other small side streets with shops, a wharf, a movie, a post office, one four-story office building, a fire department, the Dorset Hotel and that's it.

Whenever she'd come over to our table, she'd run her hand down Jordan's cheek and say something like: "How's my Jean-Paul?" She had a big crush on Jean-Paul Belmondo and Jordan reminded her of him. I guess she got that from his nose. Although Patti was only forty-four, she exaggerated her age the same way

153

she did her weight and referred to herself as if she were ancient. She'd look at Jordan and sort of growl and say, "If I were younger —or you were older—I'd run you to the firehouse and back!" Then she'd look at me and wave me away with her hand. "As for you, they'd have me in chains before I got the covers turned back!"

Although there was only two years difference in our ages, everyone always thought I was a couple of years younger than I am and that Jordan was a couple of years older than he was.

What I wouldn't give now to have one of those evenings we spent at the Flame Room of the Dorset Hotel in the heart of downtown Saypool! They weren't all just sitting around joking either.

There was one night I especially remember, involving the poor guy everyone called Crazy Andy. In the long corridor leading from the lobby to the Flame Room, there was a wide space right in front of the glass doors, and it housed a pinball machine. Andy loved it and he'd wander in all the time and play it as long as his nickels held out. He never came into the Flame Room but you could see him right through the door and if you went to the rest room you had to pass the pinball machine.

There was a tarty blonde, Eunice, who used to hang out at the Flame Room. She was always extremely well dressed and got up, hair and all, like she'd been lacquered. But I got the idea if you cracked the lacquer there just might be some little spots of decay. One Friday night when Patti was sitting at the table with Jordan and me, I saw Eunice coming back from the ladies' room. Crazy Andy must have just lit the machine up because he clapped his hands together in front of his face and stepped back a full step from the machine, accidentally landing on Eunice's foot. She let out a yowl and made a big scene, not paying any attention to his apologies. She was leaning down, rubbing her instep, and when he bent down to see if he could help, she let go of her foot and shoved him away. As she opened the door to come into the room, she said to him, "Jesus, Andy, why don't you stay out of people's way? Why don't you stay home?"

She spotted Patti sitting at our booth and came right over and plopped down next to her. She tossed a "Hi" at us and then said to

Patti, "Honey, why don't you tell Andy to keep the hell away from your hotel? Not only me, he gives everyone the creeps."

"Why don't you keep the hell away from my table!" Jordan said.

"Oh, now, *Jean-Paul!*" Patti giggled, trying to lighten it.

"What— Why, I am addressing the proprietress of the Flame Room!" Eunice snapped, outraged.

"I don't care if you're addressing the Virgin Mary," Jordan said. "You're sitting at my table and *you* give *me* the *creeps!*"

"Why, I never—I—" Eunice sputtered, standing up from the table. "You certainly are no gentleman." Then her true colors came out. "You—you're nothing but a snotty little punk."

"While you, Lady Precious Stream," Jordan said, smiling, "are absolutely enchanting!"

She stomped away and Patti and I couldn't help giggling. Lady Precious Stream—I don't know where he pulled that from.

We looked to see what happened to Andy just as he was stumbling out of sight, head down and wagging, at the far end of the lobby.

"Jesus!" Jordan said. Then: "Poor crip."

We got to talking, all three of us, about people like Andy and others we knew, including Jimmy Greer and even Dennis. And that's the first time I heard Jordan's paintbox theory.

It went like this: When we're born, when the Big Joker in the Sky checks us out for our "enchanting" stay on earth, we're each handed a little tin paintbox and inside are a couple of brushes and all these nice little squares of red, blue and yellow water paints, the primary colors. We're supposed to come down to earth and go through life painting these lovely pictures (i.e., learning, working, loving, marriage, procreating, bringing up children, etc.).

Except when you open up your paintbox, you're just liable to find your little kit's not what it's cracked up to be. Either a brush is gone or all twisted and gnarled or some of the paint is dried and chipped or perhaps even a couple of the primary colors are *missing*. Some of the paintboxes are so dented you can't even get the *lid* open!

Still, everyone's after you from the cradle to the grave, clucking and scolding if you don't please everyone by painting pretty pictures!

I loved Jordan for coming up with that theory. So did Patti. I remember when she left the table that night, she pecked us each on the cheek, Jordan last, saying, "Good night, baby!" She started to walk away, but she stopped, turned around and brushed the back of her hand down along the side of his face. "Baby?—some baby!" she said, turning to me and adding, "Oh, he's seen the elephant and heard the hooty owl, this one has."

Although I couldn't specifically translate that, I knew what she meant. You had the idea that sometime Jordan had gotten a little private peek at the *inside,* the master blueprint of life. That's one of the reasons he was so great to be with.

Incidentally, Patti used to refer to Gilford as "The Institution for the Criminally Young."

So—to get back to the institution.

13

DURING THE AFTERNOONS, when the weather was still warm enough, I'd be playing tennis, or if it was windy or raining I'd be rehearsing dear old Hamlet, so Jordan had time to himself. He was a great one for walks. He liked to walk through the woods that ran along the edge of the lake past the football field. There was a wild old boathouse down there that had been used when Gilford went in for rowing but was now just sitting there falling apart, and on warm afternoons Jordan would take a book down there and read. Sometimes on weekends, Jordan and I would walk down there and sit on the old caved-in porch overlooking the lake and talk.

One afternoon when I got back to Lincoln House after tennis I found him in the kitchen talking to the cook, Mrs. Rauscher. I'd hardly spoken to her but Jordan had a way of spotting gems and unearthing them. She was a great New England type, tall and large-boned, almost stocky, gray hair in a bun, craggy face with a wart on the side of her nose, very taciturn appearing, but when you got to know her—a dry observatory humor right beneath the surface.

She'd cooked at Lincoln House for eleven years and lived with her husband, who rented out a fleet of small boats in the summer, on the other side of the lake. Although, as I said, she seemed to be virtually speechless, in fact hardly talked to the students at all, she opened up to Jordan and told him a lot about the school and the teachers and Mr. Hoyt.

She had originally liked him when he first came to Gilford. She told Jordan he was an entirely different man before the suicide. She described the Senator's son as "a golden boy," saying she adored him and that no one ever suspected what was going on between him and the captain of the football team. She also indicated Mr. Hoyt liked him enormously and that his death and the resulting scandal had come as a terrible shock to him, had even seemed to frighten him. I remember one thing Jordan told me she'd said. "It touched something deep inside the man."

Mrs. Rauscher's sister was the Hoyts' doctor's nurse and Mrs. Hoyt had just undergone a serious hysterectomy a month or so before the start of school. She'd apparently been having an extremely rough menopause and this, together with the operation, had taken a toll on her. Jordan and I decided it was having its effect on Mr. Hoyt, too, in that his sexual activities must have been curtailed.

According to Mrs. Rauscher, Mrs. Hoyt had been quite pretty years ago and much more lively. In fact, the Hoyts had been a popular couple on campus when they'd first appeared on the scene during the previous headmaster's time. This was hard to imagine, yet Mrs. Rauscher was a square shooter and you'd take anything she said as gospel. She wasn't an idle gossip and Jordan said all this talk about the Hoyts came up because she was concerned about Mr. Hoyt and felt that running the school had become too much of a strain on him. She and Jordan struck up an immediate friendship and many afternoons he'd sit in the kitchen with her for an hour or so while she was preparing dinner.

Rehearsals went along regularly with Hamlet. I was to do the speech for the first time, Friday, November 9, at our school, when the Glee Club gave its first public concert, open to the students, their parents and friends and the town in general.

In the meantime, out of five tennis matches, we'd only lost one. The football team, on the other hand, had only won one game, against Moulton Academy, and that because three of their first-

158

string players had been shaken up in an auto accident and were out of the game. Even so, Mr. Hoyt was in a high mood with his winning points and treated the whole affair like a major legitimate victory.

Although I never knew what to expect in the way of behavior from Mr. Hoyt, I don't think I realized at the time how truly erratic he was. Probably because I was in a relatively happy state of mind, so that I tended to treat any skirmish as a minor one. Also, when you have someone to talk over your problems with, they're not nearly so bad. If I was having a sticky time with Mr. Hoyt I'd be planning to tell Jordan even while I was having it, thinking: Wait till Jordan hears about *this*.

I had gone through Frankie Spiro's routine for Jordan one Saturday evening after we'd eaten at the Flame Room and been to a good movie and he thought it was funny. Actually I'd picked my time; I wasn't taking any chances laying a bomb in front of Jordan, who had had more to drink than usual and was in a glowy mood. I'd also imitated Frankie, stutter and all, and that made it funnier than if I were just doing it on my own.

So it was on one of Mr. Hoyt's better days, actually the day after our one football victory, that I broached the possibility of doing it again. He laughed it off as a joke. "Why, Peter," he said, "you surprise me. It's coming along fine, just fine." He laughed again. "You really do surprise me at times."

And vice versa, I might have added.

When I told Jordan, he said, "Either make up your mind to do the speech trippingly on the tongue the way it's written, or turn in your tights, but forget about any takeoff."

"Why?"

"Because Reverend Davidson has a deficient sense of humor—he's as apt to laugh as a pan of cold milk."

Nevertheless, the next afternoon, when Mr. Hoyt also seemed to be in a good mood, I waited until we were finished rehearsing and I said, "Mr. Hoyt, just for the fun of it, could I go through the takeoff on Hamlet for you? I bet if you heard the whole—"

"Peter, I thought we'd been through this."

159

"Yes, I know, but I'd like to do it just once, the way it's written. I know it by heart." He didn't answer but just stood there, as if he were mulling it over. "Wouldn't that be all right? It'll only take about three minutes."

"By all means," he said coldly, starting up the aisle. "And when you're finished, turn off the lights!" And out he went.

When I told Jordan, he got a big laugh out of it. "You know something?" he said. "You really are a bulldog in disguise."

"How do you mean?"

"Old Innocent Face, but when you get something in that head of yours, you don't let go." He growled and shook his head like a dog holding on to a bone. "You're a bulldog."

From that moment on, many times he'd call me Bulldog.

A few days later, Mr. Hoyt and I had just started going over the speech when the rear door to the auditorium opened and Mrs. Hoyt stuck her head in. It was dark, except up on the stage, and Mr. Hoyt, who was sitting down, craned his neck around. "Who is it?" he asked.

"Franklyn?" she said.

"Yes . . . ?" Then recognizing her he said, almost annoyed, "What is it?"

"I've got the things."

"*Things?*" he asked, even more out of sorts.

"The things from Boston for Peter. And I've finished the jumper."

"Oh—oh, well, why didn't you say?" he asked.

"I—that's why I came over."

"Bring them down then." He looked up at me. "Peter, run over and get your tights."

I made a quick trip and took them out from under my mattress, where I'd hidden them. (I'd gotten out of rehearsing in them by saying I might as well wait until I had the top.) But this afternoon I ended up in the full outfit—black tights, a black dance belt, which had arrived from Boston along with a pair of black ballet slippers, and the black jumper, by far the most unfortunate part of the entire outfit. The neck was an oval shape and sort of low cut at that, and the sleeves were actually puffed up at the shoulder. It was also gathered in in bunches with a drawstring around the waist. If you were in a legitimate play with a full cast dressed in period it would have made a good costume for some Prince of Darkness, but to walk out onto a stage in the middle of a Glee Club concert in front of a jury of your fellow students—no, no, a thousand times no!

After I'd changed into the full costume and was standing on the stage with Mr. Hoyt sitting out in the darkened auditorium and Mrs. Hoyt plucking nervously at the jumper, circling me and tugging at the waist this way and that, my mind was scrambled with possible ways of getting out of wearing it.

"There, now," she said, giving it a final tug and taking a step back away from me.

"Yes . . . um-hmn," I heard Mr. Hoyt mumble.

"What, dear?" Mrs. Hoyt asked, shielding her eyes and squinting out at him. "Do you like it—I mean, will it do?" she asked in a tentative, whispered voice, which somehow, although I barely knew her, touched me.

"Yes, I think it will do fine, Miriam."

"Oh!" she said, flashing a nervous little smile of appreciation and then turning to me and smiling again and giving me a little nod as if the two of us had pulled it off together. Then: "Do *you* like it, Peter?" Her expression was left so hanging in anticipation of my approval that if she had asked me if I liked tongue I would have said, "Yes, can't get anough of it."

When I answered her she smiled and clasped her hands together, letting out a small but nevertheless unmistakable sigh of relief. She had a quorum.

"Come out here, Miriam. Look at it from out here," Mr. Hoyt said.

"Yes, yes, I will," she said, pleased to be asked and scurrying over to the platform and the steps leading down off the stage.

Suddenly all plots of getting out of it were knocked out of my head and I was standing there actually feeling stunned and saddened, my imagination having snatched at a picture of this odd couple attempting to save an entire school by means of little touches such as me performing "To Be or Not To Be" all got up as Hamlet.

Just then I heard a little sharp cry as Mrs. Hoyt either tripped or missed the last step and fell to one knee, saving herself from a complete fall by clutching the arm of an aisle seat.

"Miriam!" Mr. Hoyt said sharply, hurrying down the aisle as I started for the platform.

She quickly got to her feet. "No, no, I'm fine! I'm fine, dear," she said, brushing herself off.

"You really should look where you're going," he said. Then, reaching an arm out to her, he asked, "Are you all right?"

It struck me that he didn't ask her that until after he'd practically berated her.

"Yes, oh, yes, I'm fine!" she repeated, at the same time ducking a step back away from his outstretched arm and in the process bumping up against the bottom of the platform and sitting down on the steps with an "Oh, oh, dear!"

"Miriam!" he snapped, stopping and looking at her sitting there rather clumsily, and this time the word was a definite rebuke.

She got up quickly and said, "The light, I—"

"The what?" he asked, cutting her off.

"The change from the lights—up there," she said, waving a hand back toward the stage, "and the darkness down here."

"Are you all right?" he asked again, taking her by the arm this time.

She glanced quickly behind her and up at me and then back at Mr. Hoyt. "Of course," she said, and now there was a slight edge to her voice.

"That's all I want to know," he said, leading her up the aisle. When they got halfway up he turned her around and said, "Peter, stand back a bit, in the full light." When I got to the center of the stage, he said, "It looks just right—fine. How does it feel, Peter?"

I could do nothing but echo his word. "Fine," I replied.

Then he turned to her. "You worked it out very well, Miriam."

"I'm pleased you like it," she said, and she looked down, almost embarrassed.

No one spoke for a few seconds and then he said in a matter-of-fact tone, "You can go home now, Miriam," as if therapy class were over and he was dismissing her.

"Couldn't I . . . ?" she said and then broke off.

"What?" he asked.

"Could I stay and watch . . . once?" she asked.

"Well," he considered, "I suppose—Peter, would you mind?" he asked, showing genuine concern for me.

I was trapped by the mood the two of them had thrown me into. "No, that's all right."

"Are you sure?" he asked.

"Sure."

He guided her to a seat and sat down next to her. "All right, Peter—go ahead whenever you're ready."

I stood there very still and thought about—God, two people like Mr. and Mrs. Hoyt married all those years and their courtship and honeymoon and setting up their first household and how they must have been in love at first and all they must have been through—and here they were acting almost as if they were strangers, if not downright enemies.

You read about how actors use their emotions to help them in their approach to a part and I let myself use those two people sitting out there in the dark and I used my wonderment at their relationship and the sadness of it to overcome me as I said the words of "To Be or Not To Be," paraphrasing them to mean: Jesus, is this what we mean by *life!* This half-assed hell on earth? Could there possibly be anything worse than the way people get trapped together and then go on sniping and torturing each other in a hundred little ways day after day? Even in a certified hell after death with fire and never-ending tasks and the whole works?

No, it couldn't be worse. And I let my questioning of it be cynical at the very first but then I just gave up to the hopelessness, the futility of trying to outwit the Big Joker in the Sky at his own game, in effect saying: He's got us by the balls no matter which way we turn so we might as well hold good and still right where we are; it's only going to pinch and squeeze more if we try to wriggle out of it.

I said the speech very quietly and slowly and got myself so *into* it, indulged myself really, that my emotions even carried me through the lines I'd always had trouble pinning down specifically. I don't believe I moved so much as a finger. I knew what I was saying, I felt it, I didn't have to rev it all up with gestures.

When I came to the end—

> Thus conscience does make cowards of us all;
> And thus the native hue of resolution
> Is sicklied o'er with the pale cast of thought,
> And enterprises of great pith and moment
> With this regard their currents turn awry,
> And lose the name of action.

—I was saying: So we are stuck, glued, helpless, standing up to our eyeballs in our own slime and there is nothing, nothing we can do. Consequently I couldn't get myself to say the last lines:

> Soft you now!
> The fair Ophelia! Nymph, in thy orisons
> Be all my sins remember'd.

I wasn't interested in Ophelia. She had nothing to do with what I was thinking about.

So I just ended and stood there on the stage. For a moment I was almost afraid to look at them for fear they might have read my mind which, of course, was ridiculous, but still . . .

Finally I heard Mr. Hoyt clear his throat. "That was very good, Peter. Very good, indeed."

"Yes, yes, it was," Mrs. Hoyt added.

"Thank you."

And then they were getting up and Mrs. Hoyt told me how much

164

she enjoyed it again and went, leaving us alone. Mr. Hoyt walked down the aisle and stood in the separation between the first row and the edge of the stage. He looked up at me and smiled, actually a relaxed smile which was unusual for him. "So—and you were the lad who was worried about performing Hamlet's soliloquy?"

"I still am," I told him.

He frowned at my answer. "You're what?" he asked.

"I'm still worried." It may not have been good by professional standards, this rendition I'd given that day, but it was the best I'd ever done and I knew it. I also knew it was a freak, the way it happened with just the two of them sitting out there and no other audience to worry about and me in the mood they'd put me in.

Suddenly Mr. Hoyt laughed and slapped his hand down on top of the stage, surprising me. "Peter, sometimes I think you're quite a character—yes, I do."

And vice versa again.

"You've found the key, it's obvious, you just demonstrated it. If you do it as you did now we're home free. I think—I think from here on out, I'll let you call the shots as far as rehearsals." (Expressions like "home free" and "call the shots" always sounded strange coming from him.) He went on. "I suppose there's such a thing as going stale on a speech. There will be a rehearsal next Tuesday with the Glee Club to set and time out the background music. Mr. Kauffman and I have decided on Handel's "Largo." I believe it will be in fitting with the mood and still not intrude upon your performance." He walked up the steps and onto the stage and came over to me. He just looked at me for a second or two. "Well, Peter," he exhaled, slapping a hand on each shoulder and the scent of bay rum was strong, "you make a fine young Hamlet. You'll do Gilford proud." Then he shot me one of his rubber-band smiles. "Yes, you will—in spite of yourself. Well—." He seemed to be aware of his hands and took them away from me. "Yes, well," he continued very heartily, "I see no reason for you to go through it again today. Unless you want to, of course."

"No, I guess it's enough." I was still in a black mood. I wanted

165

him to leave; I didn't want to be around him because he was depressing me, every word he said.

But he waited for me to change backstage and we walked out together. When we got outside he took a deep breath of air and, putting both hands up to his chest, patted himself several times. "Umm—beautiful day, isn't it?" Then he glanced around in front of him and turned to me, saying, "It's a beautiful campus, isn't it, Peter?"

"Yes, it is," I said, but all the time I wanted to ask him how he could possibly be so happy.

See, we were missing again. Here I'd done the speech in a costume I loathed and he loved, done it well for all the wrong reasons, which I knew I wouldn't be able to repeat, and he was delighted and not paying any attention to his relationship with his wife and I couldn't get the way they acted with one another out of my mind and—we just missed.

He said again how well I'd done it, that he was glad I'd found the key, found it within myself. Then he patted me on the shoulder and went tipping along over to his house.

I walked into Lincoln House and up to my room, getting even in a blacker mood when I saw Dennis Vacarro bird-dogging Frank Dicer, of all people, in the john on the second floor and bumping into Monroe Flagler, an unfortunate walking pimple, with some kind of chalky lotion all over his face on the next flight of stairs.

Then I heard Jordan, who was sitting in his room with the door open, call out, "Alas, yon sad-assed Hamlet, I knew him well."

I looked up and almost jumped out of my shoes. One of the few times I'd forgotten about Jordan. I walked into his room and it was like stepping into a warm tub.

I was suddenly so grateful that he was there that I launched into the mock Shakespeare we'd gotten accustomed to because of the Hamlet thing: "Hark, many-diseased son of a three-legged camel. I must to the state and these shitty deeds relate!'

14

I ACTUALLY only rehearsed about four or five more times, plus one run-through with the Glee Club to time out "Largo." Nothing much out of the ordinary happened before the first performance except for Jordan having a bad day with his heart. We'd been sitting on the porch down at the boathouse one late Indian summer afternoon when the wind suddenly came up strong, aiming at us directly from across the lake.

We'd been laughing about the Terrible Twins, who, by the way, had never been seen in the nude by anyone. They were extremely shy, never showered in the gym, always did their cleaning up at Logan Hall, where they lived, either before everyone got up or late at night, never used the urinals in the john at school, always went into a booth and, in general, stood guard on one another.

Frank Dicer, who sat next to Rodney in study period had, in his usual charming way, suggested to him that the reason no one ever saw them naked was because they only had one cock between them and they had to trade off. Rodney told him to take it back but Frank kept on and they finally made a date to meet out behind school right after last class.

Both twins, of course, showed up and just as Frank was voicing his objections to three's a crowd, they jumped him and managed to leave some pretty good souvenirs about his head and face—Ronald got a bloody nose, too—before Mr. Hendrix happened by and broke it up.

Jordan and I were laughing about this and scheduling a match between the Terrible Twins and Cassius Clay when he took a coughing spell and got very short of breath. The wind didn't help him any and we decided to leave. Jordan had to stop several times as we walked up the hill, and by the time we got to the parlor in Lincoln House, his lips were that bluish color, his face was pale, and his hands were cold.

Mr. Kauffman and I got him up to bed and Mr. Kauffman left to call the doctor, over Jordan's objections that all he needed was one of his pills, which he took, and he'd be all right. I sat down in his desk chair and Jordan said, "If you've got anything to do—go ahead. I'll just alligate a while." (Jordan's way of saying lay around, derived from alligators.)

"No, I'll stick around."

"What are you going to stick around for?" he asked.

"I thought I'd just—oh, I don't know—stuff a few beans up my nose."

He could read my face like a book. It was very hard for me to get away with anything and when I did manage to fool him I considered it a major victory. "Don't worry about me." Jordan smiled. "People with chronic illnesses are the ones that hang around forever, bellyaching about their hearts and livers and kidneys, but showing up at everyone else's funerals."

"I'm not worried," I told him.

"Look at your foot. It's about to fall off." He'd remarked right after he met me that whenever I'm nervous or worried I cross my legs and shake the foot of my crossed one back and forth, a characteristic I wasn't even aware of. I glanced down and the foot was going a mile a minute, so naturally I stopped it. "Ah-ah, too late." Jordan laughed.

"I didn't know we were playing," I said, starting to shake it on purpose. Then: "You want me to stop?"

"Umm," he said, "makes me dizzy."

168

"Okay, I'll just sit here and commune."

Jordan closed his eyes for half a minute or so and when he opened them he stared up at the ceiling and then rolled them over until he saw me. He looked almost surprised. "Old Bulldog," he sighed. "I'd like to be alone—okay?"

"Oh, sure," I said, getting up. "Why didn't you say?"

He snorted. "What—" he said, stopping an obvious gasp for breath, "did you think I've been talking about—our foreign policy?"

"A million sorries, Mastah," I said, salaaming and backing toward the door.

He raised his hand and described a cross in the air with a waving gesture, like the Pope. *"Pax vobiscum pace disputandum scram."*

"Thank you, Holy Father," I whispered and backed out.

I sat in my room with the door open waiting to hear the doctor, but he didn't come by dinnertime, so I stopped by Jordan's room on the way downstairs. He was just lying in bed propped up on his pillows, his eyes half-opened. "Hi," I said.

"Hi."

"You hungry?" He just shook his head so I said, "See you later," and went downstairs to the table, but I wasn't hungry either.

The doctor, Dr. Reed, came in the middle of dinner and left about a half hour later, by which time I was waiting for him on the porch. As he came out the front door I said, "I'm a good friend of Jordan Legier's."

"Dr. Reed," he said, nodding. "Glad to meet you." And he started down the steps.

"Dr. Reed," I said, "how is he?"

"Jordan?" he asked. I wanted to say, "No, Everett Dirksen!"

"Oh, he's fine," he said, on his way again.

"But he wasn't before. He couldn't catch his breath and he looked—"

"He'll be fine," he said, stepping off onto the walk.

"I'm his best friend," I said, starting to follow him. "Is there anything I should know? I mean—like what to do if—"

"No, no," he said, waving a hand in the air without even stopping and walking on.

Jesus, how I hated him! "Oh, doctor!" I called out, dripping with sarcasm. "Thanks a lot!"

"That's all right," he said, not having caught my tone and not even turning around, but continuing to fade off into the distance with his little black bag.

That infuriated me even more. If I'd had a shotgun I'd have blown his head off. I was so angry I had to walk around the school building three times to keep from bawling. Even so, my eyes were brimming and I couldn't even look in on Jordan before study hours.

You can imagine how much I studied. Three times I went to the john with tiptoed side trips to listen at Jordan's door. I wanted to go in and check on him but if he was sleeping I didn't want to disturb him. At 10:31, however, I was gently knocking on his door.

"Come in." I opened it and he put down a book he was reading. "Hi, Bulldog." He was breathing regularly and his lips were not as blue as they'd been but he looked very tired.

"How do you feel?"

"Fine. Sit down."

"That's a great doctor you've got," I said.

"He is," Jordan said, surprising me. "He's a good doctor."

"Charming, too."

Jordan laughed. "Oh-oh, what happened—you tried pumping him?"

"No, I just introduced myself and asked—"

"You know doctors," he said.

"Yes, but thank God not like him."

"He's all right."

"I don't like him."

"So don't go to him."

"I wouldn't, not on a bet."

"Okay."

170

"He's a prick!" I said.

"Reach in my desk drawer. Have a Good and Plenty and cool off."

"I hate his guts!"

Jordan laughed and growled, shaking his head back and forth. "Atta boy, Bulldog, hang on, don't let 'em go."

I had to laugh, too. I got the Good and Plentys and we sat and talked for about ten minutes until we heard certain unmistakable footsteps coming up the stairs. "The Reverend." Jordan nodded. We both shut up and waited for his knock. "Come in," Jordan said.

The door opened but Mr. Hoyt didn't come in; he just stood in the doorway. Where I was sitting, over in Jordan's desk chair, I wasn't visible because of the way the door opened inward. "Mr. Kauffman tells me the doctor was here," Mr. Hoyt said.

The words that came out of Jordan's mouth just about knocked me out of my chair. "Mr. Kauffman's a big snitch!" Jordan said almost effeminately.

"What?" Mr. Hoyt asked, as if he hadn't heard correctly.

Jordan's lips curled into a smile and he spoke in his flattest voice, "Yes, the doctor was here." He sighed. It was really like he'd spoken to a child.

I was sitting there in shock and at the same time I realized this was the first time I'd ever heard them exchange words. Just then, Mr. Hoyt sensed someone else was in the room; he stepped one foot inside and looked over at me. "Oh," he said, "Peter . . ."

"Yes," Jordan said, "you know the Prince of Denmark?" Like he was introducing me. Mr. Hoyt swung around to face him and just as he was about to say something—I don't know what it was going to be, but it wasn't going to be pleasant—Jordan chimed in with "Peter, offer Mr. Hoyt some Good and Plentys." Again Jordan sounded a bit minty (swishy) and Mr. Hoyt was looking confused. "Go ahead, Peter," he said. Mr. Hoyt looked at me and I found myself holding the box out to him. I didn't know what was coming off. "Take one, they're good," Jordan said.

"No, thank you," Mr. Hoyt said to me. Then he turned to Jordan. "Well, are you—going to be all right?" he asked.

In a complete switch of tone, in his regular but even-more-Southern-than-usual drawl, Jordan said, "Yip, I'm gonna be just fine."

Mr. Hoyt bobbed his head. "Good night then. Good night, Peter," he added and shut the door.

When he'd started down the stairs, I whispered to Jordan, "Jesus, what was that all about?"

He simply shrugged. "Beats me."

"No, I mean—the way you talked to him! It was almost . . ."

"What?" he asked.

"Campy," I told him.

"Yeah," Jordan said, adding, "I'm a good camp."

Actually he was. I'd never noticed it much before but the more I got to know him, and the better, he'd every so often camp and do it extremely well, no self-consciousness or embarrassment. "But what made you do it?" I asked him.

"I just felt like it." He smiled.

"No, really—tell me," I said.

"Bulldog wants an answer." Jordan laughed. "I don't know—he just brings it out in me."

"Aren't you afraid of him?"

"*Afraid* of him?" Jordan asked.

"Just a little bit? I mean—doesn't he put you off?"

"Nope."

"How come?"

"I'm rich." Jordan shrugged. "He knows he's got to keep me here this year. My father didn't like my grandmother any more than she liked him, but he sure wants me to get ahold of that money. I know he's promised Gilford something if I graduate from here. The Reverend's hands are tied."

"You take the cake," I told him. "Jordan, listen, do me a favor—what happened that first day you got here?"

"I met a bulldog." He grinned.

"No, come on, you know, between the two of you?"

"He made a pass at me."

"Huh? No, really, tell me."

"It wouldn't bear repetition."

"How do you mean?"

"It wouldn't translate," he told me and with that he got up to go to the bathroom and I knew he was never going to tell me. I made an iron pledge *not* to tell him the very next thing he really wanted to know, which, of course, I never even began to keep.

The next day I was relieved to see Jordan looking much better. The following day was H-Day—Hamlet Day. I was way off my feed and the majority of my nerves were based on Jordan. I didn't want to lay an egg in front of him; I didn't want him to have to be embarrassed for me. What I remember most was my stomach. It was talking back to me all day. I pretended, of course, to be very cool but the calmer I behaved on the surface the more my stomach was giving me away. All I was doing was going over the words in my mind. I was gripped by fear of going blank. I kept remembering all the stories my father and his cronies at the Masquers tell of actors going "up" in their lines, even after appearing in a play an entire year. So all afternoon I was plagued by thoughts like:

> To be, or not to be: that is the question:
> Whether 'tis nobler in the mind to . . . to . . .
> S-P-L-A-T!

Jordan and I didn't have the last class together, so we usually met at my locker near the front door. This afternoon I waited for about five minutes and when he didn't show up I went over to Lincoln House where I found him in bed again. "Hey, Jordan— what's the matter?"

"Oh, nothing," he said. "I should have stayed in bed today. I ran out of gas midafternoon."

"You want to sleep?"

"Yeah, if you don't mind." As I started to leave, he said, "If I'm still feeling under the weather, would you mind if I didn't show up for the gala premiere?"

"No, no!" (Jordan later said I almost turned a somersault.) "No," I went on. "Who needs to listen to the Glee Club hum while I rattle off thirty-five lines? It's not exactly a hot ticket."

"But I'm your friend," he said.

"Listen, if you're not up to snuff, rest up," I told him. He winked at me and I shut the door. I had actually thought of asking Jordan not to come but I didn't want to let on to him that I was that nervous.

I could hardly touch dinner; it was like there was a catcher in my stomach all ready to throw anything back at me that I dropped down his way. Climbing the stairs afterward I was hoping I wouldn't find Jordan getting dressed to come over to the auditorium. His door was closed and I could tell from the transom his lights were off. When I walked into my room there was a small case, twenty-four boxes, of Good and Plentys on my bed, with a red ribbon around it and a note:

Feeling tired, turning in. The Good and Plenty people sent these for opening night. Don't know how *they* knew. Break a leg, Bulldog.

JORDAN

P.S. Look in after, in case I'm awake.

Right then I said to myself, I love him, I just love old Jordan.

When I'd changed into my Black Swan outfit in that little room assigned me back of the stage I started kicking myself for having lost the Battle of the Costume. The members of the Glee Club all gathered in the large music room off the other side of the stage, so I was at least unmolested by them. As I sat there, I knew I was determined about one thing—not to make a fool of myself. I finally got so nervous looking at myself in the mirror that I found a few pieces of black velvet on the closet floor and draped it so I couldn't see myself.

There was a short visit by Mr. Kauffman, looking very spruced up in a tuxedo, telling me not to worry about the timing of the background music, that he'd take care of that, and wishing me luck. About five minutes later Mr. Hoyt came by. He pointed to the material hanging over the mirror and asked what it was. "I don't want to look at myself," I told him.

"Why, Peter!" He grinned. "You're still—"

"Yes, I am. I don't want to be laughed at."

"You won't be laughed at, I assure you. If only you could catch an unbiased glimpse of yourself, you'd realize how—striking you look." I glanced down at the floor, and he took me by the arm. "You'll be fine, you'll see. Do it like you did for Mrs. Hoyt that day and you'll be fine."

"I don't think I can."

He paid no attention to that. "I'm counting on you, Peter," he said, squeezing my arm. "Good luck, lad." And he was gone.

From then until I went on I sat there in a daze. I heard the applause when Mr. Burlingame, the accompanist, came out to play his opening number and the applause when he finished and then the Glee Club was marching on and beginning their first set of numbers.

Some of the thoughts that zipped through my brain as I sat there feeling like a trapped Christian about to be thrown to the lions:

Thank God Jordan isn't here.

Maybe the furnace will blow up and we'll all be killed.

Maybe Jordan *should* be here, maybe hearing about it from the ghouls that live in Lincoln House will make it sound worse than it is.

I could find some rags in the basement and *start* a fire.

We'll all be dead in a hundred years and it won't matter, so what do I care?

A LOT!!!!!

Still, of all the thoughts, the one that persisted was: I will not make a fool of myself. No matter what—I will not make a fool out of myself. Pretty soon I heard the clomping of the Glee Club marching off and Mr. Burlingame's second solo and then they were clomping on again for the second half and it was time for me to get ready. I left the dressing room and went to stand in the wings. For a brief moment I thought of tearing over to Lincoln House and getting into my dark suit but I knew I was playing with fire as far as Mr. Hoyt was concerned and I *wasn't* rich.

There was a big hand for "Camptown Races" and it sounded like a good house and then they were into "Greensleeves" which was right before me. I went into shock about that time, most of all I remember wiping my hands off against my tights, wondering if they would ever get dry. More applause and then Mr. Kauffman put a finger up to his lips, indicating for the Glee Club to hum quietly as he started conducting them in Handel's "Largo."

The stage darkened and I took a deep breath, thinking Oh, shit! and stepped out from the wings. After a few swooping wigwags, Mr. Rush finally managed to hit me with the baby spotlight. When I got to center stage I turned front and was surprised that I could see the audience so well in spite of the light on me. The place was filled except for the last several rows and the rear sides. It was strange to see men and women and a good sprinkling of girls sitting out there after only male assemblies.

A high-pitched giggle tripped out from some dizzy girl sitting down front. Oh, God, I thought, here we go. I hadn't even opened my mouth and they were laughing. I glanced down and saw her in about the fourth row as she giggled again and her friend, another dizzy teenager, put a hand up to her mouth and elbowed her to shut up. They were obviously two dizzy girl friends who went through life giggling together. The first girl giggled again and then someone in the Glee Club behind me snorted while he was humming. It sounded like a muffled sneeze but he was obviously laughing as a result of the girls. I thought: Thanks a lot, buddy, whoever you are. Then I heard Mr. Kauffman go "Shhh!"

The girls stopped and I decided: The hell with it, just dive in. I took another deep breath and got out " 'To be, or not to be: that is the question:' "

176

Then both girls giggled; one was actually more like a squeal. I'd as soon be stoned to death as go rattling on with them giggling all the way through it, so I remembered something my father had done once in the play that Jordan had seen him in. In it he played a defrocked priest and at the beginning of the second act he's drunk in a low-type bar and when this whore says he doesn't have the look of a bum, although he's dressed like one, and asks him what he does, he jumps up on the bar and preaches a sermon.

I saw him in it dozens of times and once there was a big commotion when the curtain went up, an argument, some people had taken the wrong seats and the right people returned late and they were really having a time of it. My father was starting his sermon but the audience was wrecking it; people were shushing the ones who were making the noise and someone called out "Usher!" and pretty soon it sounded like a race riot.

What my father did was this: He jumped down off the bar, walked right up to the front of the proscenium and stared down at where the noise was coming from, just stood there and stared and stared and gradually, like a record running down, the noise dribbled away and silence took over. Finally you could hear a pin drop and then and only then did my father turn around, walk back to the bar (to great applause), jump up on it and start in on the sermon again.

So I just stopped and stared down at them. At first that brought on another little fit of giggling, but then they were tugging at one another to shut up and they finally did. I was just about to go on and some young kid, a boy, let out a laugh a few rows in back of them. I looked back to where he was sitting and this set the girls off again. Then a man in the first row laughed and for a split second I thought the whole place was going to fall apart, struck down by the mysterious giggling virus, but I decided to look back to the girls and just stare them down. I did and the man in the front row stopped laughing and turned around to see where I was looking. Now the girls were getting really embarrassed, I could tell. Pretty soon they weren't even smiling and within seconds they'd slumped way down in their seats like they wished they could fall through the

177

floor, which was much less than I wished for them. No one else was laughing either. But I even allowed time for anyone that wanted to, to break in.

When it got deadly quiet except for Handel's "Largo," I started in over again. I was angry, angry at those cretins for laughing, angry at Mr. Hoyt for making me do it and in that costume, to boot, and angriest at myself for going along with it. I said the speech bitterly through my teeth as if I were talking to morons who couldn't possibly understand the content. Although I was so angry (and nervous) that I don't recall any specific meaning I gave to any specific line I do remember that I kept looking directly at the audience, first at one section, then another, pounding it right at them and thinking: You think it's funny, but you'll all be tucked in your own little deathbeds some fine day and you'll be wondering some pretty dark thoughts about what comes after and you won't be laughing then.

They might not have understood the speech but the whole audience was quiet and they knew *something* was going on from my end. When I finished I realized the Glee Club was just about to end and I stood there very still until they did. Then the audience started to applaud. I didn't stop the show, or get a standing ovation, but the applause was solid, and as I turned to walk off, the man in the front row who had laughed bobbed up from his seat and called out "Good boy, good boy!" I got a kick out of that. I suppose he was complimenting me for bravery in action.

The minute I'd got to the little room assigned me, I stripped out of my costume, determined it was the last time I'd appear in that. The Glee Club was yodeling its way through *The Sound of Music* medley and pretty soon it was all over. To my surprise Mr. Lomax Piper, my grand old French teacher, was the first one to seek me out. He was warm and kind, saying he had no idea I had theatrical aspirations. I told him I didn't, that Mr. Hoyt had them for me. He went "Hmn" a couple of times and then he caught sight of the costume on the back of the chair. He asked if that was Mr. Hoyt's idea, too. When I told him it was, he "Hmn'd" again. Then I heard

Mr. Hoyt calling my name and he came into the room. "Oh, Mr. Piper," he said, surprised to see him. Mr. Piper said hello and then Mr. Hoyt said, "Well, Peter, considering the obstacles you had to start with, I think it went very well. Didn't you, Mr. Piper?"

"Yes, I was just telling Peter. I'll run along," he said. He started to leave, then turned around and waved a hand at the costume. "Oh, Franklyn," he said, as if he were already taking it for granted, "you're not going to make him wear that again, are you?"

Mr. Hoyt looked at the outfit for a second and then gave Mr. Piper one of his rubber-band smiles. "No, no, I think not."

"Good," Mr. Piper said and left. A-plus for Mr. Piper.

Mr. Hoyt was about to say something when a couple of the Glee Club guys came by calling my name. They broke off when they saw him and mumbled they'd see me later. "Well, Peter, I think you did very well. I felt for you, at first, but I must say you handled them, you certainly did." He shook his head as if he were getting a kick out of it. "I think just the blue suit next time." Then he stuck out his hand. "You were right about the costume—all right?" I shook his hand, surprised at his outright admission. "Well, I've got to run along. Some of the trustees are here. Thank you, Peter."

"You're welcome," I said. I was so pleased by his consideration that as he was leaving I called out his name and he turned around. "Tell Mrs. Hoyt I'm sorry it didn't work out."

He looked at me a long time, then nodded his head. "Yes, yes, I will, Peter."

Jordan was not only awake but he was sitting in his chair with his feet on top of the desk and the door ajar when I got back to the third floor. "Hear it went okay," he said.

"Not too bad."

"Well, come in!" he said, pulling me in the door and shutting it. "Give me the low-down, come on."

"Naw," I said, shaking my head, "it doesn't bear repeating."

"What?" he asked, not catching on right away.

"I mean, it wouldn't translate well," I told him, heading for the door. "Oh, by the way—thanks for the candy."

"You little bastard!" he said, coming after me and grabbing my arm. "Boy, you are some bulldog, with a dash of elephant tossed in for good measure."

We laughed and, of course, I told him the whole thing from the word go. While it hadn't been a great victory, at least it hadn't been a total rout. When I was finished, Jordan told *me* something. He'd been feeling fine, but didn't want to suggest he plain not show up for fear of letting me know he was nervous for me, which he was.

How about that for a friend!

15

THE FALL MEETING of the league Glee Clubs was scheduled right before Thanksgiving, only a couple of weeks away. In the meantime the weather was getting cold. The heat was turned off right about lights-out time, and when I'd sneak down to Jordan's room, as I did three or four nights a week, it would get chilly sitting around so I began getting in his bed.

Now we get down to the nitty-gritty. In spite of what later happened and all the talk, nothing ever took place in the way of sex. I'm not saying I'm all that pure, so I might as well admit to some masturbation sessions with Boots, my friend in California who moved away, and one episode in which an actor who has the lead in a television series, *and* a reputation for being a lady-killer, picked Boots and me up hitchhiking home from Malibu. We were sixteen at the time; we got to talking in the car and he finally asked us if we'd like to see his "pad." Talk about acting! He staged a boffo production up at his house in Laurel Canyon. Twilight swimming in his pool, with him naked, followed by a rum drink which he said had practically no alcohol content but got us all fuzzy and buzzy. Then he hauled out three albums of dirty pictures, some of them even featuring him and an equally well-known actress. When it got dark, out came a movie projector for us to see some bullfight pictures he'd taken in Tijuana. We did see some bullfighting but then he said he must have gotten the reels mixed up when this wild technicolor film came on which was a pornographic treatment of Robinson Crusoe. You can probably imagine what happened when lonely Old Rob came across his man Friday, who happened to be a colored weight lifter, swimming in a turquoise lagoon. The camera work was brilliant, no sound, but otherwise, technically, you'd have sworn a big studio like MGM had turned it out.

So, at sixteen you're horny enough to get an erection watching two parakeets do it, let alone humans, no matter what sex. This actor was a master operator. One thing led to another and he finally had his oral way with first Boots and then me. Not only that, but he gave Boots a .22 rifle and me a suede jacket. Boots wanted to contact him again but he moved away soon after and we never did.

Having told you that, I'll hope you believe me when I say Jordan and I never did anything. Jordan would hardly ever touch me, not even with his leg or arm, when I'd be in his bed. We'd just be there talking, having, as we used to call it, "News of the Week in Review," which was a post-mortem on the events of the day. Now that I look back on it, we liked each other so much I believe that's why we didn't play around, nobody wanted to chance spoiling the great relationship we had. I know that's part of it, aside from also knowing Jordan's tastes were much stronger for the opposite sex than for men. Me, too.

Mr. Kauffman would make a tour of the halls once after lights-out and sometimes twice, mainly to try to keep poor Dennis Vacarro "off the streets," as Jordan would say, but he would never open a door to anyone's room after lights-out unless there was noise or a radio playing or he could see lights through the transom. Unless there was an emergency of some sort, Mr. Hoyt hardly ever came over to Lincoln House in the evening. So Jordan and I were being cautious and feeling relatively safe about our late night talks.

I suppose any proof of either Jordan's or my heterosexual activities will be of help, so I'll tell you about what happened a week or so before the Glee Club competition. We'd been to the movies in town and afterward we stopped by the Flame Room. There were only about five people on hand and Patti was tinkling away at the piano as we walked in. She didn't break into the Jack Armstrong theme, like she always did, just glanced up and smiled very briefly, a little smile that looked like it hurt her, and went on with her playing. We took our regular booth and Jordan nodded for me to watch her. She was all dressed up in a black lace dress with like a black satin slip underneath and she had a black lace mantilla arranged over her piled-up hair. She wasn't doing anything but watching her fingers, something she never did. She'd usually be looking up and glancing around the room and smiling.

Jordan ordered and sent Patti her usual. When it was delivered, she glanced up from the piano, flicked another little smile and nodded her head. "Jean-Paul . . ." she said, but she kept on playing and didn't even sip it.

"Heavy, heavy, hangs in the air," Jordan mumbled. He was right; the atmosphere in the Flame Room was grim. After a while one man who was always at the bar called out, "Hey, Patti, give us a song. What is this?"

Patti looked over at him like she'd really been interrupted. "What?" she asked.

"I said—what goes, what is this?" the man repeated.

"Oh, *this!*" Patti said, stretching an arm out, indicating the room. "This is Forest Lawn East." Then she went back to her playing.

"It's a memory night," Jordan said. He excused himself to go over and speak with her. He leaned over the piano and, although she looked at him, she kept on noodling at the keyboard. They talked for a while and suddenly Patti let out one of her great laughs and stopped playing. She reached out a hand and brushed it down the side of Jordan's face the way she usually did when we left and I could tell from the way she was looking at him, the focus of her eyes, she wanted to kiss him that very moment. I was dying to know what Jordan had said.

Pretty soon she got up and Jordan walked her over to our booth. I remember thinking how tiny he seemed alongside her. Patti lifted her glass to take a drink and then suddenly put it down hard on the table. She snorted and turned to Jordan. "Would you believe I've hung on to this dump all this time on the million-to-one shot he might just come back?" She put a hand up to her forehead and gave a little shudder. "Oh, I must be headed round the bend. Not a postcard or a phone call in five years, and I'm sitting here waiting for him to walk in the door and say, 'Hi, Hon—sorry I took so long getting the cigarettes.'" She laughed and grabbed hold of Jordan's arm. "I ought to turn myself in; I'm a public menace running around loose. Oh, Jean-Paul," she sighed, squeezing his hand, "it's a lonely old planet, and this solo work's for the birdies. Tell me something reassuring from your reassurance book."

Jordan cocked his head at her and said, "Would you like company tonight?"

She looked at him closely and for a long time. "Tonight?" she asked. Jordan nodded. "You mean it, don't you?" He nodded again. She smiled a funny little twisted smile. "An old bag like me?"

I was feeling so for her I blurted out, "We think you're spiffy!"

This killed her. "Spiffy!" she roared, and Jordan was laughing, too. "Spiffy. I haven't heard that for— So you think Fat Patti's spiffy? When did you decide that?"

"We took a vote," I said, keeping up a front, in spite of feeling foolish for having spoken up.

When she stopped laughing she put a hand on top of Jordan's hand and said, "I'd love company."

"I'll be back," he said and called for the check.

"In that case," Patti said, grinning, "it's on the house."

Jordan and I left after she'd pecked me on the cheek and said, "We thank you for the vote."

On the way back to school I asked him if he was really going back and stay with her. When he said he was, I asked him, "If your Holiness will permit the effrontery—do you suppose you're going to conjugate the verb?" That was Jordan's way of saying "doing it."

"I suppose," he answered.

"She's a lot bigger than you," I said.

This really got a laugh from him. "It's not a wrestling match, not a contest of strength," he said. "We'll both be cooperating to the fullest extent." He laughed again. "As long as I don't lose my footing."

When we got back to Lincoln House, we checked in with Mr. Kauffman and I'd only been in bed about five minutes when Jordan came in to use my fire escape. He said good night and as I was helping him out the window I suddenly thought about his condition. "Hey, Jordan, try not to overdo it." He gave me a questioning look. "You know—conjugating the verb."

"How can you overdo the verb?"

"I mean—take it easy on your pump."

He laughed. "You nut! Besides—what a way to go!" Although I didn't think there was anything funny about what I said, I could hear him chuckling all the way down the fire escape.

He stayed all night with her and climbed in my window about five-thirty in the morning, looking tired but contented. That afternoon when we got back from classes there was a package awaiting him, a beautiful cashmere sweater and a note:

To Jean-Paul,
For consideration above and beyond the call of duty.
Love,
The Singing Nun

Jordan was a true gentleman. I was eager for a play-by-play account of the evening but he was discreet, only letting me know they'd conjugated the verb successfully and that he was fond of her.

I tell you all this because I got a letter from Patti day before yesterday in which she said she would willingly come forward to

185

attest to Jordan's and my masculinity. Patti and I also have a history, which will be coming up later, and she would certainly be a good character—and conjugation—witness.

Now to get to the Big Day itself, which is an important trigger to this whole thing. Jordan had decided not to go home for Thanksgiving, being it was nothing more than a long weekend. Instead he suggested we go down to Boston for a few days. I was looking forward to this as much as I was *not* looking forward to the Glee Club competition. Although I'd squeaked through Hamlet once without falling on my face, I still had an itchy hunch it was going to be bombs away sooner or later.

To add to this, something happened right before that made me want to help win those precious points for Mr. Hoyt even more. I hadn't realized I hadn't seen his wife around for a few days when Jordan learned from Mrs. Rauscher in one of their kitchen sessions that Mrs. Hoyt had gone away someplace "for a rest." I had noticed that Mr. Hoyt seemed distracted for several days and his concentration wasn't its usual pinpointed self.

Because there were seven schools in the league they broke up the competition into two afternoons, the Friday and Saturday before Thanksgiving. We were scheduled for Saturday afternoon, next to last. Each school was limited to eight numbers. The event was to be held at Hampton Academy, which had the best theater.

Several days before the Big Day, Mrs. Mason got me out of English class and brought me to Mr. Hoyt's office. Because of there being only eight numbers he wanted to discuss the scheduling. He had me placed between "I Won't Dance" and *The Sound of Music* medley and I told him I thought it was bad to follow "I Won't Dance"; it was too zippy and I explained to him it would be a battle to pull the audience down to the somber mood of Hamlet. He said he thought Handel's "Largo" would do that and I told him that was really part of Hamlet and would be too late to help. He asked me my suggestion; of all the numbers scheduled I picked "Lazy Afternoon." Besides being my favorite, it was soft and

186

legato and a natural lead-in to me and "Largo" and then *The Sound of Music* could pick them up for the last number.

He got a kick out of my reasoning and ended up agreeing and saying, "So, the lad who fought me every step of the way is now caught up in Hamlet, planning his strategy to the very last detail."

"No," I told him, "I'm just fighting for survival."

"Why, Peter, I don't believe you." He grinned.

"It's true. I'd pay money not to do it—if I had any," I added.

"Then why *are* you doing it?"

He completely surprised me by that. I wanted to say because he'd bullied me into it. Instead I told him, "Because you wanted me to."

If I'd been surprised by his first question, I was even more thrown by his next. "Only because of that?" he asked.

My God, I wondered if he could possibly have forgotten his attitude and threats and—I couldn't believe the way he was talking. "Yes," I said.

"That's very gratifying to hear," he said, giving me a non-rubber-band smile. He stood up from his desk, walked over to me and put a hand on my shoulder. "You're a good boy, Peter."

I walked out of his office in a daze. It wasn't possible for him to have forgotten his strong-arm campaign to force me into it and all the ploys I used to try to get out of it. Though it might seem like a small thing, this short conversation was, I believe, the first time since my opening encounter with him that I began to think he was, as Patti said about herself, "headed round the bend." It made me nervous about Mr. Hoyt.

The Big Day itself turned out to be wild. Jordan and I and most all the boarding students were transported to Hampton in buses. It was chilly gray and looked like New England was going to have its first big snow. The Hampton campus is very big and expensive-looking and their auditorium is great; actually it was a little theater all by itself, donated by an alumnus theatrical producer as a monument to himself. Inside it was all dark wood, with huge beams running across the ceiling and even a small balcony and the seats all had red covers. In a way, the inside gave the feeling of a great summer theater, only not so roughhewn, a little more solid and warm.

There were lots of dressing rooms and I was assigned a small one to myself. Four schools were performing that afternoon, and we were to go on third. I'd been more or less resigned to the experience on the bus ride over but once we were there and I saw all the other buses and the parking lot full of cars and a big crowd waiting to get in—then I got the cold sweats.

There were several rows in the back of the auditorium for the members of the Glee Clubs to occupy either before or after their turns and Jordan was sitting back there waiting for me to join him, but I decided to stick by myself in the dressing room. Because of my nerves I knew I wouldn't be concentrating on any of the other Glee Clubs and, mainly, I didn't want Jordan to see what condition I was in. I went around to the front, found him, said I'd see him afterward, and went backstage.

There was too much activity in the wings, so I shut myself up in my dressing room, off-stage right. My hands were already cold and clammy as I heard the sounds of the large audience pouring into the theater and chattering and clacking the seats up and down. I stepped in front of the mirror and my face had that tight, frightened look, like I'd had white cement poured over it. Mr. Kauffman came by to wish me luck and I asked him about the judges—who, how many, where they sat. But he just said, "Don't worry about the judges; you just worry about Peter Kilburn!" That remark was such a great comfort to me I had an impulse to say something original, like: "Go shit in your hat!" F-minus for Mr. Kauffman.

Shortly after he left I heard the buzz of the audience as the houselights dimmed and then applause when the first Glee Club clomped on and began singing a march. There was a knock on the door and Mr. Hoyt stuck his head in. A quick rubber-band smile and I could tell he'd had a little cement poured on his face, too. Being in this great theater with all the activity and their rich-looking campus made Gilford seem like a poor relation. If I sensed it, I could imagine how Mr. Hoyt felt. "Peter, not out front watch-

188

ing?" I told him no and he said that Stonehenge, the school with the magician, was on first and he thought I'd want to catch that. He was trying to be jaunty, but I could tell it was a cover-up. When I told him I didn't want to watch any of the others, he stepped inside and closed the door. "Nothing wrong?" he asked.

"Yes—I'm scared," I told him.

"Coming from a father who—"

"My father *throws up* on opening nights!" I said. "And he's a professional."

Mr. Hoyt chuckled but it was a mechanical chuckle. "Peter, you're going to be fine."

"I'd rather be dead."

Another nervous little laugh. "Nonsense, you'll be fine." He paused, then took a step toward me and I could tell how really concerned he was. "Pretend—Peter, pretend you're doing it just for Mrs. Hoyt and me, the way you did that afternoon. That was perfect." He put both hands on my shoulders and I could feel the rigidity in his fingers. "You can do that, can't you?" When I didn't answer, he gave me a little squeeze. "Can't you do it just like that, Peter?" He wasn't asking me, he was begging me.

"I'll try." There was nothing else I could say.

"Of course you will—and you'll do it." He took his hands from my shoulders. "I have confidence in you, Peter." He said it slowly, stringing the words out as if he were evaluating me and that made it almost a warning. Then a quick, hearty (forced), "Good luck, Peter!" and he turned to go.

Suddenly I was angry all over again at him for inflicting Hamlet upon me and this made me perverse. "Is Mrs. Hoyt here?" I asked, knowing full well she wasn't.

He turned around quickly and said, like it had been rehearsed, "No, she's away on a trip, family thing." He started to leave again but then he turned back to me. "However, I'm sure she's thinking about Gilford now, and if we come out of the competition with some points I know that would make her very happy, Peter."

And he was gone. That did it, that made me feel sad for her (and him again) and it served me right for opening my big mouth. I suppose if I've learned anything in this short life it's: if you want to hurt yourself and you don't know how, just take a swat at someone else and it won't be long at all before it gets back to you.

Stonehenge had been on for five or six numbers when I heard the curtains close and the opening strains of "That Old Black Magic." After about sixteen bars I heard the curtains opening, followed by a crash and then a huge uproar from the audience. My curiosity forced me to scoot out into the wings just in time to see two white doves flutter up in the air and take off out over the audience to great howls of laughter, while the magician, a chubby kid with thick glasses, was scrambling around on his hands and knees trying to corner a white rabbit that was hopping over to the piano with the obvious idea of getting under it.

The magician's own Glee Club was breaking up and the audience was actually howling. The poor guy had suffered a catastrophe. The curtains had been closed in order for two little tables holding his magic paraphernalia to be set up, only they were set right against the folds, so that when the curtains were pulled open, one of the tables got knocked off balance, over it went, and out came the doves and rabbit, and a large pitcher of colored water broke.

When he finally hauled the rabbit out from under the piano and dropped it into a top hat, the audience gave him an ovation; but it was obvious the big tricks he had up his sleeve were shot to hell. I won't go into the details of his entire tortured performance, except to say the audience was completely goosey and even when he did a simple card trick they clapped and carried on as if he were the Great Houdini. He was all shook up as he worked his way through making a bouquet of flowers disappear, some handkerchiefs tied in a row change color, and a complicated thing involving a butterfly net and some ping-pong balls which I didn't quite get because just then the doves came to life and flew in over the stage, buzzing the Glee Club, three of whom jumped down off their benches, and then zooming back out over the audience. I might add the audience

190

wasn't paying much attention to the butterfly net either. By the time the magician ended I really felt sorry for him. He'd been cheated out of his last big trick, the doves, so he used the rabbit to end with, only by that time everyone knew there *was* a rabbit and exactly where it was. He finally just gave the signal for the curtains to close and again the audience gave him an ovation and there were even a few bravos—sort of cruel ones.

I quickly ducked back into my dressing room. Although I felt sorry for him I started perking up about my own turn; I suppose it's only natural to feel good when your competition falls on his face. Before I knew it the next school was finishing, there was a short intermission and our boys were beginning. Still I stayed in my dressing room, trying to get myself into the right mood, one that would carry me through the speech. Several times, before I went to stand in the wings, I heard bursts of laughter from the audience, especially one hearty-sounding woman. Though "I Won't Dance" could possibly be described as a humorous number, I couldn't imagine what was so funny about "Gaudeamus Igitur."

As soon as they started "Lazy Afternoon" I took my place in the wings. I tossed up a quick prayer, went into a trance, and the next thing I knew Mr. Kauffman was putting his finger up to his lips for the quiet humming and I was moving like a zombie out onto the stage. When I turned front I could see, from the way the light hit me and the slant of the orchestra floor, the people in the first ten or twelve rows clearly and everything beyond faded into darkness, which was all right with Hamlet.

Right off, in about the sixth row by the left aisle, I saw a big fat lady with what looked like a tub of red poppies on her head. She had a great round jolly face and she was smiling, even sort of nodded approval at me, tipping the poppies back and forth. Actually, from what I could see of the audience, they all looked very amiable. There was almost a party atmosphere about them.

I took a deep breath and, thinking how friendly the natives were looking, said, " 'To be, or not to be: that is the question.' " Well, the big fat lady thought that was about the funniest thing she'd ever

191

heard. A great barrage of laughter came up out of her, a real
boomer, and that caused about a dozen others to laugh along.

Oh, sweet Jesus, I thought, here we go! I looked over at her and
this made her rock back and forth and let out an even louder blast.
And, as sudden as it was odd, I couldn't be angry at her. She was
just a great big heap of good-naturedness with a crazy red-poppy
hat on top—and what could you do? I knew if it got to a staring
contest I'd come out losers. I was certain she could laugh longer
than I could look. The only thing I could think of at the present
was to plow ahead:

> Whether 'tis nobler in the mind to suffer
> The slings and arrows of outrageous fortune,
> Or to take arms against a sea of troubles,
> And by opposing end them?

She was still laughing, but she was trying to bring it under control; so were the others who were laughing at her. Right about then
I started thinking of Jordan. I hadn't spotted him; I supposed he
was still sitting in the back and I was glad I couldn't see his face. I
spoke very slowly, hoping that soon all the laughter would fade and
I could at least get them from the middle of the speech on. I took a
long pause before I said:

> To die, to sleep;
> To sleep: perchance to dream: ay, there's the rub:

Nobody was making any noise, although the faces in front of me
were far from solemn.

> For in that sleep of death what dreams may come,
> When we have shuffled off this mortal coil,
> Must give us pause. There's the respect
> That makes calamity of so long life;

I stopped at that, to let it sink in, and I was just opening my
mouth to go on when one of Houdini's white doves swooped

down from the flies and whirred by my left shoulder, kind of flapping its wings, as if it were thinking of landing. It startled me so I jumped a full step to the side and that scared the bird so that it took off over the audience.

I suppose I don't have to tell you how this affected the Poppy Lady. She was off and running again, taking a majority of the audience right along with her. I was thinking seriously of shrugging and walking off, really calling it a day, when I thought: No, I can't give up like this, not in front of Jordan! I can't. Right about then the one dove had stirred the other up and the two of them made a little migratory flight in over the stage, buzzing the Glee Club and breaking them up completely and sending the Fat Lady into convulsions. As they flew back past me one of them started to land on top of the stand-up flagpole to the side of the stage. By this time the place was pandemonium and I realized Houdini had really set the mood for the afternoon and they just naturally expected to laugh at the next joker who stepped out onto the stage and that was me. I also realized I'd been playing it pretty straight and that it was a total rout, so as the bird was flapping its wings to settle on the knob atop the pole, I pantomimed machine-gunning it. That got a laugh and also frightened the bird away out over the audience with me doing my other pantomime of pulling the pin of a hand grenade with my teeth, throwing it, and then ducking back and shielding my face with my hands from the explosion. The Fat Lady really went for that one; she let out a scream of approval and started clapping her chubby hands together. Being she'd practically been elected conductor of the audience, a lot of other people applauded, too.

Right then it hit me: Frankie Spiro's routine. I certainly couldn't go on with the *real* Hamlet. He'd gone down the drain for good. And I couldn't give up and walk off. There was really nothing else to do but try it. While I was waiting for them to quiet down I thought of Mr. Hoyt and that gave me pause. Although I couldn't see him, which suited me fine, I could imagine the expression on his face and that was enough to put me off. Still, there seemed to be no alternative.

193

As they were quieting down, I got my handkerchief out and wiped off my face, exhaled a big sigh and said exaggeratedly, " 'To be, or not to be:—' " This got a little laugh, like a giggle, and then, just for insurance, I looked right down at my friend, the Fat Lady, and said, "Listen, don't laugh at the poor guy. This Hamlet really had problems." Even before I got to *one* of them I had her laughing again. "In the first place, how would you like it if your uncle came over for dinner and made a pass at *your* mother." Another laugh. "And those old castles—talk about drafty. Everyone always had a cold and Kleenex hadn't even been invented yet. That's why everyone had long, bulky sleeves with lots of extra material." Big laugh. Now she was really going and taking the audience right along with her, like the Pied Piper. I felt safe enough to look away from her and address the rest of them. "And the plumbing in those old castles—it was criminal!" Bigger laugh and I heard several snorting chokes behind me. I turned around and the guys in my Glee Club were all broken up, except for one serious prune, Burris Flintner, who was staring at me like I'd completely lost my mind, and Mr. Kauffman, who was looking like he'd been in a bad automobile wreck. He'd even stopped conducting and was standing there, arms dangling, mouth open.

When I turned to face the Glee Club I gave them a very sober look, like: what are you guys *laughing* at? This broke them up even more, and when the audience focused on me looking at them, they naturally saw the guys falling apart and this tickled them further, so that it was like a tennis match with the Glee Club and the audience laughing back and forth at one another and me, the ball in the middle.

It was freakish, the whole thing, but I was home free and I knew it. You just couldn't miss with that audience, thanks to the Poppy Lady and Houdini's doves. When they didn't get the non sequitur about not bathing from Halloween to Shrove Tuesday, which is either in April or Montana, I quickly snapped my head back to the dear Fat Lady and that set her off and got them going, too. The part about "That's a long time without soap and water, from

194

whence cometh the saying: There's something rotten in Denmark!" got a huge laugh and a few people clapped, led by Our Lady of the Poppies, as I later dubbed her to Jordan.

No need to go through the entire routine; actually I skipped some of it. Not on purpose, I just wasn't that up on it. The end, about how everyone in the castle suffered from terrible migraine headaches from figuring out how to say everything in iambic pentameter, got a big guffaw; and when I walked off bobbing my head in time with the meter and saying, "For*sooth,* I *needs* must *go* down *to* the A and *P!*" they really broke into solid applause.

When I stepped into the wings I realized how fast my heart was beating and I suddenly fell apart with nerves and stage fright. Like, if some dragon were chasing you and you broad-jumped a chasm and made it safely and *then* stopped and looked back down at what you *could* have fallen into. Now, after it was all over, I was petrified.

I turned around and looked back out onto the stage—had that been *me* out there? And there was Mr. Kauffman now looking like he'd just discovered the cure for cancer *and* won the Irish Sweepstakes at the same time, alternately applauding and waving me on for a bow. I wasn't about to go out but the more he waved the more they clapped and then someone shoved me from behind, the conductor of the next Glee Club, and I stumbled out, knees almost buckling from the shakes. I got a big hand and bowed, but I couldn't smile. My face was frozen, my mouth was glued shut, I could feel it. I caught sight of Our Lady of the Poppies, turned my body toward her and executed a very formal bow right at her, which got a roar and more applause, and walked off again.

The man who'd shoved me out was pumping my hand and congratulating me along with several fellows from his school. "I thought you were in serious trouble at first," he said. "You really had us fooled."

"Me, too," I said, but I couldn't say anything else. I heard the applause fade and our boys launch into *The Sound of Music* medley and I staggered into my dressing room and fell into a chair.

I'd no sooner sat down when Mr. Hoyt came racing in. Before he could even speak, I panted, "I quit!"

"You *quit!*" he roared and closed the door behind him. "You quit!" he repeated and then just leaned back against the door and laughed uncontrollably. Although I was in a state of shock I remember experiencing a measure of relief that at least he was laughing. You see, with Mr. Hoyt being so unpredictable, even though the routine had gone over well, still in the back of my subconscious was the notion that I might catch it from him.

But soon he was gasping my name. "Oh, Peter—Peter! You're some boy, some lad, you are." And then he was just looking at me and shaking his head. He did that for a long time, still leaning back against the door. Finally he said, "How did you ever—*ever* think to come up with that?"

"I don't know," I told him.

"You don't know," he repeated, chuckling, and I could tell he was getting a wallop out of what happened. "You don't *know!* Well, one thing you must know—you saved the day. You certainly saved the day! I never would have—" But he just broke off and shook his head again. Suddenly he took a step toward me and wagged a finger in my face. "And now, who doesn't want to be an actor?"

"Me," I said.

"You!" He laughed.

"Not in a million years."

"And why—why is that?" He laughed again.

"Because if I tried to get up out of this chair I'd fall flat on my face," I told him.

"You would, would you?" he roared. When he stopped laughing he again shook his head and kept looking at me. He took another step to me and put the palm of his hand on my cheek and jaw, almost cupped my face in his one hand it was so large. He looked at me for a long time. Then he said, "Jesus, you're some boy. Some boy!"

It was the first time I'd ever heard him swear and it surprised me. He took his hand from my face and backed a step away to look at me again. Then the door opened and our Glee Club burst in with Mr. Kauffman bringing up the rear to congratulate me. Even Mr. Hoyt's presence didn't have its usual sobering effect and they were all over me, pumping my hand and hauling me up out of the chair and whacking me on the back.

At one point I looked up and Mr. Hoyt was standing against the wall across from the door, beaming like a kid in enjoyment of their enthusiasm. They were all thronged around me, so that all I could see was his head, but I could tell he was so excited he could hardly keep still. He'd look from one face to another and then, as he moved his head around slightly, I saw his smile disappear and the next thing he was frowning.

I followed his gaze, looking outside the door, and there, maybe fifteen yards away, was Jordan leaning up against a stage flat, arms folded, looking very bored. When he saw me spot him, he raised a hand, looked at his watch and yawned. I laughed because I knew he was putting on an act and then he laughed. Mr. Hoyt glanced around at me just then and then back at Jordan and his face took on that tight look which somehow seemed to make his lips disappear. I waved to Jordan to come in but he shook his head, indicating he'd wait until the commotion was over. I looked once more at Mr. Hoyt, who was still staring out at Jordan, and then at Jordan just as he glanced at Mr. Hoyt and fixed him with that cool, almost lids-at-half-mast look. Mr. Hoyt looked back at me and I remember right then thinking, in the midst of all the noise and chatter, the guys wanting to know if I'd planned it, where I'd learned the routine, etc.—I remember thinking that Mr. Hoyt and Jordan and I were some kind of a triangle.

16

AFTER THE LAST Glee Club had finished—by this time Jordan had wandered away and I couldn't see him—there was a big hubbub backstage and Mr. Hoyt took me around introducing me to the headmasters and some teachers and chorus masters of other schools. All of them were extremely complimentary and Mr. Hoyt was beaming and treating me as if I were his own son. No doubt about it, I was excited. He'd told me the winners wouldn't be announced until the next day but he was positive we would place in the first three.

Soon all the groups were being organized and it was time to leave. I didn't meet up with Jordan until I got on the bus. It had started to snow and as I sat down next to him, he said, "I thought we'd have dinner at Thorgan's, if the snow keeps up."

"Fine," I said, realizing he was continuing the act. "I'm not too hungry right now, but I suppose I will be later on."

"I'm not either," he said. Then he turned to me and smiled. "So —whatcha been up to lately?"

"Nothing much." I shrugged.

"How's the folks?"

"They're all away on a trip."

"Oh?"

"LSD."

"Great!" Jordan said. "Been gettin' much lately?"

"*Comme ci, comme ça.*"

"Well, listen, that's better than nothing! What do you think of the world situation?" he asked.

"No doubt about it," I told him, "I think we should send all our laundry to Red China. Especially that involving night soil!"

"I'll bring that up at the next Cabinet meeting. Incidentally," and Jordan brought his voice down to a whisper, "I hear the Prez is a big fruit."

"Oh, didn't you know that? They say they can't keep him and De Gaulle off the Hot Line. They're on it for hours at a time!"

"Well, you know the French," Jordan sighed. "They're all fruity. So—who's your all-time favorite movie star?" I started to speak. "All-time!" he emphasized.

"Oh, all-*time?*" I asked. Jordan nodded. "Oh, Sandra Dee!" I said, clapping my hands together.

We went on like that until the pace got frantic and we couldn't help burst out laughing. When we calmed down Jordan put his hand on my leg and said, "Bulldog, I almost messed myself at first —that's how worried I was! You took a big dare and you won." Then he looked me in the eye and said, "I'm proud of you."

I knew he was leveling with me so I replied with a simple "Thank you."

We spent the rest of the bus ride doing a rehash—Houdini and his doves, Our Lady of the Poppies, Reverend Davidson and his reaction, etc. We'd keep getting interrupted by the guys on the bus and even Frank Dicer gave me an out-and-out compliment without the stinger in it.

We planned dinner and the late movie, which on Saturdays started at the racy hour of nine-thirty. The snow was coming down in big heavy blobs and as Jordan and I joked I was holding a secret elation inside me. I was loving the present; this was one of the all-time good times. It isn't often when you actively say to yourself that you're really eating up what's going on right at the moment, but the bus ride was one of them. Everything was in place. Outside of the Glee Club competition, I knew I'd won points with Mr. Hoyt, I was getting good grades in school, for the first time in my life I was some kind of a hero, at least for a few days, and I had one of the best friends ever right next to me. Even my father was currently behaving himself and there were several jobs on the horizon according to his last letter.

When we got back to school Jordan called Cutler Barnum to pick us up in an hour. I'd just stepped into my room after showering when there was a knock and Mr. Hoyt came in. He was still very excited. "Oh, Peter, I didn't know you were dressing." I was in my bathrobe and I said that was all right and to come in. He closed the door and smacked his hands together. "I was wondering if you'd have dinner with Headley and me. I think a celebration's in order."

"I'm sorry," I said, "but I—"

"You have dinner plans?" he asked.

I don't know what governed my wordage, but I think it just seemed simpler to say, "I've got a date."

"Oh, you have?" he asked, smiling.

"Yes," I said, immediately feeling on shaky ground.

"Well, I don't wonder. A good-looking, successful young actor like you should have a—what is it they say nowadays—a 'heavy' date?"

"Yes, I guess so," I said, now really regretting my use of the word "date" and not wanting to pursue it. You see, I didn't say I was going out to dinner with Jordan because I knew he didn't like him and everything was so perfect, even Mr. Hoyt was in an expansive mood. I didn't want to disturb the status quo.

But then he asked, "One of the town girls?"

"Well, I . . . ." I was just about to say I hadn't really meant a date, more just that I had plans for dinner, when he made that chopping gesture in the air with his flattened-out hand. "None of my business. You've certainly earned a night off from school and that ogre headmaster. Perhaps some other time?"

"Yes, I'd like to." Actually I wouldn't have minded dinner alone with Mr. Hoyt to see if I could figure out what really went on inside him, but I knew I would only be uncomfortable with him and Headley.

"Fine," he said, "we'll do it." Then he walked over to my desk and put his hands on the back of my chair. He looked down for a few seconds and then up at me. "I want you to know how very proud I am of you, Peter. That was quite a showing this afternoon. I'd like you to know how appreciative I am, how grateful the entire school is." Then he walked over and put his hands on the outside of my shoulders. "Peter, I've wanted to say one thing for a long time."

"Yes, sir?"

"Don't say 'Yes, sir' like that," he told me, but he said it gently and almost with a kind of imploring humor, if that makes sense. "I'm talking to you as a friend. I hope you consider me a friend," he said, holding me away at arm's length and looking at me closely. "Do you, Peter?"

And although I couldn't specify the category and felt more, somehow, empathy for him than direct friendship, I said, "Yes, I do now."

"Now?" he said, smiling. "That's one thing I've wanted to talk about. Perhaps—perhaps I was a bit off in my judgment of you when you first arrived here. I'm sorry if I was. I hope you'll excuse that."

"Yes, I do."

"Good," he said, squeezing my shoulders. We both remained standing there and it was funny but the one goal I'd had my heart set on so strongly from the very beginning, to get him to change his mind about me, had been achieved and even more—I'd heard a direct apology from him—but still, instead of feeling jubilant I felt a little uneasy.

After a while I began to wonder how long we'd stay like that and suddenly I was struck by the way he was looking at me, and in an instant—like a quick flash of memory association—I realized it was the same way Patti had looked at Jordan that night at the

201

piano and then I remembered the way he'd put his hand on my cheek in the dressing room that afternoon. Right then I felt he had an impulse to—I don't know—hug me, or perhaps even kiss me. Finally he said, "You're a remarkable boy, Peter."

I couldn't help it and I shivered, not from fear or even repulsion, just from the strange realization that Mr. Hoyt, our "ogre," our Reverend Davidson, had this impulse. Ask me how I knew and I couldn't tell you but I felt it strongly. He noticed my shiver and said "Cold?"

"I guess I'm still a little wet," I said, which was the truth because I was feeling that chill that comes when you've let the water just stay on you without thoroughly drying.

"Well, better get dressed," he said, taking his hands from my shoulders. Then right away he switched to his hearty headmaster gear. "Bundle up, lad, when you go out. Winter's here. Have a good time, Peter. See you tomorrow. We'll have that dinner soon!" And then he was out the door and tilting down the hall.

I was left standing there in the remains of that most peculiar moment, but I didn't have time to dwell on it because right after he left, a lot of the guys were in and out of my room and soon it was time for Jordan and me to take off. Although my encounter with Mr. Hoyt was still very much with me I didn't go into it with Jordan outside of saying Mr. Hoyt had asked me to have dinner with him and Headley. I didn't want to chance dampening the tone of the evening. "Listen," Jordan said, "that sounds like a funfest. I'd certainly understand if you'd rather."

"No, some other time. I'm too jazzed up already and you know what a madcap Headley is. I'd get completely out of hand."

I left it at that. The road up the side of the mountain to Thorgan's was already being sanded and Cutler Barnum said this first heavy snow was bound to keep up for several days. We got a table by the window and being so high up and not able to see to the bottom of the ski slope through the thick flakes—it was like we were sitting right up in the clouds.

Jordan ordered his drink and my ginger ale. I'd just gotten my twenty-five-dollar allowance from Milton Bigelow, and because I'd had my little triumph courtesy of Frankie Spiro, I asked Jordan if I couldn't please take him to dinner. Surprisingly enough he said sure and with that reached in his pocket, took out an envelope and handed it to me. "If you'll take this," he said.

I opened it up and there were lots of crisp twenty-dollar bills inside. I counted them—two hundred dollars. "What's the pay-off for?" I asked. "I haven't even pulled the job yet."

"No pay-off. I thought it would be easier while we're down in Boston if we each had our own money."

"How could we each have our own when it all belongs to you?" I asked, putting the envelope down in front of him.

"Don't make waves," Jordan warned.

"I'm not, but thanks to you I still have the nest egg I saved up last summer. Anyhow, two hundred dollars, we're only going to be there a few days."

"So—Boston's not a free port."

"I'll use my money," I told him.

"Supposing I want to do something out of the ordinary, extravagant, why should you have to pay for it?"

"I'm a big spender." I shrugged.

"I'm a bigger one," he said, putting the envelope back in front of me, "so try to be gracious and accept it and forget about it."

"Jordan, honestly, I'd feel funny. You keep it and if I run out I'll borrow some."

Jordan shook his head. "It's more fun if we each pay our own as we go and don't have to worry about what the hell we're doing."

"But it's *not* my own."

"It is if you'll just take it. Besides, the trip to Boston was my idea." I opened my mouth to speak, but his patience was running out. "Take it and don't let's louse up dinner, okay? I haven't even had time to sip my drink."

I looked around the table. "It isn't even *here* yet."

We laughed and he insisted I take the money, repeating he was loaded and saying that of my many virtues, graciousness was not one of them. By that time our drinks had arrived and he sneaked a little bourbon in my ginger ale and offered up a toast to Our Lady of the Poppies. We were about to drink when Jordan glanced over and said, "Well, well, Reverend Davidson steps out!"

I turned and he was just being led in by the hostess with Headley bringing up the rear. Right away, I wanted to disappear. He was seated four tables in toward the center of the room from us. He hadn't seen us though and as long as I knew he was bound to eventually, I was caught up in the suspense of when exactly that would be.

"What's the matter?" Jordan asked.

"Nothing," I said, looking away from Mr. Hoyt's table.

"Nothing to fear from the Rev. You're his boy now."

"Yes." I smiled kind of sickly.

"What's the matter?" Jordan asked again.

"I told you, nothing. I just never expected to see him up here." I turned to look again just as Jordan was saying something about how it was a free country and sure enough Mr. Hoyt had spotted us. He was holding the menu up but he was looking at me and he was not looking pleased. Just then Headley glanced up from his menu, noticed his father's expression and followed his gaze. He brought us into focus with all that magnified glass he wore and gave us a squinty nod of recognition. I nodded back and Mr. Hoyt looked down at his menu without acknowledging it. Again Jordan asked me what was the matter and this time I told him. I thought he'd be annoyed with me for letting myself get involved in such a stupid, half-assed deception and also pick me up for avoiding saying I was having dinner with him. Instead, he got a big kick out of it and laughed. "If I'm the hottest date you can come up with, you're in big trouble. If I'd have known, I'd have ordered a corsage." He started to lift up out of his chair. "I think I'll just ask them to join—"

"Jordan, don't!" I said, grabbing his arm.

"Peter, I was only kidding," he said, surprised at the strength with which I'd grabbed him.

We finally settled down to eating, only my heart wasn't in it; although I tried not to let it show, Jordan was aware of my one-track mind because as soon as we finished dessert he said, "Pay the check and I'll phone Cutler. We'll wait in the lounge. Maybe we can have a laugh or two out there." He left the table.

All during dinner I'd every so often looked over toward Mr. Hoyt and if he happened to be looking in my direction he'd glance away. To my knowledge he never exchanged a word with his son, who acted as if he were alone no matter how many people were around. When I'd paid the check and was leaving, I thought to stop by and maybe say some little thing but the atmosphere was so chilly I was sure I'd say the *wrong* little thing, so I skipped it and walked out by an aisle several tables away from them.

As Jordan and I were waiting in the lounge he said, "Look, I know something's still bothering you."

"Yes, I'm kicking myself for not just saying I was having dinner with you instead of letting him go on with that whole date thing."

"Look, Peter, he was the one that went on with it. That's his problem, not yours. He's got a lot of problems you don't have."

"What do you mean?"

"I think he's getting hung up on you," Jordan said.

"Why do you say that?" I asked, remembering the feeling I got from the way he looked at me in my room.

"Sweet Jesus," Jordan laughed, "I'm not blind. I see the way he keeps his eye on you all the time and from the way he was sitting over there at that table—he's acting like some jilted high-school girl." Jordan patted me on the arm. "Now you be kind to the Reverend. Don't you go breaking his heart."

I had the feeling Jordan was sort of not kidding as much as he was kidding. When we left Thorgan's I almost forgot about it. The movie starred Simone Signoret, a favorite of mine, so I loaded up with Good and Plentys and had a whopping good time. It was still snowing when we got out and we walked home with Ed Anders, who was all excited about skiing the next day, and Wiley Bevan, who was all excited because Betty Thorn, the town whore, had stepped on his heel coming out of the theater and said "Excuse me." He interpreted that as some sort of mystic sign that she was bird-dogging him.

The excitement of the day had me bushed, also I hadn't slept too well the night before, so we didn't have News of the Week in Review in Jordan's room, which turned out to be just as well. Right after I'd gotten in bed, Jordan came by and opened my door. "Hey, Peter . . ."

"Yes?"

"You have a good sleep, hear? You did well today, so don't you worry about the Rev. You did well today," he repeated. We said good night and he left. He was perceptive, just a little thing like putting a friend at ease was important to him.

I was close to sleep when I heard Mr. Hoyt's footsteps coming down the hall. He knocked gently, then opened the door and flicked on the lights. I sat up in bed and rubbed my eyes. "Did I waken you?"

"No, sir."

He looked around the room as if he'd expected to find someone there. "I had a call from one of the judges, telling me Gilford placed second in the competition. I thought you might want to know," he added.

"Yes," I said, "I'm glad."

He just stood there and stared at me. I had the feeling he was saying in that stare: "How was your heavy date?" After a while I became extremely ill at ease. "Mr. Hoyt—" I said, not knowing exactly what I would say, which turned out not to matter because he cut me off with a brisk "Good night, Peter!" and quickly walked down the hall.

After I'd turned out the lights and gotten back into bed I lay there thinking about Mr. Hoyt and Jordan's remark about how he was behaving like a schoolgirl. It was partially true. If he wasn't exactly sulking, he was certainly pulling some kind of a scene. I thought of how the scales had tipped from our first meeting and in a way I was getting a certain confused pleasure out of it. That was only because I had no idea how serious it was.

17

I DIDN'T SEE Mr. Hoyt the next day, Sunday. Mr. Kauffman had spread the word that we'd taken second place and I was still basking in my share of glory. The snow kept up and in the afternoon Ed Anders organized a group to go skiing at the slope nearest town. Jordan was curled up in his room, glued to a book, so I went along and got on skis for the first time, ably assisted by Ed, who turned out to be an excellent instructor. He was easygoing and patient and when I finally made it down the beginner's slope without falling, except at the bottom, you'd have thought from the reception I'd just qualified for the Olympics.

I got ski fever that afternoon. About five o'clock I got too frisky, having made it down the beginner's slope several times without mishap, and decided to try the regular slope. Even Ed Anders said to wait until the next day but I was determined, especially since it didn't look too steep and everyone else was doing well, including some kids only ten and twelve (who'd probably been born on skis).

Ed and I started together at the top but pretty soon I was going much faster than I'd bargained for. Ed was right along with me calling out instructions: "Bend at the knees . . . not so rigid . . . lean into it." But I just froze finally and instead of riding it down I tried to spread my skis out in back and point in at the toes as I'd done on the beginner's slope, but I was going too fast and ended by crossing my skis and taking a lulu of a spill in which I did a lopsided somersault before I hit ground again.

I could feel it in my back right away—a sick, hollow sensation at the bottom of my spine. Ed Anders was quick to the rescue, and when I could barely walk, he borrowed a car from one of the town kids and drove me to a doctor. He kept berating himself for letting me try the regular slope and I kept telling him it was nobody's fault but mine, which was true, and telling *myself* I would never walk again and planning my life as a paraplegic and wondering if being a paraplegic meant I'd never be able to conjugate the verb.

Dr. Horton, I thanked God, was not the same one that took care of Jordan. After working over me and moving my legs every which way and taking X-rays, he assured me I'd simply sprained my back, that it would bother me for a few days but it would be fine. He taped me up, gave me some pain pills, a few sleeping pills, and told me to stay in bed until he came to see me the next afternoon.

What got me was Jordan. He was all bundled up and standing out on the porch waiting for me. The other guys had come back from the slope and the word had got around. He trotted over to the car while Ed went inside to round up some fellows to carry me upstairs. "Hi," he said. "Didn't you know you have to ski at least two days before you start jumping off mountains?" Although he was kidding, I could tell by his face he was concerned. "What did the doctor say?" I told him I'd just sprained it; Jordan sighed and put a hand up to his chest. "When Burt said you couldn't walk— thank God," he added.

Ed came back with three guys and they made a seat with their hands and carried me up to my room with Mr. Kauffman hovering over them, clucking and telling them not to drop me. "We can't let anything happen to our very own Hamlet," he said, at which point Jordan and I couldn't help but smile. Everyone came in to see me after dinner. Jimmy Greer presented me with a sketch of a skier (me) flying down a slope ass-over-teakettle, Dennis Vacarro brought me some fudge his aunt had sent him, Ed Anders gave me

208

a book on skiing (too late), and lots of other fellows looked in on me. I acknowledged that they weren't such a bad group after all. I was even getting to feel affectionate toward their various nuttyisms. My back began really bothering me after a while so I took a sleeping pill and conked out, with Jordan sitting at my desk reading.

The next morning he checked on me before and after breakfast. When they all left for classes I went back to sleep. After a while I was awakened by the feeling there was someone in the room with me. I looked to the door, which was open, but I couldn't see anyone. Then I heard Mr. Hoyt say my name. It gave me a start and I turned my head to see him sitting in a chair pulled way up even with the head of my bed. He was very solicitous, asking how I felt and saying he was sorry he hadn't been around on Sunday, that that's why he hadn't come to see me before. Then he said, "I saw Mrs. Hoyt. She was most pleased to hear the news of you and the Glee Club and sent you her congratulations." I thanked him and we sat for a while without saying anything. After a while he said he'd better be getting back to school, but that he'd see me in the afternoon when Dr. Horton came by. He didn't seem to have any traces left of his Saturday night attitude and even asked if there was anything I wanted before he left.

He and the doctor came over about four in the afternoon and the doctor had me walk up and down the hall. I was already worried about our trip to Boston, so I tried to walk as well as I could but my back was really quite sore and the doctor could tell. He got a heating pad for me, told me to stay in bed except for going to the john and said he'd see me the next day.

That evening, although my appetite returned and I ate most of the dinner Mrs. Rauscher brought up, I still didn't feel like tap dancing. I told Jordan, being that the long Thanksgiving weekend was beginning the day after next, maybe he might as well go home because I didn't think I'd be up to Boston. He said he'd wait and see how I felt but I told him he'd better try to get plane reservations before it was too late. The heating pad helped some but I still couldn't get in any one position long without my back aching, so I took another sleeping pill.

Tuesday afternoon the doctor came again and checked my back, which wasn't aching so much but was terribly stiff when I tried to walk. I told him about Boston and he strongly advised against it, saying he wanted to leave me taped up until Friday. I actually didn't feel like any trip so I told Jordan I'd stick around school, after all it was only a long weekend, and I'd see him on Sunday night. He said he'd think about it. After study hours he came by to say he'd be flying down to New Orleans in the morning if I was positive I didn't want company. I told him I'd get some reading done and get back into shape.

Some of the kids who lived nearby were picked up by their parents that evening, and Mr. Hoyt dropped in to say that several students were staying at school over the holidays and that he and Headley were going to be away Thanksgiving Day but Mr. Lomax Piper, who lived in town, was coming over to preside at turkey dinner. As he was leaving the room he turned and said, "It doesn't seem fair, does it, Peter? For all you did, you get rewarded with a sprained back. We'll make it up to you."

The next morning when I woke up I was feeling a little better but when Jordan came in to say goodbye, all dressed up in a dark-gray suit and his best cashmere overcoat, I didn't tell him for fear of making him feel badly about leaving. I suddenly got very shy with him as we were saying goodbye.

After he left, around ten, I really got hit by a case of the blues. The place was deadly quiet, even Mr. Kauffman had gone. With all the boarders out, the house smelled differently. You could actually smell the wood and the wax and the bareness. I heard footsteps coming up the stairs and down the hall and then Dennis Vacarro was standing in my doorway all bundled up and carrying ice skates. "Hi," he said. "I'm staying, too. My mother's gone down to Key West to see if she can talk my father into coming back. They met on Thanksgiving at a USO party when he was in the service."

"I hope it works out."

210

"I hope so," Dennis said, "but I don't imagine it will." He looked back down the hall. "Holidays always seem to be lonelier than—just regular days, don't they?"

"Yes, I guess they do."

"I'm going ice skating. I'll see you later." But he stood right where he was. "Peter?"

"Yes?"

"If you think holidays are lonely, too, maybe I could—you know, stay up here with you tonight?"

"Dennis, look—"

"I don't mean to do anything, not if you don't want me to. I could just bring my mattress up here and blankets and put them on the floor. Just for company."

"Dennis, I really don't sleep well in the same room with anyone."

"Yes, well, but if you get lonely. Don't decide now. Wait and see. And I'll see you later." He hurried off down the hall, not wanting to hear a definite no.

That little encounter did nothing to pick up my spirits. I also realized my back wasn't feeling as chipper as I'd imagined. I was suddenly bitterly disappointed that I wasn't in Boston with Jordan. I was missing him already and I began to think how much I'd miss him when school was over and we'd each go our own way. I started worrying about what was going to happen to me when I was out of high school. Then I started thinking of my father: would he be broke and more or less unemployed the rest of his days? I even began thinking of my mother and what if she hadn't died and I suppose I just plain started to feeling sorry for myself and wishing I had a huge regular family instead of my rather unfatherish, albeit special, father, and my dotty grandfather who keeps thinking *I'm* my father. As usual when I work myself up to a real depression, I got sleepy and soon I'd flopped over on the bed and slipped off into one of those steam-heated midmorning naps.

I was awakened by music—loud strains of *Turandot*. I got up, all groggy, and staggered out into the hall. For a moment I thought

I might be dreaming but I could feel the stiffness in my back and the tape made me walk funny. I followed the music to Jordan's door, which was closed. I opened it and there he was in his green Chinese kimono with the gold dragon propped up in bed grinning at me. I was still sleepy. "Jordan . . . ?"

"No, I'm Gloria Okon for Pratfall, the new fun wax for the entire household!"

I looked outside the windows; it was still snowing. "No planes?"

"Are you kidding?" he asked. "You didn't think I'd abandon you up here in the frozen tundra!"

"But—I mean, you said goodbye and you were all dressed up and—"

"I was all dressed up to go down to the village and pick up the *Turandot* I ordered for you." He cocked his head and looked at me sideways. "You actually thought I was pulling out on you, didn't you?" It was obvious I had, so there was no use bluffing. "Dumbhead!" he said.

How about that! We sat in Jordan's room almost all day and I played the entire album of *Turandot* three times. We had a wild talk session covering God, sex, crime, war, etc., etc. I remember expressing one favorite theory of mine: that maybe if Jesus would bestir himself and make another guest appearance on earth everyone might straighten up and fly right for a while. To which Jordan replied, "Do you think Jesus was smart?"

"Above average, I'd say."

"There's your answer for why he's not making any more surprise appearances."

"How's that?"

"Look what they did to him the *first* time!" He held up his hands, palms facing me. "Those nails smart something fierce. He needs to be crucified *twice?*"

I remember it as an all-time great afternoon. Jordan on sex: If everyone were allowed to conjugate the verb with anyone they wanted, any time, any place they chose, the perverse compulsion would go out of sex and people would stop forcing themselves to

212

conjugate with chippies and small boys and chickens and raping eighty-seven-year-old women in basement laundry rooms and only do it with people they were really attracted to and cared about.

Jordan on war: If you believe in the Bible, it said "Thou shalt not kill." Period. Paragraph. It did not say "Thou shalt not kill except, but, unless or however . . ." Some more on war and human relations: If we don't get along with someone, why can't we just *not* talk; why do we have to go around tripping one another?

Jordan on homosexuality: Any man who says he wouldn't whack off with Cary Grant is either a liar or can't get it up.

Jordan on God: I believe in him with all my heart—because I'm scared shitless *not* to.

During the afternoon he hit on a plan. He found out that Dennis Vacarro and the Terrible Twins and he and I were the only students left on campus so he talked to Mrs. Rauscher and phoned Mr. Lomax Piper, letting them both off the hook for Thanksgiving dinner the next day, and reserving a table for the five of us at Thorgan's, to be his guests, of course.

Thanksgiving Day my back was feeling even better and Jordan and I took a walk down to the boathouse. The lake was frozen over and way out in the middle there were little, like outhouses, set up and lots of old geezers were perched out there fishing through the ice. They looked silly sitting out there on regular chairs in the middle of the lake. It was cold and windy so we cleared off the snow from one of the porch doors and went inside and sat talking for a while. The main floor of the boathouse was built up over a slip of water. In rowing days years ago the boats were brought right in and stacked up down there. An old dilapidated wood stairway led down to the slips and we could hear the ice creaking below us. We both agreed there was something spooky about that old boathouse in the winter. There was even a leftover smell of summer mildew that seemed to haunt the place. I remember Jordan telling me a ghost story his grandmother had passed on to him about her mother and I was not overly sad when he suggested we walk back up to school.

I never would have guessed I had a story coming up that would make his grandmother's look like something out of "Peanuts."

Jordan treated us to a great spread that evening at Thorgan's. There was night skiing going on with all sorts of lights strung down the mountain and it was all very New-England-Christmas-card-looking. Dennis Vacarro was visibly excited and the Terrible Twins were, too, except you got the feeling they were wondering what the pay-off was, like were they going to get stuck with the bill or both have to submit to Dennis or carry hot money over the border into Canada or something. Jordan and I got a kick out of the way they ordered. Rodney would say "Shrimp cocktail" and then Ronald would say "Shrimp cocktail," then Rodney would say "Cream of celery soup" and Ronald would say "Cream of celery soup," etc. As they went on, Jordan and I were looking at each other, building up suspense as to wouldn't one of them just differ in one thing, salad dressing or flavor of ice cream, but they stuck together, ordering like that through the entire full-course dinner. Why they just didn't ditto one whole order we didn't know.

When we left Thorgan's, Jordan had Cutler Barnum drop us off for a nightcap at the Flame Room. As we walked down the corridor with the cocktail lounge and Patti and the bar in sight through the glass doors, that's when the Terrible Twins' nostrils flared like they were being led to slaughter. It was obvious they'd never been in the Flame Room and weren't about to enter such a disreputable place now. When Jordan opened the door they both pulled back, dug in their heels and started talking at once. "Oh, well, we better get back." "Yes, we—oh, dinner was great, Jordan, but—" "Yes, yes, it was, but we don't drink and—" "No, we won't drink and, well, we really ought to get back."

Jordan took it easy with them, simply saying he'd like to have them join us but he'd understand if they didn't care to. They both fell all over themselves thanking him and took off like a couple of antelope.

Dennis Vacarro was fascinated, though, and Patti was in a high good mood and blasted into our Jack Armstrong entrance music.

Dennis couldn't take his eyes off her; he especially went for her "risqué ditties." His face was wide-open and he was really glowing. I realized he was actually quite good-looking when he didn't have that damp, furtive, hungry look about him. Several times he'd suddenly turn to us and say, "This is one of the best times I've ever had up here," or "This is one great Thanksgiving." Because Mr. Kauffman was away we didn't worry about getting back on time and we stayed until about one o'clock. We might have stayed later than that but a strange thing happened. Patti had finished her funny songs and was tinkling her way through some standards. She was singing "I Get a Kick Out of You" when suddenly a gulp came out of Dennis. He kind of choked it back, then a real sob burst out of him. I looked at him and the tears were streaming down his face. He put a hand up to his mouth, said a smothered "Excuse me!" and stumbled up from the booth and out the door. Jordan left a twenty-dollar bill on the table and was quick after him. I paid the check and by the time I met them outside Dennis was shaking his head and apologizing, saying what a rat he was and how it had been one of the best evenings ever. "Honest, you guys," he kept saying. What he did tell us was that "Kick out of You" was his father's favorite song and it just set him off hearing it.

Jordan put an arm over his shoulder and we walked back to school. It was a quiet, snowy, small-town night and nobody talked for a while. Then Dennis sighed and said, "Sometimes I wonder how beautiful nature can be and how unbeautiful people can be. Like me, all screwed-up. It's like I don't belong in it." I felt so for him I nudged him in the side with my elbow. Dennis went on talking, saying he'd gotten one postcard when his father first went to Key West. "Key West is the end of the line and your dad is here," it said, and he'd never heard another word from him.

As we neared school I saw the lights on in Mr. Hoyt's parlor. Right away I got nervous. I motioned toward the house and indicated to Jordan like it might be a good idea to take his arm from around Dennis' shoulder. Jordan caught on but he only laughed and kept walking the way he was. I had a hunch that when Mr.

Hoyt had got back to Saypool he'd checked the house and, when we weren't home, was probably watching for us.

Up on the second floor of Lincoln House, Dennis really got to me. He reached out, very formally, and shook hands with us, saying good night and thanking us. When he withdrew his hand he stood there for a minute and looked down at the floor. Then he looked up at us and smiled and said, "You guys are really my friends, aren't you?" We both said sure and then he gave us a bigger smile, shook his head and added, "I mean—you really are!"

"Till death do us part." Jordan laughed. Dennis laughed, too, and walked toward his room and we started up to our floor. "Hey," he said. We stopped and turned around. "You guys stay together, don't you?" he asked. I guess I looked confused, because he nodded his head up and said, "I mean—upstairs."

"No," Jordan said matter-of-factly.

He looked at us and hunched up his shoulders. "How come?"

"Just the breaks." Jordan shrugged.

"I would if I were you guys," Dennis said. "Don't you get lonesome?"

"Sometimes," Jordan said.

"At night I get so lonesome sometimes I . . ." He just stopped and contemplated the degree. After a while he looked down the hall. "Especially—you know, when everybody isn't here." He jabbed a finger at the door next to his. "Frank Dicer's room," he said. Then he smiled ruefully. "My floor's so empty I even miss Frank Dicer."

"Yes," Jordan said, "he's enchanting."

"Yeah." Dennis laughed. "Well, are you going to take showers or anything?"

"No," Jordan said.

"Oh . . . well, still—I'll probably come upstairs to brush my teeth. Okay?"

"Sure," we both said. When Jordan and I got up to the third floor I asked, "News of the Week in Review?"

"Yes, but after Dennis goes to bed," Jordan said.

216

After I brushed my teeth, I got into my pajamas and lay down on my bed. I heard Dennis come upstairs and I could hear Jordan and him talking in the john, their voices, that is, not their conversation. After a while I heard Dennis go downstairs and then Jordan came by my room. "Okay if we skip News of the Week?" I said sure and asked him if he felt all right. "Oh, yeah," he said. Then after a moment: "Dennis is going to stay with me."

"He is?" I said, sitting up in bed. "How come?"

Jordan shrugged. "I don't know. He didn't even ask. He wanted to ask so badly but he didn't. And that's what—He really got to me tonight." Jordan looked at me and I think he was waiting for me to say something, but I didn't. "Besides, what the heck—it's Thanksgiving," he added.

"Sure." I smiled at him. "Anyway, I've got my heating pad," I said, patting it with my hand. We both laughed and said good night. A little while after Jordan had gone I heard Dennis come upstairs. I got into bed with my heating pad and was just lying there thinking how much I admired Jordan and how great it was to have such an unusual friend when I heard the footsteps coming up the stairs. I was immediately frightened for Jordan but the steps came right down the hall and stopped in front of my room. There was a gentle knock and the door opened a crack. "Peter," Mr. Hoyt whispered.

"Yes?"

"I came by when I got back but you weren't in. I wanted to check on your back. How is it?"

"Much better."

"May I turn on the light?" he asked. I said yes and he did. Although he tried not to show he was scanning my room I could tell he was taking it in. "The doctor's coming tomorrow?" I said he was. "Good. I'm glad you're feeling better." I knew he'd seen us come back and I knew he was curious as to what we'd done. "I spoke with Mr. Piper," he said.

"We all went out to dinner," I told him, not wanting to talk much because I was so concerned about Jordan and Dennis that I

217

wanted to say something to throw him off the track, at the same time knowing the less I said the better it would be.

"Did the twins go, too?" he asked, and now I was positive he'd seen us come back and therefore had seen Jordan's arm around Dennis.

"Yes, we all went."

"I see," he said. "I'm glad you're feeling better," he repeated. "See you tomorrow." He switched off the light and closed the door. I lay there very still, listening to him walk down the hall and then stop outside Jordan's door. My heart was pounding for a second or two until I heard his footsteps go on downstairs and I could tell from the sound that he was going all the way down without stopping at the second floor and checking on Dennis. By that time I was damp from perspiration. I lay there for perhaps a minute but I just had to get up and move—from nervous relief.

I opened my door and stuck my head out just as Jordan poked his head out at the end of the hall. We looked at one another, sighed and smiled. Jordan stepped out into the hall, looked up at the Big Joker in the Sky and crossed himself. We both waved good night and went back into our rooms.

The next day Dennis was walking around on a cloud. I was curious, of course, to know what had taken place and if there'd been conjugating of any sort, which I guessed to be one-sided; still anyone that wouldn't be interested in the details wouldn't be human. But the gentleman in Jordan was always there. We discussed how we both felt when we heard the Reverend's footsteps and Jordan did say he and Dennis had talked until almost five that morning, but that was all. I knew if he wanted to say more he would have. I also didn't want to lose points by asking any leading questions.

My back was feeling pretty good but it was still a little stiff the next morning. In the afternoon Dr. Horton came by and gave me a good checking over, bending my legs and all, and then decided to take off the tape, which was a project I didn't enjoy. Mr. Hoyt arrived and Dr. Horton said it would be good for me to have an alcohol rubdown to stimulate circulation but not for several hours as my skin was still sensitive from having the tape stripped off. Mr. Hoyt said he'd see I got a rubdown and they left together.

That evening, Friday, Mr. Piper came over and had dinner with the Terrible Twins, Dennis, Jordan and me. He told stories of the time he spent in France and stayed on and we all watched television in the parlor together. He left around eleven and my back was feeling stiff by that time; I told Jordan I thought I'd get into bed with my heating pad. We'd spent the past two days together so there wasn't any need for News of the Week in Review and we said good night. I got into bed, switched on the heating pad and began to read, when I heard "the" footsteps.

Mr. Hoyt opened the door. He was carrying a large bottle and a towel but he was, as always, dressed in a dark suit. "Your rubdown, Peter." I'd completely forgotten about it; it also never occurred to me that he was going to give it. I told him he didn't have to bother, that I was using the heating pad and it felt pretty good. "Doctor's orders," he said, taking off his coat and rolling up his shirt sleeves. "We want you back in shape by the time school starts. Now, you'd better take off your pajama tops and get over on your stomach."

I don't have any kind of a complex about people touching me but the idea that he, Franklyn Hoyt, was going to be applying his hands to my back was something I never would have thought of in my wildest imagination. As I got into position and heard him drag over the desk chair and settle himself in it, I realized I was tensing up as much as if I were expecting a snake to be dropped on me.

"After all you've done for Gilford, the least I can do is give your back a rub," he said. The first splash of alcohol was cold. I shivered and made a little sound. He chuckled and I felt his huge hands on my back. I shivered again just from the size of them as he started to rub the small of my back. "Cold, I know." He sort of laughed and went on rubbing. Right away he started talking over the Glee Club competition. It was like we'd never discussed it and I guessed his enthusiasm for the performance had been cut in half by what happened that night at Thorgan's and now he was over that slight and it was released again. It was obvious he was still excited and impressed, and after he'd gone on about his reactions sitting out there in the audience, he asked me if I had stage fright as badly as I claimed how I'd dare to switch to an untested routine. I told him it was just timing and the mood of the audience and an intuition that the *real* Hamlet would be a disaster more than a feeling that the satire would be a smash. He was in a talkative mood as he went on rubbing my back with those huge hands of his. At one point it occurred to me—I'm having News of the Week in Review with Reverand Davidson! Finally the talk ran down and he asked if the massage made my back feel good. I told him yes and thanked him, thinking perhaps it was over, but then he put some alcohol up between my shoulder blades and started massaging my neck and shoulders. "You just relax, go to sleep if you can, Peter."

There was something gratifying in the idea that this man who had treated me like sewage when I first arrived was now making a special effort to rub my back. He didn't speak again and after a while I'm not sure whether I drifted off to sleep or just to that area where you're half in, half out. The next thing I was aware of was that he'd stopped. I remember lying there, my chest flat down on the sheet, my head turned to the wall, certain that he'd gone and vaguely thinking about getting up to turn off the light and putting on my pajama tops. But instead I just lay there for a while.

Then I must have actually gone to sleep because it was a light touch on my back that awakened me. For a second I thought perhaps Jordan had come in to find out what the Reverend had been up to, so I played it very cool and just continued lying there with my eyes closed. I felt it again, a finger lightly tracing down from my shoulder to the small of my back and then it was gone.

After a few seconds I turned my head the other way around and opened my eyes. Mr. Hoyt was sitting in the chair staring at my back, the same way he'd been staring at me that day up on the stage. I'm sure he was completely oblivious of the fact that I'd turned my head and was looking at him. His shoulders were slumped forward and his arms were hanging down between his

220

legs, hands clasped. As I watched him he smiled, not at me, but at my back, and raised his hand, slowly bringing it over toward me. Before he was just about to touch me, he glanced up and saw me looking at him. "Oh . . ." he said. He stopped smiling and withdrew his hand, clasping it with his other hand, between his legs again. He glanced down at his hands and then back up at me. He smiled again, not a tight rubber-band smile, but still a very brief little smile, and cleared his throat. "I'll be going now," he said very softly. He gathered up his things and slowly walked to the door. He opened it, started to go out, then remembered the light and flicked it off and left, closing the door gently behind him.

I listened to him walking down the hall, slowly, not at all the usual sounds of his footsteps, and then downstairs. I lay there for a long time, experiencing both a sad and an eerie feeling. For a while I considered going down to Jordan's room to talk it over but finally I just pulled the covers up over me and went to sleep.

18

I TOLD Jordan about it the next day, Saturday. When I finished he sat there very quietly. "What do you think?" I finally asked him.

"I think," he said, "you should have a bodyguard at all times."

"Oh, come on, now you're—"

"You asked me and I told you."

"But he's married, with a son," I said.

Jordan laughed. "So? What does that mean?"

"Besides, he's death on that sort of thing, you can tell."

"The real Reverend Davidson was death on loose women and look what happened to him."

"I don't like to think about it. How can you tell for sure?" I asked him.

"How can you be so naïve?" he asked me.

"I know, but some people are what they seem to be, no matter what it is. Others keep you—"

At that point Dennis barged in and we didn't continue. Also, I don't think I wanted to pursue it. I was starting to feel uneasy because I was beginning to believe there might be some truth to what Jordan said.

That afternoon I passed Mr. Hoyt as he was walking from his house to the school building. He was clipping along, using his trademark walk, and he shot me a very brisk "How's the back?" "Fine," I told him and on he went without another word, as if he only had a nodding acquaintance with me. His attitude was so different I wondered if I'd imagined the night before.

Jordan and I were going out to dinner that night. As we were coming downstairs, he dashed back up to get his glasses and I kept on coming down. When I stepped off the bottom landing I saw that Mr. Hoyt and Headley had come over to preside at dinner for the strays. They were in the dining room but they hadn't started eating yet. "Peter," Mr. Hoyt said, standing up and pulling out a chair next to him, just as Mrs. Rauscher came in from the kitchen with a platter of something and Jordan stepped down off the last step. The expression on Mr. Hoyt's face changed immediately. "We're going out to dinner," I said.

"I see." Then: "Whom did you sign out with?"

"Mr. Kauffman's not here," I said.

"Therefore you should sign out with me."

Jordan spoke up. "I told Mrs. Rauscher."

"Yes, he did," Mrs. Rauscher added.

"I wasn't asking you, Mrs. Rauscher," he said, without even looking at her, keeping his eyes on Jordan. "That was considerate to Mrs. Rauscher but not to the rest of us."

"I didn't think you'd want to be bothered," Jordan said, very straightforward.

"Bothered!" Mr. Hoyt snapped. He turned to Mrs. Rauscher, who was just standing there, and waved a hand at her. "Well . . . get on with the serving." He glanced back at Jordan. "Bothered?" he repeated.

"Yes," Jordan said, and I could tell he was angry about Mr. Hoyt's rudeness to Mrs. Rauscher. "Besides," he smiled very coolly and went on almost in his camp voice, "everyone knows Peter and I go out every Saturday night."

Now Mr. Hoyt was furious. "Whether everyone knows it or not you will sign out with your housemaster, and in the event he is not here—with me. Do you understand that?"

223

"Yes, sir," Jordan replied, pulling in.

"You may go now," Mr. Hoyt said.

As soon as we got outside I asked Jordan why in the name of God he had to say what he did. "I didn't like the way he spoke to Mrs. Rauscher."

"Yes, but why bait him? He's just going to take it out on us."

Jordan shrugged. "He's going to take it out on us anyway." Then he laughed. "What he'd like to do is take it out on *you!*"

"Oh, Subtle One," I said. Finally we both got to laughing but that evening was when it became most unfunny.

We got home about a quarter to twelve. My back had stood up fairly well for most of the day but it was tired from the double feature and wanted to lie down. Again Jordan and I skipped News of the Week in Review. I took a hot shower to relax my back and got into bed on top of the heating pad. I was feeling clean and snug and I knew I wouldn't even read. I went right off to sleep.

The next thing I knew, the lights were on and Mr. Hoyt was standing in the doorway with another bottle of alcohol and a large bathtowel. He was wearing a blue sweater with elbow patches, a blue shirt open at the neck, old gray flannels and tennis shoes. I suppose it was the combination of not expecting him at all, the unusual way he was dressed, and my complete sleepiness that convinced me I was dreaming. I must have smiled and I believe I even mumbled, "Hi, Rev."

"Smile on, fair Hamlet," he said, grinning back at me.

This did nothing to dispel my illusion and I just lay there grinning about having a dream based on the rubdown of the night before. He closed the door and walked over toward my bed, picking up my desk chair and bringing it with him. "Tops off," he said and I still grinned, going along with the dream. I undid the buttons, rolled over on my stomach and sort of tried to pull my arms out of the sleeves. He helped tug the tops off me in a sort of playful way. I giggled and he laughed, too. Then I remember smelling his bay rum and thinking what a detailed dream it was—I could even *smell* the Reverend.

224

"Jesus!" I shouted as I felt the icy splash of alcohol on my back.
"Peter!" he said.

I swung around and looked at him frowning at me. "Cold," I said
and I was truly masking my surprise that he was actually there in
person, all set to give me another rubdown. I guess I wasn't doing
such a good job of it because he said, "What is it, Peter?"

"The cold, it surprised me."

"Still, there's no excuse for that sort of language. Over," he said
and I flipped back on my stomach. "It's the company you keep.
You never used to speak like that." He'd only known me a short
time before Jordan came, so what was he talking about? "I've been
meaning to speak with you about this Legier boy. He's not your
sort." He started in on my back. "Not good company for you to
keep. Not good for the school, in fact. A boy like that, a spoiled,
decadent weakling. I'm surprised you've taken up with him." He
paused, then gave me a glancing swat on the back. "Did you hear
me?" Before I could even answer, he'd leaned down close by my
shoulder and repeated, "Did you hear me?"

"Yes, sir," I answered. He snorted, "That's better!" and I got a
definite whiff of liquor on his breath before he straightened up and
went on rubbing my back. Right away the danger sign lit up. I
wondered whether he was actually drunk or if he'd just had a drink
or two. I'd never heard any rumors about him and alcohol.

"I suppose you think a young man like that is sophisticated.
You'll discover as you get older there's a difference between true
sophistication and decadence, without regard for any of the moral
principles that govern decent conduct." I gathered I was in for a
lecture and no answers were required but then he said, "Are you
listening to me?"

"Yes, sir."

Another little swat on the back and a deep exhaling breath. "All
right, then!" Now I realized he'd either had more than one or two
or else he wasn't used to drinking and they'd gone to his head.
Although his speech was not noticeably thick, the snorts in between
phrases and the fact that he was not one to give playful swats were

225

giveaways. "At any rate," he went on, "you'd do well to slack off with him. There's nothing to be gained by a relationship with a person of his inclinations. Young as he is, he *is* what he *is* and nothing's going to change him. I suppose you think he's clever and amusing—well, don't you?"

"He does have a good sense of humor," I ventured.

"Hah—humor! It's a sickness. I won't even discuss it with you." Thank God, I thought. I was suddenly annoyed. I'd been all warm and comfortable in my sleep and now I was feeling cranky and—like when a dog or a cat's asleep and you insist he wake up and play, so you keep after him, blowing in his face, tickling his whiskers and talking *at* him.

Then he spoke in a completely different tone of voice. "Quiet . . . the school's peaceful when the boys are gone, isn't it, Peter?"

"Yes, it is."

"The first year Miriam—Mrs. Hoyt—and I came to Gilford, we stayed here all that summer. Such a quiet, peaceful summer it was." He stopped massaging and didn't say anything for a long while, as if he were summoning back the quiet of that summer. "Those early days . . ." More quiet, then he sighed. "Well, time turns back for no man, hmn . . ." He went on with the massage. "Sometime you must tell me about your childhood. Interesting how a boy with a background like yours turns out to have the right qualities and a boy like that, coming from wealth, with every possible advantage, turns out"—he hesitated, then said—"spotted with decay."

I wanted to say, simply: "He's a good friend." But I knew, although this was the first time he'd spoken to me of Jordan, there was no reasoning with him. I knew he hated him.

"How's the back?" he asked.

"Fine, I think it's all better," I said, hoping against hope he'd say, "Oh, in that case," and pack up and leave. I knew this session was leading to nothing but trouble.

No such luck. "Backs are tricky," he said, "but we'll get you

226

fixed up." Then he went to work seriously on me. Again he told me to relax and go to sleep. And I thought perhaps that would be the easiest way out. So I turned facing toward the wall and crossed my arms up over my head and told myself to go to sleep. I wondered if Jordan had heard Mr. Hoyt's footsteps and what he was thinking. No, don't wonder anything, just *go to sleep!* I might have actually made it if I hadn't become aware of Mr. Hoyt's breathing. At first I thought I was noticing the sound of it because we weren't talking, but I realized after a while it was definitely irregular and shaky. He put more alcohol on and gradually worked his way up my back toward my shoulders. By that time he was leaning over my head and his breathing sounded very heavy, as if it were being magnified. I could also smell his breath again. He stayed around my shoulders for a long time, working them vigorously at first, almost to the point of hurting, and eventually decreasing until he was kneading them gently, and finally he stopped.

But I could tell he was still leaning over me. Then he whispered my name. "Peter . . . ?" I was wide awake but I thought I'd pretend to be asleep and he'd undoubtedly leave. He leaned way over by my face and whispered my name again. I almost suspended breathing for the few seconds he remained close by my cheek, so close I could feel the heat from his face. I concentrated hard on not letting my eyelids flutter.

Then I sensed him pull away and heard him stand up. I felt a breeze of relief until I realized he hadn't taken a step, he was just standing there. I thought of cruelty to dumb animals again, why, I don't know. Come on, I thought, don't stretch it out. Finally he walked slowly over to the door and switched off the light. I'd hardly had time to give thanks when he walked back across the room and sat down again.

This threw me completely. The longer he sat there the more nervous I became. I could hear his breathing every so often but now it seemed regular, not heavy and shaky like before. Gradually I synchronized my breathing to go along with his, thinking that if I couldn't hear him I might forget he was sitting there and be able to

227

sleep. I might have known it wouldn't work because I was far too uneasy to sleep with him in the room. I sneaked my eyes open and was surprised at how light it was with the lights out. From my position I couldn't see out the window, but I could tell the moon was out from the night shadows on the wall and ceiling.

About that time I heard him moving on the chair and then another cold splash of alcohol hit the small of my back. It got the top part of my pajama bottoms wet and I felt his hands touch them, then tug them loose and peel them down a ways from my waist. I started to get panicky as he spread the alcohol around the top part of my backside.

I couldn't have been more awake now if I'd just taken an amphetamine spansule and hopped out of a cold shower. My mind was clicking away like crazy. All sorts of things: Mr. Hoyt, I sprained my *back,* not my ass—honestly. Because that's what he was rubbing now. And I was wondering how long he would keep at it, when he started to work up my back again. I was also wondering if he could possibly think I was asleep, because he was using very firm, circular strokes. In fact, if he kept it up I had the idea he'd rub the skin raw.

But he didn't. He stopped, picked up the bottle and dumped about a full pint in the small of my back so that it splashed right over my behind and trickled down in the crack, running down between my legs and wetting more of my pajama bottoms. He felt around with his hand, sort of grunted, as if to say, Um-hmn, they're wet all right, and then started tugging them down farther.

The marathon was on. I pressed down against the mattress with all my might, still pretending to be asleep, although you'd have to be under general anesthesia to sleep through that deluge. Nevertheless I was committed to sleep. He curled those huge fingers down under the waistband of my pajamas and, in spite of my efforts, managed to tug them all the way down off my backside, so they were finally resting halfway along my legs down by my knees.

And there I was—lying bare-ass in all my glory in the moonlight. He then slipped his hand down sideways between my legs. He

228

could feel the sheet was wet and then he started to work his hand up closer and I knew pretty soon he was bound to touch my testicles, which were also wet from the alcohol.

Just about then I realized I was getting an erection. I began to get terrified. First, I couldn't help wondering about the perversity of why I was getting it; but I didn't have too much time to spend on that, because what I was really terrified about was that he would find out, would somehow touch it, and that's what frightened me. Of course as soon as I realize it was happening and told myself not to get an erection, then it became fully hard instantly. Like that old saying: think of anything but a hippopotamus. If you think of a hippopotamus, you'll be killed. So, of course, all you see in your mind's eye is an entire thundering herd of hippopotamuses.

He was slow and gentle with his hand now as he kind of massaged the inner part of my upper legs, more squeezed and pressed against one side and then the other, than massaged them. I tried thinking of all sorts of things to lose my erection before he might get to it: people throwing up, whole *armies* throwing up into trenches, me throwing up, the Hiroshima Maidens, sharks, runover things on the highway, etc. Same old thing—hippopotamuses. Then he wiggled his fingers and touched my testicles, brushed a finger lightly against them and froze, just letting his hand rest there.

Talk about freezing. I think both of us stopped breathing. All I could think of was—what next? I was thankful that my erection was pointed upward under me toward my navel, instead of scrunched around sideways or even pointed backward as sometimes happens when you're sleeping.

Looking back on it, I'm sure what made me excited was not my wanting anything to happen, because I didn't, but a combination of knowing what *he* wanted and fear. I was frightened of him, frightened of his looks, that raised spot on his forehead and the size of his hands. Most of all, I was frightened of the unpredictableness of his actions and of the god-awful conflicts that must go on in his brain. And of the results, now that he'd been drinking.

I've read about danger making people sexy, of certain people

229

who can only do it in situations where they might be found out, like behind giant billboards right next to busy highways and in movie theaters and subway toilets, etc. So, lying there on the bed with Mr. Hoyt's hand wedged down between my legs and all sorts of thoughts racing through my head at one millionth of a second, it occurred to me that maybe I was a Danger Nut. Maybe I'd end up dragging little girls under train trestles and into hall broom closets. As if I didn't have enough to worry about.

It also occurred to me that in my panic that Mr. Hoyt's hand should do no further exploring, I had tightened my buttocks and maybe I was holding his hand there. Nobody could pretend to be sleeping with a tightened buttocks—as if they could pretend to be sleeping with their headmaster's fingers resting alongside their testicles, for God's sake! Still I was going to keep up the sleeping pretense, no matter what. Mainly because I couldn't figure out what else to do; the only alternative was to blow the whistle on him and I couldn't think of a right way to go about it. I began thinking how to relax my buttocks and legs without being noticed. I was concentrating on this feat when Mr. Hoyt suddenly let out a long sort of shaky sigh and I used the sound of the sigh to relax on, as if the sound of his own sigh would block off his sense of feel.

Still his hand rested there, all moist and slippery right up between my legs, but he was careful not to move his fingers at all, hadn't in fact, moved them an iota since they'd come to rest up against me where they were. After a while the two fingers that were touching me gave like a small tremor, then another larger one, a twitch, and he slid his hand out and away from me.

Now what, I wondered. He cleared his throat and I heard a little sucking wet sound as he parted his lips. I was positive he was going to say something and I dreaded whatever it might be because I knew I'd be no good whatsoever if I was called on to reply. But he didn't speak, just continued sitting there.

The town clock struck two. Two o'clock and all's *not* well. I squeezed my eyes shut and clenched my teeth. Make him leave! I wondered how long he'd been there. Over an hour, at least. As the clock was striking I was sure when he heard how late it was he'd go.

But those good old intuitions of mine were way out of whack that night. I heard the chair creak, and just as I was thinking, Hallelujah! I felt another large splash of alcohol on my back. This time I almost shouted out "No! No! Stop it!" It had gone on far too long and my nerves were unraveling and curling up at the ends. I could hardly believe he was going to stick with it. But he even poured another little splash on and that, together with the first, was enough to spill over my back, around my waist and run down under my stomach.

He went right after it, feeling around my waist, then patting the sheet and feeling the dampness, and pretty soon he'd started to work his hand down under my stomach. I pressed down again with all my might to keep him from getting under me but the alcohol made his hand so slippery he managed to get the ends of his fingers between the mattress and my belly. I had my arms folded up above my head and there was an iron railing running across the top of the bed with smaller iron tubing running down from it. I sneaked my hands around two of these and grabbed on for dear life, so I'd be able to hold my own and stay on my stomach because I could tell he was trying to get leverage to turn me over on my back.

Now I could hear his breathing again—heavy. He'd every so often slip his hand out from under me and work around my waist to my back, but then he'd get right back and slip it, flattened out, under my stomach again. My hands were gripping the metal tubing like I was holding on to a life raft in a monsoon and he was just about breaking his wrist trying to lift me up off the bed with that one hand under my stomach. I knew if he escalated the war and put both hands under me he could flip me over like a hot cake.

Then a crazy thing happened. My nerves finally snapped and I got completely punchy. I suddenly felt myself starting to giggle, way down inside of me at first, but I could tell it wanted to come out. It was a dangerous sensation and I couldn't account for it, which made it even more dangerous. Then I could feel his fingers wiggling under my stomach, very close to my erection, which even my increasing panic hadn't ruined, and on top of everything else I got just plain physically ticklish and I could feel my stomach heaving up and down.

Now I was swinging out of control and I had to act fast. The only thing to do was to pretend I was having a nightmare, which I promptly did. I quickly snorted and shifted my weight around and had a few mild convulsions and muttered incoherently, as if to say: "What? . . . Huh? . . . Where am I? . . . Hmn. . . . Oh oh, yeah. . . ."

That did it. The minute I started he withdrew and I could feel him sitting there watching me. When I quieted down he said my name softly again. "Peter?" But I didn't reply. I was so afraid of any words between us. I was thinking of what it would be like when we saw each other in the cold light of day, when school had come to life again—that if we hadn't documented the experience with words we could pretend it hadn't really happened. Otherwise how do you look at someone? What eyes do you use? And even more crucial—how do they look at you?

So, instead of turning around and sitting up and even saying something like, "Oh, Mr. Hoyt, I was asleep . . ." I just lay still like I'd gone off again, figuring he would certainly leave now. Also, I was sure he couldn't have any rubbing alcohol left, not the way he'd been throwing it around.

But as soon as I'd settled down from my "nightmare," I felt his hands on my back again. Only now, there was a difference; it was like they didn't know what they were doing there. Then the weirdest thing happened. I felt his fists clench up and rest on my spine, and for a second I thought he was going to smash them down on me. I couldn't help stiffening. But then I heard a long, shaky, almost shuddering sigh come out of him and his fists disappeared and I felt the palms of his hands once more. I could feel next the weight as he leaned over and put his head down on top of his hands.

He sighed again, a smaller sigh, maybe it was just an expelling of air because of his condition, and I could feel his breath graze my back. After while he raised his head off his hands and with several fingers brushed away a small spot on my back, as if he were clearing a little area of sand.

Then he bent down and kissed that spot. Not a real out-and-out kiss, just pressed his lips gently against the small of my back, left them there a second, during which I stopped breathing completely, and then he stood up.

I heard his feet catch on the chair and the scrape of it on the floor and then he left the room and I listened to his footsteps go along the hall and fade away down the stairs before I finally turned around and sat up in bed.

He hadn't even closed the door. After a while I got up and shut it. On the way back I stepped on something. I turned on my desk lamp and saw the towel all bunched up on the floor and the empty bottle of alcohol. I picked them up. The towel was monogrammed with his initials: F.P.H. I don't know why, but I put it and the bottle in my closet behind my suitcases.

When I got back into bed I was filled with such a strange feeling I couldn't fall sleep. I heard the town clock strike three and then four. I couldn't get over the thousands of miles of difference between the way he acted around school and the way he was that night—especially that kiss on my back. Now I knew for sure he was a deeply troubled man and, most of all, I felt that the relationship between us was full of danger.

19

THE NEXT MORNING, Sunday, Jordan came to my room way before it was time to get up. I could just about manage to open my eyes. "I heard the Reverend *as*cend, I was awake reading for over an hour, but I never heard him *de*scend." Jordan glanced around the room. "In the closet?" he asked.

"No." I was so groggy I could barely smile. "But I've got headlines for News of the Week in Review."

He hummed the Fate Theme from *Carmen,* ending up with "You look beat."

"I am. I'm going to sleep some more."

"See you when you get up." Jordan started toward the door, but then turned back. "You okay?" I nodded. "The Rev didn't violate you?"

"Not quite," I said.

Jordan let out a low whistle. "Holy Smoley—don't sleep *too* long, hear?"

I got up after eleven. As soon as I'd scrounged up some breakfast, Jordan started to haul me up to his room but I suggested we walk down to the boathouse. I didn't want to chance seeing Mr. Hoyt if he happened to come around. Mainly because when something like that happens you're bound to look at someone with different eyes and I wanted time to rehearse keeping my eyes the way they were before.

We sat all huddled up in the boathouse and I told Jordan the entire episode, with one exception: I didn't say anything about feeling sorry for Mr. Hoyt because of the way Jordan had reacted when I first told him about the Hamlet thing. He was a great listener, no smart remarks or interruptions, just fastened his eyes on you and let you pour it out. When I got through he looked down at the planks on the floor and shook his head. "The poor Rev."

"You say it like you just found out," I said. "You told me—"

"Yes, but he's in bad shape," he replied. Again I told Jordan how it just didn't figure, with him being so up-tight about things like that. "Exactly why it does figure," Jordan said. "Like guys who don't have a problem, if they come into contact with anything homosexual, they can just shrug it off. They can even have friends who swing that way and it doesn't drive them up the wall. But someone with a little iggie about it, who's fighting it off, they're the ones always screaming about the 'goddam faggots' and beating them up."

"But what about the guy who killed himself here? The Reverend's never gotten over that little episode, so how could he ever—"

"Sure he's never gotten over that. *Especially* that. What about those two guys? Nobody would have ever called them 'fruits'—they were attractive, popular, masculine. All his years at prep schools, the Rev must have seen a lot of non-fruity guys he thought were fooling around. I'll bet way deep down a little voice keeps nattering away at him: 'Hmn, it might not be all *that* bad. Maybe the Greeks had something there.' But this isn't Greece; it's the good old ballsy, arm-punching U.S.A. Even worse for him. I mean, for God's sake, the Rev's in charge of turning today's boys into tomorrow's men! So how long can you keep a little iggie like that bottled up? That's a bad trip to be on—a long one, too."

"You really think?" I asked.

"I really think," Jordan said. Then he looked me in the eye. "I feel sorry for him."

"Jesus, so do I." He must have seen the relief on my face; I was glad to hear Jordan say that. "What should I do?" I asked.

"Don't sprain your back again, that's number one."

We both laughed and I said, "How about me getting an erection?"

"Didn't you know?" Jordan said. Then he glanced around the boathouse and spoke in his purry, secret Southern voice. "Baby, we're all animals! Animals is what we are. It's a wonder we're not all running around bare-ass, sniffing at one another and peeing on everything in sight!"

We discussed Mr. Hoyt for a while longer and both decided the probability of another incident was slim, that what had happened was a freakish slip. What we had coming up, however, was worse than if there'd been a reoccurrence. Surprise—just when you're expecting one thing, you can be sure when you turn the corner you won't find it. You'll find another. It's the old shell game, and if anyone knows how to run it, it's the Big Joker in the Sky.

I didn't see Mr. Hoyt all day. I should add that I wasn't exactly looking for him. In the evening the rest of the boarding guys started trickling in from vacation, good old Mr. Kauffman was back, and by ten there was the usual amount of noise and horsing around. About a half hour after lights-out, there was a crash and slamming around down on the second floor you wouldn't believe. It came from Herb Sloan and Warren Glover's room at the end of the hall and sounded, from the yelling and crashing, like someone was trying to break in a wild stallion. I met Ed Anders in the hall and we picked up Jordan, who was just coming out of his door, and went down. Mr. Kauffman was banging on their door with both fists and shouting, "Boys! Boys! Stop it, stop it at once!"

By this time Dennis and Jimmy Greer were there and Ed was taking over, yelling for them to open up and cut it out. Jordan and I looked at each other because Herb and Warren were both good friends and kind of quiet and dull and the noise coming from their room was incredible. There was another crash and a scuffle and we heard Frank Dicer screaming "You bastards! You pricks!" Finally the door was unlocked by Lee Galonka, of all people, and there was Frank Dicer pinned down on the floor by Herb and Warren. Frank was the only one who seemed mad, so mad that tears were running down his cheeks. The other guys were excited because it was obvious he'd tried to beat all three of them up, but they were really looking amused beneath the surface.

As soon as we went in the room they let go of Frank, who immediately took a wild swing at Herb and was prevented from a swipe at Warren by Ed, who bent Frank's arm behind his back and hustled him out with Frank screaming "You turds! You bastards!" etc. There was a flurry of postfight excitement but nobody would tell what caused it. Lee and Herb and Warren would only snicker and say they'd just gotten into a fight, which was obvious, and all Frank Dicer would do was curse them out. Mr. Kauffman couldn't get anything from them, so he finally made us all go to our rooms for another try at lights-out.

Jordan and I were itching to know what had happened; all we knew was that the three of them, everyone in fact, hated Frank Dicer. But none of them were scrappers, so what were they doing locked in a room with him? Mr. Kauffman was patrolling the halls, clucking and fussing, so although I knew Jordan and I would have to have News of the Week in Review, I knew it would have to wait until Mr. Kauffman was tucked away in his room on the second floor.

By the time I got to Jordan's room he'd got the whole story from Lee Galonka in the john. The heat in Lincoln House was turned off and Jordan told me to pile into bed, which I did. Then he told me what it was all about. Frank Dicer was always teasing Lee Galonka, and calling Herb "Eight Eyes" because he wore bifocals, and referring to Warren as "Dopey" because he was short and had big ears and a wild-looking grin. So Herb had met a friend over the holidays who went to Andover and told him of a trick they pulled on a hated character there. A little game called "Circle Jerk."

They got to talking to Frank before lights-out about masturbating and how fast they could "come." Frank Dicer would always

237

claim he could do anything better, bigger and faster than anyone else. So Herbie said why didn't they, after lights-out, forgather and each put five bucks in the kitty, sit around in a circle in the dark on the floor and each one masturbate. The first one to come was to announce himself and he'd collect the money. Sordid as this sounds, the contest was entered into. When the lights were out, the other three all made a lot of noise, pounding their fists against their legs and heavy breathing, but they actually didn't even undo their pajamas. When Frank Dicer yelled the magic words, Herb quick flicked on the lights and there Frank was in all his glory. Warren made a face at the sight and shoved the kitty at him, saying, "Take the money and see a psychiatrist. You must have some kind of a problem, jerking off in public like this."

That crack, together with the fact that none of them had even begun and were all just sitting around grinning that Frank had been duped, drove him crazy and that's when he tried to beat them all up.

Jordan and I got a huge kick out of what had happened and we lay there awarding A-plusses to Larry Olivier, Herb and Warren. About that time we heard footsteps and doors opening on the second floor and then we recognized the voices of Mr. Hoyt, Mr. Kauffman, Frank Dicer and Herb and Warren. It was obvious Mr. Kauffman had run to Mr. Hoyt, who was trying, we could hear, to get Frank Dicer to admit they'd been gambling (Frank was a known cardshark) in Herb and Warren's room. Jordan laughed and said, "He'd mess himself if he knew the real reason." Frank was saying no, they were just arguing, and Mr. Hoyt wanted to know what about and why in that room with the door locked. A lot of mumbling and then Mr. Hoyt was coming upstairs, telling Mr. Kauffman to stay there and swearing he'd get to the bottom of it.

Jordan and I froze in bed. We heard Mr. Hoyt walk down to Lee Galonka's room and go in. "What if he happens to look in on me?" Jordan whispered he didn't think after last night he would, besides I wasn't involved in this. We lay there quietly; all we could hear were faint voices and after a while Mr. Hoyt left Lee's room and walked very quickly back down the hall to what we thought were the stairs. Instead, the door was flung open, Mr. Hoyt said, "Jordan Legier!" and he switched on the lights. There we were, lying side by side in bed.

The look on his face will always be with me. First surprise, turning quickly to shock, then the coldest, most angry, knowing look I've ever seen. He just stood there staring at us, aiming a laser beam that could have sliced steel. After a while he began nodding his head up and down like a judge who'd just decided on the verdict —guilty—and also the penalty—death. I glanced over at Jordan, who was sitting up slightly. I was still lying down prone, being too frozen to move. Jordan was looking, on the surface at least, as cool as ever and when he saw me looking at him he even smiled slightly. Mr. Hoyt then made a little snorting sound.

Still no one spoke and I was wondering when someone would, although I had a hunch it wouldn't be me. Time ticked on and Jordan finally said, "Won't you come in?"

"Don't speak to me that way!" Mr. Hoyt hissed, although Jordan had said it very straight, no shadings whatsoever.

"Sorry," Jordan said very seriously.

Mr. Hoyt snapped his head to me, fixing me with a narrow-eyed stare. It suddenly struck me this was the first time I'd seen him since the night before and all sorts of unhealthy thoughts started colliding in my head. "Sit up! You might at least have the—Sit up!" he shouted at me.

I sat up quickly as I heard a door open down the hall and Wiley Bevan say, "What the hell's going—" but he must have seen Mr. Hoyt because he broke off and shut the door immediately.

Mr. Hoyt looked back at Jordan and started nodding his head again. "I might have known. I might have known."

"You might have known what?" Jordan asked coolly, yet seriously.

"Careful, young man—careful! You'll be sorry enough about this as it is without giving me any smart talk!"

"Sorry enough about what?" Jordan asked as I heard someone coming upstairs.

"That's *enough!*" Mr. Hoyt shouted, taking a step into the room and swinging the door shut after him. "You'll speak to me only when requested and not until!" He was furious; his breathing was shaky and I was praying Jordan wouldn't answer him back.

There was a knock and Mr. Kauffman said, "Mr. Hoyt?" Mr. Hoyt snatched the door open as Mr. Kauffman said, "I was wondering if—"

"Look at this!" Mr. Hoyt snapped, waving an arm toward us. "This should give you something to *wonder* about. A pretty sight, isn't it?" Mr. Kauffman's face was registering the proper amount of shock. "A pretty sight indeed! Did you have any idea, Mr. Kauffman, that dirty little games such as this—"

"The dirty little games are in your mind," Jordan said, not sarcastically, just straight-on. Even so, it was enough to make me almost wet the bed.

"Quiet! You be *quiet!* Mr. Hoyt boomed, and you could almost see the flames coming out of his nostrils. Mr. Kauffman took a step backward and winced. Now Mr. Hoyt was so livid I thought he'd explode right there and splatter all over the walls. "Go to your room," he said to me. "The two of you be at my house at seven-thirty." It was obvious he was too enraged to have any further discussion that evening. I scooted out of bed and out the door and he practically stepped on my heels as I was leaving. He whizzed down the stairs without another word and I heard the front door slam from my room.

I needn't add this was a second night of little sleep. In spite of being innocent of the charge I knew Mr. Hoyt was harboring against us, I still felt guilty. I knew what he was thinking: that I had played it cool the night of the rubdown and then turned around and went to bed with Jordan, which was literally true but not biblically. I was dreading the A.M. meeting and I'm not sure I wouldn't have preferred facing Mr. Hoyt alone rather than with Jordan, whose calm and bravery and, in a way, insolence in front of Mr. Hoyt only made me more aware of my own cowardice, besides making me nervous Jordan might say something that would cause a real earthquake, like: "I hear rubdowns are all the rage this year!"

By the way, how Mr. Hoyt happened to come to Jordan's room: He'd tricked Lee Galonka by telling him that although none of the principals in the fight would admit it, he knew for a certainty what they were up to. Unbeknown to Lee, he was referring to gambling, but Lee, in his dumbness, thinking Jordan had squealed, said something about: "Oh, I hope you don't believe that nutty story Jordan Legier told you." Whereupon Mr. Hoyt came straight to Jordan's room to find out what story that was. Our little scene took precedence, however, and nobody heard much more about the fight, except for underground word spreading among the students.

I was awake at six, so I could be sure to get a good hour or so of heavy worrying under my belt. No use wasting precious daylight hours in sleeping. I waited until six-thirty and went to Jordan's room. Sound asleep. I made about three trips, like every ten minutes, before I finally awakened him. When I did, he appeared to be sleepily content. "Jordan, what are we going to tell him?" I asked.

"The truth." He smiled at me.

"Oh, boy, I'm glad I caught you before we went over. I feel so much better just talking it over with you," I said facetiously.

"Good, any time you're in the neighborhood drop around." He grinned.

"No, honestly—what will we say?"

"Bulldog, we can't know that until we know what *he's* going to say."

"Promise me one thing—no matter how angry you get, don't bring up the rubdowns." The second I was saying it I knew I was off-base. Jordan stopped smiling.

"What do you think I am?" he asked. "That's your affair—sorry about the word—not mine."

When we were cleaning up I could tell the guys in Lincoln House knew something was up, but they weren't sure what, and the Dicer incident clouded things, which was all right with me. Walking over to Mr. Hoyt's, I asked Jordan if he wasn't nervous. "Yes, a little, but only because he's crackers," he said, using the English term we both got a kick out of.

Mr. Hoyt was ready to pounce. The second we stepped onto the porch the door was snatched open. "In there," he said, indicating his study. He was still coldly furious. We walked in and sat in chairs in front of his desk and he sat down behind it. He looked from one to the other of us, a look again of contemptuousness, and then started in. He was holding in his anger as much as possible but it prickled behind each word as he told us he knew what we were up to, and *had* been up to ever since Jordan arrived, that it was as obvious as it was disgusting, that he, as headmaster, would not tolerate such degeneracy, that the school had a reputation to uphold, etc. He said he'd considered holding us up as an example to the other students, but he'd decided that would only undermine the morals *and* morale of the school which this year was doing so well in the league that he didn't want to shake the foundations by "airing this nasty little scandal."

As he went on I couldn't believe that the same man who'd come to my room drunk only two nights ago and gone through that entire pitiful, horny rubdown scene was speaking this way in front of me. My mind became crammed with thoughts: Could he actually believe I wasn't aware of what that rubdown had nearly turned into? And if Jordan and I were as intimate as he'd decided, could he possibly imagine I hadn't told Jordan about it? Then, suddenly, there was no more worrying about Jordan bringing it up and I was the one who felt a voice inside wanting to yell out: "Jesus, what about *you!* Who do you think you're talking to? How can you be such a phenomenal hyprocrite!" It was then I thought if he'd completely erased from his mind his own behavior—well, I could only think of words like psychopath and schizoid.

After a while, something—his change of tone, I suppose—caused me to tune back in to him. He'd talked some of his anger away and was speaking now in the righteous manner of a headmaster (or Reverend Davidson), putting most of the blame on Jordan, saying he was older than me and more experienced, that he had undoubtedly indulged in all sorts of questionable practices, that he had thought I was more decent, but I was obviously weaker and more impressionable than he'd imagined. Toward the end he turned to

242

me and said, "Peter, your part in this messy business comes as a grave disappointment to me."

He wound up saying we had better watch our steps, that we were on probation, that we were forbidden to ever be in each other's rooms after lights-out and he strongly suggested we keep out of each other's rooms at any other time. He said he was being lenient but this was his one and only warning, that any further insubordination by either one would result in that person's expulsion. When he was finished he just sat there staring at us. Now he was looking almost pleased with himself. He picked up a pencil and turned it over in his fingers. Then, focusing on Jordan, he said, "What have you got to say for yourselves?"

Jordan smiled. "I would have thought you would have asked that first. It's too late now. You've said it all."

Mr. Hoyt slammed the pencil down on his desk and was on his feet. "You don't even bother to deny it then. You sit calmly in front of me with a smile on your—"

Jordan was on his feet, standing right in front of him. "There is nothing to deny. The only rule we've broken is to be in each other's rooms after lights-out. If you want an apology for that—"

"You lie! In bed together like that! And you tell me—"

"I do not lie." Jordan stood right up to him. "I'm sure I've done many things you'd disapprove of—there's no use going into that— but having anything to do with Peter in the way you're suggesting is not one of them." He paused and looked him straight in the eye. "I tell you that."

"You're a very cool, collected young man, a very cool liar."

"I do not lie," Jordan repeated. Then he braced his hands on the desk, leaned in toward Mr. Hoyt and took a deep breath. "I wouldn't bother lying to you."

Mr. Hoyt had slapped him so quickly and I had stood up just as quickly and shouted "Stop it!" that the moment was over before I knew it had happened, and I was standing there, wondering if it *had* happened. We all just stood there, the three sides of a lopsided triangle. I glanced at Jordan's face. It was like a piece of amused

243

rock. Oh, God, what a look! Nobody spoke. Finally Jordan said, "I'll be leaving now."

Mr. Hoyt got a strange expression on his face. "Not the school, you won't," he said warningly.

"Oh, no," Jordan said. "Leave Gilford?" And he turned and began walking out. "It's an en*chan*-ting place. En*chant*-ing atmosphere," he added and he was gone.

Jordan had come out on top in some weird way and I was left standing there, wanting very badly to hold up my end. Mr. Hoyt looked at the door for a long time before he turned to face me and waved an arm out after Jordan. "Oh, Peter," he said, shaking his head, "that boy, can't you see what a—"

"He's my friend," I surprised (and pleased) myself by saying.

He looked at me for a second, then jerked his head back like the remark had stung him on the end of his nose. "Get out!" he said.

I turned and left.

20

IN A COUPLE of days it was December, only a few weeks until Christmas vacation. Now we went into a strange period with Mr. Hoyt; I don't believe any words were exchanged between him and either Jordan or me. Although we rarely had News of the Week in Review after lights-out, our friendship grew even stronger. Twice Mr. Hoyt checked on me. Once I was asleep when the light awakened me and I squinted over at him. He turned the light out and shut the door without saying a word. The second time, I was reading after hours when I heard his footsteps coming up the stairs. I switched off the bed lamp and was just lying there when he opened the door and turned on the overhead light. I stared at him and he stared at me for a few seconds and again he left without words.

Things hit a snag for my father in California and the play he was supposed to do in the East was postponed again. But I got a letter saying Milton Bigelow had staked him to a trip to New York and he'd arrive the 20th of December and we'd spend Christmas together. I wasn't looking forward to this. When he's not working, my father is distracted and unhappy and that's when the heavy drinking is liable to start. I discussed this with Jordan, who said I'd be more than welcome to come to New Orleans with him. If my father had been rehearsing and busy, this would have been fine, but

I felt I couldn't leave him when he would need someone around. Then about the middle of December I got a call from my father, all excited because he'd gotten a couple of weeks' work in a picture to be filmed partly in the Philippines. He was to play a retired admiral and he was leaving the next day. They'd told the cast and technicians they'd try to get back to California for Christmas but it depended upon the shooting weather. He'd send me money for the trip to California and I could come out and see all my friends (?) and stay in the apartment until he came home. This plan filled me with emptiness. I told him, as long as it was uncertain, I had a good friend who'd invited me to his family for Christmas. He said that was fine, then suddenly moaned, "So, you don't want to see your poor old dad, eh? Oh . . . oh, dear, bread and beer," in a senile, quavering voice that was part of a humorous act he'd put on. We laughed and he said by all means to go with Jordan, that he'd send me a check for the trip. He was so excited to be working I knew he wouldn't be upset at my suggestion.

So Jordan and I made our plans. About five day before the start of vacation, Jordan had a letter from the one brother he loved, saying he and his wife were going on a Caribbean cruise over the holidays and wouldn't be home with the family. This was a Friday and Jordan was upset. At Thorgan's that night he was very quiet, just sat there sipping his drink and looking out at the night skiing. Suddenly he let out a little sound and shook his head. "What's the matter with me? Listen, Bulldog—you can't be serious about spending ten whole days in New Orleans with my *family*."

"Sure," I said, confused.

"Oh, you might get a kick out of *meeting* the Little Foxes, but ten whole *days* with them!"

"What are you talking about?"

"Let's take up where we left off Thanksgiving, go to Boston, then maybe down to New York."

That was fine by me, great in fact. I asked if he was serious and he assured me he was. Although I was curious to see his parents in action I was sure I wouldn't be falling in love with them. I asked him if he could get out of going home easily. He laughed and snapped his fingers. "No problem," he said. Then his face changed expression so quickly I almost did a double take. On the surface was a kind of bemused expression, wry smile and all, but bleeding through was a vulnerable— I only looked at his eyes for a fraction of a second. I couldn't have looked longer; I would have felt like a Peeping Tom. "I don't suppose there'll be any great slashing of wrists," he said. I knew from the way he said it, no matter how unaffected he pretended to be, way down deep the idea that he could easily get out of going home to the Little Foxes hurt him.

So we planned to take in Boston for a week and then move on to New York. My father sent me a check for one hundred and eighty-six dollars; how he arrived at that figure I'll never know. I'd given Jordan back his Thanksgiving money but I still had most of my summer money so I was in good shape. In the mail arrived a Christmas card signed, "Merry Christmas—Louise." (Wiley Bevan's waitress.) A check for five hundred dollars fell out of it, Jordan's check. I went right to his room and we entered into a big hassle about that and I gave it back. It popped up that night stapled to my French lesson, right inside the book. I then tore it up, hauled a chair down the hall, climbed up and threw the pieces through the open transom above the door. To my surprise Jordan didn't say a word about the money that evening or the next morning. In the afternoon, during study period, he walked up to Mr. Hines's desk, spoke to him and was excused. I was worried that he wasn't feeling well. Soon as classes were over I tore up to the third floor, but he wasn't in his room.

I walked down the hall to my room and when I opened the door all you could see was green stuff, dollar bills all over the bed, the desk, covering the floor, on the window sills, hanging from the curtains, in the wastebasket. I quickly shut the door and fell down on the bed howling with laughter. Five hundred one-dollar bills! Then I heard Jordan laughing in the closet. When he came out and we were gathering up the money, he explained that I'd accepted an invitation to stay at his house and since the invitation was rescinded and switched to another locale I was manner-bound to accept the same hospitality. This argument, together with the gesture of going to the bank and buying five hundred one-dollar bills, made me accept. Even so, I felt uneasy and knew I'd use up my own money first before dipping into his.

There were several Christmas functions and a party before school let out, and although Mr. Hoyt was still ignoring us on the surface, I could feel his eyes when I wasn't looking at him. He was treating us as outcasts and Jordan dubbed us the Terrible Twins II. I wondered if he'd learn of our fairly unorthodox plans, but that seemed unlikely, what with the confusion and high holiday spirits the last few days of school. The day we left I'll admit I was on the lookout for him when we went down to meet Cutler Barnum, but he wasn't in sight. Cutler told us on the way to the train that Mrs. Hoyt had come back home for Christmas vacation that day and that she was going to a rest home in Connecticut when school started.

I'll do my best to make short work of the Christmas vacation. It's necessary to give you a few high points and the over-all impression so you'll know to what extent the time spent with Jordan heightened the loss that was to come so soon and was responsible in large degree for what happened to Mr. Hoyt.

Oddly enough, summoning up words to describe it is not easy; because every moment, perfect as it was, is gone and sorely missed and deeply remembered and you wonder if the good times will ever return. Setting down the bad times isn't nearly as difficult. Put them down, explain them, and try to forget them. You certainly don't miss them like the good times. I'll try to make them brief, like a list.

Boston item: A party given by some former school friends of Jordan's in Cambridge where, when we entered, they all lit up like sparklers. You could tell the way they felt about him; they were all over him like hot soup.

Walks, museums, fine restaurants, shopping, presents you wouldn't believe, great talks always, and people-watching. Jordan and I would sit in the lobby of the Statler an hour at a time and watch all the nutty, funny, strange, sad, happy people go by and make up stories about them.

Christmas Eve item: A tryout musical based on *A Tale of Two Cities* with tons of scenery and revolving stages that got stuck three times and shook and shuddered and gave the singers and dancers the carefree, devil-may-care appearance of earthquake victims, and a leading man who got progressively drunk during the show and ended up screaming "Shit, shit, shit!" during a crowd scene in which he must have thought he couldn't be heard but could. It was such a stupendous disaster we almost went back to see it again.

Evening of December 26: Jordan had a date with a former girl friend and asked if I'd mind if they went out alone, but he said would I please be in our room by eleven, there was a chance of joining them at a party. At eleven-fifteen there was a knock on the door. I opened it and an extremely pretty girl, brown hair, big brown eyes, fair skin, small perfect nose, pretty, pretty, pretty, was standing there with a Pan Am bag. "I'm Peggy," she said in a tiny voice. "Poor Peter, Jordan told me about your back," she went on, walking right into the room and taking off her coat, "so Peggy's here to give you a rubdown." I laughed and she asked what was so funny. Then I thought it was some kind of a joke and I'd better go along with it, so I just followed her directions and stripped to my shorts and lay down on the bed. She got right to work on my back —such tiny hands she had—and any minute I was expecting Jordan and his date to come in, which was probably an added reason why I got excited so fast, and after about five minutes of massage she suddenly fell down on top of me, clinging to my back and kissing my shoulders and saying, "Oh, pretty Peter, pretty Peter. Peter's back is made of satin." The next thing she was getting out of her clothes and then we were kissing and she was mumbling, "Make patty-cakes with Peggy, make nice patty-cakes with Peggy," and soon we were conjugating the verb and I realized it was no joke.

(I had had one previous conjugation with a nymphomaniac coed from UCLA who had approached Boots about me at State Beach, but it was extremely sordid. Boots had hardly introduced us when she dragged me right out of the surf and into one of those tacky one-room linoleum beach apartments in Santa Monica. She knocked me down the minute we got in the door. She was bigger than me and forceful, even overpowering, clawing and biting and bouncing me up off her until I thought I'd crack my head on the slanted ceiling and both of us sandy and damp and covered with sun-tan oil. I had no control over the event. It was like doing it with a lady tumbler and I was one of the barrels she was flipping about.)

Peggy was different, like a little girl, soft and croony and so tiny she made me feel like a lumberjack, which was not bad in that situation, and when we finished she still clung to me and caressed my back, saying, "Peter makes good patty-cakes." Then she said she had to get cleaned up and did I feel up to making a "goodbye patty-cake" in the shower with her. I did and we did, which turned out to be a little more complicated than the first patty-cake, but she was extremely agile and it was successful nevertheless. Afterward, she dressed, packed up her Pan Am bag, thanked me for the nice patty-cakes and kissed me goodbye with one last "Pretty Peter" and was gone, saying she didn't want to be late for her next appointment, which remark I was grateful she left for the end. She arrived at eleven-fifteen; it was now only seven of twelve and we'd had a massage and two patty-cakes, one under the shower. I had to lie down. I was dizzy.

Jordan didn't show up until the next morning. "How's the back?" he asked, which brought on a quick News of the Week in Review and the information that she was known as Baby Peggy (there was a silent-film star named Baby Peggy), actually twenty-eight, who worked for a madam that can be reached by calling the Around-the-Clock Answering Service. She would be a good heterosexual character witness, being that she praised the patty-cakes.

Last Boston item: That afternoon Jordan was reading *The New York Times* when he suddenly let out a gasp, looked at his watch and said he had to make a few private phone calls and would I

mind leaving the hotel room and maybe go people-watching for fifteen minutes. This was unusual for him, but I quick got out and
took the magazine I was reading down to the lobby. About a half
hour later I was paged to the house phone. It was Jordan. "Christ,
Peter, will you get up here and pack! We've got to catch the six
o'clock shuttle to New York!"

He sounded truly excited. It was already ten after five. He was
almost packed by the time I got upstairs. "What's up?" I asked, but
he just said he had to get to New York and to get a move on. When
we'd checked out and piled into a cab, he leaned forward and said
in his most grave Southern voice, "Sir, my friend's mother was in
that awful elevator accident down in New York. She's not expected
to last the night. I'd appreciate your getting us to the airport as
quickly as possible."

"Yes . . . yes," the cabbie said, glancing back at me. "Elevator accident?" he asked. "Yes," Jordan said, wincing and patting
him on the shoulder as if to say: "You understand, it's too brutal
to discuss in front of him." The cabdriver practically drove over
cars and under trucks and we made the six o'clock shuttle. As we
got on the plane, Jordan said, "Sorry to use your mother, but I
didn't want to put my mouth on anyone living." The trip is short
but it was foggy in New York and we circled for almost fifteen
minutes before landing. By this time Jordan was in a highly agitated state. He raced two ancient ladies to a cab, yanking me along
with him and shoving me inside right ahead of them. The cabby
had seen this and was just about to open his mouth when Jordan
reached up with a clutching hand and panted, "Sorry, but my friend
here—little sister fell out of a four-story window—not expected to
last much longer—could you please get us to Sixty-fifth and Broadway right away!" The driver expelled a hissing sound of regret
through his teeth, said "Yeah . . . yeah . . . sure!" and took off
with a screeching of tires. I was bursting to know what the *real*
emergency was but I realized if Jordan had wanted to talk he certainly would have by now, so, although I was eaten up by curiosity,
I kept my cool. The driver tore from La Guardia to the Triborough

Bridge, down the East River Drive and then battled to get cross-town. Jordan was sitting way up in his seat after we got to the West Side. He said "Right here!" and dropped a ten and a five over to the cabby; then we were piling out with our suitcases in front of Lincoln Center. The driver caught on and was calling out "You smart little bastards!" as we raced across the plaza with Jordan laughing. "We made it! We made it!"

"Made what—what?" I yelled, following him.

"Take a look!" he called back, pointing to the poster as we neared the Metropolitan.

It was *Turandot* with Birgit Nilsson and Franco Corelli. How about that!

Jordan had seen it was playing in the *Times* and had phoned the son of one of Rudolf Bing's right-hand men whom he'd gone to school with and arranged tickets. He quick picked them up while the bells were ringing and the last of the crowd was squeezing in. We checked our suitcases with a cranky attendant who muttered something about it not being Grand Central Station and were ushered to our seats just as the conductor came out and the lights dimmed.

I was close to being in heaven. That great music started; we were off and away and I don't mean to sound melodramatic but I was transported. I wasn't sitting in my seat. I was floating up in the air all over the opera house. It's strange but, as hooked as I am on the opera and especially seeing it for the first time, toward the end of the second act, although I was still seeing and hearing it—Birgit Nilsson singing *In Questa Reggia* could blast out another Panama Canal—even so, part of me, my mind, left the opera and I started thinking about all sorts of things: my life so far, imaginings about my mother, my father, my old friend Boots, California, Gilford, Jimmy and Dennis and Mr. Hoyt. Then I got to thinking that here I was, plopped down in the Metropolitan Opera House at *Turandot,* totally unexpectedly, and it was then I began to acknowledge that my life might not be all laughs and patty-cakes and pennies from heaven, but it certainly had its share of surprises.

Jordan and I had a great walk-around and talk during intermis-

252

sion, and when the third act started, I looked over at him sitting there next to me and then I began acknowledging that this was surely one of the richest times yet, and I got attacked by goose flesh all over. The next thing I was thanking God for being right where I was at that very moment and having this fantastically unusual friend sitting next to me. It's beautiful when you can stop and say to yourself: This moment is it, this is perfect. I suppose it was catching because soon I was thanking God for all sorts of things, for being young and healthy and that all my parts operated correctly during patty-cake and for my father's job (may it lead to another), and then Franco Corelli had launched into *Nessun Dorma,* which gets me anyhow but now simply flattened me, and I was filling up, up, up and then spilling over and the tears were splashing down my face and I was choking back a few sobs.

I glanced over at Jordan, hoping he wasn't noticing me, but he looked over at me just at that point. In the short time I allowed our eyes to meet he winked at me and when I looked back to the stage he reached over and held my hand, which killed me even more, and I just sat there and let the tears roll down until I started getting extremely wet, at which point I took my hand from Jordan's, fished out my handkerchief and went about mopping-up exercises. I finally simmered down and refocused on the opera itself, enjoying it thoroughly.

So—New York, room at the Warwick, five times to the theater, Modern Museum, Metropolitan, Frick, etc., long walks, phone call to my father, who got back the 28th, visit to friends of Jordan's, visit to an old actress friend of my father's, all kinds of people-watching. Most of all, the greatest companionship imaginable, laughs mixed with such other moments I wouldn't even know how to begin putting them down. And we agreed on most everything. For instance, I like nuns, but they make me laugh. Jordan and I would have to cross the street to get away from each other when we'd see two or three approaching. It was brutal. All sorts of other things: We loved feisty older people that look like they'd as soon crack you with their canes as lean on them, drunken bums who admit to being drunk, big buxom redheads, good-hearted waitresses that treat you as if they'd just finished conjugating with you and the next step was naturally to feed you. We both hated: pigeons, box-office people, women that shake cans in front of theaters for causes (Jordan put his cigarette out on top of one—can, not lady—who pestered him), most doormen, German accents, and, oddly enough, most all little kids whom most people coo over but who are a nuisance and make very little sense to have around unless you require someone to trip over and yell at continuously. I know I'll change later as soon as I make one of my own.

Last vacation item: New Year's Eve. We hadn't talked about what we'd do. The afternoon was overcast but mild and we took a walk in Central Park. Later on Jordan took a nap and I read. When he awakened he put on his dragon robe and just sort of paced around the room, stopping every now and then and staring out the window and down at Sixth Avenue. Finally he said, "I think I'll call the Little Foxes." I asked him if he wanted me to leave and he said no. He lit a cigarette and gave the operator the information and while he was waiting for the call to be put through he lit another one, while the first one was laying on the ashtray right in front of him.

"Hello," he said. "Oh, Barry, hi. This is Jordan. . . . Fine. . . . No, I'm feeling fine. . . . Oh, nothing in particular. Dad around? . . . Oh, I see. . . ." Then a little laugh. "Yes, I know. . . . Well, what about Mother? . . . Oh. . . . Yes. . . . No, no, just tell them I called to say Happy New Year. . . . Yes, . . . Yes, you too." He hung up and walked back to the window.

"They out?" I asked.

"No, my father's splicing film down in the basement. He's a camera bug and that's one time he doesn't like to be disturbed—when he's splicing film. My mother's resting up for the big night." He looked down at the street again and then said, "I don't like New Year's Eve."

"I don't either," I told him. "I've never had a good one yet, except maybe the night Boots and I took in two double features. Even then I got a headache."

254

"I've had two good ones, one in Boston, one in Paris. I still don't like them. They're too . . ." He broke off and hunched up his shoulders.

"Too what?" I asked.

"Too—I don't know—what *might* have been or what *should* be." Although I couldn't translate that specifically, I knew what he meant. It was getting to be that murky winter twilight hour, all chilly gray. Jordan looked out the window again. Then he suddenly said, "I wonder how many more New Years I'll be seeing in?"

He never spoke like that; I was so taken off guard I said something brilliant, like: "Tons."

"No, I wonder . . ." he said very calmly, like he really would like to know.

"Oh, Jesus, Jordan!" It spooked me.

He turned around. "Listen," he said almost chidingly, "if I can't say it to you, who can I say it to?"

"Me," I agreed.

"All right, then." And this was the only time he talked about death. He smiled at me. "Funny, to think about checking out when I'm enjoying. When I'm depressed or disgusted or even sick, I never give it a thought. I suppose I don't give a damn then. Hmn . . . if you knew you were going tomorrow, what would you do tonight?" he asked me.

"Faint!" I said, not wanting to continue in this vein at all.

He laughed. "Listen, Bulldog, would you do me a favor?" I told him sure, glad to be off the subject, I thought. "If anything ever happens to me, would you take whatever money I have on me and my—"

"Jordan, stop it, will you!"

"Ah-ah," he said, holding up his hand, "just hear me out."

"I'd really rather skip—"

"Peter, I mean it!" He said it so sharply that I clammed up and he went on. "If anything ever does, I want you to take my wallet, my watch and my ring. I'd want you to have them. Okay?"

"What about your gold fillings?" I asked him.

He grinned at me. "Okay, but you heard me," he said, pointing a finger at me. Then he clapped his hands together. "Now, let's have us a New Year's Eve we won't ever forget."

And we did. A swim and steam bath at the New York Athletic Club, which his uncle belonged to, a fantastic dinner at La Fonda del Sol, then Jordan said, "Let's not be in a stupid club or a bar at midnight. Let's just take in the town, wing it." We took a cab to Washington Square and began walking around. The Village gets A-plus for people-watching. You can't be sure of anyone without a score card and on New Year's Eve it was especially juicy. In only about forty-five minutes we had seen:

Two Lesbians slugging it out in the middle of MacDougal Street over a very pretty young girl who sat on the curb watching them, all the time combing her long blond hair.

A priest pull up in a Corvair and quickly change clothes in his car, emerging in black boots, jeans, a turtle-neck sweater and an old Army-type Eisenhower jacket.

An Afghan dog going up to a drunk who was leaning against a building and peeing on the drunk's leg. The guy who was walking the dog acted like the drunk was a post and the *drunk* wasn't even aware it was happening.

Three college guys had set up a stand, some kind of a homemade scale like a weighing machine. Instead of GUESS YOUR WEIGHT, their sign said: GUESS YOUR SEX—and underneath it: WE ARE RIGHT AT LEAST 25% OF THE TIME.

The most frightening was a fight between a couple we couldn't see in a walk-up sixth-floor apartment. There was a whole cheering section standing on the sidewalk opposite their windows and you could hear him call her a whore about twenty times and she kept yelling, "If I'm a whore, you're my pimp!" All the while they were having a contest to see who could throw more of the other person's possessions out the front windows: it was raining books, records, two cameras, a mantel clock, glasses, a knitting basket, clothes, and finally a wild scream from the woman followed by a huge gray cat.

256

Jordan and I had turned and were traveling fast away before the cat hit. But we heard it and the stunned silence from the crowd. From the heightened sounds coming from the apartment I wouldn't be surprised if she killed the guy. "I need a drink," Jordan said as we turned a corner onto a side street.

"Hey, pretty little white pussycats!" we heard a voice call out. We looked up and a very good-looking colored man and a beautiful colored woman were drinking out on the fire escape of a loft building right above us. He had on a red shirt and she wore a green knitted dress. "Come on up, have a toddy, you pretty little white pussycats," the colored man said laughing.

Jordan called up in an outrageous Southern accent, "You got any watty-mell-lawn and frahd chick-ken?"

"Jordan!" I said, elbowing him.

But the man was howling with laughter, the woman, also, both screaming for us to come up. Jordan laughed, too. "Hey," he called up, "if we come up, y'all gotta sing and dance for us. You know, that great little shuffle step y'all do?" Yes, yes, they were laughing and waving us up but Jordan wouldn't stop. I was standing there with my mouth open as he went on. "I bet y'all really dig swinging around on that fahr escape, huh? You people shore like to climb around a lot. I mean y'all ain't down out of the trees more'n a hunert years or so—right? I betcha you got little vestigial remnants of tails you hide back here, huh?" he said, patting his behind. This really killed them and the guy said, "Get your ass up here, white boy!"

"I hear," Jordan continued, "that all you guys got some kind of stuff you rub on yo'self that makes white women do it to you, just a whiff and they all lay down and start yellin'—sock it to me, Sweet Black Baby!"

Then the colored man choked on his drink and the woman was patting him on the back with one hand and waving us up with the other. As we were climbing the stairs I asked Jordan what got into him but he just laughed and said, "They're swingers. I could tell right off."

The door opened on the third floor and the red shirt and green dress were still laughing and then they were all over Jordan, hugging and kissing him and then me. They hauled us into this huge loft which we learned was Bo-Bo's (the red shirt) and Wilma's (the green dress) dance studio. They were married and the place was jammed with about a hundred and fifty people, all sizes, shapes and colors, students, actors, actresses, writers, painters and just people.

Bo-Bo and Wilma were charmers, getting us paper cups of purple-looking punch and dragging us around, introducing us like we were the guests of honor. It was the friendliest party I'd ever been to. Jordan and I got separated early on and I found myself standing by half a dozen people seated on the floor listening to a very elegant woman dressed in a Chinese silk outfit, red pants and a mandarin top. She must have been in her seventies and when she noticed me standing there she stopped her story, waved an arm and said, "Sit down, angel." I did and she went on in the most civilized serious manner telling about how she'd poisoned her first husband in Italy years ago. "Poisoned—really poisoned?" a young girl asked. The woman looked at her for a long moment and said, "That's what I said, my dear." Then she turned to a colored man and said, "Isn't that what I just said?" He assured her it was and then the young girl asked, "But how could you *do* that? I mean take a person's *life!*" "My dear," the woman sighed, "I just finished telling you—he was not a very *nice* person!" I dug her, as she went on saying that, of course, that was many years ago and you couldn't do that any more because they can detect everything nowadays and it's too risky. "If it weren't," she added, waving a hand in the direction of a much younger sleek gentleman talking to a long-haired mess of a boy, "number five wouldn't be making goggle eyes at everything in pants." She shook her head. "No, number five would have been dispatched long ago." She held her hands out in front of her, palms up, and said, as if she were talking about the hopelessness of the war in Viet Nam, "But, you see, that's what I'm talking about. One can no longer do that; one has to suffer in silence. It's the age of compromise."

Just as I was relishing, again, the *unusualness* of being there in that loft, listening to this woman bemoan the fact that we can no longer knock one another off, it was midnight and an epidemic of kissing and noise swept the loft like the plague. Everyone was up on their feet kissing everyone else and eventually the woman who'd been talking grabbed hold of me and kissed me quite aggressively and I was aware of the bristles of hair around her leathery lips and then she put her hand on my privates and squeezed them and I lost all the respect I'd been harboring for her. Thank God somebody, a young colored boy, cut in on us. She went to kiss him but he grabbed me instead and then a colored girl tapped me next and then I tapped a redhead and horns were blowing and two bongo drums had started and I suddenly wanted to find Jordan.

I bobbed around on tiptoe and finally saw him standing up on something in the corner, craning and looking and he spotted me and smiled. He hopped down and we plowed through the crowd and met toward the middle of the room. We threw our arms around one another and we kissed. It was a real kiss, and no matter what anybody might think, a perfectly right and fitting expression of our friendship for that time and place and for us. That's the only time there was any physical intimacy between us. Enough said. When it was over, Jordan laughed and said, *"You* don't tell the Rev, *I* won't tell the Rev."

Pretty soon the general kissing stopped and a trio joined the two bongo drummers and dancing began. Those who weren't dancing moved to the sides of the room and sat on the floor. Jordan and I found a place and squeezed down just as a very tall vampire-looking girl came over to Jordan and handed him two cigarettes. "Thank you, Marion," he said. "Happy New Year, Jordan." She smiled and walked away. I asked him where he knew her from and he said nowhere, he'd just been talking to her before midnight. He handed me a cigarette. "One for you, one for me."

"They're homemade."

"Yes," Jordan said, "they don't package marijuana yet."

And they were and we did, Jordan claiming they were much better for us than the punch, which he said was lethal. He showed me how to do it, inhaling with the smoke and how to suck in and hold it down, no easy feat without coughing. So we smoked, sitting side by side and watching the dancers. When I'd finished my cigarette and was experiencing nothing but a hot, parched throat and a stuffy sensation in my stomach, Jordan turned to me and asked if I was feeling anything yet. "Nothing out of the ordinary," I told him.

"You will. Give it time."

Just then the drummers went into a solo and the crowd moved away from the floor while Bo-Bo and Wilma began a great exhibition together and suddenly I thought I was going to slide down the floor and join them. "Time!" I said, reaching over and grabbing Jordan's knee.

"You all right?" he asked.

"Sure," I said, "it's just the way the floor slants."

"Easy, just relax, give in, go with it."

And after that first moment, that first big tilt, which had me scared, things gradually evened off to a lovely liquid hazy feeling of lightness, like I was sitting on a cushion of air. "Umm," I mumbled, loving it.

"What?" Jordan asked, grinning.

"Ummmmmmmmmm," I repeated, wagging my head.

"Good Bulldog," Jordan said, patting me.

I took to it like Good and Plentys. I sat there watching Bo-Bo and Wilma, and soon they were joined by several of their students, whom they led in combinations of Afro-Cuban-jazz steps. It was unbelievable. The more frenetic the drummers and the wilder the dancing, the calmer, more cozily secure I was feeling. And then I was looking at the people sitting along the opposite side of the room—they seemed to be sitting on air, too—and loving them, feeling they were all my friends and that they loved me, too. And I thought of my enemies and all the people who'd ever given me trouble and that included Mr. Hoyt. I was sure if I could confront them for a moment, all differences would be settled.

Then one of the dancers slipped and fell down, an easy fall and she quickly got up, but that just set me off and I started to giggle and I looked at Jordan who began to laugh at me giggling. When we finally stopped, I looked around at all the people again and I began to feel I was harboring tons of very warm secrets way down inside me—secrets about what, I didn't know, but they were incubating inside me and when they were fully hatched I felt I just might tell a few of them. Or maybe I wouldn't, maybe I'd hoard them. I leaned over to Jordan and said, "I have secrets."

"I'm not afraid," he said.

"Me either."

We had a small giggle about this. Later on I looked across the room just as the woman who'd felt my parts handed her husband a drink and pecked him on the cheek. I started to laugh again, and when Jordan asked me what it was, I pointed over and whispered, "That woman's poisoning her husband!" That struck him as fairly jolly, too, and we chuckled about that for a while. The dancing ended about this time and we all applauded. People circulated around the room and a record player was turned on and general dancing began. Jordan and I sat there on the floor for an hour or so, having a warm, hazy session of people-watching, which was almost like being at the movies. We'd mumble a comment and nod and laugh or just grin. After a while I was getting both drowsy and hungry, and when I mentioned this to Jordan, he said he was drowsy, too. We found Bo-Bo and Wilma and thanked them for asking us in. They kissed us goodbye like we were old friends and told us to come back when we were in the neighborhood.

Outside on the street I still felt high, as if I were walking on the deck of a gently rolling ship. Jordan did, too, because we kept bumping shoulders and laughing. I got an insane craving for a hot-fudge sundae and after a few blocks we fell into Howard Johnson's on Sixth Avenue. The place was jumping and we sat at the counter waiting to give our orders. There was an empty seat next to me and in front of it, leaning up against the side of a Coke machine, was a cardboard cutout, head and shoulders about half size, of a grinning waiter with some slogan about "Always Pleased to Serve You" printed below.

261

A man of about fifty, bombed out of his mind, staggered over and after about three passes at the stool finally managed to climb up on it. Already Jordan and I were grinning, but then the drunk snorted, looked at me, took in all the activity behind the counter, which seemed to make him dizzy, then ducked his head back, blinked his eyes and brought the cutout of the waiter into focus. He broke into a big smile, lurched forward until his face was only about six inches from the cutout and said, "How's about a chocolate malted for your Uncle Dudley?" He belched, said "S'cuse me" to the cutout and sat back to wait.

That did it—instant hysteria. It would have been funny anyhow but in my weakened slug-nutty condition it absolutely fractured me. Jordan was right along with me and pretty soon we were off the stools, howling with laughter and stumbling out onto the sidewalk. We had no control at all. We were hanging on to a lamppost and we'd run down and for a split second we'd stop. Then one of us would let out a shriek and we'd be off and away again. We ended up sitting on the curb, holding our stomachs and rocking back and forth. We laughed like that for at least a half hour, until I was as physically exhausted as if I'd swum the English Channel.

We finally hailed a cab and alternately giggled and moaned all the way to the hotel. When the elevator door opened, there was a woman holding a leash with one of those tiny hairless Mexican Chihuahuas on the end of it. The dog was shivering so hard it couldn't take a step. "Come on, Fred," the woman said in a great whiskey voice, yanking it out of the elevator. Jordan and I were roaring again, all the way up in the elevator, down the hall and into our room. I clawed my clothes off, fell into bed and laughed myself to sleep.

We slept until noon. I woke up happy. No hang-over from marijuana. Jordan, however, was looking pale and tired, with that slight blue tint to his lips and a tight look around his mouth. He said he felt all right, just worn out from the pace of the whole vacation. I was a little tired myself and my stomach ached from all that laughing, like I'd done several thousand sit-ups. In the late afternoon

Jordan perked up, and being it was our last night in New York, we went to a Chinese restaurant and took in an Andy Warhol movie which unfortunately was about fifty times more boring than it was dirty.

Back in our room, Jordan was in bed reading and I was packing. Suddenly, as I was wondering how I was going to get everything in my suitcase (every time Jordan saw something he liked for himself, he'd buy one for me), I had an overpowering sensation: Don't go back up there, don't you or Jordan go back! For a few seconds it was so strong I lay down on the bed to think about it. As soon as I was concentrating on this feeling, it struck me silly. Just like Jordan's knocked out physically from this two weeks, you're punchy in the head, I told myself.

That night when the lights were off, Jordan whispered, "Bulldog?" and reached over between the beds and took my hand. "Thanks for a dandy vacation."

He was thanking *me!*

I thanked him. Then I thanked *HIM* for Jordan, who mumbled something about being back with the Rev soon. I almost mentioned the feeling I'd had before, but I didn't. Instead I thanked God again and told him he was getting nothing but A-plusses lately and asked him to keep up the good work.

Ask and ye shan't receive!

21

THIS MORNING a phone call from you. Knowing you'll be here within two weeks gives me a shot in the arm. I'm feeling "up." I'll be keeping my fingers crossed regarding your jury. (Not that my opinion makes any difference, but I'm sure Caroline Wilk did it. From what I've read about her aunt and uncle, they deserved to have it done to them.)

As you'll see when I drop all this on you, I've been typing away like a demon. Without the pills I couldn't, but with them it keeps splashing out and I feel lighter and lighter the farther along I get. Now it's compulsive. If they took my typewriter and paper away I'd scratch the rest of it out on the wall of this cell with a nail.

My father writes every couple of days and keeps sending me prayer cards and medals and rosaries. I wish he'd stop this. It makes me feel like he's hoping I'll "go to God" before they strap me into the electric chair. I'm thinking of asking him to stop—only I can't figure out whether it makes him feel better to send them or makes me more depressed to receive them.

The next evening Jordan and I were back at school. Getting off the train and the ride back with Cutler Barnum, who told us Mr. Hoyt had driven Mrs. Hoyt to Connecticut the day before, being checked in by Mr. Kauffman, all goosey and wearing a loud checkered vest the local librarian had given him, then going upstairs and seeing Frank Dicer elbowing Lee Galonka away from the second-floor john mirror, where he'd been combing his hair for a few hours, being warmly greeted by Dennis Vacarro and Jimmy Greer and hearing that first welcoming barrage from Ed Anders' room, which sounded like a series of tugboat blasts—all of this struck Jordan and me the same way. We both agreed coming back to Gilford was like returning to visit a pack of daffy relatives you had funny childhood memories of and were getting a kick out of seeing again but that didn't necessarily mean you wanted to settle down for a long stay.

When I went to bed that night I lay there thinking of the complete difference between our Boston and New York—scenes, I suppose you'd call them—and this eccentric cut-off-from-the-world scene at Gilford. I was part of both, yet they were so different it seemed that one should be reality and the other some kind of made-up crazy-quilt world. I lay there wondering which was which. I didn't even hear footsteps, I was thinking so hard. The door opened and Jordan stuck his head in. "Hi," he said.

"Hi—come in."

"No, better not. First night—the Rev might be on the prowl." There was a pause. Then Jordan said, "Jesus, I had a good time."

"Me, too."

"Listen," he whispered, "I've been thinking—this summer, after graduation, I'll be stinking rich. What about Europe? Ah-ah, before you say anything, I've got it all figured out. I wouldn't *get* the money if I didn't graduate. I wouldn't have stuck it out if you hadn't been here. Conclusion: you're actually entitled to half. Fat chance," he snorted. "You'll settle for a trip to Europe!" He waited for me to speak, to protest, but I just lay there smiling. Jordan walked over to my bed and flipped his hand against my foot. "So—Europe this summer?"

I put on a great big yawn and spoke in the middle of it: "Yeah . . . I suppose."

He laughed and walked toward the door. "Oh, it won't be as bad as all that." Then he left. I lay there grinning and aiming a few more bouquets at God. I was inundating him lately.

In another one of his unexpected reverses, Mr. Hoyt took me completely by surprise the next day when I saw him in the hall before morning chapel. "Peter," he said, smiling and extending his hand, which I shook, "did you have a good vacation?" I told him I did and he asked if I went all the way to California.

"No, just New York."

"How's your father?"

"Fine." I saw no reason to say Jordan and I had spent the vacation together on the loose, and I wasn't lying. I didn't say I'd been with my father, only that he was fine.

"It's good to see you, Peter. We must get together soon and discuss plans for your new monologue. I believe a humorous one, on a slightly higher level perhaps, Twain or even a contemporary, Thurber or S. J. Perelman. Think it over. See if you can come up with something you like." He gave me a pat on the shoulder and left.

He hadn't spoken to me for weeks before vacation and now this display, glad to see me, how's the father, and plans for a new monologue (that cast a shadow or two). When I told Jordan, he said it might have been better for me if he'd continued the Cold War. Mr. Hoyt didn't accord Jordan any such welcome but he did nod to him and mumble his name when he saw him.

The first week went quickly. Mr. Hoyt was busy with all sorts of projects and seemed to be in one of his cheerier manic-energy periods. After chapel, the morning assembly was like a pep rally, with announcements about ski meets, hockey games, the Glee Club rehearsals and other activities. There was also one outside announcement that caught Jordan's and my fancy: *"Winona, the Winnipesaukee Maiden,* an Indian pageant of early New Hampshire, written and acted by local talent and produced by the Northern New Hampshire Women's Association." It was to pre-empt the movie on Sunday night at Guild Hall and Jordan and I built it up to a huge event, treating it as a big Broadway opening night. Students could purchase tickets at half price but we agreed we'd pay one hundred dollars apiece *not* to miss it, if we had to. We'd built it up so in our minds that at dinner before, we agreed we were in for a letdown; we were positive it couldn't be anywhere near as bad as we hoped it would be.

We were wrong. It lived up to all our expectations and then some.

First off, it was a packed house. Not many Gilford students, mostly townspeople and country folk. Five minutes after we'd taken our seats in about the twelfth row on the side, Mr. Hoyt, all civic-spirited, came tilting down the aisle with Headley and sat several rows ahead of us, over in the center. I was hoping the lights would dim and we'd get under way immediately but no such luck. He was glancing around, dispensing rubber-band smiles, and soon he looked back and spotted us. Although he gave me a tight little nod, the fact that Jordan and I were together registered on his face and he turned front again. It was supposed to start at eight-thirty but it wasn't until ten of nine that the pitiful little orchestra, three women and four men, all very thin if not downright skinny and unfortunate-looking to boot, straggled out and took their places on folding chairs.

"Holy Smoley," Jordan whispered, "the UQ (Ugly Quotient) is fierce." As they started warming up, he said, "The Buchenwald String Ensemble will now—" but I was already swatting him to be quiet for fear of laughing out loud. After they'd tootled around for a few minutes, a little old lady conductor with frizzy white hair, looking like a plucked chicken, marched out, tripped, recovered and put her music in front of her on a metal stand which promptly collapsed. She and the violinist were all rear ends and elbows picking it up and Jordan and I were giggling. Finally she got herself pulled together and gave the orchestra a one, two, three count with her baton and we were under way. The first few bars were so hideous that I whispered to Jordan, "Overture by Ed Anders!"

That started him off and within seconds we were in deep trouble. Especially after the narrator, a very prim, tall, tight-ass-looking man, came out. He was all serious business but when he opened his mouth and spoke I thought Jordan and I would have to

267

leave immediately. He had the most sibilant "s" I've ever heard. The Hollywood Freeway at rush hour with every car having a slow flat tire couldn't have sent up more of a hissing sound. "Many moonsss ago in thisss land of mountainsss and lakesss dwelt a beautiful maiden, Winona, daughter of the proud chief of the Winnipesaukeesss. Ssso awe-inssspiring wasss her beauty that warriorsss from tribesss to the north, sssouth, eassst and wessst—"

Jordan and I were clutching at each other and the curtains opened and there stood Winona in the center of the stage, about five-three, very plump, sort of pleasant round face, if you could get the terror off it, and eyes as crossed as a Siamese cat. Sitting around her in a semicircle were twelve extremely uneasy and unlikely-looking Indians, all with wild New England Yankee non-Indian faces and bodies. This sight did nothing to help Jordan and me control ourselves as the narrator hissed on, explaining how braves were paddling canoes over every possible body of water for hundreds of miles to woo "the beautiful Winona," but she would have none of them, she was waiting for true love. To help matters, Jordan leaned over and whispered, "How many 's'es' in Winona?"

Things went from bad to worse. Winona sang about how "true love would fly in like a dove" in a high, reedy little voice that was pleasant enough except that her eyes *double* crossed on the high notes and she sharped them, too. True love did appear in the form of a hawk-nosed tenor who looked at everyone else on the stage as if they'd been dead for several days in extremely hot weather. He had only scorn for them and it was obvious everyone else in the cast loathed him. He was completely stuck on himself and sang a love song to Winona without looking at her once. The tribal council then executed a "Dance of Joy" that turned out to be a spastic free-for-all. Also, the stage of Guild Hall must not have been swept in many moons because great clouds of dust spread up and fanned out in the air. Several Indians and the narrator sneezed and Jordan was clutching at my knee and we were shaking the entire row of seats.

When the dance was finished I thought maybe we could settle down, but as the applause faded, the Indians on stage just stood

268

there and gradually they were all looking down at the drummer, who was sitting there looking up at them. I noticed the tenor really giving him the evil eye and then the conductoress was going "Pssst!" to attract the drummer's attention, but he kept on staring up at the stage waiting for the show to go on. Finally, just as the conductoress whispered "Bernard!" the tenor said, in a snide, disgusted manner, "I *thought* I heard the drums of war!"

"Ohh!" the drummer gasped, making a lunge for the tom-toms which he proceeded to beat the hell out of, as if he could make up in noise for what he'd lost in time. Even the audience, who'd taken all the rest as if it were the original company of *My Fair Lady,* laughed at this. But whereas they managed to settle down, Jordan and I were hopelessly lost. We just kept on, and when the tenor said superciliously, *"Now* I hear the drums of war!" Jordan let out a yelp and I thought he'd fall off his seat.

I glanced over and Mr. Hoyt was looking around at us. I tried to shush Jordan but that only made him laugh more, and when the villain, a brave from the warlike Mohawks arrived to claim Winona, and turned out to be a fat New England businessman that no amount of war paint could disguise, I knew we were finished. Every time we'd start to simmer down, the narrator would come out with a few lines and we'd be off again. Now Mr. Hoyt was really keeping tabs on us and I started to sweat blood, which only made me laugh more. Finally all the men went off stage for a council to decide whether Winona should marry the tenor and have all hell break loose or whether to let her go to the Mohawks and avoid a war. Then came the capper.

Twelve squaws and about six little kids came on and don't you know who one of the squaws was—Our Lady of the Poppies! She didn't have her hat on but you couldn't miss her round pumpkin face, still grinning as I fondly remembered her, all two hundred pounds wrapped in suede and lots of beads and a few feathers in her hair. Jordan and I nudged one another at the same time and blurted out "Our Lady of the Poppies!" The squaws all stood in line and started a song called "The Winnipesaukees Are a Peaceful Tribe." About five lines into it, Our Lady of the Poppies spotted someone she knew down front in the audience and took time out to wave and give them a big smile and this killed me. Now I was whooping and hollering, Jordan, too, and a woman in front turned around and gave us such a hatchet-faced look of disgust that I was up and climbing over some very cranky people and scooting up the aisle with Jordan fast after me.

We tore out into the lobby and hung on to each other, howling and gasping. We couldn't believe the good fortune that had sent us Our Lady of the Poppies. We tried going in a couple of times and standing in the back but we couldn't make it for very long. The last time, the villain and his witch doctor had all the Winnipesaukees huddled in a corner telling them in no uncertain terms that there'd be a lot of funerals before there'd be any wedding between Winona and the tenor. The witch doctor was shaking dead things in their faces, and as he and the villain left to summon the entire warlike nation of Mohawks, the Winnipesaukees were all crouched together in terror. All but Our Lady of the Poppies. She was standing there grinning after them for all she was worth, happy as a clam. I thought she might even wave goodbye and Jordan and I had to leave again.

We hid out during intermission so we wouldn't have to see Mr. Hoyt and waited until everyone was inside before we returned. Mr. Hoyt was on the sharp lookout and threw us one of his more disapproving glances, which we pretended not to see as we walked solemnly down the aisle and took our seats.

I guess the whole evening had gotten to me because I started shaking as soon as the Buchenwald String Ensemble straggled out to take their seats. Jordan punched me on the leg, hard, a real corker. It hit a nerve spot, really hurting and, of course, making me laugh all the more.

I won't inflict the whole second act on you. We managed to stay in our seats but there were enough goodies to keep us in a constant state of hysteria. The people seated around us hated us, you could feel the waves, and that only intensified the pain. Several times I thought we'd have to make a dash for it, especially when the squaws had a number preparing for Winona's wedding and each

270

one stepped out for a solo couplet and Our Lady of the Poppies muffed her lines completely. Instead of being embarrassed, she had a whale of a good laugh about it and Jordan and I were stomping our feet and holding our hands over our faces. Right toward the end, Winona's father, the chief, stuck his foot through a papier-mâché rock and that was a laugh riot, being he had one hell of a time getting it out.

By the final curtain, I was wringing wet from perspiration and had what felt like a migraine headache. We quickly got up to leave during the curtain calls so we wouldn't bump into Mr. Hoyt, who had never stopped glancing around. We were actually weak as we staggered out into the fresh air and down the steps. The cold felt good.

Jordan was breathing hard on the way home and we stopped several times. I was worried but he tossed it off, saying he was feeling fine, that "opening nights" always took their toll. When we got back to Lincoln House it was time for lights-out. Mr. Kauffman and the town librarian were watching TV in the parlor and it looked like he had a little romance going.

Although we were both tired, it wasn't possible after the performance we'd witnessed not to have News of the Week in Review, so after Mr. Kauffman had made a quick tour of the halls, I tiptoed down to Jordan's room. He was taking a pill. I was concerned that he might be going to have an attack but he said no, only one for protection, he was really just pooped from the pageant. We got into bed and I thought we'd start in doing an autopsy right away but instead we both chuckled and lay there next to each other.

I really don't think we had any energy to dive into it. I remember lying there thinking how great it was that the combination of Jordan and me somehow just made unusual things happen for us. I remember a feeling of almost swelling up with that idea. Finally I raised up on an elbow and whispered to Jordan, "We really do have some good times, don't we?"

"You bet your ass," he said, reaching over and patting my leg, and I noticed how cold his fingers were.

I lay back down and—

271

(Oh, God—I'm bawling my eyes out and I've already had two pills today. All I can hear in my head is my own voice saying over and over again: "Oh, God, Oh, God, Oh, God!")

I lay back down and I could hear Jordan breathing heavily but regularly, it seemed, and the sound of it was soothing and like my own breathing and I went to sleep.

The light woke me up. For a split second I didn't know where I was. Yes, Jordan's room. I looked up to see Mr. Hoyt standing in the doorway. Mr. Kauffman was behind him, peering over his shoulder. I glanced over at Jordan. He was asleep and now breathing strangely, little jerky, panting breaths. I looked back at Mr. Hoyt. His expression wasn't one of anger or surprise—just deeply, seriously set. I sat up and looked over at Jordan again. I suppose it was the movement together with the bright light that caused his eyes to flutter. I noticed his color now, the lips blue and that white, drawn look in the lower cheeks and jaw and a waxy sheen on his forehead. He blinked and even before he saw me he muttered "Hey . . ." Then he opened his eyes and I could tell he was seeing me in a groggy way, but not clearly. "Hey," he said again. "Bulldog." I knew he wasn't aware there was something going on, something more than just Bulldog.

Still no one else had spoken.

Jordan raised his head; his eyes were still fluttering and focusing at the same time. He shook his head and finally he saw Mr. Hoyt. He said "Hey" again, bigger, almost a gasp, and with a sort of humor behind it that said: Oh-oh, big trouble.

I looked back at Mr. Hoyt. He hadn't moved a muscle and it didn't seem like he was even about to. Jordan shrugged and before I knew it he was reaching over and yanking the covers off us, saying, "No problem—sleeping—nothing going on."

I was aware of the breeze, the cold, and looked down to see that I was in a semi-erect state and that it was angling out of my pajamas, the fly of which had lost all but one button at the laundry. I hardly ever wake up without an erection and there it was. Jordan saw it, too, and as I was yanking back the covers, which gesture

272

made it seem even worse, I was also looking up to see if Mr. Hoyt had noticed. I heard Jordan sort of chuckle—"Oops!"

Mr. Hoyt's expression, one of deep disgust, was evidence he had taken in everything. Jordan coughed and lay back down as Mr. Hoyt snapped "Sit up!" and then turned to Mr. Kauffman and said "Go downstairs."

"Mr. Hoyt, I—"

"Downstairs," he said in a deadly calm voice. Mr. Kauffman disappeared and Mr. Hoyt kept staring at us. I looked over at Jordan again. He had lain all the way back down and put a hand up to his chest. He was not breathing right at all, his breaths were too irregular. He coughed again and put his hand up to his mouth. His eyelids began to flutter like they had when he was first waking up. But now he was lying there just like no one else was in the room. Suddenly I got very scared.

"I think he's sick," I said to Mr. Hoyt.

"Sick?" he replied, with cool amusement. "Yes, I'd say he was sick," he added, still smiling. The smile snapped shut, and as Jordan mumbled "Hey . . ." again, Mr. Hoyt spoke to me. "Go to your room!" I looked from Jordan to him and he repeated, "Go to your room!" His voice was still cold and controlled.

"Yes, sir." I got up out of bed and started across to the left of him. He stepped away from the door and into the room. When I was about passing him, I looked back at Jordan, who was just lying there, not really knowing what was going on. "Mr. Hoyt, I don't think he's feeling—"

He gave me a full backhand in the face, so quickly and with such force that it caught me completely off guard and I went off balance, bumping up against the dresser. It stunned me for a few seconds and I stood there with a hand up to my face. "I said get back to your room." All his anger was in that blow because his voice was still that impersonal, strange hollow sound. Then he was walking to the bed. "Get up!" he said. "Get up and get dressed!" He stood there looking down at Jordan, who coughed again and then raised his hand up to his forehead. As he did this, Mr. Hoyt grabbed his

273

forearm and yanked him up and over toward the outer side of the bed, so that he was angled across the width of it.

Jordan's eyes opened wide and there was panic in them. I knew he'd forgotten what was going on and this abrupt gesture had taken him by surprise.

"Don't hurt him," I said. Mr. Hoyt snapped his head around. Now the anger was showing in his face and in his breathing. "He's sick. Please don't hurt him," I repeated.

Mr. Hoyt dropped Jordan's arm—Jordan flopped back down on the bed like a rag doll—and started after me. I quickly turned and went down the hall to my room. When I'd shut the door I stood there behind it, listening. The thing I heard most was the thumping of my own heart. I couldn't make out much of anything else until eventually I heard the door open and the shuffling sound of the two of them going down the stairs.

As soon as they hit the second floor I went down the hall to the bathroom, which had windows overlooking the quad and the walk between Lincoln House and Mr. Hoyt's. I heard the front door slam and was able to see them after they'd gotten off the porch and away from the building. Mr. Hoyt had a hand under Jordan's armpit. He was holding him up high on that side so that Jordan was walking all lopsided. He was also so much shorter than Mr. Hoyt he was dangling as if Mr. Hoyt had hold of a puppet. At one point, Jordan stumbled and his knees buckled and I let out a little sound. But Mr. Hoyt had a firm grasp and jerked him upright, still sort of dragging him along without even stopping to see how he was. When they got about three quarters of the way along the path, something happened. Although I couldn't hear, it looked to me like Jordan stopped, pulled back and said something to Mr. Hoyt, who then also stopped and in a brusque movement threw Jordan's arm down by his side. They stood there for a second staring at each other, then Mr. Hoyt walked on and Jordan followed. He was weaving like he was drunk. Mr. Hoyt stopped at the intersection of the path that led to the porch in front of his house, and when Jordan staggered up even with him, he again grabbed Jordan by the

274

arm and hauled him around front of the house where I couldn't see them any more.

Right then I wanted to kill Mr. Hoyt, but my concern for Jordan wiped out that moment and I stayed by the windows, staring over at the house as the lights went on in the study. I don't know how long I remained there, just looking over as if I were going to see something, which was impossible because all the windows had shades plus drapes or curtains and they were all drawn.

After a while I looked at my watch, almost one-thirty. I went back to my room and lay down knowing I wouldn't be able to sleep. After a while I got up and turned on my desk lamp. My desk was cluttered with books and papers, all sorts of homework, and over to the side I noticed a book I hadn't seen before and a note sticking out of it. The book was a collection of Mark Twain's humor and the note was from Mr. Hoyt, saying he thought we'd find something excellent and we'd discuss it after I'd had a chance to look through the book.

I'd been out of my room until early that evening when I got dressed to go with Jordan. I supposed Mr. Hoyt had left it there in the afternoon and maybe that's why he'd dropped by, either to see if I'd found anything in it or else to bawl me out for our conduct at the pageant. I lay back down on my bed and kept hoping I'd hear Jordan's footsteps coming back upstairs—then I'd know he was all right.

When the town clock struck two I got up and went into the bathroom again. Looking across, I saw that the lights were now on in the study, the front parlor, on the porch and in one of the bedrooms upstairs. I didn't like the look of the lights. I stayed there worrying over that for a while and got so restless I finally went back to my room. I just paced around for fifteen or twenty minutes, made another trip to the bathroom—lights still on—back to my room and it was either start shouting and breaking things or put my clothes on and go over there.

I dressed quickly and climbed down the fire escape. The snow had piled up thick around by that side of the house and I waded

275

through a deep drift of it. The moon was out above the clouds and it wasn't too dark. I followed the path over to Mr. Hoyt's until I was standing next to the study windows. I stepped up close to them but the drapes were thick and full and there wasn't even a sliver of an opening to look through. I pressed my head right up by the windows and stood very quietly but I couldn't hear anything, not a sound, voices or anything. After a minute or so I heard footsteps upstairs in the bedroom above the study. I stepped back and looked up at those windows and I could see the shadows of curtains behind the shades, nothing more.

I was wondering what I could possibly do when I heard a car pulling up out front. I stepped back close to the house. When the car door slammed I edged forward and moved out behind a clump of bushes. I could make out the form of a man walking up the path toward the front porch. He was carrying a bag and I was certain it was the doctor. I ducked back against the house as I heard him step up on the porch and the door opened and mumbled voices and the door shut again. Then I could hear footsteps going up the stairs and I imagined Jordan was in the bedroom with the lights on right above the study.

It was good news that the doctor was there. At least Mr. Hoyt would realize Jordan was really sick and that meant he wouldn't be losing his temper and smacking him around. With these thoughts I returned to Lincoln House and climbed back up the fire escape.

I got out of my clothes, but I might as well have stayed in them for all the sleep I knew I wouldn't be getting. I didn't even lie down. I just sort of wandered around the room and kept telling myself that, rules or no, in any kind of a decent society if a person's best friend was sick the most natural thing would be to go to where he was and find out *how* he was. And stick with him. But no, not here at Gilford. Living naked in the jungle, grubbing for roots and berries and eating bugs and ducking pythons and panthers and all the other charmers was more civilized than existing in a place where you had to stare out of bathroom windows, scramble up and down fire escapes and turn yourself into a Peeping Tom because your closest friend might be having a serious heart attack.

Naturally I kept padding down to the john every now and then. Finally around four-thirty when I looked over, all the lights were out except on the porch. I interpreted this as a good sign. By this time I was groggy. I went back and fell into bed but I didn't go to sleep before having a few words with—rather at—the Big Joker in the Sky.

The words added up to: Look, I know how you love to play the old switcheroo game. You've really been raining the good times on us; now maybe you think you've got us sufficiently distracted to surprise us by dropping a few tons of elephant shit down the chimney. Well, we're not fooled, we've got one eye cocked, so save it for someone else.

In effect, I was trying to head him off at the pass. Fat chance!

22

FIRST THING next morning I checked Jordan's room. I didn't think he'd be there and he wasn't. In the parlor before breakfast I saw Mr. Kauffman. "Mr. Kauffman, have you heard anything about Jordan?" He looked at me and shook his silly head. "How could a bright, talented boy like you let yourself—" I turned and walked toward the stairs. "Peter, I'm *speaking* to you!" he said petulantly. I swung around. "Mr. Kauffman, I asked *you* a question!" I realized after I'd said it I had actually mimicked him. I almost laughed as I trotted up the stairs. I was beginning not to care about any regular behavior.

Jimmy Greer came up to me all concerned, asking me if it was true Jordan was sick. I told him I thought so, but I didn't know how bad it was. At the breakfast table Ed Anders asked about him, and Logan Tinney, who had the room next to Jordan's, also said, "What was going on last night with Mr. Hoyt and you two?" I mumbled something about Jordan not feeling well and Mr. Hoyt coming to see what was the matter. "Not quite what I was talking about," he said in a knowing way. After breakfast, as I was going up past the second floor, I heard Frank Dicer laughing. "Yeah, I hear he caught 'em with their pants down."

Morning chapel turned out to be even more "en*chan*-ting" than usual. Mr. Hoyt came striding on like he was about to lead the

Charge of the Light Brigade and started reading from the *Old* Testament—which my father refers to as that horror-book predecessor of Edgar Allan Poe—about the cities of Sodom and Gomorrah and the wickedness of the men that dwelt there and— Oh-oh, I thought, this is no coincidence! When he got through with the text, he closed the book and braced his hands against the lectern. He stared out over the faithful assembled for a full thirty seconds before opening up with his big guns.

Finally he sighed and said, "Sodom and Gomorrah—the ancient story of unnatural acts between men, men so wicked and depraved that God saw fit to destroy the very cities they inhabited. I thought for a long time before bringing out into the light of day the reason for the choice of this particular text. I feel it must be spoken of, however." Now another long pause. "Last night . . . two of the boarding students were caught in bed together."

He stopped—a huge pause, dramatic and drawn-out—to let this bit of news sink in. If I was embarrassed, I believe the rest of the students were, too. The ones who had an inkling of whom he was speaking of, mostly boarding students, had the kindness or subtlety or *something* not to turn around during the pause itself. But when he finally went on, pulling all the stops out and saying he realized we were living in an age of total permissiveness about sex, normal sex, but he didn't believe we'd gone so far that society was willing to close its eyes to the sins that beset Sodom and Gomorrah, etc.— well, when he got into this, then the heads gradually began swiveling around and the eyes were taking little pot-shot glances at me.

I can't say I wasn't embarrassed. I was, of course. But it was my anger at his libelous conclusions about us—Caught in bed, doing what? Sleeping!—that made my face sting, my ears burn red-hot and caused a ringing sensation in my head so that after a while I wasn't really tuned in to the specific inky stains he was squirting all over Jordan and me. Most of all, again I wanted to shout out: "Hypocrite—what about my back? Oh, Guardian of the Golden Morals! Let's talk now about rubdowns, you ——!" (Fill in the blank with any dirty word or series of them.)

When I noticed Mr. Lomax Piper looking at me from the stage, I started to pay attention to Mr. Hoyt's words again as he was saying one of the students had no scruples whatsoever and had cast some sort of a spell by means of his rebellious nature and so-called sophisticated personality upon the other boy. And that oddly enough, this first boy, splotched with decay, even as God had struck down the cities of Sodom and Gomorrah, so had he struck this boy down by inflicting him with chronic ill-health.

He went on drawing this parallel between Jordan and Sodom and Gomorrah and managed to leave no doubt about just who we were. He might as well have had two mounted blown-up photographs of us and a pointer.

It finally occurred to me that I should simply stand up and walk out, but I suddenly got confused wondering about what Jordan would have done. With him not there, if I walked out I'd be doing it for him, too, and I wasn't sure that's how he would have reacted. He might just have sat there giving the lie to it with that half-crooked smile of his. Also, it struck me that maybe getting up and walking out would be like admitting it. I got so confused thinking about the alternatives that I missed his windup. Suddenly it was all over.

No one spoke to me as we filed out. Drumming through my brain was: Keep your cool. I refused to go stumbling around blushing all day and not looking at people. I didn't know how to keep from blushing but I did know how to keep my eyes working. Just look at people when they looked at me and not take my eyes away, simply look at them as if to say: "Yes, that's me, that's Peter Kilburn, and no matter what he said, I'm still a person, he hasn't erased me, and I hope to God you judge me as you see me, on your own grounds, not by that Bible-thumping pagan." (I read that phrase somewhere.)

I saw Mrs. Mason in the hall and went straight up to her. She never attended morning assembly and I could tell by her hello she hadn't yet gotten a whiff of Sodom and Gomorrah. "I wonder if you know how Jordan Legier is?" I asked her.

"Well, I'm sure he's doing nicely," she said.

280

"How do you mean nicely?" I asked her. "Didn't he have a heart attack? He's not in school this morning."

Then she got cute. "That doesn't necessarily mean he's had a heart attack, does it?"

I remember speaking very much on a level. "I don't know, that's what I'm asking you." But I could feel my eyes narrowing.

Now she was being the grownup speaking to a child. "I don't believe you should worry so much about Jordan Legier. He'll be fine." (Undertones of something there.) "You just keep your mind on Peter Kilburn," she said, patting my arm and giving me that professional-department-store-saleslady smile. Having made her little put-down, she switched to another gear completely. "Oh, Peter, Mr. Hoyt received a letter from the Lions Club requesting you to perform your monologue at their jamboree next month. They're willing to donate one hundred dollars to our athletic fund in return. What do you think of that?"

"No," I said.

She looked confused. "What?" she asked.

"No, I won't do it," I said. Then I turned and went to my first class. Mr. Piper did me the great favor of not calling on me once. I was so struck by this consideration that I went up to him after class. You don't have to protest to someone you feel on the same wave length with, so I said very calmly, "Mr. Piper, what he said isn't true. We were in the same bed, that's all." I wouldn't go on until he reacted. After a moment he smiled and said, "If you tell me that, I believe you."

"He is my best friend, though. And he's sick. I think he's at Mr. Hoyt's. There seems to be a big secret about not saying how he is and I won't be able to concentrate on anything until I know. You could do me a great favor if you'd find out and tell me."

"I'll do what I can," he said.

I thanked him and left. I suppose the bulldog in me will out. I sat through the next two classes and I might as well have been wrapped up in a plastic bag in the freezer for all I was absorbing. Although I knew I couldn't expect Mr. Piper to suspend his classes and conduct a research campaign for me, I also knew I couldn't wait any longer. So after third period I left the building and walked toward Mr. Hoyt's. I got halfway there when I heard his front door shut and then Mr. Hoyt came around the corner. I kept on walking, but he stopped several steps in front of me. "You wanted to speak with me?" he asked coldly.

"I wanted to find out how Jordan is."

"What!" he snapped. "You left school without permission to—"

"All I want to know is if he's all right." I couldn't look at him, all I could do was look slightly past him and down. "That's all I want to know—if he's all right." I think he saw determination behind the words and maybe a preview of coming hysterics.

"Your little 'friend' is all right. He's back in his room. One of you will be moving. I don't know which yet." I could feel him staring at me. "I'll be speaking with you later. Now get back to your classes."

I went gladly. The relief I felt was like somebody had emptied all the rocks out of my stomach. There was only a short period before lunch and as soon as morning classes were over I raced over to Lincoln House. Mrs. Rauscher came out of his door as I reached the top of the stairs. She shook her head, said "Peter . . ." and walked past me. I've seen granite faces before, but never like that. When I walked in the room and saw Jordan I knew why.

He was propped up in bed against four or five pillows. His head was turned to the right and on the left side of his face, running across from his sideburn to the high point of his cheek under his eye, was a nasty-looking bruise, dark blue with yellow and purple splotched through it. There was some medication which made it shiny and probably made it look worse than it was. Even though Mrs. Rauscher had just been in the room, Jordan's eyes were closed. When I shut the door, he turned his head and looked over at me. "Bulldog, I've been waiting for you." He saw the look on my face as I was taking in the bruise. "It's not all that bad."

"Jesus, did he do that?" I asked, sitting down on a chair next to the bed. "Jesus!" I could feel tears of anger wanting to come out.

"Just a love tap from the Reverend."

"Love tap! Jesus—when did he do that?"

"Doesn't matter," Jordan sighed.

"Doesn't *matter!*" I said.

"Hey, baby," he whispered and made a little quieting gesture with his hand, "no fireworks, huh? I'm nice and tired." I said okay. Then I guess he thought he'd hurt my feelings. He looked over and smiled. "No . . . no, you see, he wanted me to tell him, like with details and graphs, what dirty little deeds we indulged in. I didn't want to pleasure him, didn't want the Rev to get all hot, so I refused. He just got impatient, that's all." All I could do was keep saying "Jesus!" Jordan turned his head away from me and coughed. When he turned back he said, "I don't know if I can stick him out, Bulldog. See—he really got an F-minus."

"We'll leave. We'll both go!" I jumped in.

"We'll see. Maybe not, though—it gives the Hun in me something to chew on." I asked him what he meant by the Hun in him. "We all have to hate now and then. Sometimes it's good to have a great big dead-on target to aim it at. Gets it all out of you, like a good purge. That way you don't spread it around in little dinky ways on people you like. We'll see. I just want to get my second wind. Then we'll see."

I looked at him closely. His color wasn't good at all and the skin seemed drawn very tightly over his face. "Jordan, can I ask you a question?"

He smiled without opening his eyes. "You will anyhow, so go ahead."

"Shouldn't you be in a hospital?"

"Ahh! I've been through this a hundred times. Long as I'm quiet a while, I'll be fine."

"But you'd be quieter in a hospital."

He shook his head. "Don't like hospitals. They remind me of my mortality." I thought about that and Jordan just lay there. After a while he said, "So—talk to me."

I didn't want to tell him about morning chapel for fear of upsetting him, that could wait. Finally I said, "You *really* look like Jean-

Paul Belmondo with that bruise. I hope you slugged him back," I added kiddingly. "Just think, you spent the night at the Rev's. How was it?"

That great twisted smile. "En*chan*-ting."

"He give you a rubdown?"

"Nope, I don't think he'd mind open-heart surgery, though—zap!" And he pantomimed yanking his heart out of his chest.

We kidded easy like that and then we just sat there quietly. Jordan looked like he might go to sleep so I told him I'd go down and have lunch. He looked over at me and nodded. When I got to the door he said "Hey!" I turned around and he reached his hand over and patted his night table. "You remember what I told you in New York?" I asked him what he meant. "This junk," he said, and I realized he was patting his wallet and watch and ring.

"Oh, Jesus, Jordan—stop it! That's not even funny."

"Sorry," he said, "but remember—"

"Ghoul!" I could hear him laughing as I went downstairs. The fellows at our table came through with flying colors for once. They didn't know what to talk about, that was obvious, but at least no one brought up morning chapel.

During afternoon classes my main project was keeping my spine erect and my head up and my eyes open and on a straight line with whatever or whomever I looked at. Nobody went out of their way to speak to me and the teachers took it easy as far as calling on me. After school I saw Mrs. Mason again. She came over to my locker, and by her attitude, chilly, and eyes looking right past me, I knew she'd heard of our terrible crimes against nature. She told me Mr. Hoyt was busy—just then I saw him walk around the corner and go into his office with two elderly men—but that tomorrow he expected me in his office after last class. She ended up by saying, "I didn't tell Mr. Hoyt of your refusal to appear for the Lions, you're in enough trouble as it is. I'd change my mind about that if I were you."

I don't know what prompted my answer, but I said, "I wish you were."

"What?" Then she looked at me for the first time. "Why, Peter —what's come over you?" It was a rhetorical question and she walked away, shaking her head and making little clucking sounds.

Jordan was sleeping when I looked in on him. Most of the fellows on our floor were out, engaged in a sport or activity of some sort, but I stayed in my room. Just before dinner I heard footsteps coming up the stairs and I peeked out to see the doctor going into Jordan's room. Right away I went down to the second-floor landing to wait for him. After about five minutes, Mr. Kauffman came out of his room. "Oh—Peter," he said, looking all surprised. "What are you doing here?"

His attitude annoyed me. "I live here," I told him.

"What?" (Everyone was asking me what!)

"My room's right up there," I said, pointing up the stairs.

"Hmn . . . not for long," he muttered and went down to the first floor.

In another ten minutes the doctor came downstairs on his way out. I said hello and he just nodded and smiled and started to go on by. I plunged right in. "Doctor, I know you're busy but I'm his best friend and all I want—"

"Peter?" he asked, surprising me. "Are you Peter?" I nodded and said yes. "Jordan said to be on the lookout for you." Then he really smiled and suddenly I liked him. "He's doing all right," the doctor said. "It's just a case of exhaustion. Apparently you two had quite a vacation." I said we did and he went on reassuring me that he was much better than last night, all he needed was a few days rest and he'd be up and about. We spoke a little longer and he left, saying it was nice meeting me and not to worry.

After dinner Mr. Kauffman informed me I'd be moving to Logan Hall the next afternoon. Jordan's lights were out so I didn't bother him. I took a little walk for myself down by the football field and then was when I first noticed the weather. It was cloudy but unseasonably warm, almost muggy. The top few inches of snow was sinking down in little pockmarks, like someone had poured a quick splash of warm water over it. The snow wasn't that clean white flaky stuff; it was turning dappled-gray. It looked sick, if you can imagine sick snow.

I looked up at the school. After a while I began shaking my head: the weather was sick, the school was sick, Jordan was sick, my father was basically sick, Mr. Hoyt was really sick, then there was Jimmy and Dennis and—"Sick, sick, sick," I said out loud.

When I got back to Lincoln House, Jordan's lights were still out. As soon as study hours were over I started to check again, just as Jordan, in his green kimono, stepped out into the hall. We both grinned and he walked down to my room. "Long time no see," I said.

"Heap big sleep—many moons pass," he replied. He told me he felt much better. He didn't look much better but I didn't tell him that. He looked very fragile and much thinner than usual, but he was in good spirits. He wanted to talk about our trip to Europe, so most of the time was spent discussing where we'd go and what we'd do. Just before lights-out I remembered I was moving to Logan Hall the next day and I told Jordan. "The Reverend's gonna force us to shack up in a motel," he laughed, adding, "the turd!" As he was going out the door he suddenly turned around and snapped his fingers. "I got it! Wherever we go this summer we'll bombard him with postcards—no, *pictures* of the two of us! Holding hands and standing in front of the Arc de Triomphe, the Tower of London, the Colosseum, the Pyramids—'Love, Peter and Jordan,' we'll sign them. It'll drive him mad." We loved that idea. We had a good laugh about it and said good night.

Because of the events of the day I was bushed. After lights-out I was almost asleep when I heard someone creaking around out in the hall. A few minutes later I heard them creaking downstairs and about ten minutes after that the fun started. I heard Lee Galonka, who had a reputation for being a sack-hound and often going to sleep *before* lights-out, muttering out in the hall. "Oh. . . . Oh, Jesus. . . . Oh, *Jesus*. . . . Oh, no. . . . Oh, my God!"

I got out of bed and stepped out into the hall just as Wiley Bevan came out of his room. We both saw Larry Olivier stagger into the

286

john and we followed him as far as the doorway. Lee was gaping into one of the mirrors and picking at his hair with his fingers. Even with only the night light on I could see it was tangled and snagged like those pictures you see of Medusa. He was muttering and cursing and then he started clawing at his hair and soon it looked like he was trying to tear it out and sobbing at the same time. I said, "Lee—Lee, what is it?"

He turned and stepped toward me, really wild-eyed. "Chewing gum! Some rotten filthy bastard put chewing gum all over my pillow while I was *sleeping!* While I was *sleeping!*" he cried out.

And some rotten filthy bastard named Frank Dicer had indeed put chewing gum on his pillow while he was sleeping—a lot of it. Although none of us exactly worshiped Lee Galonka—I mean he wasn't our favorite movie star *yet*—still the sight of him and the pain on his face prevented me from laughing. Not Wiley Bevan, though; he started gasping, and when Lee wailed that he'd have to cut it all off, Wiley put his hands up to his mouth and ran back to his room.

Just then it must have struck Lee who it was. "Dicer, that sadistic bastard Dicer!" And he was moving down the hall like he was on wheels with me after him. "I'll kill him, I'll kill him," he said through his teeth. As he reached the banister I said, "Now, look, Lee—" but he swung around, eyes blazing, and whispered like a madman, "I'll kill him!" and started downstairs.

"But Mr. Kauffman's down—"

"I'll kill them all!" he said, which did strike me funny while down the stairs he went just as Jordan opened his door. "What the hell's up?" he asked. I'd just finished giving him the word when we heard the first crashing around and yowls from Frank Dicer. Having been in our share of trouble, we ducked into Jordan's room and shut the door, staying right behind it, however, all the better to listen. The level of noise increased on the second floor and doors started opening on the third floor and all the guys were gathering at the head of the stairs. From what we could hear it was more than just Lee and Frank Dicer and we imagined Herb and Warren, Lee's confederates in the Circle Jerk Conspiracy, had joined in with Lee against Frank. Then we heard Ed Anders, in the role of Big Brother, start down the stairs shouting, "What the hell's going on down there?" Next Ed was calling out for Mr. Kauffman, but someone shouted back that Mr. Kauffman had gone over to Logan Hall. At this news, which meant there was no adult in the building, Jordan and I grinned at each other like you do when you're watching a catastrophe that you don't mind is taking place.

Next thing Frank Dicer shrieked out, "Not my balls—no, no, not my nuts!"

"Cut 'em off, do you think?" Jordan whispered.

"You said he ought to be sterilized," I told him.

"Yeah, but I didn't think they'd *do* it!"

We heard a couple more guys clomping down the stairs. Whoever had Frank Dicer where the hair was short wasn't letting go because he was still protesting loudly and then we heard a huge crash that sounded like a bureau tipped over and Frank Dicer screamed, "Oh—oh, my toe! Jesus, my toe!"

"Well, listen," Jordan said, "better his *toe!*"

With that we were laughing as we heard Ed Anders plowing into the melee, trying to stop them, and then there was a lot of thumping and knocking about and Ed Anders was shouting for someone to get Mr. Hoyt and pretty soon Frank Dicer screamed out, "Lee! . . . Lee, not my fish—my *fish!*" And there was this awful crash of glass, which represented the end of his aquarium and that really drove him crazy. Jordan grabbed my arm. "His balls, his toe, and now his fish—is nothing sacred!"

Now the battle was joined and it reached fantastic proportions, beyond our wildest dreams, with Jordan whispering things like: "And so on this day of our Lord, Monday, January twelfth, Gilford Academy came down like a house of cards." He turned to me and said, "Good night, David!"

"Good night, Chet!"

I was just suggesting that we go down as a U.N. Inspection Team when we heard a door slam and Mr. Hoyt boom out,

"What's going on here?" I think Mr. Kauffman and he came in together because I could hear him clucking as sort of an obbligato to Mr. Hoyt. Talk about a cease-fire! The battle stopped dead. A couple of guys came scooting upstairs as Mr. Hoyt demanded an explanation and then everyone was talking at once and it sounded unbelievably juvenile with Lee Galonka whining about "Gum in my hair!" and Frank Dicer yapping about ". . . care what they do to me, but leave my fish alone!" and Mr. Kauffman swearing when he'd left for Logan Hall it was "quiet as a tomb."

Jordan said, "Isn't it great! If we'd planned a little celebration for the Rev, it couldn't have turned out better." I agreed and said I'd better hotfoot it back to my room in case he came up to the third floor for a mass interrogation. I walked toward the door but Jordan reached out and touched my arm. "Listen, we better not chance News of the Week, but if you wake up early, come on down and crawl in." I told him okay and Jordan added, "I hate it that you're moving!"

"Me, too."

As I reached for the doorknob, Mr. Hoyt really started bellowing at them. You could almost feel the house shake, and Jordan whispered, "Hey, Bulldog!"

"Yeah?"

"Wild!" he said, jabbing a finger down toward the second floor. "Isn't it wild?"

I pulled his old act of being bored. "Feh!" I said, shrugging and then yawning. I quietly opened the door and crept down the hall to my room while Mr. Hoyt was at the height of reading the riot act to them.

Oh, God, if only we knew when we were saying goodbye to someone.

23

INSIDE MY ROOM I could still hear Mr. Hoyt ranting away and then all the guys started yelling at one another and he had to shout them down. Pretty soon he was hauling Larry Olivier upstairs, really chewing him out and also bawling out Ed Anders for being at Gilford four years and not being able to control the dormitory. It was a good half hour before doors were slammed, lights were out and quiet was restored.

When I got into bed I was chuckling and counting my blessings. "Oh, you were doing *what?*" says the Big Joker. Yes, that's what I was doing, remembering how blue I was feeling standing down by the athletic field, looking up at school and thinking about how everything and everybody was sick.

Now Jordan was feeling better and we'd had this nifty "happening," which would be known as the Great Chewing Gum Incident. We were off and running again. I went to sleep with a smile, knowing the Reverend had been handed an upset and sure that morning would fill us in on all sorts of gory details about who was on who's side and why. And probably bring about a few retaliatory attacks. In fact, this might be the beginning of an endless Tong War here at Lincoln House.

It was about five-thirty when I opened my eyes. I felt wide

awake immediately, which was unusual for me; I usually lie around in a coma for a while. I had to pee, which is not unusual, so I went down to the john. The only sound was the muffled snoring coming from Ed Anders' room. I was on my way back to bed when I got to thinking about how this was the last morning I'd be waking up at Lincoln House. I stopped and looked down the hall toward Jordan's room. He'd said if I woke up early to come down and crawl in and that's what I decided to do.

When I opened his door there was enough soft night light from the hall so that I could see he was asleep, lying on his right side over near the wall and facing it. His left arm was stretched up across his face and his hand touched the rail at the head of the bed. I walked very quietly across the floor and slipped in under the covers carefully; nevertheless, despite quietly and carefully, I was hoping he'd wake up. The sheets were cold and fresh where he hadn't been lying.

Come on, move a little, Jordan, and find out I'm here. I cleared my throat. Then the complete quiet in the room and throughout the building got to me and reminded me it was the ungodly hour of five-thirty. I looked out the window, still pitch-black. I lay there thinking how the whole country, half the world probably, was asleep, and I just let that silence of the early morning seep into me and soon, without moving a muscle, I was asleep myself.

When I woke up I was surprised I wasn't in my room, then I remembered. I looked over at Jordan and he was in the same position, still on his side with his arm stretched up across his cheek. I glanced up at his hand; his fingers were curled over the metal railing. I turned my head the other way around. Outside the window it still wasn't light; it wasn't black either, but a sort of murky dark gray. I checked my watch, straining to see the time, twenty after six. My watch had been losing time lately, so I glanced at Jordan's watch on the little stand next to his bed with his pills and wallet and ring and a glass of water.

Something happened. It will sound strange. I couldn't make out the dial so I leaned over to reach for it. In moving, stretching way

291

out to the left with my arm, my right leg slid over and just as I picked up the watch and the gold band was cold to the touch, my right foot brushed up against Jordan's leg, the calf of it, and it, too, was cold, extremely cold. But then I knew his circulation at times was very poor. I took my foot away and as I was straining to see the face of his watch I was thinking I had a nerve to come down to his room so early in the first place. His watch read a little after four; I held it up to my ear and it had stopped.

Right then the lack of hearing it tick reminded me of how quiet it was in the room. There was only the faint tick of my watch and my breathing. That was all.

I suddenly froze. It was then it struck me I couldn't remember hearing any breathing from Jordan. Dumb bastard, I told myself, you get too melodramatic. Many times you don't hear people breathing unless you make an effort and listen for it.

I put his watch back down and lay there very quietly. I could hear my breathing and feel my heart pounding more than usual—because I'd given myself a scary moment thinking what I just had. I held my breath, but I couldn't hear another sound. When I'd held it as long as I could, I exhaled and heard myself say "Jordan . . . ?" in a weird hollow way. This, the sound of my own voice, frightened me more than the silence and I quickly turned over to look at him, still lying there in that same position, not changed an inch. I moved my foot over slowly and felt the skin all over my body tighten and I thought I might yell out until I touched him, his leg, that is, and—oh, God, he was so cold!

And I thought, almost knew, he was dead.

Now—I can't explain it—it was like someone had struck me a blow on the back of the neck, sending little deadening waves up and down my spine and around in my head. But these waves, numbing as they were, didn't stop me from moving. I quickly slipped out of bed and stood up, yet I wasn't terrified, felt no urge to call out. The realization that Jordan might be dead, that was too much in itself to take in, too overpowering to allow for any emotions—fright, panic, sadness. The creeping awareness that death was in the room filled the time.

Like the end of the world might be. Just a moment to comprehend that the world was ending, over for all time, yes, this is it, so—what could you possibly do?

I looked at Jordan lying there, turned away from me in the semi-darkness, and although I couldn't see his face, still not a move, nothing, and then, even though I knew, came a backlash, a moment when I couldn't believe it. I grabbed at it—perhaps the early hour, the winter quiet, the murky predawn. Tricks. No, this is too much, it couldn't be, not Jordan.

I sat down gently on the bed and leaned over toward him. "Jordan . . ." I said. Then I said his word—"Hey!"—the same way he used it, tough, just the opposite of when he'd camp. "Hey!" I said, like a sharp whisper. "Hey! Hey, Jordan!"

No movement, no tricks, I couldn't fool myself.

Now his position looked strained to me, like he was holding on to that railing for dear life, or else trying to pull himself up. It was grotesque and I wanted to relieve him of it.

I reached over and touched his hand, the one holding the rail. As I was freeing his fingers I was thinking: His fingers are cold and fairly firm in their hold, but they're not clammy or clenched, I'm not having to *pry* them from around the metal. If he'd been playing games or fooling me, he'd have tried to scare me, but not if it were for real.

When I'd loosened his fingers, I said "There" and took my hand away. His arm flopped down in front of him and the weight of it caused his body to turn more, just a bit farther over on his side, away from me. At the same time a small sigh, sort of high, almost like he was going "Hmnn . . ." escaped him.

I jumped up from the bed this time. "Jordan!" I said. "It's me—Peter!" A moment of uneasiness, and although I'd never been close to a dead person before, except for funerals, I suppose all I've read and things I've heard told me that there is sometimes a breath, that is, air, released after death if the person is moved.

Still, I didn't want him moving any more by himself. I sat back down on the bed and put my hand on his shoulder, as if to steady him. I kept my hand there for a long time. I wanted to turn him over; at the same time I became aware again of the darkness and, although it was getting a shade lighter, I didn't want to *imagine* what I was seeing. I wanted to be sure, so I got up to turn on a light. Contradictorily, although I didn't want to be tricked by the darkness, I also didn't want too bright a light. I went to his bureau and turned on a lamp which had a small yellowish bulb. It gave off a soft glow and I went back to the bed.

Looking back, it hadn't occurred to me once to tell anyone. It was like there was all the time in the world. Even more—there was no time. Time didn't matter if Jordan was gone.

There he was, lying on his side, now with his arm down, looking so relaxed he really could have been sleeping. But I wanted to see his face. I couldn't just leave him there without *looking* at him. I reached across and took him by the shoulder and carefully turned him over on his back.

A sudden jolt—his eyes were open. He'd looked so like he was sleeping I suppose I just took it for granted his eyes would be closed. I can't say if there was expression in them of fear or pain or whatever; I was so surprised they were open, that's all I was aware of. It looked unnatural and I quickly reached over with two fingers and gently pressed the lids closed. I took my hand away and the next shock was seeing the bruise on his cheek. I'd forgotten about that. There was nothing to be done, so I tried not to dwell on it. Because he'd been on his side with his legs bent, now that he was on his back his knees were sticking up and I pressed down, straightening his legs out, and now he looked completely relaxed.

And then I noticed his mouth. His lips were slightly parted and over at the left corner, nearest me, his mouth had that slight tug over and down, like that crooked smile of his, only not so much, perhaps the tag end of a smile.

That got me. That's when the—oh, God, he looked so young and frail lying there, even with the tug of his mouth and the bruise and that little flattened-out place on the side of his nose. And I thought: There he is, all there like he always was, light-brown hair, a little of it down across his forehead, that smooth ivory skin, the odd nose

294

and that mouth. All there but I'd never see them working again, never see the cool look or that wise expression or the campy one or the tough one. For a moment I wished I hadn't closed his eyes. I'd never see them again.

There I sat, just looking at him, looking at him closely. I know I was looking for some sort of sign, not necessarily for him to *give* me a sign, just to see a sign of—what I don't know. There is such wonderment in death. And mystery. Was he really gone for all time? Or was there some part of him still inside there, inhabiting his body? I thought there must be. He didn't look like you hear people say—a wax figure or an empty shell. He didn't even look sick. He looked younger and more fragile than usual but he looked so much like *Jordan,* like he might just open his eyes and say "Hey!"

For a split second I imagined his mouth moved or something in the lower part of his face changed expression. I leaned in closer and, of course, it hadn't. If you stare at anything long enough you imagine you see change and it's probably the involuntary movement of your own eyes from keeping them fixed for so long. But still I kept focused on him.

You know what startled me more than anything? I heard a toilet flush and a john door bang shut and I jumped up from the bed. Then I heard footsteps walk down the hall and I realized where I was, here on the third floor of Lincoln House in Jordan's room and the only one in the world with the knowledge of what had happened.

A few seconds later I heard someone moving down on the second floor. The entire house would be waking up soon. I knew right then this was the time to say my private goodbye to Jordan.

One thing about death, no matter all the others—the sadness, the wonder, the shock or the fright—is simply the pure *importance* of it. I've heard people say you don't feel the importance of someone's death until way later. I did. I felt it, I was filled up with the importance of Jordan's death right then, all the time I was with him.

I sat down on the bed again. All I could say, or did say, at that moment was "Hey . . ." Talk about the inadequacy of words—what could I possibly say? I reached over and touched his face, drew my hand down the side of his cheek to his chin. Then I leaned over closer and traced one finger very lightly down his nose and over that little flattened-out place. The feeling I had was one of smiling, although I probably didn't.

Then I had an idea I might just lean right up close to him and kiss him, just press my lips against his cheek for a second. But I didn't. Something kept me from it. Not fear of kissing a dead person. I don't know what it was.

I wish I had. If it had shown respect and love for him and saying goodbye—then I wish I'd done it.

Instead, I took his hand and just held it a while. If this all seems like it was so calm on my part, the only explanation is that the wonderment and importance of Jordan's death gripped me strong, almost hypnotized me. I knew what I was doing, what was going on, but it was like there was a big bell jar clapped over Jordan and me. It was my time with him and I knew it.

Again it was only outside sound that made me move. Another trip by somebody down the hall to the john.

I sighed "Well . . ." and stood up. I stood there looking down at him and from way back in my childhood came the memory of my father saying " 'Good night, sweet prince' " as he'd bend over and kiss me and tuck me in and then I heard myself saying " 'Good night, sweet—' "

But I stopped. I wanted to say my own—thing, word, not copy my father. So I started in again and said, "Good night, sweet—"

And I realized what with Bulldog and the Reverend and the Terrible Twins and Larry Olivier and all the rest, we never had a name for Jordan. He was simply Jordan, is what he was. So I said, "Good night, sweet Jordan," only his name went so fast run together with the phrase that I said just his name again, separating it into two syllables—"Jor-dan . . ."—and it reminded me of the way he said "en*chan*-ting" so I added that: "En*chan*-ting."

It occurred to me I was acting very calm and yet crazy at the same time. It was all slow motion and like I was outside the room watching myself down the long end of a telescope. Although I was sure I'd pay for his death with all the emotion in me, now was still not the time and in some weird way I knew it.

I walked to the door and suddenly I thought, No, you can't just walk out without looking back. I told myself right then I wouldn't be around when whoever else had to see him walked in. I knew I'd have to tell someone but I didn't want to be there when other people were looking at him or any of the formalities were being attended to. I looked back toward the bed and then around the room at his things, his stereo, his typewriter, his desk and books and then I noticed his green dragon kimono over the back of a chair. I got it and spread it on top of the covers, over him, but it looked wrong, so I just picked it up by the collar, like you'd take it off a hook, and laid it on the bed next to him. Stepping back, I bumped the leg of the nightstand.

There was his watch and ring and wallet. I glanced at his face and the tug in his mouth said "Take it, Bulldog" and I knew he'd been serious and wanted me to have them, so without hesitation I picked them up.

I heard someone else moving about on the third floor. I walked quickly to the door and left the room. Halfway down the hall and Philip Simmons came out of the john. "Hey," he whispered, "how about last night? Galonka's hair and Dicer's *fish!* Really wild, huh?"

"Yes," I said and walked to my room.

Once inside with the door closed I put the ring and watch and wallet in a bureau drawer under my shirts. I quickly got dressed and suddenly I knew I wouldn't be staying at Gilford. I knew I wouldn't leave right that moment because I was starting to feel all tight and shaky inside. I opened the drawer and took the money out of the wallet—two hundred and sixty dollars. I jammed it into my pocket, for some reason, instead of taking the whole thing, and put the wallet back under my shirts.

I walked out of my room and avoided even looking at Jordan's door as I went quickly down to the second floor where Frank Dicer was just coming out of his room with a cut on his lip and a black eye. I thought way back to him calling Jordan "Blue Lips" and hated him all over again. I stared at him all sleepy and squinty-eyed sore and said "Prick!"

"Huh?" he asked, stopping and blinking at me.

"Prick!" I mouthed clearly and went on down to the first floor. Going out the door I asked myself where I was going. I had to think for a few seconds. No, not to tell Mr. Hoyt. Tell who? I closed the door and stood in the parlor. Mr. Kauffman? No, he was too ineffectual. I thought of telling either Jimmy Greer or Dennis and having them pass it on. No, they were screwed-up enough as it was. I quickly walked back up to the second floor and knocked on Mr. Kauffman's door. "Yes?" I heard him ask. "Just a minute." But I opened the door and there he was in a gray sweat suit on his hands and knees just about to get up from a vinyl exercise pad. There was an instruction manual spread out on the floor in front of him. He looked so ridiculous it stopped me for a moment. "Morning exercises, keep in shape," he panted, getting up.

"Jordan's dead," I said.

He looked at me and almost smiled. "What—what are you—"

"Jordan's dead—in his room." With that I was off and down the stairs with him coming out in the hall and calling my name. Then I was outside and trotting down the path toward the headmaster's house and the street. Looking at his house reminded me of how he'd dragged Jordan over there in the middle of the night and I could feel my anger rising and I thought: No, why should he get off? I ran around to his porch, up the steps and rang the bell, once, twice, three times, and then I started banging on the door without even waiting for anyone to come. Finally the door opened and there was Mr. Hoyt in an ugly bathrobe, a glass of juice in his hand.

"Peter?" he said. I just looked at him and he said, "What's the meaning of this?" He glanced down to check his watch.

298

"You—you did it!" I said. "You did it!" He looked back up at me but didn't say anything. "Jordan's dead. Are you happy?" I asked him, hating him the longer I was looking at him. "Are you good and happy?"

He looked terribly confused. "Peter?"

"I said—he's *dead!*" Suddenly I was all wound up. I could feel it. "You let up on him now?" I couldn't stop thinking about that bruise on his cheek. "You going to drag him out in the middle of the night any more? Are you? Or you going to let up on him now? Are you?" I was shouting.

He stepped out toward me. "Peter!" he said. He didn't know what was happening.

Just then Headley came up behind him. He, too, in a bathrobe, looking all prim, glasses on. "Father, what's the matter?"

"Ass-hole!" I shouted at him, and in response to his look I yelled it again: "Ass-hole!" Then I turned and ran down off the steps with Mr. Hoyt calling my name and shouting for me to come back. I could tell he'd come down off the porch and he finally yelled, "Peter—Peter, where are you going?"

With that I stopped and turned around. "You go over there and shake him up good! Give him what for! You go over and really give him *hell,* smack him around, see what you can do to the *other* side of his face!" And I realized I was not only screaming, I was starting to cry.

I took off at a run down the street. I could feel myself gulping and choking it back but I couldn't and wouldn't let it out until I got someplace. The effort of running helped me keep it in check. Now it was getting light and I didn't want any part of the day. As I was running I began wondering where I was running to. I think I had in the back of my mind to go to Mr. Lomax Piper's halfway up the hill on the other side of the village. Passing Guild Hall, I saw Crazy Andy pawing through a trash can and I immediately thought of the Flame Room and I knew I would go to Patti.

When I ran into the lobby the old man behind the desk was asleep. I kept on right across to the stairs leading up to Patti's suite on the second floor. Then I heard him mumbling, "Hey, there—Say—who's there?" I tore up the stairs, down the hall and started banging on her door, shouting for Patti, and when I heard the desk clerk coming up the stairs after me, I tried the door, which was open, and went in, just as some guy, all sleepy and naked, appeared in the doorway to her bedroom.

"Patti—where's Patti?" I asked. He was rubbing his eyes and looking confused and I heard Patti's sleepy voice ask who was there. I shouted who it was and when she said my name back, I let it out: "Jordan's dead! Patti, Jordan's dead!"

Just then the desk clerk came in and there I was standing between the naked man and him and they both looked like they were going to grab me, but right away Patti came up behind the naked man, pulling a robe on over her. "Peter," she said, "what?"

I ran to her. "Jordan's dead!" And she threw her arms around me as the two men came over and started to pull me away.

"Leave him alone!" she snapped. "Leave him alone!" She told the desk clerk to go downstairs. Then she said, "Paul, get your clothes. I'll see you later." He started to protest but she made it plain she wanted him out of there quick.

By this time I was falling apart. I couldn't keep it in any longer. She held on to me for dear life. I don't remember the man leaving but pretty soon she was leading me into the bedroom and we were sitting on the bed. When I finally stopped and began pulling myself together, she whispered "Tell me" and I did manage to get the main points out. Every once in a while I could feel myself shaking and trembling and I thought I'd start choking again but she was holding both my hands and when this would happen she'd squeeze them very hard and this helped me get through it.

After I'd finished, she put her arms around me again and held me very close to her for a long while. Then she told me to stay there and she left the room. She came back with a glass. "Brandy," she said. "Drink it."

I took a big swallow and the minute it hit my stomach it started back up. I ran to the bathroom with her after me and was sick to

300

my stomach with her holding on and steadying me. Loathing the act of throwing up, this brought me to my senses and as soon as I was finished I was flooding her with apologies, not only for that but for getting her and her friend out of bed. This made her laugh and she gave me a wet towel to wash my face with and brought me back into her bedroom and sat me down on the bed again.

She brushed her hand down my cheek the way she used to do with Jordan. I was feeling hollow and raw, like a cantaloupe that had been split in half and scraped. She said, "A good sleep is what you need, Peter. Would you like a good sleep?" I nodded yes and she went to the bathroom and came back with water and a pill. "This will do the trick." When I'd taken it she undressed me, except for my shorts, and put me to bed. "Patti will stay right here, right with you," she said. It was a very short time until I was out. I do remember her rubbing my forehead gently with one hand and holding one of my hands with the other. And I remember at one point squeezing her hand and saying "Oh, boy . . ."

"What?" she asked.

"I'd like to kill him," I mumbled.

"Kill him?" she asked.

"Mr. Hoyt," I added, looking up at her.

And I remember her smiling down at me. "Later, baby," she said, "later." That's all I remember.

If she is called as a witness, I suppose it would be better to skip this part of our conversation, but you'll know about that.

24

THE PILL was a whopper. I think I must have tried to wake up for a long time but I couldn't manage it. When I finally did struggle through and open my eyes I didn't know where I was, not at all. I was on my stomach, head turned to the side; the flowered draperies and the strong smell of perfume had me completely confused and I lay there for a while, eyes half closed, dredging around in my mind for a clue. I knew something had happened, something was wrong, but I didn't pinpoint it until I heard the sound of paper rustling and turned my head the other way to see Patti sitting in a chair over by the far wall reading a magazine. She heard me moving and lowered the magazine. "Baby . . ." She smiled at me.

Immediately I remembered. "Oh, Patti . . ." I said. And she was over to the bed and holding me. I'm afraid I was crying again and there was Patti caressing me and kissing me all over, on my cheek and neck and forehead and then my mouth. And, oddly enough, soon I was kissing her in return and right then there seemed very little difference between crying and making love. Soon, without a word between us—maybe only Patti saying my name several times—she was lying next to me and I welcomed her, wanting to bury myself in her, so as not to have to just lie there awake and remember about Jordan.

302

Although it seems strange now, thinking about it and putting it down, at the time it didn't. Perhaps if I'd been thinking about it *then,* it might have, but there was very little thinking going on—it just happened.

Soon she was undressing and then we were actually conjugating and it was anything but tender. There was fierceness in it. Not that I'm that experienced, but there was something more than just love-making going on, which I still can't understand. It was like something that *had* to be worked out. Even, in a degree, as if I were punishing myself or her and also for the first time I was more aware of wanting to ignite my partner than I was dwelling on my own sensations. I drove and slammed at her and she matched my energy and came back up to meet me each time. I knew maybe this was crude love-making and if it was I wanted it not to be halfway, no accident, and so I increased the attack and pounded and pounded until I could see a glazed look in her eyes and ripples shuddering up her body from her stomach to her breasts and extending all the way over to her shoulders and there were still no words between us until the rhythm was unbelievably violent and she started saying "Yes . . . yes . . . yes . . . yes" and then I was saying it, too, and we ended up screaming out animal sounds and then we were lying there all sweaty and heaving and it was like the task had been worked out.

We didn't even speak about it, and when we'd recovered, our whole relationship changed and she was my mother, leading me to the shower, regulating the water, and later handing me towels and even helping to dry me. After I was dressed I looked at my watch: quarter to five. Patti came to me and took my hands. "What now, baby?"

"I don't know."

"Would you like to stay here tonight?"

"No, I think maybe I should go back. There might be—I don't know—something I should do." I was feeling bits of guilt, thinking I'd somehow been remiss, although I couldn't think of anything I actually could have done. His family? I didn't know them. Stay

303

with him? No, not with the others around. And you don't go to the undertaker's with someone.

Patti walked me out to the street. It was cloudy and, as it had been the day before, unseasonably warm. She even commented on it, saying it would wreck the ski business if it kept up. She kissed me goodbye and said to call her later on, if I wanted to, and to let her know if there was a service for Jordan.

Walking back to school, I even worked up some perspiration it was so muggy. I passed Mr. Hoyt's, all quiet. I walked into Lincoln House and Philip Simmons and Logan Tinney were playing Scrabble. I couldn't believe it; I was really stopped for a moment. Jordan had only died that morning right upstairs and they were sitting around playing Scrabble. They looked up at me and Philip said "Oh . . . hi." Logan Tinney added, "They've been looking all over for you."

I only nodded and walked upstairs, wondering if either one of *them* had died, would Jordan and I be playing games? I thought no, we'd tend to be quiet. On the second floor I heard a blast of laughter coming from Herb and Warren's room. They both liked Jordan, I knew they did, and I wondered what in Christ's name they were laughing about. Frank Dicer came out of his room carrying a new aquarium. He hadn't forgotten what I'd called him that morning, because when he saw me he did a big take and stepped toward me. Before he could say anything I heard Mr. Kauffman calling my name. I turned around and his door was open. "Peter, where have you been? Mr. Hoyt's terribly upset, we've all been upset. Come in." I stepped into his room. "Peter, you shouldn't just disappear like that, you know that. Where were you?"

I found myself staring at him. My God, he was an adult and the first thing he could do was give me a lecture. Mr. Kauffman then said, in his petulant way, "Where were you, Peter? You might as well tell me. Mr. Hoyt will only—"

A blast of music—it was Petula Clark singing—came from somebody's room nearby and a wild thought suddenly occurred to me. I looked at Mr. Kauffman and said, "Jordan *is* dead, isn't he?"

"What?" he asked.

"Jordan did *die,* didn't he?"

"Why, Peter, you know that." He wasn't getting my point.

"Oh," I said and started to walk out.

"I'll have to call Mr. Hoyt and—Peter, are you all right?"

"Oh, dandy!" I said. Then I remembered and turned back. "Where is he?"

"Mr. Hoyt?" he asked.

"No—Jordan! Where is *Jordan?*" I couldn't believe him.

"Why, he's—I suppose he's—" I could tell he was wondering whether to tell me even a simple fact without Mr. Hoyt's permission.

"Where *is* he?" I asked again, taking a step back into the room.

Mr. Kauffman looked at his watch. "Mr. Hines should be leaving Saypool right about now. He's accompanying the body to Boston. One of Jordan's brothers is meeting him there and flying him back to New Orleans. Does that answer your question?" Although he'd told me, he wasn't that pleased about it.

"Yes, thank you." As I was leaving he was going on about how, of course, he'd have to call Mr. Hoyt right away and tell him I was back.

I couldn't get over the swiftness. I mean he was already gone. I started thinking about death certificates and autopsies and embalming and all sorts of morose things and shook my head to clear these thoughts away.

The sight of Jordan's room at the top of the stairs stopped me cold. The door was open and his special bed had been replaced by a regular one like mine. There was a mattress rolled up, tied with a cord. Outside of that and the chair, desk and bureau, the room was stripped, every trace of him was gone. I went in and closed the door. I just stood there staring at the bareness, not a remnant of Jordan on the bureau or desk or—I saw something glimmer on the floor by the head of the bed. I went over, bent down and picked up a safety pin.

It was unbelievable that this soon there wasn't even a hint that

Jordan had ever lived there. I don't know what I thought I'd find but—something, not all antiseptic and emptied like it was. I opened his closet door and it was as bare as the room. There were some little cubbyhole shelves built into the right wall. I could see in the three top ones but not in the bottom two. I stuck my hand back in the fourth and then jammed it back in the fifth and felt something.

I pulled out one of Jordan's black cashmere socks. I felt the softness of it, just a sock—still, it was his. I thought of the bureau drawers and went through each one, even running my hand over the shelving paper in case anything had worked its way underneath, but there was nothing. Over to the desk next. The middle drawer on the left jammed when I tried to pull it out. I stuck my hand in and up under and felt some paper stuck up in the runner. I eased it out; it was only a small piece that had been ripped at a jagged angle off a larger piece of lined yellow paper. I smoothed it out and saw Jordan's meticulous handwriting. It read:

> If I write this st—
> and the character of—
> contain much of Peter in—
> also the tenacious struggle ag—
> with parts of my Italian friend Rober—

To discover my name made me smile. He'd never spoken of writing, but from this he obviously was thinking of it. I went through the rest of the drawers and found an old stale Good and Plenty in the last one. Lastly, I looked in the wastebasket—empty. Before I left I put the safety pin, the sock, the piece of paper and the candy on top of the desk and looked at them. I don't know why but, as stupid as it was, for a moment they made me feel good. Especially the sight of my name in his handwriting. I smiled again—The Jordan Legier Memorial Collection. And part of my smiling was acknowledging that Jordan would have smiled at this, too. I picked them all up and walked out of the room, trying not to see any more of the bareness.

306

Jimmy Greer, his face all blotchy and eyes red, came out of the john. We said hi and he just sighed and shook his head. I said, "I'll see you later," and when I started to walk away he said, "Pa-Peter . . ."

"Yes?"

"Before the da-doctor came, I went in there." He hesitated a second. "I ta-touched him—just his leg."

"I touched him, too."

"I wasn't afraid, like I thought."

"Either was I."

"No, you wa-wouldn't be—with Jordan, would you?"

I told him no and walked away. Ed Anders' door was open a crack and I could hear several voices. I stopped and listened, thinking they probably were talking about Jordan. But Ed Anders was complaining about the warm weather, saying if it rained it would wreck the snow and they'd have to cancel the ski meet.

I quickly went to my room and just as quickly stopped dead. My desk and bureau drawers were all opened. Before I even looked under my shirts I felt sick. I knew the wallet and ring and watch would be gone. Even so, I dug around furiously, finally dumping all the shirts out onto the floor. Jordan's things weren't there.

Immediately I was filled with rage, so much so I felt dizzy, like I was going to keel over. And, yes, I could feel the rotten tears welling up again. This probably blocked my senses because I didn't even hear his footsteps. Suddenly the door was flung open and there was Mr. Hoyt.

He came into the room in a hurry, like he didn't really expect to find me there. But then he took his time, shutting the door, backing up against it and leaning there with his arms crossed. I'll forget many things in time about this experience, I'm sure, the sights and sounds that are so with me now and even the appearances of people, but I'll never forget that long look he gave me. Never. He wasn't particularly angry. He was looking, or doing his best to look, grave. But it was behind the put-on look that I saw. Behind it was the look of someone who'd just been dealt a terrific poker hand against somebody he knew he was going to wipe out, but he hadn't declared it yet. He was relishing it, maybe without even consciously realizing it, but that's what was there. Way down deep inside I could tell he was delighted Jordan was gone. Because he knew he could never lick Jordan, never really win with him. But now Jordan was out of the picture forever. Besides that, Mr. Hoyt was extremely relieved I was back. And alone. I knew he felt he had me to himself now.

The essence I absorbed from the way he was looking at me was dirty and perverse and, to be quite truthful, savage in the most civilized way. He kept staring at me and I tried to look back at him with eyes that would tell him exactly what I was seeing in him. He must have sensed something because after a while he frowned.

Then I suddenly remembered. "You took them," I said.

"What?"

"You took them," I repeated, indicating the drawer and the shirts all over the floor.

"Oh . . . yes, of course."

"Why?"

"Why?" he asked, almost smiling and as if it were obvious. "Come to my study in ten minutes." With that, he turned and left.

A far less stormy meeting than I'd expected, a really harmless encounter, I suppose it must seem. Yet his manner, together with the act of rifling through my things, so sickened me that while he was still walking down the hall I knew I was finished with him and the school. I knew it. I also knew I'd take no more from him, no more lectures, no rules or regulations, no more slurs or insinuations. Standing there, after he'd left, it was like I was already gone. I didn't feel sorry for him any more, I didn't want to please him, I wasn't even afraid of him. I was still angry, because of what he'd done, but, most of all, I realized I was full up to my throat with his behavior.

The lack of respect I had for him also triggered a reckless feeling. As fed up with him as I was, I'd just as soon go out with a bang and it occurred to me it might be great if he kicked me out.

I wanted him to pay his share of Jordan's death.

Now I thought I'd just have my last little meeting with him. Why not? I was leaving. If he wouldn't kick me out, I'd pack up and walk out. But I didn't want to sneak away.

I got an idea and pulled down my suitcases and took out the loud plaid jacket I'd worn for that first interview with him—and hadn't worn since. I put it on and then I got his monogrammed towel and the empty rubbing-alcohol bottle and put them in a paper bag and started over.

A light drizzle was falling now, like little messy gnats hitting you in the face. I hurried across the quad and up on his porch. A few seconds after I rang the bell Headley opened the door. His small face got even smaller when he saw me. "Oh, it's you," he said.

"Yes, it's me."

Mr. Hoyt's voice came from the study. "Show Peter in here, son."

The old-fashioned sound of "son" did something to me. I looked at Headley and whispered "Crap!"

"Huh?" he asked, leaning forward. I shoved my face right up close to him and whispered it again. Headley ducked his head back and his eyes showed that he clearly thought I'd flipped. He quickly turned and led me to the study.

The minute I walked in I saw a little jolt of something on Mr. Hoyt's face at the sight of my sports coat. Was it new or—then I caught the flash of recognition, which he quickly hid, searching my face now to see if my attitude matched my jacket. The point had been made and that allowed me to feel good enough to look perfectly cool. He told Headley to close the door and then said, "Sit down, Peter." I did, placing the paper bag on the floor next to me. "Now, would you like to tell me where you were all day?"

I opened my mouth to tell a lie or the truth or whatever but I knew there could be very few specifics left between us and that wasn't important enough to be one of them. I ended up by just sighing.

309

"What does that mean?" he asked.

"It doesn't matter," I said, almost mumbled.

He pursed his mouth and said, "I see." And I was thinking, Um-hmn, I—*inside*—match the jacket. *Comprende?* Now I could tell he was sorting through his bag of tactics. He decided to throw me a bone. "I'm aware of how you must be feeling." But he couldn't leave it like that, he had to add, "Especially in light of your unusual relationship."

"Yes," I was quick to pick it up, "it was unusual, but not the way you mean."

"Have it your way."

"No, I'm telling you." I felt this was my final interview and I wanted it straight. I suppose it was important because of the point I was going to make about him.

"And you expect me to believe that?"

"No—except it happens to be the truth."

"I see it's impossible to speak with you on that score."

"Yes," I agreed with him.

That stopped him for a moment. "No matter, it's immaterial now. That's over and done with. And a good thing for you. In years to come you'll realize this, too." He went on to say how when anyone as young as Jordan dies suddenly it's "regrettable" and that he was certainly possessed of a "quick, agile mind" but that wasn't to be confused with true intelligence and (again) sophistication, that "the boy" was basically lost, his values were warped, and he would have been doomed to a misspent life anyhow, so that, who knows, perhaps he was better off.

That was wrapping it up neatly and tying it in a bow.

This led to me. I would certainly be better off. Jordan was a bad influence on me. Look how well I was doing at school, what a fine attitude I'd taken on, but when Jordan arrived, things had changed, my own values began disintegrating. Now, although his death would take me a few weeks to get over, we'd be back where we were before. We had more than half the school year ahead of us, there was the next Glee Club competition, the spring tennis season, so much to look forward to.

When he was speaking of these things, I had the feeling of being coaxed back into my cage. I could hear heavy rain now, sloshing against the side of the house. I looked over and noticed Jordan's stereo set on a table near the windows. Mr. Hoyt caught this and stopped talking. When I looked back at him he was smiling in a patronizing way. I noticed how thin and rubbery his lips were, like lips drawn on an animated cartoon character. He stood up, walking to the set and placing a hand on it. "I got it for you. When I spoke to his mother she said if there was anything the friend with whom he spent the Christmas holidays wanted, to pick it out." He looked at me for a knowing moment. "Another thing you lied about."

"I didn't lie about it."

He took a step toward me. "Don't contradict me!"

"I didn't lie about it!"

"You lied by omission." Now he was suddenly angry. "Spending the Christmas holidays in a hotel with him in New York City!" His mouth pursed in distaste. "I can just imagine what went on."

"One of the best times I ever had."

"I'll just bet!" he spat out. He suddenly sprang over to me, grabbing me by the wrist and bending back my arm. "Admit it, admit you had an affair with him!"

Even though I was leaning back, cowering almost, from the suddenness of his move, I managed to speak in a calm voice. "I didn't. We didn't."

"Ahh!" He threw my arm down in disgust and walked away. "Anyhow, he's dead," he said in a loud voice. Then he muttered almost to himself, "He's dead." He wheeled around and almost shouted, "Isn't he?"

"Yes."

"Yes," he said. Once more he stepped toward me. "So there's no point in denying—denying," he said, grabbing my wrist again. "Why do you persist in lying about something that—" He jerked my arm back again. *"Why!"*

Then he saw the look on my face. I must have forgotten how disturbed I considered him to be, but now I remembered and it must have been on my face. He didn't continue, just held my arm

311

back, and I could tell he was outside himself looking in on him bending my arm back for the second time within a minute. I think even he was puzzled by it and finally he just let go and walked back to the stereo set. "Anyway, it's yours. I thought you'd—"

"I don't want it." I didn't want him giving me anything of Jordan's.

He spun around. "You don't want it! You wanted his Tiffany watch and his ring and his wallet—stealing from a dead person! Aren't you—"

I jumped up from the chair. "No, he gave them to me!"

"When—after he died?"

"In New York. He said if anything ever happened to him to take them. Again the other day, he pointed and said 'don't forget'!"

"I find that hard to believe."

Suddenly I was furious at him again for taking them, and furious for Jordan, who wouldn't have liked it at all. "You find everything hard to believe!" I was almost choking. "You went through my things and *took* them!"

Now a sneaky, dirty look from him. "If he gave them to you, why did you hide them underneath—"

I didn't even let him finish. "Because I know *you!*" I shouted at him. "Because they were *mine!*"

He ignored it. "There was money in his wallet, wasn't there?" Another step toward me. "Wasn't there?"

"Yes, there was. I don't *lie* to you!"

"You'll have to give it to me, I'll send it on—"

"No!"

"You'll give me the money," he said, holding out his hand.

"No, he wanted me to have it. Jordan wanted it!" I was still shouting at him. "He wanted me to have those things and you took them!" He moved closer and for some reason that huge hand held out in front of me drove me crazy. "You took them—goddam you!"

Before I could say anything else he'd struck me, an openhanded slap but so strong it lifted me up off my feet and knocked me down.

312

As I lay there on the floor he came toward me. "Get away!" I kicked at him with my foot and he stopped.

I think he was shaken by what he'd done. He said "Peter . . ." and started toward me once more. "Get away, stay away!" I kicked at him again and he stepped back.

Though my face stung and my head was ringing, I was glad he'd hit me. That finalized things and I felt great relief, and when he next said "You're upset!" and walked around toward his desk, I actually laughed, a couple of gulps of laughter came out of me as I thought: You just clobbered me and *I'm* upset!

"What are you laughing at?" he asked.

Now I was feeling reckless again. "You!" I said and laughed again.

"Get up," he said.

"Yes, sir!" I almost sprang up.

"Sit down, Peter."

"Yes, sir!" I said, but I was mocking him.

He sat down behind his desk and clasped his hands together and he knew it. He shook his head and after a while he sighed. "Of course, of course, this—what happened today is bound to have a deep effect on you. I know that. I'm sorry I slapped you, Peter. I understand how you—" He broke off for a moment and waved a hand in the air. "When all this is past and digested, in its perspective, I'm sure we can be friends again." He looked up at me and even smiled.

In an instant I was saddened because now he was trying to treat me like a human being. God, my emotions were flicking off and on like a defective light bulb. "I know we'll be friends, won't we, Peter?"

"Oh . . ." It came out of me like a groan and hung there.

"What is it?" he asked.

I didn't want him to try even. I knew it was over. Not lying became important. "I don't think," I mumbled. I was staring down at my lap when I said it but then I did glance up and he was looking confused. Right then I thought of telling him I was leaving, but I

313

knew from the way it had gone so far, he wouldn't take it from me. Also, suddenly I thought about Jordan: Jordan's gone. What am I doing playing out this scene with Mr. Hoyt? Just leave, Jordan's dead, so what does all this matter!

To my surprise, Mr. Hoyt was standing and saying, "Well, I know . . . You need a good sleep, Peter. You take it easy for a while. If you feel you want to talk to someone in the next few days, I want you to come to me." He held out his hand. I stood up in reflex and looked at it. He was offering it in friendship and I took it in farewell.

My eye caught sight of the paper bag. Whereas I'd thought to present him with the towel and the bottle in anger, even revenge, and had anticipated the look on his face when he saw them, now I only wanted, in effect, to say: Goodbye and I know, have known, and will remember—that's how it is.

I picked the bag up and held it out to him. "Here," I said very softly, "I believe these are yours." Then I turned and left and as I walked from his study to the front door I could hear the paper bag crackle. Nearing the door, I had an impulse to snatch it open and run, thinking I would hear his voice calling me back. But he didn't. It was very quiet.

Outside, the rain was plopping down in heavy blobs, almost slush. There was the normal buzz when I opened the door to Lincoln House. They were all eating. Then complete silence as they turned and saw me. When I got to the doorway of the dining room there wasn't as much as the sound of a dish or a fork for a second. They were all looking at me and I was looking back at them. Mrs. Rauscher opened the pantry door and took one step into the room. All of her rocky New England features had melted into a lump of crying-pink dough. She said "Peter . . ." and ducked back into the pantry. After that a few fellows mumbled my name. I was almost thinking of going in and sitting down but then I saw Jordan's chair at our table, empty and cold-looking, and I turned and trotted upstairs.

On the way to my room I was telling myself, in Jordan's words:

Baby, get out of here, go, flee, fly away. Don't get involved in any more crazy mental sleight of hand, make your mind work for you. And I did. I shifted gears into practical. Before even reaching my door I swung around and went down to Mr. Kauffman's room. I knew this was my chance to phone, while he was eating, so I called Cutler Barnum and told him to meet me in a half hour three street lights up along the main road on the side of school away from town. He'd heard about Jordan, and when he asked if I was going to the funeral, I just said yes.

Back in my room I packed like the Chinese were coming. I'd collected so much what with all the Christmas presents Jordan had given me that it was difficult to get everything in. I left all my books and some old clothes and even my tennis racquet. The rest I crammed into my two suitcases. That, along with my typewriter, was it. I made two trips down the fire escape in the rain and left my things by the side of the house.

Coming down the stairs I passed some of the fellows along with Mr. Kauffman, who asked me where I was going. I said I was supposed to go back over to Mr. Hoyt's. Several guys were in the parlor and I walked out without saying anything. I went around the side of the house, gathered up my things and took off toward the back dirt road that led in from the street to the gym.

I'd only just reached the appointed street light when Cutler pulled up. He told me he was sorry about Jordan, that he was an odd little fellow but he had a big spirit. I think he sensed my mood because he didn't say much else. I knew I'd missed the one evening train to Boston so I had him drive me to Theron, about twenty-some miles away, which was a stop for buses. Cutler, who was up on everything, said the next bus to Boston was at ten after nine. It was a little after seven; by the time we got there I'd only have an hour or so to wait.

As we neared Theron, Cutler talked about the weather and how this would ruin the winter business unless there was a sudden freeze. He said folks were already taking the little wooden fishing shacks in off the lake, which was unusual for January. When he left me off he shook my hand and absolutely refused to take any money. "Nope, this one's on me," he said. I protested that it was over twenty rough miles of driving both ways but he said, "Nope, this one's for Jordan. Now, Peter," he added, "you say goodbye to that little fella for me, will you?" I told him I would, feeling like a rat because I wasn't going to the funeral.

The bus terminal was appropriately tacky, one huge room with a lunch counter and magazine stand to one side, a ticket booth, some lockers, some wooden benches, a couple of johns and that was it. It was way overheated and had a peculiar smell like perfumed bubble gum.

After I bought my ticket and made sure about the bus, I sat down on a bench. I felt hollow and dead and, in spite of all the sleep I'd had, drowsy. The heat in there was suffocating. I thought I'd take a walk but when I opened the door it was raining hard again. I didn't have a hat or umbrella and I didn't want a soggy bus trip, so I went back to the bench and sat down.

I didn't mean to fall asleep, but I did.

25

I WAS YANKED UP and standing on my feet before I was wide awake. Mr. Hoyt had me by the arm. The first thing I noticed after he shook me and I was able to focus my eyes—he was holding me up close to him—was the contrast between the flush of his face and the deadly white of that spot on his forehead. The moment he saw I was even vaguely awake he began hauling me out of the terminal. He had a superman grip on me. I was so completely stunned and groggy that I just let him drag me out.

As he opened the front door and shoved me in the car, I saw my bags and typewriter in a jumble on the back seat. He'd thrown them there before grabbing me. He was usually a cautious driver but the car took off with a lurch. After we got going I could hear heavy, quick breaths wheezing out of his nostrils.

He was in a highly explosive state, so I just sat there very still, looking straight ahead. I wondered how he knew where to find me, but I supposed once somebody saw my room and knew I was gone, it wasn't hard to figure I'd try to get to Boston and there were only buses and that meant Theron. I was kicking myself for not using my head. I should have had Cutler drive me to the New Hampshire Turnpike, which was about fifteen miles away, and hitchhiked, instead of going to sleep like a dodo in that ridiculous bus station.

As we were leaving Theron I thought I smelled wine fumes, like the night of the rubdown. The minute I became aware of that I was reminded that I'd given him the towel and the alcohol bottle. I wondered if what had set him off was that, or me running away—or both.

The car was stuffy. His breathing was not leveling off and I was sure of the wine now. Still there hadn't been a word between us. Soon we were driving through the rugged countryside, still heavy with snow in spite of the rain. Suspense was building up as to when he'd speak. I sneaked a look at him. I could see the muscles of his face, how taut they were and how stony his profile. He was gripping the steering wheel like he was holding a jet airliner on course through a hurricane. I could imagine him ripping it off.

He sensed me watching him and looked over, a quick swing of his head and right back again. I was so curious to catch his expression that I didn't look away. There wasn't much to see on his face except the rigidness that comes with fury. The only other thing I noticed: his brown eyes actually flashed green. It could have been the combination of the night and the dashboard lights but I believe it was from pure anger.

The next series of events were memorable for their timing. Once more I faced front, just staring at the steady sweep of the windshield wipers and listening to the whoosh they made. Then, in my peripheral vision, and somehow connected with the first look, his head darted around for another glance at me, which he held a bit longer before turning back. I didn't look at him directly this time, nor the next time he looked over, nor the third, each glance coming closer together in sequence and yet each one held longer on me. I knew something was building up but I had no idea until, instead of another look, he expelled a large breath and then slashed his right arm over and hit me a backhanded blow on my upper lip and nose.

My head snapped back and I must have made a sound—I don't know—I certainly put a hand up to my face as I felt my nose go all hot and the blood gush out of it.

Just then, and surprising me as much as when he hit me, he slammed the car to a skidding halt—we were going fairly fast—

318

and jerked the hand brake on as he turned his whole body toward me and shouted as loudly as if he were screaming from one mountaintop to another: "Who do you think you are!" I was backed up against the door, still with my hand up to my nose and the blood dripping down over my fingers. He seemed not to even notice this. Instead, he made an abrupt false start toward me, which made me duck back even more, and shouted out again: "Answer me! *Who do you think you are!*" The force of it left my eardrums ringing. All I could do was shake my head at him.

As abruptly as the attack had come on, he snorted, turned front and started the car up again. It was only then that my face began to hurt; my lip and nose were aching and I could feel a throb in them, like my pulsebeat. I fumbled around for a handkerchief but I didn't have one. Without a word, Mr. Hoyt jammed one over at me. I took it and mopped myself up, wiped off my chin and right hand, and then just held it pressed up to my nose to try to stop the blood, which had poured all down the front of me.

We drove along in silence except for the muffled noise of the windshield wipers and the slick sticky sound of tires on wet pavement. After a while the throbbing in my face turned to a numb ache. Sitting in that car about as miserable as I'd ever felt, I started thinking about Jordan. I hadn't forgotten his death. But now again I was consciously thinking about *him,* all cold in a box, traveling in a baggage car to Boston, or being shunted from the railroad station to the airport and hoisted up into the cargo section of a plane. And here I was trapped in this car with this poor fucked-up man I could partially understand but never completely, going back to a school I could never in a million years stay in. Both of us on the road. Where we didn't want to be and where we had no control.

And I started to sob—I would have sold my soul not to let it happen in front of him—but I couldn't hold it back. It wasn't because he'd hit me and it hurt, but I was crying over Jordan and me and our plans. We'd been ambushed, shot down. As if we were walking along a beach having the greatest time of our lives and a tidal wave reared up out of nowhere and wiped us out.

Then as suddenly as he'd stopped the car before, he did it again, veering this time up on some sort of a bank to the side of the road. The bumping made me turn and look out the window, which is why I didn't see his right arm shoot out and around my shoulder. I pulled away but he was strong and, almost in the manner of a hammer-lock hold, cricked his arm around my neck and forced me off balance toward him until I was almost lying down with my cheek jammed up against his side.

This stopped any sobbing I was doing. I just froze with the handkerchief still up against my nose. I was wondering what he'd do next. What he did was say my name, "Peter . . . oh, Peter . . . ," with unmistakable remorse. With his other hand he began stroking my hair. I could feel that huge hand, cupped, travel over my head and feel the tremor in the fingers, then feel it leave and come back over me again. After a while he said "There . . . there . . ." the way you would to a child, but there wasn't anything to say it about because I wasn't crying or doing anything now, except trying to breathe regularly in that awkward position.

In a flash I remembered my father and a cocker spaniel I had when I was a kid. The puppy was cute and loved me but it was frightened of my father, especially when he'd be drinking. My father was wild about that dog and when he'd had a few drinks he'd always want to hold it and play with it, but the puppy would get away from him and hide under the furniture. My father would haul it out and force it to stay in his arms and he'd be cooing over it, telling it how much he loved it, and when the dog would wriggle and keep trying to get away, all that affection would suddenly turn sour and my father would hit it; once he almost smothered it and once he even kicked it across the room. All my father wanted was for that puppy to accept his affection.

This struck me very strong while Mr. Hoyt was holding me like that for—I don't know how long—maybe five minutes. Just as I was feeling my nose again to see if the bleeding had stopped, he said, "There, it's all right, you'll be all right."

I remembered lying there on the floor of his study earlier that evening and in the one bit of thinking that was like my old self, I thought: Yes, I'll be all right, if you'll stop beating me up.

320

He stroked my head several more times, still holding me firmly in the crook of his arm, and then I felt him gradually ease his hold until I could tell he'd let me sit up and pull away from him, which I finally did. Soon as I was sitting up, he started the car and we bumped down off the bank and were on the road again. I touched my nose with my fingers and I could tell from the warm sticky feel of it that it had stopped bleeding. I went about pulling the rest of myself together, straightening my clothes, and got another surprise when he began talking in a very calm low matter-of-fact voice, a bit thicker and slower than usual, as if the only thing we'd been through was a flat tire. "We'll forget all about today. And when it's behind us, you'll tell me about you and Jordan. Everything, all of it, the truth. It won't be nearly as difficult as you imagine. You'll see. And we'll be friends again. I'll be your friend, a good friend." He went on about the Glee Club and my new monologue and then suddenly he was talking about how beautiful the spring was in New Hampshire. I was grateful he didn't require an answer of me. I knew I couldn't talk to him; I wouldn't know which voice to use. After a while, he said, "Perhaps Mrs. Hoyt will be back by then and we can—Mrs. Hoyt's very fond of you, too, Peter—and perhaps one weekend we can drive up into the White Mountains or down by the seashore. So you see . . ." He broke off as if he'd lost his place. He was quiet until he reached over and put his hand on my leg. "You cause in me . . ." Again he stopped. More silence and finally he patted me on the knee and took his hand away.

I was frightened. Just to think of the pulls and tugs, like riptides, that must be going on inside of him was scary. Dense as I might have been about him before, I knew for certain he didn't really care if Mrs. Hoyt ever came back, that what he wanted deep down was to take me up into the mountains or down by the seashore. But that he could never admit it to me—no matter what he thought I'd done —and he probably could never admit it to himself. I also knew I could never really speak to him again. How can you talk to someone when you know what their real meaning is and they won't ever acknowledge it to you—and you can't.

Approaching the village, I got a sick feeling in my stomach.

Now, without Jordan to talk over and share and make light of Mr. Hoyt and the school and students—like an experience you were getting through together—it was no longer funny at all and I was back in nightmare territory alone. You can be scared in the dark if you're with someone so that it has a little humor, but if you're solo, it's not funny.

"We're home," he said, pulling up in front of his house.

Home!

I stepped out of the car and got my things and he came around and took hold of my large suitcase and the typewriter. "Peter, would you like to come in for a cup of cocoa or a bite of something?"

"I'm tired," I said, finding it impossible to look at him.

"Yes. Here, I'll walk you over."

"I can manage."

"I'll come with you."

The lights were on in Lincoln House. Study hours were about over. When we got up on the porch and just as I reached for the front door, he grabbed hold of my arm. I was so conditioned that I flinched and swung around before he could turn me, if that's what he would have done. He was surprised and then I believe annoyed. He said my name like he was asking: Why did you do that? I was allergic to him touching me and it must have shown in my expression. He said my name again, as if it were a question: "Peter?"

Jesus, what does he want of me! "What?" I asked and it must have sounded sharp because a snap came into his eyes and he phrased the question I'd already translated. "What is it?"

There we were asking questions back at one another. The loud and clear answer to his, of course, was: *You!* I didn't say it, but it was there, again for him to see. He reached out for me and suddenly his hands were the hands that had dragged Jordan over in the middle of the night and hit Jordan. "Don't!" I said, pulling back and bumping up against the door.

He didn't touch me but I felt he wanted to slap me again. "Now listen to me, Peter. You won't try anything like this again, will

you?" His saying it only made me think of how soon. I suppose this made me hesitate a second too long for him. "Peter, I'm speaking to you! Answer me—no more running off!"

I looked at him and said no, but as I was saying it, it even sounded to me like yes.

He kept his eyes fixed on me. "I'm serious. No more nonsense. You've indulged yourself enough for one day. You'll be checked on so don't try any—" His impatience with my attitude made him stop. "Do you understand me?"

"Yes."

He didn't speak for a long moment, during which I knew he was weighing about whether he could trust me or not. Finally he said, "All right, get up to your room."

I turned and opened the door. He stood there very still and watched me put my things inside. When I'd closed the door and managed to pick up both suitcases and the typewriter, I walked to the foot of the stairs and looked up them. The effort, together with the lack of any desire to climb them, stopped me. I turned and glanced back to the porch. He was still standing there, staring at me.

Crazily enough, I felt this smile crawling over my face, and as soon as I realized it, I turned and went up the stairs. I heaved a sigh of relief after I cleared the second floor without seeing anyone. The door to Mr. Kauffman's room was mercifully closed. Turning the landing on the top stairs, I saw a piece of paper stuck to Jordan's door. There was printing in black crayon: *This Room Is Haunted!* It was the work of some moron who'd disguised his writing by printing in quavery lines. I ripped it off and threw it in the hall wastebasket. A shower in the john was running and Ed Anders' door was open but he was standing on his bed, his back to me, tacking a pennant to the wall.

I quickly went into my room and shut the door, thanking God I'd made it up two flights and down the hall without having anyone see me, especially without having to speak to anyone. I put my bags down, switched on the light and switched it right off again. I

323

realized word of my running away must have got around and if the lights were on someone was bound to come snooping around and want to hash it over.

It wasn't too long before lights-out. I went over to my bed and just sat there in the dark. Outside of a recurrent moment of anger about the piece of paper on Jordan's door, I really sat in a stupor, thinking it wasn't his room that was haunted, it was the entire school. Doomed and demented, more than haunted. I became terribly anxious sitting there. I was only existing moment to moment until lights-out when I could get away. Every time I'd hear footsteps in the hall I'd tense up, saying to myself: No, no don't come in *here!* I sat there with my eyes shut, willing them away. And no one came. At one point Ed Anders stepped out into the hall for a short blast, but he went right back into his room.

With Jordan not there I felt the foundation was gone, and I began thinking if I didn't get out soon, the building would actually collapse and come crashing down. A crazy notion and I acknowledged it as crazy but still I couldn't get it out of my mind and pretty soon I was grasping the edge of the bed with both hands and feeling the perspiration break out on my forehead and around my neck. I took one hand and felt my nose, dried and stuck with little flecks of blood, and my upper lip, swollen and numb.

I would like to have showered and cleaned up but I didn't want to chance any encounters. Then I made up one of those dizzy step-on-a-crack-break-your-mother's-back things: if no one came to my room before lights-out, I'd get away safely. For the last ten minutes I was practically holding my breath. There's always a flurry of activity right before bedtime, trips to the john, last-minute room visits. This night, and I liked to think because of Jordan, it was a bit more subdued than usual. Sitting there, waiting for the hall lights to go out, I was dripping with perspiration. They hadn't reduced the heat to go with this warm spell and my room was steamy-hot and even seemed stuffier sitting there with all my clothes on in the dark. I got this suffocating sensation and consciously had to make my breathing deep and regular.

324

Quite a few footsteps out in the hall now but not much talk. Then the lights went out. I exhaled in relief as the footsteps led back to their rooms and doors were closed. I was just telling myself I'd made it when one pair of footsteps came up the stairs and down the hall to my room.

The door opened and the light went on. It was Mr. Kauffman. He looked at me sitting there like I was, on the bed, and said, "Mr. Hoyt told me you were back." He ducked his head out and squinted at me. "Peter, your nose, what happened?"

"I—bumped it."

He took a step forward. "Bumped—" But his foot struck one of my suitcases. He looked down at my things, then back up at me, fully dressed. "Why aren't you ready for bed, Peter?" He glanced down at them again. "Aren't you going to unpack?"

"Yes."

"When?"

"In the morning." The words were coming out by rote, the fewest, simplest, easiest answers that occurred to me.

"Don't you think you'd better undress and get ready for bed?"

I stood up. "Yes." I took off my jacket.

"And, Peter, whatever you did to your face—you'd better wash up, too."

"Yes, I will." I started taking off my tie and shirt. He stood there watching me for a moment. "All right, then," he finally said and left. I decided I would clean up so when I was hitchhiking I wouldn't scare prospective rides away. I got my towel and comb and walked quietly to the bathroom. By the time I'd sponged the dried blood off me and washed my sore lip and nose and combed my hair, I didn't look too badly out of whack. My upper lip was swollen but I figured at night no one's going to notice that much.

Back in my room I decided to consolidate my things into one suitcase, even forfeit my typewriter, that's how badly I wanted out of there. When I'd done this, which took about ten minutes of sorting out and repacking, I got dressed again and turned out the lights.

Odd, but it never occurred to me for a moment to stay there a day or so, to play it cool, and then leave. If I had, all this probably wouldn't have happened. It was like a prison break the night before execution—now or never. I stood there another few minutes, firming my plan. I'd cut across the back part of the school away from town, walk to a gas station about a quarter of a mile away where there was a phone booth, call Cutler and have him drive me to the turnpike where I'd hitch to Boston.

I went to my door and listened. I could hear Ed Anders snoring already. Lights-out and all's well. I went to the window, eased it open, got my bag and stepped out onto the fire escape. The drizzle had stopped and now a brisk wind was blowing. The sky was completely overcast with heavy, billowy clouds moving fast. If it hadn't been for the many fields and stretches of snow which outlined where buildings and trees and paths *weren't,* it would have been an extremely dark night; that is, it was a dark night, but the snow helped distinguish landmarks. It felt good to be out of the stuffy house and I liked the wind. There's about a four-foot drop from the last rung where the fire escape leads down right by the corner of the building. I swung my suitcase out and let it fall. I hung for a moment from one of the rungs and let myself drop easily to the ground, facing away from the corner. I straightened up from the crouched position I'd landed in and had just picked up my suitcase when a pair of hands grabbed me from behind.

Right away I knew it was him; still it was so unexpected I reacted violently, wrenching my body from his grasp, at the same time swinging my suitcase out and slamming it back as hard as I could against Mr. Hoyt's side, right below his shoulder, knocking him up against the building.

There hadn't been a sound uttered. We stood there for a moment with only the wind between us. As soon as he took his first step, I flung the suitcase directly at his face and took off. I heard him grunt when it hit him but then, as I turned to the left, thinking to angle over in front of the gym to the back road and cut over to the left again toward the street, I could tell he was running along parallel to my left and behind me but not far enough behind to enable

326

me to cut over. The only course open to me was to keep running the way I was over toward the gym and somehow lose him.

I keep thinking in my mind now—even though it's over and done with—if only he hadn't kept after me!

26

I TRIED NOT to let the snow slow me down; I was leaping over and through it, all mushy from the rain. I hit the cleared path leading to the main doors of the gym, veered off on the one that ran all the way around the building and tore around the corner without even looking back to see how close he was. An error, but all I could think of was whipping around the gym with him behind me so I could get running ahead and out toward the street and the town.

The gym, like the main school building, was on a rise. I followed the path close up against the outside wall and turned again, running along the back of the gym where the snow hadn't been cleared too well. When I was about halfway to the end, Mr. Hoyt came around the far corner, the one I was headed for; he'd anticipated what I was trying to do and had cut me off. I pulled up short, then swung around wide out of the path to turn around and run back. I misjudged where the hill sloped away steep, because of all the snow, and one leg buckled and down I went, rolling a full turn over on my side, my head tilted downhill. I looked up to see him bearing down on me.

I scrambled to my feet, but he must have dived at me. I heard him grunt "Bastard!" as he grabbed my coat and then down we both went. It was a hard fall and we rolled a couple of turns down the hillside with me ending up on my back and him below me. As I was starting to raise myself up, he sprang forward and landed on top of me. The force of him snapped me flat down and the back of my head hit hard on the ground and left me stunned. I don't know whether I was actually out for a few moments or just lying there dazed but the next thing I was aware of was the pressure of his hands on my head.

He had one huge hand on each side of my face, holding my head upright and steady. When I opened my eyes he was right over me, pressing his mouth down toward my lips. I smelled his sour wine breath and squirmed, ducking my head back and forth from side to side with him exerting all the pressure in his hands to force my head upright. "Is this—this—what he did—hmn?—like this?" I screamed no, meaning no and for him not to do it, and kept fighting to move my head. "No? No? . . . What was it like? . . . Wasn't it like this—hmn, hmn?" And for a brief second I felt his thin lips, cold and rubbery and tough, press down on my mouth. An awful moment—shuddering—like lizards and snakes crawling all over me. I jerked my head to the side and then he was pressing his lips down against my cheek and making eerie muffled humming sounds. "Hmn?—Hmn?—Hmn?"—meaning: Like this, like this, like this?

Just as he was about to touch his lips to mine again, I opened my mouth and screamed with every ounce of energy in me, not words or anything, just a wild, bloodcurdling scream. I could feel the blast of air strike his face and bounce back in mine. It surprised him. He ducked his head up and looked down at me. Then he laughed, a dirty laugh. "You didn't protest when that nasty little—"

I wouldn't have him speak of Jordan. I made a claw out of my right hand and slammed it up, digging my fingers into his face and dragging them down. I felt one finger pop into something jellylike, and when he cried out, I realized it was his eye, the corner of it. I quickly jabbed to do it again, but his eyelid was closed by then. Still it hurt him and he groaned in pain. By this time I was tearing at his nose; I would have ripped his whole face open to silence anything he might say about Jordan.

He rolled off me to get away from my hands. When I tried to stand up he made a grab and caught hold of my pants. I kicked him in the shoulder with my free foot and he grunted and let go, but this caused me to stumble and fall downhill again. By the time I got to my feet he was up, too, one hand to his eye, but above me on the hill and stepping off right after me. With him having the advantage of being above me, it was impossible to cut across the slope and run uphill against him. The only thing to do was keep on running down the long, easy hillside leading to the football field and the woods beyond.

As shaken as I was, I was suddenly elated that I'd inflicted some damage on him. I was pretty sure I could run faster than him, so I had in mind to put as much distance as possible between us. I opened up and ran as fast as I could, following more or less the dirt road which hadn't been plowed but which at least was more regular beneath the snow than the hillside itself. The wind was at my back, blowing hard down toward the lake and helping me. Halfway down to the field I heard him shout my name several times, telling me to stop. Even if he'd had a gun, I wouldn't have stopped. He didn't keep yelling for long, though, and all I could hear was my own breathing under the wind and the sloshing sounds that running through the snow made.

When I got to the bottom, at the edge of the football field, I stopped and turned to see how far ahead of him I was. Not as much as I thought. He was coming at a good clip, part of his strange tilted-forward walk was in his run and he was flapping along like Ichabod Crane. When he saw me stop, he jogged to a halt, too, and put a hand up to his eye. "Peter—stop—come here!" I thought how hard he was panting and realized I was breathing just as hard. He dropped his hand from his face and called out "Peter?" once more, like a question. A big gust of wind blew his overcoat out behind him. Standing on the hill higher than me, he looked even taller, and with his coat flapping out behind him, it was like he had wings and could swoop right down on me.

I turned, took a deep breath and charged out across the solid mass of snow that was the football field, angling across toward

330

where the narrow path led into the woods running alongside the lake. I'd follow the path a ways, then cut over to the left through the woods until I hit an old trail in the middle, double back and lose him completely.

Suddenly the idea of Mr. Hoyt chasing me across the football field in the middle of winter struck me funny. I laughed and that made me sprint even faster until I reached the small opening where the path led in through the woods. I stopped to check how far he was from me. I'd gained some distance now that we were on level ground. He was loping along across the field and I had an insane desire to run back past him, mimicking his unique gallop, which of course I never would have carried out, especially when it came to me that what I was doing was just *standing* there watching him come at me.

Just then he stumbled and went down on his hands and knees in the snow. I laughed again, and with Jordan's probable words, Run, Bulldog, run! and the thought, Reverend Davidson, this is the last you'll see of me, I took off into the woods.

I'd hurt his eye and he was falling all over himself. Again I experienced that reckless sensation I'd felt earlier. As if now, with Jordan gone, the lines sharply drawn and the chase on, the warden and the escaping convict, there was nothing I wouldn't do to get away from him. Not only that, if I could possibly torment him while doing it, so much the better. I started fantasizing a scene of me crisscrossing back and forth in the woods until I'd run him ragged and he'd finally be lying there helpless in the snow gasping for breath. Then I'd saunter up, stand over him and aim one long, cool look down at him and sort of strut away. But I didn't stop with that notion. I think it was the idea of us wrestling on that hillside and now a physical chase, like kids, that struck me silly. Soon I was plowing through the woods having all sorts of brain waves, wild mental pictures of me zooming off in a private plane with him tearing across the airstrip after me, of him dashing out on a wharf and me gunning a speedboat away in the nick of time. When it got that bad I stopped and came back to reality.

The trees were thinner at the beginning of the woods, but the farther in the path went, the thicker they got until I was forced to slow way up and pick my way over big clumps of leaves and snow and dead branches that had fallen down. The wind seemed like it was at the top of the trees; it made a faint whistling sound up there. I was making a lot of noise crashing along the path and I stopped and listened. There was only the wind; I couldn't hear him. I turned around and, of course, I couldn't see him either.

In an instant, I was terrified. Now that I was in the woods, cut off from the sight and sound of him, playing hide-and-seek, there was something eerie about it. No more thoughts of teasing him. It was serious. I remembered the feel of his weight on top of me and the touch of his lips. I shuddered. No more games—just get away from him. I grabbed hold of the trunk of a scrub pine and stood very still, straining to catch some sound he might be making, but all I could hear was the wind. I glanced up, wishing it would cut out for a second. Then I thought maybe he'd stopped at the edge of the woods, hadn't even followed me into them, thinking it would be better to go back and get a couple of the other teachers or even call the police.

As I was trying to second-guess him, I heard a distant crackling sound way back along the path. I strained to see but couldn't. Another sound, louder, this time of branches snapping and I took off again. Then I heard him call my name. He sounded far behind me but just knowing he'd actually followed me into the woods made me sprint. I was leaping over mounds of snow and branches and I was making good time. I came to a little dipping turn in the path, a gully no more than three or four feet, and then the path leveled off again. When I hit it, I didn't trip or anything, I just wasn't prepared for the give under the snow and my right ankle snapped over to the side and down I went with a yelp.

A stupid fall, no reason. My body landed easily but immediately I felt a sharp pain in my ankle, very sharp. Oh, Jesus, I thought, come on, give me a break! I sat there holding my ankle with both hands, rocking back and forth and cursing. Now, more than anything, I was mad. I just felt: Okay, I've had enough, let me off the hook. Then I heard him shout "Peter!" way in the distance. Not only was my ankle hurting, but my nose and lip, where he'd hit me, were aching again and I was wet and cold. I turned all my fury on him. Leave me alone, stop it, the game is over, you sadistic bastard! Goddam you! And I mean God *DAMN* you, and if He won't, I will. And then he shouted my name again, loud, shrill and wild-sounding. I got to my feet, although my ankle was killing me, and started gimping away, and I thought: You son of a bitch, if I get run over by a train at the next turn in this fucking path and my leg is cut off and I'm lying there in pieces I'll still pick up the bloody stump and chop you over the head with it if you come near me.

What I did see at the next turn was the old boathouse jutting out over the lake. Each time I put my weight on my right foot a pain would circle around my ankle and shoot up my leg. I wondered if I'd broken it but figured no, I wouldn't be able to use it at all if it were broken. I must have sprained it. A sprained ankle—what a dizzy simple-tit thing to be downed by! I wouldn't—couldn't—let him catch me because I'd sprained my son-of-a-bitching ankle. That would be too rotten. I went off balance and fell over, steadying myself against a boulder to the side of the path. "Shit!" I shouted out. "Shit!" And hobbled on, telling myself if you have to do something badly enough, you do it, even if you have a broken *neck!*

A wide wooden walk led to the boathouse up ahead to my right. By this time, no matter what I told myself, I knew I'd never make it farther along the path without him catching me. Like a wounded animal, I headed for shelter. A metal railing sided the walk leading to the building and I used it for support, pulling myself along. A big gust of wind howled over across the lake, and just as I thought I heard my name being called again, a wooden shutter banged shut and open and shut again and I couldn't be sure.

The snow was thick on the porch and there was a drift of it up against the wide doors which I cleared away as best I could, kicking at it with my good foot. The doors themselves were stuck from all the winter weather and I had to shoulder them hard to get them to give at all. One, two, three, I slammed my whole weight against them and, of course, they swung in and I ended up on the floor. This latest fall was so ridiculous that I actually laughed at myself lying there on my side. I just stayed on the floor nodding my head: why not, it figures!

Then I did hear him call out my name. It didn't sound too close, still it was enough to make me get up and quickly shut the doors. I stood there, leaning up against them. It was pitch-black inside the boathouse. I felt sheltered and even warm, what with the wind outside. In an instant it came to me what I'd do. He didn't know I'd sprained my ankle, so he'd naturally think I'd run on farther along the path and maybe even through the woods toward the dirt road that bordered the other side. Already I was moving toward the windows at that part of the boathouse overlooking the path and the woods. As soon as I could see him go past, I'd let him get ahead a ways, then I'd leave and double back. Instead of climbing the hill, I'd circle around the edge of the lake below the school toward town, cut across that part of the campus beyond Logan Hall and quick scoot over to Patti's. No one would think of looking for me there. She'd help me get transportation to Boston; she might even drive me there herself. Especially when I explained to her about Mr. Hoyt and I had the battered face and ankle to prove it.

I took my place by the window and looked down along the wooden runway to the path and the next moment my great plans were shot to hell. Leading directly up to the doors were my messy footprints, the only ones. Nobody'd been walking down around there in that weather. A perfect set of tracks leading smack to me.

And there he was, coming along the path about twenty yards from the walk. Instinctively—not that he could have seen me from that distance—I ducked back away from the window. If anyone ever prayed, it was me. I was beaming them up to heaven that he wouldn't notice those footprints, that he'd keep on going right past them. After a few moments I couldn't stand not watching, so I edged up to the window and peeked out through the broken shutter.

334

He was standing at the foot of the walk, facing the boathouse. But one hand was up to his eye and he didn't seem to be looking anywhere, just pressing his hand against his eye and forehead. A gust of wind swatted the trees near him and some snow drifted down and swept across his face and shoulders. He brought his hand down and gave a little shake of his head.

Oh, Jesus—suddenly he was a monster standing there, so tall and gaunt, like a huge stunned crazy giant that had just escaped from a madhouse and hadn't decided what to do. Maybe that's what he *was* doing, deciding whether to look for me inside or go back to school and get someone.

I prayed for him to turn and follow the path and I wasn't praying to God now but to Mr. Hoyt himself, silently begging him to go away and leave me alone, at the same time saying: If you come in here after me, I'll kill you. From what he'd done and said on that hillside I knew he'd gone all out of control and you can't reason with a crazy person.

He put a hand up to his eye again; after a moment he brushed the snow off his shoulder. Then he lowered his arm and stood there with those huge hands hanging down at his sides. His shoulders gave a sudden jerking motion and he started up the walk toward me.

27

BY THE TIME he'd taken his second step I was skittering across the large main room toward the old stairway, with several steps missing, that led down to the boat slips and the lake which came in underneath the boathouse floor. My bum foot broke through one of the wooden planks going down and although I felt a sharp pain I didn't fall and I didn't let it stop me. I went down the rest of it crablike. It was quite steep, but I hung on to the rusted metal railing.

At the bottom was a wooden walkway that ran around the boat slips on three sides in a U-shape. Most of it was pretty well rotted away. All in the middle was water, now frozen over, where canoes and small motor boats used to come right in and tie up. The end that used to be open and lead out to the lake had been all boarded up, so you couldn't get out that way unless the water wasn't frozen, then you could swim underwater a yard or so and make it. But in winter it was like one huge barn with walkways on both sides and at one end and then an ice floor below them. I could feel the walkway cracking under my feet, so I sat down and eased myself off it and let myself drop to the ice.

Just then I heard the doors open up above and footsteps on the floor over me. A shutter banged outside several times, then everything was quiet.

"Peter!" he called out and the word echoed around the upstairs and ran down the stairway. "Peter!" His voice was hoarse and there was something frantic in the way he called it out, almost screamed it, the third time: *"Peter!"*

I started to move away from where the stairs led down over to the corner and bumped into the bow of an old rowboat that was half sunk and sticking up out of the ice. I remembered seeing it when Jordan and I had been down there. This made me take a heavy, lurching side step and I heard the ice crack. I stopped and probed around with my good foot. It felt solid enough despite the warm spell the last two days. I remembered seeing ponds and lakes melt around the edges first and I wondered if the fact that this slip of water was sheltered and warmer than the lake outside would make it dangerous. Still, I would risk it rather than let him get at me. I moved toward the far inside end, opposite from the boarded-up side. There was another loud crack but I didn't feel anything give. He took a few more steps upstairs and I wondered if he'd heard the ice. Then everything was quiet, except for the wind, which was having a good time playing around the building, creaking it and banging a shutter now and then.

"Peter?" He said my name tentatively this time, like maybe he doubted I was there. I didn't hear a match being struck but I saw a faint glow seep down from the stairs, just enough to show the few top steps, nothing more. I cursed the inventor of matches, at the same time hoping he only had one of those used-up books with one or two matches left.

I picked my way over the ice carefully until I could feel the far corner where the two wooden walkways met. I turned around and leaned up against them. Now I was as far away from the stairway as I could get. His match went out and it was black again. He said my name tentatively once more. Then the faint glow of another match and slow, halting footsteps, the way you walk when you're trying to keep something lighted and look around at the same time. Dark again, but now I could hear him moving toward the stairs. A kicking, scraping sound—he'd bumped into an old chair or table—and he muttered something but kept on coming and I could tell he was close to the top of them. He stopped and struck a match, but the lighted head broke off so there was only a little spiral of flame looping down the steps and darkness again.

The last one, make it the last!

But he struck another and it took. I could only see his feet and part of his legs, about up to his knees, as he stood on the floor above. I was surprised at the strong shaft of light that flickered down the stairs.

"Peter!" He screamed my name out this time, still frantic, but now it was angry, too, and so loud I jumped back and bumped up against the walk. Then he took one step down and the light was gone.

I began to tremble. Not that I wasn't scared all along, but now I was terrified. And you know what I thought? Of all the ridiculous things I never even had or knew? I thought: I want my mother. Eighteen years old and been around and seen a lot of weird things, especially in California, been seduced by a TV star, even found Jordan dead, and suddenly: I want my mother. Isn't that ridiculous?

He was having trouble with the stairs, the same rotted boards that gave me trouble, and when he didn't light another match I was sure he must be out of them. I heard a board splinter and he crashed through down to the next step and muttered "Jesus!" Then all was quiet. Until he lit another match, which surprised me, and said my name again. There he was on the next-to-the-bottom step, holding the match out in front of him, looking ahead toward the boarded-up end, not at me. The light was strong where he was and I used this opportunity to get my bearings. I saw the sunken rowboat and also a dilapidated canoe a little farther beyond it and to the side. I glanced around and piled up on the wooden walk a yard or so from my right shoulder was a stack of old oars, paddles and a couple of boat hooks. Right away I thought to grab one but I didn't want to attract his attention by moving or noise of any kind.

He stepped down on the walk itself, looked out over the ice directly in front of him and then turned and looked back and to the

338

right of where I was. I could see him plainly, see a splotch of blood in the corner of his eye and down the side of his nose. But with him holding the match out in front of him and by the expression on his face I could tell he wasn't seeing me back in the dark corner.

I held my breath and remained perfectly still as he moved back along the walkway. The flame flickered and he stopped, staring ahead where there were some old barrels stacked up. I quickly glanced to my right to see if I'd be able to grab something in a hurry. That little movement, even though he wasn't looking at me, must have caught his attention or maybe he just sensed it. He turned his head slowly and looked right over where I was, right at me, but I must have been more in the shadow than I thought because there wasn't a trace of anything on his face as the flame died out.

Black again. I slid over a step nearer the oars piled up at shoulder level on the walk. The ice cracked. He struck another match. The flame flared up, then steadied, and he was still looking right at me. He blinked his eyes, moved them slowly, looking over past me, then quickly brought them back, ducked his head out, squinted and saw me. It was like a double take.

He frowned for a second, then his face relaxed, and there we were staring at each other. He just kept looking at me with kind of cool, mad, almost amused, eyes. Then he smiled, not a big smile, just in his lips. I quick reached to my right, without taking my eyes off him, and grabbed at random at the pile. I got the wood handle of a boat hook and yanked it out, knocking a couple of oars onto the ice, and stood there with it in my hand.

Now he really smiled, a big smile, which struck me as crazy, and he made a little chuckling sound. The match went out and he laughed. Standing there in the dark, listening to the ragged ends of his laughter, I could feel the skin all over my body tighten up and prickle. All dark and quiet again. I waited for him to strike another match, but he didn't. I waited for him to speak; I was sure he'd issue an order of some sort, but the silence just stretched on. I tried to imagine what he was waiting for. I figured he'd seen me crouched back in the corner there, obviously frightened, like some trapped rabbit, and perhaps he was waiting for me to beg, to whimper out some little plea for mercy.

Again I got angry at him for scaring me. And I thought: If you're waiting for me to speak, if that's what you want, I'll keep quiet as long as you.

The wind stirred up outside and I couldn't even hear him breathing. Wild how your emotions change in an instant. The next thing I knew my ankle was sending pains up my leg again; for a while I'd forgotten all about it. Now the anger I was feeling about being scared doubled as I became aware of hurting. And standing there in the dark I began to shake in a sort of frightened rage.

He jumped down onto the ice. I heard him grunt when he hit and the ice cracked again, a sharp warning crack of a sound.

"Get away, keep away!" I shouted, raising the boat hook.

He didn't say anything. I think he laughed or chuckled again as he lunged at me, which I couldn't see, only feel as he got me around the shoulders before I could swing the hook. And down we went on the ice with him all over me again and me yelling for him to stop, to get away. I'd been so surprised I hadn't had time to use the boat hook, but when I was falling I still hung on to it. Now I let it go because I needed both hands to fight him off.

No one who knew him at school, none of the teachers or students will believe this (I hardly do), but again he pressed himself down on me, only this time he was muttering all sorts of filthy things it seems indecent to repeat, now that he's dead, but it's the truth. And always between trying to hold my head still and making those little humming "Hmn? Hmn?" sounds. "Did you stick that —— of yours up that hermaphrodite's ——? Hmn? Hmn?"

Ask me, when I've used some pretty rough words before, why I can't quote him here and I can't tell you. I can only say it would make me sick. He kept on saying these filthy things and I kept fighting him off, clawing at his face and squirming, and when he couldn't bring his lips down to meet mine he suddenly jammed his hand down between my legs, at first just grinding his hand down on

340

me and then grabbing hold, clutching me, like he wanted to rip everything off. And then the sounds coming from him were indescribable.

The pain was immediate and intense and gave me a burst of strength to get away from him. I brought my knees up and kicked and clubbed him with my fists and when I'd managed to push him off me I kept kicking with my feet, even the bad one. I inflicted some damage, I know, from the sounds he was making.

I felt for the boat hook, grabbed it, got to my feet and jumped clear of him out farther on the ice. Then I went a little crazy because I took a position backed up against part of the rowboat, shouting at him that if he came near me I'd kill him and then finally just chanting: "I'll kill you, I'll kill you, I'll kill you!" And he was cursing and yelling at me but I didn't want to hear him so I screamed even louder, "I'll kill you! I'll kill you!" and although I couldn't see him I knew he'd be getting up from the ice and I began slashing the boat hook back and forth in front of me every time I shouted.

Even when I felt the ice crack under me and a giving sensation I kept on and suddenly I connected with him. I must have gotten him in the body, the fleshy part, because it was a soft thwumping sound and feeling as he cried out and then moaned "Peter—no!" But I couldn't stop. I swung again and this time there was a hard hollow crack of a sound and I knew I'd hit him in the head. A terrible deadly blow, so hard my hands and forearms stung from it. A short howl, sliced in two right at an ungodly high shriek that I'll never forget, as he fell heavily and the ice cracked and gave.

I dropped the boat hook and grabbed the bow of the rowboat. There were a few more snapping sounds and I could hear part of him sloshing in the water and feel the ice crack and give out in front of the boat, but still it supported me.

Then an awful sound from him, a choking gasp, a gurgle, again cut off abruptly, and more sloshing in the water and then silence.

I was terrified at what I'd done. Right away I wanted to save him. I remember hearing myself say "No, wait!" as I stepped forward to find him. Only two or three edging steps and the ice, already broken through ahead of me, chipped off under my feet and I went down in the water.

I don't even remember the cold. I could barely touch bottom; the water in that part must have been a little over five feet deep. I swung my arm out and found him, one leg, angled up out of the water. I bounced forward on the balls of my feet and brought my hands up to get him by the waist or shoulders and somehow pull him up onto the ice or over by the walk, but when I got up toward his shoulders my hand struck the edge of the ice and there was no more of his body. What I mean is—when he fell through the ice and choked and gasped he went down and his head came up under where the ice hadn't broken yet.

I grabbed hold of the back of his coat with both hands and tugged. His head and shoulders popped out from under the ice with a burbling sound and I could feel the buoyancy of him floating free.

Then the job of getting him someplace. The worst time of my life, trying to manage him there in the water. He was floating face down, so first I turned him over, only I flipped him too hard and he went all the way over and ended up face down again with a splash. "No, here . . ." I said, "here!" and I tugged at him again, turning him over easier and steadying him with a hand under his back. "Mr. Hoyt . . . Mr. Hoyt . . ." Now talking to him like nothing had happened, like I was trying to get his attention in a roomful of people. I could feel his legs sink down, and although I had a gruesome hunch, I wouldn't give in to it and I kept talking to him, asking him to answer me, could he try to stand, please say something!

I'd only struck him twice, only twice! But I couldn't fool myself. His weight was dead and lifeless and he must be, too. Not being able to really see him, only to feel the different parts of him, was even more frightening. I reached out to get a better hold and my hand got his shoulder and then I moved it over toward his face and my fingers touched that awful warm pulpy place on the side of his head. I cried out, letting go of him and backing away.

342

Still I couldn't just leave him there in the water. I had to at least get him up on something. Then I just went wild, reaching forward and grabbing him every which way, his arm, then his coat, and pulling and tugging and trying to get him back to the edge of the unbroken ice, and to cover up my absolute falling apart I kept screaming "I'm sorry! I'm sorry!" Screaming and thrashing and I'd back up to the ice and try to hoist myself up but the edge would crack off and splinter until the water was over my head and I lost my footing and went under, letting go of him again. When I got to where I could stand I couldn't find him for a second, and when I did, I grabbed his hair and it was all wet and matted and slipped out of my fingers. I was terrified of touching that bloody part and then—suddenly—I just had to get away from him!

I plunged back and bumped into the partly submerged rowboat. I scrambled up over it, just hauled myself up and climbed over on the other side of it where the ice was still solid, crawling at first and then getting footing, and even as I was running and sliding it was cracking more but I reached the wooden walk and pulled myself up on it, stumbled to the stairs and crashed up them as if all the ghouls in the world were chasing me and I was hollering and screaming— what I don't know—to keep them away. When a board snapped I just clambered up over splintering wood until I got to the top floor —I think I could have flown—and tore to the front doors, almost went through them, until I was out on the porch and could see.

Just to be able to see! I alternately ran and limped my way to the path and along it. Nothing could have stopped me, not my foot or the fact that I was freezing and sopping wet. I stopped when I got to the football field. I had no breath left. I turned and glanced back and imagined I could see him coming along the path after me and —breath or no—I went charging up the hill. I tripped a couple of times, even went down in the snow, but I'd just scramble up and go on.

I could see the lights on in Mr. Kauffman's room as I came around the front of Lincoln House. When I opened the door I even fell in on the living-room floor. I made it up the stairs and flung open the door to his room. He was in his robe and already on his feet with a book in his hand. He must have heard me coming. "In the boathouse—in the water," I gasped. He shook his head, just taking in the sight of me. "Mr. Hoyt—in the water—get him out!"

Then I was down on the floor and he was holding me, then covering me with a blanket, and all I could do was shiver and mutter gibberish which I could no more tell you the meaning of than I could describe the moment of my birth.

I vaguely remember the whole building coming to life, people dashing in and looking at me and rushing around and finally Ed Anders and Mr. Hines hauling me onto Mr. Kauffman's bed and trying to get my clothes off and dry me and me only fighting them off. I had enough of the nightmare and wanted out of it—like I was still in the water with him and fighting to get out.

And then being grabbed and forced over on my back and looking up to see a doctor, Jordan's doctor, and I was glad to see him because I knew he'd give me something to end the nightmare; but even though I wanted whatever it would be I couldn't stop struggling to get away from the body in the water until I was overpowered by hands and arms and held down and then I was out.

28

It was light when I woke up and two men in uniform, and one not, were in the room. The sheriff came over to the bed and asked me if I could get up and dress. I said yes. My ankle had been taped up and I wondered how they knew. There were fresh clothes laid out and while I put them on I noticed my bags and typewriter there on the floor.

Mr. Kauffman was sitting in a chair in his front room when we came in. He was blank-faced and his eyes were red, but he stood up. When we looked at each other, he cleared his throat but he didn't know what to say. The men stopped; they knew *something* had to be said. Mr. Kauffman looked from one to the other of them and cleared his throat again. "You should have seen him with our Glee Club," he said to the sheriff. He turned to the policemen. "Hamlet, only it was . . . he . . . he was so . . ." But he just let it drop. He looked down at the floor, then up at me. "Goodbye, Peter." He held out his hand. We shook hands very formally, like we were meeting for the first time instead of saying goodbye.

What gave me a jolt was the activity the second we stepped out of the front door. All sorts of photographers—I don't know where they'd been—flashbulbs going off and yelling at me to look at them. The sheriff lost no time hustling me inside the car. There wasn't a student in sight and I wondered where they all were.

Driving out of Saypool and just as I was beginning to think how nobody would believe me, I mean the truth about what happened, the sheriff asked me if I wanted to tell him the whole story, get it off my chest. I shook my head no.

"You did kill him, though, didn't you, Peter?" I told him yes. Twice more during the drive to Concord he asked me if I'd tell him all about it, but I shook my head no again. I couldn't then. It was too soon and it was too complicated.

The roads were messy and the drive was long; they stopped once for coffee. I thought the building they finally pulled up to was the police station. It looked like that kind of an official place, big and gray and granite. They took me up the steps and inside and down a long green corridor and then into a bare room. I wasn't paying much attention, just being led. The room had a funny smell and the sheriff indicated a bench. He and one of the policemen sat on either side of me and the third one left.

We just sat there until a frosted-glass door swung open and a stretcher was wheeled in with a sheet over it. I stood up immediately. I knew what was underneath. The sheriff was right up next to me. He held one arm and the cop held the other while an attendant pulled the sheet back.

I don't think they had done anything to him. He was still in those same wet clothes—awful, it was an awful sight. His head, the side all mashed in and the blood coagulated. His skin was blue-white and the stubble of his beard looked heavy coming through it. His lips were drawn tight and they were blue, too—the color of Jordan's lips when he was sick. I shivered.

"Did you do that, Peter?" the sheriff asked me. The yes I said stuck in my throat and I turned my head to the side. "Take him away," the sheriff said and they wheeled the stretcher out.

They led me back down the hall and outside. When we got to the bottom of the front steps, the sheriff stopped me and turned me toward him. "Suppose we stop off and get something to eat and you tell me the whole story, Peter."

I actually smiled; I don't think I laughed. "What?" he asked. I looked back up the steps as if to say: "You show me *that*—and then you want me to sit down over a steak and talk about it?"

The sheriff got my point, even patted me on the back as we were getting back in the car for the trip to jail. That must have been when the one cop said I laughed right after looking at the body. Enchanting—how people interpret you.

You see, that's one of the things that worries me. If a little incident like that can be twisted and used against me, what about the reports of Jordan and me "caught" in bed together, the Sodom and Gomorrah assembly with the entire school in on it, and all that Mr. Kauffman and some of the students have told them.

I wake up some nights rolling in sweat, thinking there's nobody who was around us that would possibly believe, let alone understand, the truth. Not a soul. What went on between Jordan and Mr. Hoyt and me was unspoken. There could be no witnesses. No one knew about the rubdowns, to say nothing of the undercurrents, but Jordan—and he's gone. Who would ever believe Mr. Hoyt would try to kiss me, would say the things he said and grab me where he did?

I wouldn't believe it if I hadn't been there.

Why do I have no doubts that you will believe me and understand when you've read this, and still—why am I so frightened that twelve men and women won't?

I wish I weren't frightened. The other morning I woke up about four, clammy wet and all jitters from My Great Trial Nightmare (an every three-or-four-night favorite). I popped out of bed and stood there barefoot and shaking. When I'd calmed down and given myself a nervous little laugh that I'd actually thought it was real—ha-ha, you poor dumdum!—I walked over to my table and sat down. I dug through a manila envelope until I found the small snapshot I keep of Jordan, in which his eyes match that crooked half-smile and his image gives off a quiet, cool, completely—*who he is*. For the first time since all this happened it suddenly occurred to me: God, play it like Jordan would, take his sense of—personal dignity, is what it was—and just fill yourself up with it. Pretend Jordan's got his eye cocked on you and act the way you would if he were watching. I found myself smiling at the picture. Later, I dried myself off, got into a fresh t-shirt and shorts and climbed back into bed where I actually slept another hour or so. I'm trying to use that part of Jordan more and more. I think it's working.

Two days since I finished and tomorrow you arrive. One or two thoughts:

Writing it all down in detail, although it kept my mind on it, somehow it also kept my mind off it. I mean the reasons, the consequences and the future. I was riveted to just setting it down as it happened. Now my mind is wandering, snatching at odd little bits and pieces of the whole. I don't have any control over it. The way I feel the last few days, I think maybe I ought to take up bead-stringing or the mandolin. Little isolated scenes keep popping up. Funny how you store away the sight and feel of the important moments in your memory. The good times are there to be called on; they jump up like they've been waiting. But there's a catch: the bad times have a way of popping up without an invitation.

So often now I can't help thinking of how fast everything can change and of the whopping surprises in store for us. One day your paint box is all tidy and filled with the greatest colors and your brushes are clean and things are nifty; the next day a steam roller has mangled the whole works but you can't even worry about that because the whole world is upside down and you're hanging on for dear life. If that can happen in a day or two, what will the years bring?

Don't answer!

Other times I try to keep thinking that maybe I've had my share of rotten surprises for the time being, and maybe some of the surprises coming up will just have to be good ones.

Hopefully yours,